R.D. PITTMAN

NEW EARTH: PROJECT O.N.E.

Fiction Caveat
This is a work of fiction. Names, characters, places, and incidents either are the product of the author's imagination or are used factiously, and any resemblance to actual persons, living or dead, business establishments, events, or locales is entirely coincidental

Acknowledgements

THE NEW EARTH TRILOGY

These trilogies are a work of fiction; nonetheless, I strived to be as accurate as possible when utilizing facts and figures, to lend more credence to the stories. To that end, I should note that all of the military references were obtained from the official websites of the various armed services. The Army, Navy, Air Force, and Marine websites were invaluable in providing detailed information regarding force strengths and mission imperatives, as well as historical perspectives. I would like to thank the Public Affairs office of Nellis Air Force Base for its assistance and input. Much thanks to the US Department of Agriculture and the Bureau of Land Management for their website content that enabled me to provide realistic portrayals of agriculture and mining related issues that formed the basis of a significant part of these books.

My editor, Dave King, of Dave King Editorial Services was no less an important part of this effort than I was as the writer. While his editing was professional, it was also comfortable. His ideas about character and plot development were invaluable, and his patience was greatly appreciated. I can't imagine what it would have been like without his input and guidance.

No writer can ever freely admit that he or she did it on their own. There are always one or more persons that have a significant impact on the finished novel. Mine continues to be my best friend in life, someone I've known for forty-four years, and loved from the beginning...my wife Sharon. There was never a moment that she didn't praise me, remind me to take a break, rub my neck and back, put drops and warm hand towels on my eyes, and give me those wonderful loving hugs and kisses. Even when she wasn't there...she was there.

To my very best friend, my soulmate, my wife Sharon,
I lovingly dedicate this book.

Chapter 1

WE ARE IN CRISIS MODE

Alex was on his way home to Sacramento after having looked at an investment property in Pasadena. It was in a neighborhood that was already on its way to recovery, but he thought it was still priced low enough to leave room for potential upswing. It wouldn't make a killing, but at his point in life, he didn't need to make a killing. A comfortable profit was enough. He tapped the button that woke up the voice-activated phone system in the dash of his rented Smart Car.

"Call Curt" The phone ring seemed odd, like a violin out of tune, and then "That's right, at Mauna Kea. It was the Keck, last Thursday's scan."

That wasn't his son Curt, unless Curt had picked up the phone without realizing there was an incoming call. But Mauna Kea? The Keck? Why was that familiar?

"Eldon I'm absolutely positive, I got the data yesterday. At least a couple of dozen, maybe more, hitting over six days. They're coming, and there is nothing we can do about it."

There was panic in the voice. Whatever he had dropped in on, it was serious.

Then another voice. "Listen, get off this phone, meet me at the office—no meet me at Coco's at, say, three o'clock."

"The one in Glendale?"

"Yes."

"Okay see you at three…This is unbelievable, I just can't—

"Jeffrey, shut up and get off the phone now."

The line went dead.

Alex pulled off the highway, turned off the ignition and sat there for a moment. Whatever it was he'd overheard, it had unsettled him so much he couldn't remember ever feeling this unnerved. Not since Iraq. That was what had gotten him so rattled—he remembered hearing exactly that tone of voice from field commanders who were coming under fire when they didn't expect it.

After taking several deep breaths he switched his in-dash information center to the Internet and queried Mauna Kea and Keck. The Keck Observatory was part of the Mauna Kea observatories in Hawaii, jointly run by Cal-Tech. He then queried staff at Cal-Tech, the science division, and put in a search for first name Eldon—how many could there be? It came back Eldon Huart, Chair, Astrophysics Department. He then queried Jeffrey, Astrophysics Department and found Jeffrey Macklin, Professor and Director of something called the NEO Project. Alex queried NEO, Astrophysics Department and got NEO or Near Earth Object. The NEO project was a program that scanned for comets and asteroids that crossed the earth's orbit.

They're coming, and there's nothing we can do about it.

Now he wasn't rattled. He was scared.

It was 2:16 p.m. when Alex started his car, pulled back on to the freeway and looked for the nearest exit to take him to Glendale. As he raced down the Pasadena freeway he saw the sign, —Coco's next exit. As Alex pulled into the restaurant parking lot, he saw a white four-door hybrid with a Cal-Tech logo on the door pulling into a parking spot.

Alex pulled next to it and shut the car off. He had to compose himself. His heart was pounding again he could feel it in his temples, a level of adrenaline he hadn't experienced in more than ten years. He glanced at the clock. About fifteen minutes to the meeting. Should he approach these two people and tell them he overheard their entire conversation? But why should he get involved? Also, it could have just been some kind of sick fraternity joke, couldn't it? Alex wasn't a man to jump to conclusions, his career in the Air Force had taught him to carefully consider a situation, to weigh all the facts and then make an informed decision.

No, if this is for real he had to know, there were too many loved ones at home potentially at risk.

The man who got out of the Cal-Tech car was tall and thin, sparse gray hair, kind of stooped over. He looked like a college professor. Alex got out of his car and followed the man into the restaurant.

When the hostess asked if the two of them were together, Alex almost jumped in and said yes, but thought better of it.

"How many in your party?" she asked the professor.

"I'm supposed to meet another gentleman here at three."

"Oh, are you Professor Huart?"

"Yes."

"Your party is already here. He wanted a secluded place to sit, so follow me."

Alex watched as she walked Professor Huart into a far corner of the restaurant where another man sat alone, then led both of them to a private dining room with double doors. It was secluded, all right. She then seated Alex well away from the private dining room. Alex gathered his thoughts, after a few minutes he got up, and pushed through the double doors.

Professor Huart looked up and stopped talking to Professor Macklin.

"Yes, can I help you sir?"

"My name is Alex Hanken, Professor Huart, and you must be Professor Macklin,"

Macklin looked nothing like a professor. More like a linebacker.

"Excuse me, uh Mr. Hanken was it? We're having a very private conversation."

Alex leaned forward with his hands on their table. "I know, I was driving down the Pasadena Freeway, trying to call my son in Sacramento, and my car phone system inadvertently picked up your conversation."

"And what conversation was that Mr. Hanken?" Huart asked.

"The one about a near earth object event that was picked up by the Mauna Kea Observatory, and how it's coming at us. Professor Macklin you seemed extremely confident and also in a complete panic."

"Are you a reporter Mr. Hanken?"

"No I'm a retired Air Force Major General from Sacramento."

"Then how did you get our names? We didn't mention our names?"

"Look, there is not much you can't find on the internet Professor Huart. Or should I call you Eldon?"

"Give it up Eldon," Macklin said. "He knows."

Huart seemed to collapse. "Sit down Mr. Hanken."

"Please call me Alex." Alex slid into a seat. "I'm not here as an adversary or to gain an advantage. I'm involved whether any of us likes it or not."

"Okay," Huart said. "To start with Jeffrey and I both hold top-secret clearances because of the nature of the work we do, I could call the appropriate authorities and have you detained indefinitely. You know that, don't you?"

"Of course that would take some doing I'm not a former two striper, but I have no plans to run out of this restaurant and start yelling the sky is falling. I've flown combat missions during Desert Storm, so I'm not easily scared, but the conversation I overheard between you two gentlemen is more than a little disturbing."

"Mr. Hanken, I need your full name and address." Huart pulled out a Blackberry and began entering text. "If someone wishes to give you additional information beyond what you think you know you will be contacted. We are under no circumstances going to discuss this with you. I hope you understand."

Alex nodded. "I understand. I also hold a top-secret clearance. Here's my card with my address and phone number, gentleman good day." Alex turned and walked out of the restaurant to the car, where he sat, trembling slightly, and tried to collect his thoughts.

Then unexpectedly he smiled. Maybe that property in Pasadena didn't have so much upside potential. What with the world ending and all.

Jeremy turned to Eldon. "What were you thinking? This guy knows what's going on and he's a general in the Air Force," Macklin said, "with a top security clearance…and you know we could use a little help on this one."

"He says he has a security clearance. Do you have the skills and experience to do a complete background check on him?"

Jeremy massaged his forehead, then shrugged his shoulders. This was all still so much.

"I didn't think so," Eldon said. We'll let the professionals handle Mr. Hanken. We have a job to do and that is to brief the president and his staff on what is coming and what, if anything, can be done about it. Do you understand?"

"Yes, I guess you're right, Eldon. God, we had such hopes for comet Sedna/Kern. A close pass, a chance to sample the tail. And now…"

"Jeffrey, what's your analysis of the mechanics of this?"

Macklin wiped his brow. "We knew Sedna/Kern p236 was going to make a near pass at Jupiter that would slow it down and send it into earth-intercept orbit, but we didn't calculate what would happen when it hit the asteroid belt. It must have hit something dead on, and the resulting debris cloud affected others. Right now we have some forty asteroids of various sizes that have been catapulted directly into earth's orbital plane. Some, if not all, will impact the earth in August 2017, within a six day period. It's still too early to predict exact impact points, but there will be massive damage to the affected areas."

"So…."

"Yeah. It's the end of the world."

As Alex vectored his private plane toward Sacramento, he was glad for the computer-assisted avionics, because his mind was still racing. Was this the Extinction Event prophets had foretold for centuries? How did you prepare? Was there any point to preparing? And who would he talk to? Who could he talk to, now that Ellen was gone? Curt?

Alex didn't remember pulling into the garage at his home in suburban Granite Bay. He immediately went to his bathroom medicine cabinet and pulled out the sleeping pills his doctor had prescribed for him after Ellen's death. He had used them once and hated the wooly- headed feeling they left him with, and didn't like the idea of using a crutch, so he'd never taken another. But now things were different. He knew damn well he wouldn't sleep without them, and he needed to be alert for …whatever. So he downed two with a shot of scotch and was deeply asleep within minutes.

Alex began to stir around 10:20 the next morning. Which was strange, since he normally never slept past six a.m. And why was his head so fuzzy?

Then it all came back to him—the overheard conversation, the meeting at the restaurant, everything. But it was just a dream, it must have been. But it was so vivid!

Alex stumbled into the kitchen to start a pot of coffee and noticed his message light blinking. The first message was from Curt, asking him to call when he got home, then a Democratic fundraiser asking for more donations, and then reality hit.

"Alex, this is Professor Huart. Things are moving faster than I thought. Jeffrey and I are leaving this afternoon for D.C. You might expect a visit sooner than expected. I just wanted to give you a heads up. Hope your trip went well. Goodbye for now."

Alex felt faint. And just then, Curt walked in.

"Dad what the hell happened, are you okay?"

"Yeah…I…I'm just a little tired, you know that trip to Pasadena really got to me."

Alex sat down and asked Curt to pour him some coffee. His first, almost automatic, instinct was to tell him everything. They'd never kept secrets from one another. But no, not yet. When the time was right. What could he tell him anyway, that he overheard two eccentric professors discussing the end of all mankind? Alex needed more concrete proof. He'd call Roger in Admiral Torrance's office and make his own inquiries.

"So Dad, did you look at that piece of property?" Curt asked. "What did you think?"

"It looks better in pictures than in person. There's a lot of restoration work to be done, and the immediate area is in fairly run down condition. I'm going to pass on that property." None of this was true, but there was no need to make any investments now. If anything did survive who would care? "I got your message. Was there anything in particular you needed?"

"Nah. Just to talk. You know."

Alex did know. Since Ellen's death, he and Curt had developed a strong bond.

Alex managed to hold it together through two cups of coffee and some small talk. But he was relieved when Curt finally said he had some errands to run and left.

Six days. Professor Macklin had told Professor Huart on the phone. The asteroids would be striking the earth over a period of six days. That's how long it took God to make Earth! How ironic. Alex went outside on the back patio and pulled a chair out toward the pool, so he could see the sky. Where would they come from? What would it look like? What was it like to be incinerated?

He wouldn't let it get to that point. If there were no other choice, he would take himself out of the picture.

He tried not to think about it anymore, Alex went to his favorite restaurant, a small place that specialized in Italian cooking. Maybe he would make it his last meal if it came to that.

He returned home, read the newspaper, and went to bed with only one sleeping pill and no Scotch chaser this time. He would call Roger at the Pentagon in the morning. If there was something going on or on the radar screen this man would know it.

His sleep was filled with horrific imagery that he could not erase as he tossed fitfully throughout the night.

"Alex Hanken how the hell are you, this can't be you, I have you third on my list to call today, you're not only the best damn logistics mind I ever met, but now you are some kind of psychic."

"I'm on your call list? Roger, what's going on?"

"I'm not the one you want to talk to. Please hold for the Chairman."

"Roger, wait—

But Roger was already gone. A few moments later, Alex heard the familiar voice of Admiral Evan Torrance, Chairman of the Joint Chiefs of Staff.

"Alex," he said, "What a hell of coincidence. We've got something important to ask of you."

"Is it about incoming asteroids?"

"How the hell—

Alex relayed the conversation between the two professors. There was silence for a moment, then…"Goddamn scientists. Alex get your butt on a plane to Andrews AFB pronto, leave right now, drop whatever you're doing, talk to no one about this. You are hereby put on notice that this is covered by the US Secrets Act. You're in Sacramento right?"

"Yes sir."

"All right get to Beale AFB, I'll have a staff Lear waiting for you."

"Yes sir, I'll leave immediately."

Okay, obviously Admiral Torrance knew what was going on. And he had some role for Alex to play. Alex found himself relieved for the first time in the last two days. Actually having something to do meant that, at least he wasn't going to be helpless.

After a little thought, Alex packed his uniform which still fit him like a glove, a few days' necessaries, and headed out the door for Beale AFB. Roger had mentioned logistics. When Alex had been assigned to Southern Command in 1992, he'd headed up logistics for the upcoming Iraq war. The air and ground war was short-lived, but Alex had proved invaluable to the upper brass, and Admiral Torrance had noticed. Now the Admiral was the man in charge, with the entire military at his disposal. It was flattering that he would come to Alex with this.

Of course, with something like this, you'd want to go with someone you could trust. This all had to be need-to-know.

Alex rolled up to the front gate at Beale AFB and an airman with an M-16 assault rifle stepped toward his car. Alex showed him his identification card.

"Yes sir, General Hanken, we've been expecting you. If you'll follow that air police car, he'll escort you to the flight line where base Commander Campbell is waiting."

"Thank you airman."

The air police car sped off with his light bar flashing with Alex following closely behind. They traversed the expansive base in minutes winding between hangars until finally stopping by an awaiting C-21 Lear. An airman came forward, threw a salute, and grabbed Alex's bags. Then the base commander introduced himself shouting over the Lear's engines that were in warm up stage.

"General Hanken, when the Chairman of the Joint Chiefs of Staff calls and says do something, you don't question it, you just do it. I took the liberty of having my pilot and co-pilot available to fly you there is that okay?"

"I appreciate your help General Campbell, I have a lot on my mind right now and I could use the time to relax a little, thank you."

With that Alex boarded the plane and after a short preflight check the sleek jet lifted off for the six hour flight to Andrews AFB. It was 10:30 a.m. there on the west coast, it would be dark by the time he landed and walked into the Pentagon.

Alex tried his best to clear his mind, but there were too many things coming at him. He thought of the tough times the country had been through these last few years. For the seventh year in a row the United States congress promised to tackle the energy crisis facing the nation, and it looked like they weren't getting any further than they ever had. While most of the industrialized nations had already put in place new and innovative approaches to curb their nation's dependence on imported oil, the US was still embroiled in special interest infighting over environmental issues versus costs. Crude oil traded at three-hundred dollars a barrel and gasoline prices at the pump reached eleven dollars a gallon. Still, the oil companies insisted the rise in prices was a supply and demand issue, never mind the fact that the five largest domestic oil companies made a combined $185 billion dollars in profits the previous year. The US economy had slipped into a deep recession in early 2007, in late 2008 the entire world's financial system seized, drastic moves by central banks across the globe averted the potential calamity, but the die was cast. Millions had lost their jobs, the US automobile industry had to be bailed out along with nearly all of the large banks, and the national debt soared undermining the dollar.

Austerity measures had only prolonged the problem, cutting social services without creating jobs. Talk of more government intervention and nationalizing of certain industries sparked sharp debates among those moneyed interests that would be affected. The US was on the brink of financial collapse until the Saudi's and the Chinese recognized that a healthy US economy was in their best interest, and pumped six trillion dollars into the US in 2013. It staved off the worst of the disaster but didn't solve the underlying problem. The airlines, crippled by rising fuel costs and the prolonged recession, were nationalized in 2014.

And this steaming mass of conflicting interests, dwindling resources and unparalleled greed competed against a healthy world economy that was needed to stave off the disaster. But now that was assuming a disaster of another kind could be staved off, a disaster that would make all others pale by comparison.

Chapter 2

FINDING COVER

President Owen Betts slumped at his desk in the oval office, oblivious to the array of advisors on the couch in front of him. So many questions kept circling in his mind. How could they prepare? Could they prepare? How do you break it to the world's population that civilization might end without creating a panic that would, itself, end civilization? How could he maintain enough control to save what could be saved? Clearly this all had to be kept under wraps now—you don't tell people a disaster is coming until you can tell them what can be done to avert it. Should he tell other heads of state? They would need a chance to prepare, but the more people who knew; the more likely it was the news would leak.

What about the upcoming election campaign? Should he run again? It would be a huge distraction, but it might create a frenzy of investigations if he announced he wasn't running. Somebody would probably break under the pressure, that famous unnamed White House source.

The President rose from his desk and walked to the windows that looked out onto the White House grounds, his hands clasped behind his back. He stood there for a few moments, then turned to National Security Advisor, Arlen Hendry.

"Arlen, implement COP at Mount Weather. Selection only—no contacts, just compile the lists and locations, and give me time-frames for implementation and the hierarchy who are essential to implementation. Can you have that to me end of business tomorrow?"

"It will be on your desk, Mr. President."

"Allen," the President said. "Mount Weather is your facility; I want you to put in place an operational readiness test that is to last at least one year. That way you can ramp up operations without raising suspicions of the staff."

FEMA Director Allen Haverty nodded. "That will be no problem. I will set it in motion immediately."

"Gentlemen, I cannot emphasize how critically important secrecy is in these early days of preparation. Robert track news leaks and shut down any sources of potential early disclosure. Do what you deem is necessary. Constitutional guarantees are essentially suspended, involuntary detention is on the table, do you understand?"

"Yes Mr. President," Attorney General Simons replied.

"Admiral Torrance, work closely with Arlen on military redeployment without raising concerns or suspicions of your command staff, I know that won't be easy, but we will need our troops here on US soil. Has your man from California arrived yet?"

"He just landed twenty minutes ago. I understand they've put him in the Roosevelt room."

"Bring him in; I'd like to meet him."

Two minutes later, the secretary ushered a stranger into the office. He was in civvies, looking a bit rumpled, but you could still see the military bearing under the clothes. Old habits die hard.

"Mr. President," Torrance said, "May I introduce Major General Alex Hanken."

"General, Admiral Torrance told me of your inadvertent eavesdropping on the two professors. Probably just as well. You know the situation we're facing."

"Yes sir."

"What you need to do is direct a total redeployment of our military forces back to stateside. We may need them here at home. Then, we'll need survival shelters for key government, military, and civilian personnel along with all the attendant supplies and equipment to literally restart the country. It's a pretty tall order, so we managed to push through an order to congress to jumpstart you to a four star, you'll need the muscle of the rank to deal with some of the lower ranking generals. So how say ye General Hanken?"

"Mr. President, it will be my honor to serve our country."

"Good, Evan and Arlen will fill you in on the details the next few days." The President then moved to the center of the room. "Gentlemen, diplomatic missions worldwide are going to start getting inquiries as to why we are redeploying our military. Any suggestions as to how we respond?"

After some thought. "Sir if I may?"

The President glanced back at Hanken. "Go ahead General."

"Simply put, we can't afford to be the world's policeman any more. Or less simply put, we are maximizing our utilization of existing manpower and resources to better meet present-day challenges affecting our country."

Torrance smiled. "I couldn't have said it better Mr. President."

"Evan, you didn't tell me that Alex was a politician as well, though that statement was a little concise for a politician. But it's a start." President Betts paused until he had everyone's undivided attention. "Gentlemen, thank you all. We all know what we have to do, and we have precious little time to do it in. So get started. Evan a moment?"

The others filed out while Admiral Torrance stayed standing. When they were gone, the President waved Torrance into a seat. "Quite an impressive man, Hanken. Good choice."

"Thank you sir," Torrance said. "Actually he was my third, after a former Quartermaster Corps General and a logistics chief from Halliburton."

"Really? Why him then?"

"He called my office before we had a chance to contact the other two, and I learned he already knew about the ....upcoming event. I knew this had to be need-to-know as possible, so I brought him on board."

"Oh. Well I would have liked first choice on this, but you're right about the security. He'll have to do."

Alex was parked on an uncomfortable chair in a nondescript office in the Pentagon. There was a briefing book and a carafe of coffee in front of him, and a stack of briefing books to his right. He'd been getting up to speed for about six hours now, and still felt like he was only scratching the surface.

At the moment it was the Mount Weather facility located about 45 miles west of Washington D.C. in the mountains of Virginia, 1,725 feet above sea level. Mount Weather was central to COP–Continuity of Operations, the government's plan to restore order to the country after a calamitous event by ensuring the executive branch, key military and civilian personnel survived. The facility itself was located 1,400 feet underground, was originally built in the heyday of the cold war but underwent extensive reconstruction beginning in 1993. There were now dorms for staff instead of cots, cafeterias, meeting rooms, self-contained power generators, food and equipment warehouses, even an electric tram. Not to mention a fully equipped ER and operating room, to be staffed by surgeons covering several disciplines, and a complete two chair dental clinic. There was an extremely sophisticated communications system linked to satellites and high gain microwave antennae, an onsite full production television studio for broadcasting, a four-lane bowling alley, a theater with over two thousand movie titles, a video game arcade, and a putting green with an electronic golf driving range. As this was to be the nerve center for the government after a disaster, there existed a massive computer complex with a network of petascale processor computers running everything.

The President, the Supreme Court justices and cabinet members had private rooms. The facility got its water from an underground freshwater lake, and there were sufficient stores of food to last the entire staff nine months. Staffing levels were projected to be somewhere between thirteen hundred and twenty one hundred total which included a thirty-five man Marine detachment and fifteen Navy Seals. The facility was spread out on five levels taking the total depth of the facility to almost fifteen hundred feet or about two hundred fifty feet above sea level. A guillotine gate and a ten foot high, twenty foot wide, five foot thick blast door that took nearly fifteen minutes to open or close protected Mount Weather's entrance. The Congress, key administration, and military staff were to be sent to several other locations in Maryland, Virginia, and Pennsylvania though their facilities were not nearly as nice or sophisticated as Mount Weather's.

And yet, sophisticated as the facility was, it was only the beginning. It would keep the executive and judicial branches alive, and the others would preserve the legislative. But what good were the three branches of government if there were no people to govern. Or if the people were teetering at starvation levels. That was the real problem he had to tackle.

And then there was the knowledge that was hanging around in the back of his brain, the dark, brooding facts that he wasn't ready to consciously face.

No matter what he did, people would die in the tens or hundreds of millions, or even billions. The very best he could hope for—the very best—was to save enough pieces that humanity would recover and not be wiped from the face of the earth.

He poured another cup of coffee and pulled down another briefing book, this one on how Japan rebuilt its infrastructure after the bombings that ended WWII.

Admiral Torrance and Arlen Hendry strolled along the path leading around the White House.

"So," Hendry said. "Does the President really believe we can keep this under wraps once we start moving pieces around?"

"We'd better, for all our sakes. Otherwise we could end up turning our guns on our own people. I'd rather turn my gun on myself."

"Evan," Hendry said slowly, we both know a lot of people are going to die anyway. Panic will set in at some point," Hendry took in the beauty of the rose garden and tried to imagine what things would look like just a few years hence. "I can't help but wonder if there is a history to be written afterwards how will we be portrayed? Hitler could come off looking like a saint compared to us!"

"Yeah. Listen, call me when you're going to get started, and I'll go over the force level reports for redeployment contingency plans."

"How soon can your man Hanken have those plans ready?"

"I'm shooting for seventy-two hours."

"You think Hanken is up to this?"

"I do. Remember he masterminded the movement of nearly two hundred thousand troops for the Iraq War that included all the various coalition troops, along with tanks, planes, field hospitals, maintenance units, supply trucks and ships, their routes, and all the attendant critical personnel to support each segmented mission. Yes I'd say he is up to it."

"All right then. My office annex on Thursday, say around nine a.m."

"See you then."

Ted Jeffers, FBI Director, wondered why the Attorney General Simons had asked for an immediate meeting with him, and was surprised to see Donald Cray, the CIA Director, waiting in the outer office when he arrived. Attorney General Simon's secretary showed them both in immediately.

"Ted, Don," Simons said. "Thanks for coming on such short notice. Let's step into my secure office for this conversation."

As they seated themselves in the smaller, electronically-shielded inner chamber, Jeffers got a sick feeling in his stomach he was going to be asked to break the law somehow. This time he would refuse.

"Gentlemen, I am hereby putting you on notice that under the US Secrets Act the President has granted me discretion to discuss a matter of urgent national security, and you are on notice that, under no circumstances, may you discuss with any other individual, unless authorized to do so directly by the President or his designee, the contents of what I am going to divulge to you. Nor are you to take any action that could arouse suspicions concerning this matter. This conversation is being recorded, do you agree to continue?"

Both men acknowledged by answering yes.

The Attorney General then proceeded to lay out for them what was coming. Cray began wringing his hands. Jeffers kept shifting in his chair from one side to the other, fighting the urge to get up and do something...anything.

Simons quoted the President as saying the Constitution was essentially suspended. They had to do whatever was necessary to keep anyone unauthorized from learning anything about this. He provided a list of the known persons who knew of this matter and ordered them all to be put under heavy surveillance.

"Bob," Cray said with a voice laced with iron control, "Just how far do we go to keep this out of the public eye?"

"Don, listen carefully. You are authorized to use any and all means at your disposal to carry out your objectives."

"Forced detention?" Jeffers asked.

"Yes."

"Terminal force?" Cray asked.

"Yes. Even against the innocent. Gentlemen, consider what happens if this gets out. We're talking total anarchy, food riots, murder sprees, chaos at home and abroad, and a complete and total breakdown of civilized behavior worldwide. One possible result would be that no one—none of humanity—survives. We are the best and last hope for any possible recovery after the event, the front line of defense."

"Sir," Jeffers asked. "Our families?"

"Immediate families will be assigned as critical personnel to the Mount Weather facility."

"Immediate families?"

"Spouse and children only. I'll need immediate action plans on your parts to be submitted in person by Thursday at 10:00 a.m. That's all."

As Jeffers and Cray walked down the long corridor of the Justice Department Jeffers was the first to speak.

"Holy Christ Don."

"I know."

"How am I going to keep 6,500 agents from finding out if I've got them out there trying to stop the revealing of something they're not supposed to know anything about? That makes no fucking sense!"

Cray held up a hand. "Ted, I'm...I'm still trying to restart my heart. I haven't thought that far ahead yet."

"Well, think. I've been given an impossible task. Any help with it would be appreciated."

"Okay, look. Remember the broken pie theory? Give each a little piece, not the whole thing. The whole pie gets eaten, but not by any one individual. Set up your teams, give them each a separate task, but have them report results directly to you, and not share with anybody else in the department."

"Yeah. I'd already gotten that far, but I can just imagine my senior guys and gals chafing for trying to hide something from them. They're smart enough that they don't follow orders blindly."

"Let them chafe. We're talking terminal Cretaceous Event here, a change in ownership. If we don't survive, it will just be the goddamn roaches and ants left. Besides you've got the easy job. When we start military redeployments, I'm going to have every agent of every major power, friendly and unfriendly, sniffing around to find out why. At least your people are under your orders."

"This could be the world's largest and last cluster fuck," Jeffers said. "Jesus mother of God, I've never ordered someone killed."

"Well Ted, come down to our range at Langley and we will show you how to kill with the best of them."

Jeffers stopped. He was scared to death and Cray was joking about it all? Maybe that's what he had to do to stay in his job. Maybe Jeffers should try it.

Chapter 3

KEEPERS OF THE TRUTH

★ ★ ★ ★

FEMA Director Allen Haverty was busy compiling his punch list for the Mount Weather COP ramp up. His staff, already at work on details of the fictional one-year operational test, had less than twenty-four hours to get him their plans for the individual areas of responsibility. Keep them busy enough and they won't have time to ask questions.

But in the back of his mind, he was sure there was something he was overlooking. Maybe it was just the rush making him think something was missing. But if there was something, he was hoping whatever it was would be revealed in the plans he would receive from his staff within the next day. In the meantime, he buzzed his secretary and asked her to contact the National Security Advisor's office.

"Arlen, this is Haverty over at FEMA."

"Good morning Allen."

"It's about money. Ramping up Mount Weather puts me beyond my budgetary guidelines by at least a factor of two. How will we explain that to the GAO?"

"We won't have to because we now have an off-budget fund we will be tapping as we go along, besides we got the GAO to buy in yesterday. They're on the team."

"This just keeps getting bigger by the minute. Have someone send me a list of the accounts to be charged?"

"Of course."

Tim Greenberg, President Betts Chief of Staff was reviewing what might be the most frightening Power Point presentation he had seen in his life. It was prepared by the National Science Foundation Committee, which was comprised of some of the leading scientists in the nation. The purpose of the presentation was to advise the President and his cabinet of various impact scenarios of an incoming asteroid swarm. All hypothetical, but it was this presentation that most of their contingency planning would be based on.

Besides being frightening, Greenberg thought the report was too technical, entirely too many formulas, and not enough basic impact analysis. The scientists didn't have to show their work, just give the President an insight into what to expect. He returned the presentation to the committee chair with a note suggesting that they downplay the technical side. Rather, provide more concrete input on potential damage to infrastructure, loss of life grids, and ongoing post event environmental issues. Greenberg went into the Oval Office and told the President he'd called for another draft.

"Tim," the President said, "how are you feeling about all of this?"

The question touched him. With everything going on, the president was still concerned with him.

Or maybe he was making sure he was still sane.

"About like you might expect, sir," Greenberg said. "I can't sleep at night, I worry about my family, and I keep replaying scenes from the movies 2012, Armageddon, and Deep Impact. I just can't believe this is happening."

"I suppose that is the natural reaction. But imagine what happens when this finally goes public, not just here in America, but across the globe."

Oh, that was it. The President just wanted to bounce ideas off of him.

"Tim, before we can attempt to convince the people that we can and will survive, we have to have a survival strategy in place that's fair yet does what's necessary. We don't have the luxury of turning inward and thinking of how it will impact us personally, we have to think of our country and our citizens. I know you, we go way back together, you are tough as nails, and I'm going to need you now more than ever."

"I know Mr. President; it's just so hard to fathom this. But I'll be here for you and as always we will get through this. Is there any hope that we can stop these things or divert them somehow?"

"I've got NASA and the DOD putting together several scenarios to present to me tomorrow, I think you have them on the agenda along with The JPL in Livermore. The JPL will outline potential defense scenarios for the incoming threat, so we'll just have to wait and see."

Louis Felson wanted a little more insight into an upcoming PBS special on the "Life of an Asteroid". Felson had produced several award winning earth and the universe oriented specials over the years for PBS. That's why he was contacting one of his subject matter experts at the National Science Foundation.

"Hi, Chris, it's Louis Felson with PBS, I need to pick your brain again about an upcoming special. Guess what it's called 'The Life of an Asteroid.'"

There was silence at the other end.

"Hello…Chris you there?"

"Louis is this some kind of joke?"

"What joke already?"

"I…listen——I can't talk right now, no, I mean I can't talk about this period."

The line was silent. Felson hung up the phone. What could Chris be thinking they had worked together for years? Oh my God——

Felson sat at his bistro type table and munched on a sandwich contemplating how he could verify his suspicions. He finished eating, downed his pino grigio, and decided to call his buddy at the Washington Post, but before he could dial the number his doorbell rang. When Felson opened the door, he was confronted with two very official looking men.

"What's going on here?" he said. Without a word they handcuffed him, put a black bag over his head, and took him away. What the hell…

It was because he knew. They were shutting him up because he knew. Felson didn't know whether to be more scared of their silencing him or of what they were silencing him about.

They dragged him out to a car—an SUV from the height—and started driving. He could tell by the direction of the turns that they were not headed to FBI headquarters. The ride length convinced Felson he was being taken out of the DC area, maybe Baltimore, maybe Langley. He could hear other traffic now, trucks, air brakes, then an overhead door opening. He felt the attitude of the car change they were going up some kind of steep grade, and then the car stopped. Doors opened, someone grabbed him and pulled him out of his seat.

"Hey, you know you can get a ticket for not putting a seat belt on someone you just kidnapped," he yelled.

No response.

He was led down a hallway, then through a door, and placed in a metal chair, black bag still over his head, hands handcuffed behind his back. Then silence.

"Hey is anybody there?" he screamed.

Minutes passed that seemed like hours…then he heard a click and felt a warm sensation on his face through the nylon bag over his head. He heard footsteps, big feet it sounded like. Then the bag was pulled off his head, and the lights were so bright he had to close his eyes. The lights were focused directly on his face.

Then a booming voice. "Mr. Felson, how are you today?"

"I am a United States citizen, I've done nothing wrong, you have no right to hold me against my will." It was worth a try.

"Ah, now that is where you are wrong," the deep pitched voice explained. "You see Mr. Felson, there are circumstances that require us to override your personal rights in the interest of National Security. Do you understand Mr. Felson?"

Just how deep did the security go? "Do you know what's happening?"

The man walked around behind him and unlocked the handcuffs but kept a hand on his shoulder. That hand was enough to hold him in his seat. "I do. And the people whom you will meet directly do as well. And no one else will. We intend to keep it that way."

"How long do we have?"

"I don't know. They don't tell me everything."

"Listen, I'd like to help."

The deep voice nodded. "I'll pass that along. But there may be nothing you can do." The man turned to leave.

Felson jumped up and grabbed his arm. "Wait! You can't leave me in here alone; I've got to do something."

The man shook his head. "I'm sorry, Mr. Felson, but we have no choice at this point. But don't worry, I suspect you won't be alone for long. In fact I'm afraid it's going to get crowded in here before we're done."

Eldon Huart nervously scoured the figures before him hoping to find some evidence of error, but was having no luck. The earth would be hit by multiple asteroids. Nothing between them and earth was strong enough to stop them. His phone rang and he picked it up reflexively.

"Eldon Huart."

"Eldon, it is Ivan Borosky calling from Russia."

Oh damn. He took a quick breath to force some calm into his voice. "Ivan, how are you, it is so good to hear from you, what time is it there?"

"It's 9:30 at night here in St. Petersburg. Eldon I have some disturbing news that I want to share with you before I take it to our people."

"Yes go on," Huart knew what was coming. Well, at least he didn't have to lie to an old friend.

"The Ussuriysk Astrophysical Observatory has been tracking a mass of asteroids that apparently were accelerated by a massive solar flair. Eldon we have gone over the calculations many times, these asteroids—thirty or forty of them—are going to hit earth sometime in late summer of 2017. I fear it will be the end of life on earth as we know it, Eldon are you there?"

"Yes. Can you send me your numbers so I can go over them first?"

"My friend that is why I called, I knew you would offer your help in this matter. You knew didn't you?"

"We're still double checking the simulations. You've got to be sure with something like this, which is why your numbers would be helpful." Eldon thought of the tap on his phone, of the security officials who had read him the riot act. He hated what he was about to do, but he had no choice. "Who knows about this besides you Ivan?"

"Just me and my assistant Anna."

"Okay, I'm going to give you the entry code and a password to our computer here at Cal Tech; I want you to send your data to it. Then let me run some simulations and get back to you before you report this to anyone."

"Thank you my friend, I have the codes now. You think maybe in a couple of days you can get back to me."

"I'll run it until we get the answer, if I have to stay up all 48 hours."

"Ah, I know you will. Thank you my friend. Goodbye."

Borosky called Anna to let her know that Professor Huart of Cal-Tech would verify the data and get back to them within 48 hours. Then, exhausted from the previous days of running calculations repeatedly, he decided to retire early.

Sometime toward dawn, the sound of a dog barking in the neighbor's backyard woke him.

"Damn dog," he grumbled as he shuffled along into the kitchen to make some coffee, and then walked into the bathroom to wash his face. The dog had stopped barking. With the towel draped around his neck, he looked out the tiny bathroom window into the backyard of his neighbor. He heard a small tinkle of glass breaking.

It was the last thing he ever heard.

Something brushed Anna Kinova's face as she turned over in bed. Then the pressure of a hand over her mouth brought her out of her light sleep. The man grabbed her forcefully, shoved a rag into her mouth, put a pillowcase over her head, and then tied her hands behind her. She tried to talk, tried to beg, but she couldn't. Her mind raced with everything she'd ever learned about how to protect yourself in a situation like this—just give in, give them what they want, stay alive as long as possible.

He shoved her into the trunk of a waiting car. Terrified, she couldn't keep her mind off what she'd heard about the sex slave trade, she had heard about that from a few of her girlfriends. It was a growing problem in Russia, and more importantly it was run by the Russian Mob, and they were ruthless in their treatment of women.

Then she overheard the two men talking, and they were speaking perfect English. What was going on here?

The car pulled away. She shivered from more than fear. It was in the middle of winter and freezing cold outside, all she had on was her bedclothes, and the trunk of the car was not heated.

Presently, the terrain became rough; she could tell by the bumps and gravel hitting the wheel wells. She hoped they would stop soon, so she could ask for some warm clothes. She got her wish; the car made a sharp left turn, and came to a stop. She could hear what sounded like rushing water. Nothing happened for a few minutes, then she heard a car door open, it was the passenger door. The trunk lid opened, and a man picked her up, slung her over his shoulder, and carried her to the edge of the dam walkway. And then—

She was falling. The last thing she thought before her body crashed into the concrete wall of the dam was, they had never said a word to her.

Sergeant Andrade Kolna arrived at the scene and took charge from the uniforms who had answered the call about a dog shot in the head. One of the uniforms had noticed a heat plume coming out of the window of the house next door and was able to see the occupant lying on the floor in a pool of blood.

One of the uniforms finished working the jimmy and the door swung open. Andrade went in first. Somewhere deeper in the house he could hear the distinctive whistle of escaping steam He found his way to the kitchen to turn off the burner under the pot. Now there was complete silence.

"No one touch anything," he said to the uniforms who had followed him. "We don't know if this was a suicide or a homicide yet." That was purely pro forma. Suicides rarely shot the neighbor's dog first.

He entered the bathroom, stepped around the pool of blood that had formed on the floor, and checked Borosky's neck for a pulse. There was none. It had not been long since he died; his body still had a little heat in it. After taking pictures of the position of the body, Kolna rolled Borosky's body over on to its back, and saw the bullet wound just above the right eyebrow. He then looked at the hole in the bathroom window, very neat, little breakage. A very precise shot... with a high powered weapon.

"This man was murdered, there is no suicide here," he said. "You there, you talked to the neighbor, did he hear any shots this morning?"

"No sergeant and his dog was definitely shot."

"Two known shots fired in a very short time period, in the same vicinity, and no one heard any shots fired. Does that include the people across the street, and on the other side of this house?"

"Yes sergeant, I have talked to both households, no one in those homes heard a shot either."

"A high velocity bullet like that would have to come from a specially made gun with a silencer. This man was assassinated by a professional." Mob or someone else?

"Do we know who he is yet?"

"Yes, his identification papers say he is Ivan Borosky. He also has a badge over here on his desk that indicates he works at the Russian Academy of Sciences. According to this article in the paper that he saved, he is a professor of astrophysics at the institute."

So why would the Mob be shooting astrophysicists? Why would anyone?

"Okay, get on the line to the institute, see if he has any colleagues that are there and can give us some background. Also ask if any of his coworkers are absent from work today."

Kolna continued to walk around Borosky's house looking for any clues to aid in the investigation. There were no signs of a lavish lifestyle. Gambling? A drug habit? He was interrupted by one of his investigators with news that the institute had reported Borosky's assistant Anna Kinova was not at work as usual, and did not answer her home or cell phone. Kolna took down her address and announced that he was going to this address to follow-up on a lead. He ordered two of the uniforms and one of the investigators to stay on scene and recover evidence, while he and the other investigator went to Kinova's house, hopefully for some answers.

When Andrade found Kinova's front door slightly ajar, he feared the worst. The small house was only a one bedroom; she had done a decent job of making it seem comfortable. When he walked into the bedroom, he could see signs of a struggle... the bed sheet still had her fingernail trails in it from being dragged out of bed. But no body.

Still he was sure there was a body. He asked for the major crime lab people to come on board on this one. They needed to turn both houses upside down for any clues and to contact him as soon as they found something of importance. Kolna had a suspicion this might be a major case in the making, something just didn't fit.

Don Cray grabbed Ted Jeffers when he was on his way out the door, and pulled him aside into the courtyard.

"Ted, one of your boys went off the reservation yesterday."

"Oh yeah who?"

"Huart."

"How?"

"One of our listening posts picked up a call into Huart's office from a Russian named Ivan Borosky. This Borosky guy is a Professor of astrophysics in St. Petersburg, Russia, he and his assistant stumbled onto our little problem, and he called Huart to have him verify his findings and Huart agreed."

"Damn!"

"No, Huart did all right. He got Borosky to admit no one knew about it but him and his assistant. Problem is, he gave the Russian access codes to the Cal Tech main frame, so he could send the data directly to the system."

"Oh, Jesus Christ!"

"Look, we wiped the trail clean today, even washed the incoming call out of the trunk system so the road ends at the British Isles Atlantic cable. You need to get a hold of your boy Huart, and do some major counseling."

"What about Borosky and his assistant?"

"I said the trail is clean Ted."

"Thanks, I'll take it from here."

There was a faint knock at his door and his secretary peaked in and said, "Professor Huart there's a man here to see you, and he showed me an FBI badge."

Huart swallowed hard and told her to show him in.

The agent waited until his secretary had left and closed the door. "Professor Huart did you have a conversation with an Ivan Borosky yesterday?"

"Uh, yes I did." Huart felt a hot flash come across his face.

"Did you provide him with access codes to the Cal Tech main frame?"

"Yes, but that was only to verify what he already knew. He is a longtime friend and a professional colleague as well," Huart was feeling more ill by the moment.

"Who would we contact so that we can erase the data input from Borosky?"

"Well, I suppose Chad Cummings. He heads up the data services division."

"Do you realize that you have violated the US Secrets Act?"

Huart's left arm began to tingle. Then it felt like someone was pushing with all their strength down on his chest. His eyes became unfocused, then darkness.

"Are you telling me that the guy dropped dead right in front of you?" Jeffers asked.

"Yes sir."

"What about the data?"

"Removed with no trace sir."

"Okay, good job and stay alert; Macklin is still bouncing around there also."

"I will sir, and thank you."

Kolna strolled into the major case squad office and was met by the lead investigator, Detective Vasily Kernoff.

"Sergeant Kolna what I am about to tell you is to stay within this room. You are to consider this a state secret. We found Anna Kinova's laptop computer under her bed. It seems she kept a daily diary of her life on the laptop. Day before yesterday she made this entry into her diary."

He gave Kolna a printout to read. The more he read the faster his pulse became, and by the time he finished he felt he was going to hyperventilate. What he told him next stirred Kolna to anger.

"They checked Borosky's telephone records and found an outgoing call the day before his death that mysteriously dead-ended at a phone hub in London, England. Yet at Cal Tech, in Pasadena, California, Professor Huart died suddenly of a heart attack yesterday. The data transmissions she mentions being sent to Huart has also mysteriously vanished with no record of its having been sent or received. Although Anna entered the exact time it was sent in her diary. Both of their offices at the institute have been burglarized, files have been taken and their computers wiped totally clean. We don't have any clue what they were working on that was so important Borosky would contact Huart for help. Finally, this morning they pulled Anna's body out of the river. She had been bound and gagged and thrown off of the dam walkway down onto the spillway."

"Goddamn it, this is the CIA and you and I both know it," Kolna was furious.

"Yes sergeant, I'm certain it was their involvement, and that is why it is out of our hands and in the big black building. It's FSB business now."

"CIA." Kolna could barely say it, he was so furious.

Ted Jeffers and Don Cray were having lunch, when a man came up to them and sat down unannounced Jeffers recoiled but Don Cray just smiled.

"Don your people really fucked up in St Petersburg, the Kremlin is getting involved and it's going to the very top of both governments." The man got up and walked away.

"Don, who the hell was that?"

"I don't know his real name. Someone on the Russian side." Ted don't get your panties all in a wad. Eat your lunch. In the old days we called it flushing out the quail. You ever hunt Ted?"

"No, I'm a fisherman."

"When you go quail hunting they usually huddle in a covey under a tree or in the underbrush. What you do is shoot in their general direction and see what flies out. That's what the Russians are doing; they want something to fly out. They're pissed off because we pulled off a major operation right under their noses. They'll get over it. And if they don't, well, in a few years it's going to be moot, isn't it?"

Unknown to Cray at that time was the fact that the Kremlin was more than just a little miffed at the CIA pulling off a caper on their soil... the Russians were deeply suspicious of US motives.

Chapter 4

FIND A HOLE AND CLIMB IN

★ ★ ★ ★

"**G**entleman, please be seated." The President waved his people back into their seats. Around the situation room table were the best and brightest minds in the country. If anyone could do anything about this threat, it would be them.

"Gentleman, we are here today to discuss strategies on how best to defend this world against what appears to be a potential catastrophic event coming this way in the summer of 2017. I now open the meeting by having Professor Conley discuss the threat we face."

"Thank you Mr. President." Professor Andrew Conley, MIT and Cal State, rose and cleared his throat. Our latest data show the mass of asteroids still on track for an orbital coincidence in July 2017. Here is the main issue that you need to consider. Imagine if you will a 3-D image of a box drawn into outer space, this box is approximately 22,000 by 16,000 miles in cross section and 1.9 million miles long. Asteroids of varying sizes are dispersed throughout this box. Some are tumbling at a slow rate and others at a high rate of speed. Many are in free spin with no discernible orbit structure around any of the other asteroids."

Conley discussed trajectory analysis, asteroid composition, and impact scenarios both in space and on earth. It was frightening stuff, but the most frightening thing was that, given the number of asteroids and their motion relative to one another, it was impossible to predict precisely where any one of them would hit.

Eric Karinsky, head of new technology development at JPL then rose.

"Mr. President, let me get to my points right away. Our strategies must fall into two categories, delaying and object destruction. Destruction, despite what you've seen in the movies, is not practical, as it leaves a debris cloud still heading toward earth. A delaying strategy relies on the fact that the earth moves one planetary diameter every seven minutes. If we can delay, or alter an object's trajectory slightly, we could cause it to miss the earth entirely. The vector and the velocity of the incoming object must be calculated correctly to implement such a strategy, which is within our capabilities. But the action to be taken must be done far enough away from the earth for the effect to be realized. On this question, I defer to my colleague."

NASA Chief Tom Benson stood and addressed the group, whose anxiety seemed to grow by the minute.

"Our part of this mission is to provide the delivery platform to implement whatever strategy is finally agreed upon. Mr. President, with the global financial meltdown and our own economy under such duress these past years, our new orbital and deep space craft development programs were left unfunded and essentially mothballed. For us to resurrect this program and bring it to fruition would take three years at a minimum, well past the event date. We are therefore left with the three space shuttles that are currently in storage. Crew must be trained, the shuttles themselves, the Atlantis, Discovery, and Endeavor, must be thoroughly gone through, new systems and any modifications necessary will take us perilously close to impact time. We must develop the strategy quickly and adopt an aggressive timeline; otherwise we are courting disaster before the impact itself."

"If I may, Mr. President," Ted Jeffers said. "If we were to ramp up our space program that aggressively while pleading poverty as the reason for pulling our troops back, there would be no way to maintain secrecy, the media would be all over us."

"Good point Ted; let's say we have decided to embark on a commercial endeavor that will drive revenue to the treasury, instead of draining it. How's that sound?"

"Well, Mr. President if you can sell it we can protect it from early disclosure."

"Good man."

"General Pontius," Admiral Torrance asked. "How's the railgun project progressed?"

"We have had success in disabling satellites; the system itself is reliable and accurate. The problem Admiral is that these are smaller objects than the majority of the asteroids coming in at us. They weren't moving at a high rate of speed and none of them were tumbling as many of the asteroids are."

"Mr. President," Karinsky spoke up. "Redstone Arsenal has an inventory of around one hundred twenty high explosive bombs called MOAB's. They can produce a non-nuclear explosion, that, if it were close enough to an object, could alter even the largest of the asteroids vector and/or velocity."

"Professor Conley," the President asked. "How far out would we have to go to lay a minefield for this box you described?"

"At a minimum you would want to start at least a half a million miles from the moon, so around seven hundred fifty thousand to a million miles out."

"Tom, can the shuttles go that far out into space and return safely?"

"Yes and no. We would have to place fuel depots along the path that far out. We would not return the shuttles to earth but keep them docked at the space station, which means outfitting the station with supplies and personnel to service the shuttles. We would have to start that almost immediately upon the shuttle's readiness to fly. We have to get the ordinance up to a storage location near the space station and then, begin sorties to the box and deploy the bombs with remote detonation capability. That could be done, but, I can't guarantee complete safety given the time frames we will be operating under."

"Then so be it. Start getting the shuttles back to readiness and laying out what you need from DOD. Ted do the best you can with regards to security. I know there are other scenarios that could be considered, but time and technology are our constraints. As you work on this plan, think about a backup plan. Does everyone understand?"

All of them nodded.

"Then get to it and God help us all."

While the rest filed out, Admiral Torrance stayed in his seat.

"Mr. President," he said, "you know as well as I do that something on this scale has never been attempted before. It will not work. There are too many moving parts."

"Don't you think I know that?" President Betts got himself under control. There was no reason to get mad at Torrance over this. "We can't possibly hope to deflect them all, that's why you have to step up the redeployment and survival plans. But if we can stop some of them, it may make a difference. Where are you on planning?"

"Arlen and I are meeting Monday. We'll be ready to kick it off when you give the go ahead."

"Don't wait for my go ahead, just get it done. We have a little less than eighteen months to get all our troops back here on American soil, devise and construct sufficient survival sites, all the while keeping it under wraps from the world until we are ready... Lord give us the strength!"

Alex was typing out detailed instructions for the data clerks on how to input the data into the format he wanted. Once he had that in place, the computers would take over and Alex could get some much needed sleep. It was going on a day and half without sleep. He had been moved to a more spacious office with windows and a couch that had been calling to him for hours.

Howard Carney, the Deputy Defense Secretary, knocked twice.

"General Hanken I see you have been busy for last few days, can I have a word with you."

"Of course and call me Alex."

Carney came in and dropped into Alex's couch. "Alex, when you have finished with the redeployment plans, we need to get to work on the survival facilities and the post event preparedness plans. Our friends at Homeland Security have punch lists of things to consider in surviving a catastrophic event. There are also military considerations we must take into account, troop concentrations, equipment relocation, air and sea power restructuring, our nuclear forces disposition. They tell me that you are a genius at this. Well we're going to need all the genius you can muster to prepare for the stateside influx of troops and equipment, while preparing suitable survival shelters nationwide. Now I know I've said a lot, but I wanted to put you on notice that Admiral Torrance and the President are going to put you in charge and I'm to be your liaison to the Admiral."

"Howard you weren't kidding…that is a lot."

"We'd bring someone else in, but you can appreciate—."

"Yes, need-to-know. I'll need funding and all military echelons have got to respect any requests I make of them."

"Funding's unlimited. You want it; just tell me when and where. As far as the echelons go, Admiral Torrance will be sending out a wire to all commands worldwide that you act and speak for the him and under no circumstances is anyone to question your authority."

"That sounds perfect Howard. Now if you don't mind I haven't slept in thirty-six hours and you're sitting on my bed. I have a long presentation to give tomorrow for the President, Admiral Torrance, and his Chiefs of Staff, and it would be a good idea not to nod off in the middle of it."

Carney stood up and brushed off the cushion. "I will be there myself, so sleep well Alex."

Alex had been asleep for about five hours when Howard Carney shook him awake.

"Alex, I'm sorry to wake you but we've got a problem. Your son Curt has put out an all points missing persons report on you. He thinks you've been kidnapped or something worse."

Alex scrubbed his hands over his face and tried to think. "Jeez that's my fault. He has called several times on my cell and left voicemails, I was just too busy to respond. How do you want to handle this?

"Call your son and tell him you are okay. You are in Washington D.C. doing some consulting work for a defense contractor."

"That won't fly. We always let each other know where we are at all times. But didn't someone say at some point that our immediate families would be brought into the shelters?"

"That's right."

"Well, my son is a telecommunications and data transmission wizard. I am going to need an industry expert like him. Can we bring him on board early?"

"Sure, but he has to abide by the US Secrets Act."

"Go get him Howard and bring him here. Be sure to tell the person that talks to him that I said 'Now is not the time for questions, just get on the plane.' He'll know it's me."

"Okay Alex go back to sleep."

Curt was talking on the phone with his fiancée, Cynthia, when a knock came at his condo's door. "Call you back, love."

When he opened the door there stood two extremely large men in Marine fatigues.

"Are you Curt Hanken?"

"Yes. What's this about?"

"A message from your father. 'Now is not the time for questions just get on the plane.'"

It took a moment to sink in. That was what his father said to him when they were leaving for a surprise trip to Disneyland when he was eight. It had become a running joke between them over the years. His father needed him, and needed him now.

"Let me get a few clothes and my laptop and I'll be right with you."

When Curt arrived at Andrews AFB a few hours later he was met by Howard Carney, who explained that his dad had been tapped to oversee a worldwide troop redeployment. Astonishing. But then, his dad had been a whiz at deployment.

Howard took Curt to the Pentagon's dignitary guest quarters and told him to be patient that Alex was giving a very lengthy debrief to the President at this very moment, and he would tell Alex that he had arrived safely.

Fifteen minutes later, Carney arrived at the briefing and nodded briefly to Alex. Curt had arrived with no problems. Good. Alex nodded back without breaking stride.

"As you can see we don't have sufficient naval transports to hit a twelve month timeframe for men and equipment, though we can get all of our Air Force planes back to the US. What I recommend is that we concentrate on the Korea's, Japan, and the Philippines first, then start on the Middle East moving most of the land based equipment that you see on the legend to Germany, Italy and France, where we have the installations in place and the room to store them. We can leave a token security force behind at each installation, much as we are going to do at the limited number of embassies we will maintain. I have intentionally placed most of the redeployed Air Force and Army personnel at US facilities away from the coasts for obvious reasons. Under this scenario we can accomplish all of this in seven months. That's all gentlemen."

There was the contemplative silence, then suddenly questions began to fly back and forth among the Chiefs of Staff and for a good hour they exchanged concerns with Alex, Admiral Torrance, and the President. Finally the President stood up and walked to the screen where Alex's plans were displayed.

"Gentleman, remember this is survival. This is about ensuring the US is still around after July, 2017, so let's get it done."

The President left the secure debriefing room as Torrance stood up along with all the others in the room. Torrance then addressed the group.

"Men, we've got our marching orders. There is zero tolerance for missed deadlines. General Hanken has absolute authority from the President and me to accomplish the intended outcomes. Nearly eighty percent of the armed forces will come under his control including the land based nuclear forces along with the air wings that have nuclear capabilities. The sea based naval forces will remain under my control. You Chiefs of Staff are there to ensure your line people are cooperating fully with General Hanken. That concludes this meeting, now get to work."

As Alex waited for his superiors to file out of the oval office first, Admiral Torrance buttonholed him.

"Well done, Alex. I'm sure you need to get some rest, so I won't hold you long. Howard told me about your son. If you think he can add value to your efforts then bring him on board."

"Thank you sir."

"We've already run a background on him. He is everything you said."

"But."

"His fiancé's parents seem to be...on the seamier side of society. We wouldn't want your son, or Cynthia—is it? To be compromised in any way."

Of course. He should have warned them. "Admiral I'll handle it, don't worry. They're both good kids and very talented."

"I know you will, Alex. Now go to your son and get some rest. That's an order."

"Yes, sir."

Ten minutes later Alex was flying back to the Pentagon on the President's chopper. God, had it only been three weeks since he'd invited Curt and Cynthia over for the celebration dinner?

"Hey, there's the new graduate." He kissed Cynthia's cheek. She'd just received her Master's degree in mathematics from Cal State Sacramento. Curt had asked him to make a big deal out of it since her parents had hardly paid any attention to her for years— not since Curt told him that Cynthia had returned from a family visit sporting a bruise. Alex had visited Cynthia's father, who was drunk at the time, to make sure that bruise was the last. Since then

Cynthia had hardly seen her parents. But he was happy to pick up the slack.

"You know," Cynthia said after diner. "I think you would really like this lady at school. She is 44, a widow, one grown daughter, pretty as a picture."

"Cynthia I—"

"I told her about you, and she said she would be interested in meeting you. How about it Dad, I'll give her your phone number?"

Alex's stomach had tightened. He just wasn't up for this. He was perfectly comfortable living alone and why rock the boat?

"Cynthia she sounds very nice and under normal circumstances...I'd be interested. But right now I have a lot of things on my plate that I'm dealing with—and, no, Curt, it's not about your mom. I am over Ellen's passing...I'm just very busy right now."

At the time, it had been a lie. He still couldn't see himself with another woman, not after he'd botched things so thoroughly with Ellen. All those years she'd hinted, then suggested, then demanded, and finally almost begged that he spend more time with her and Curt. And he'd always intended to, but something always seemed to come up. Until it was too late.

He hoped he'd changed since then. After Ellen's death, he'd retired and spent as much time with Curt as he could. But he still had his doubts.

Of course, now it was all moot. Like it or not, he was going to be phenomenally busy right up until the moment of impact. And then, the real work would begin. He realized the chopper was hovering above the Pentagon landing pad, too pressed for time, he leapt the few feet to the ground and hurried to meet Curt. He found him.

"No, sweetheart, there's nothing to worry about. I was told Dad was summoned to a special meeting of former Air Force generals to discuss better retirement options for the military, and his cell phone went on the blink. That's why I couldn't get a hold of him. Listen, here he is. I'll call you back later...I love you too....Yes I will, talk to you later, bye."

Alex gave Curt a brief man hug, careful not to make it longer or harder than usual.

"How was the trip?"

"Good…Dad what the hell is going on?"

"Hey, let's go have dinner some place special, like the War Room. I'll call the cafeteria and they will send us a feast. How's that sound?"

"It sounds like you're stalling me. What are you involved in? It's more than just this—

"Not now son, let's go eat and enjoy our dinner okay? Give me fifteen to clean up and we'll head down to the big room."

When they arrived at the War Room, cafeteria personnel were hurriedly setting up a table in an adjacent room for them. A half hour later a five course meal was delivered with steak and lobster—Curt's favorites—as entrees. Alex dismissed the attendant so he and Curt could speak privately.

"Curt you know I love you don't you?"

"Okay, you're not making me any calmer."

"And you know I would never intentionally hurt you."

"Dad—

"Let me finish. Do you trust me?"

"I have always trusted you."

"Well, then listen to me when I tell you that I am involved in something, if I were to tell you more, I would violate the US Secrets Act."

Curt stared for a moment, then took a gulp of his wine.

"Dad what the hell have they got you doing?"

"Curt it's the biggest thing since God created the earth."

"Okay, let me put it right back on you. Do you trust me?"

"That's dirty pool, Curt."

"And that's not an answer. Do you trust me to keep something secret?"

"Yes."

"Then tell your only living son what his father is involved in, so I don't have to worry about you disappearing into the night."

Alex realized Curt was not going to let up. He was his father's son.

"Okay," he said, "sit back and let me tell you the tale. It's a shame to waste all that good food though. You're not going to want to eat when I'm done."

He told Curt the events of the last few days, giving things in order in which he'd found them out. As he did Curt went from stunned to, visibly shaking to, holding his hand to his mouth to keep from retching.

Alex finished and waited for Curt to respond. Curt sat there for a moment then recovered and looked his dad straight in the eye.

"Dad, if there is a chance the world is going to end, I want to spend every last day with you."

And after everything else, that was the one thing Alex couldn't handle. The tears began to roll down his cheeks, visions of Ellen and Curt together tore at his heart…He stammered, trying to compose himself…eventually he felt he could safely speak. "Okay, then, I've already gotten clearance for you and Cynthia. You will be on my team. Do you think…can…would Cynthia want to be involved in this?"

"Dad how could…We may all turn into dust molecules in two years, but we could push up our wedding date, and work as a married couple until the end or the new beginning, whichever. At least we would all be together as a family."

"This is a big step. You can't turn back once you go on that list, do you understand that?"

"Sure."

"This is not going to be a vacation; we are in a race to save as much as we can from total annihilation. What we do will form the foundation of a new America. There will be some very difficult decisions that have to be made about who gets to survive in a shelter and who will be left exposed to…whatever may come. And before then, there is no way to make this public without massive outbreaks of lawlessness. That's why they need extreme secrecy and why I'm bringing the armed forces home. Nationwide civil unrest could very well doom all of us before the event even occurs. And that is why you and Cynthia cannot under any circumstances discuss this with anyone other than designated personnel. No friends, not her family, no one."

"You're right Dad," he said. People will go absolutely over the edge when this comes out. So what can I do?"

"We'll need redundant data and telecommunications capabilities among the survival facilities. The military has their interfacing systems already in place throughout the various commands. I'm going to need a stand-alone system that can interface with the defense systems."

"Okay. But you're talking about some serious money. And what kind of timeframe are you looking at?"

"I gave them a seven month pipeline on the redeployment plan. It probably needs to coincide with that as well."

"And the money?"

"Money is no object."

Eventually, they ate, rather quietly, since most of the obvious questions didn't have answers. They were just finishing when Alex got a call that Howard Carney wanted to meet him. He sent Curt off to start looking over briefing books then went to his office to meet Carney.

Carney was on the couch working on a tablet, but he put it away when Alex walked in.

"Alex. I just heard from the joint chiefs. They've accepted your redeployment plan with no major modifications, and the troop movements are already underway. Now we need to start on the survival shelters."

Alex nodded. A week of nearly nonstop work resulting in one of the largest, most complex, yet cleanest and most efficient redeployment plans ever developed, and not even an "attaboy." This brave new world had a pace all its own, and he was going to have to adjust.

Carney was still talking. "I have a contact that you should bring in on your team; Dr. Sandra Chenowith. She's at UC Davis and is recognized as one of the foremost experts on crop cultivation and ecosystems, especially as it relates to disaster recovery methodology."

"UC Davis? That's just west of where we all live."

"Is it? Good. Your first assignment?"

"Sorry. Go ahead."

"BLM has control of some 600,000 acres in five western states. The Homeland security people targeted several abandoned mines around Coeur d' Alene, Idaho, as ideal for survival shelters and military depots. Until we can determine a good headquarters for you why don't you operate out of Sacramento. Our contact at the BLM in Coeur d' Alene is Pete Cernak. He's a mining engineer with thirty years of experience."

"Yes that sounds like a good plan. You'll get me the contact numbers before Curt and I leave?"

"They're already in your phone. Start packing. Oh, by the way, I've already set up a contract for your Lear." He consulted his tablet. It's at the Sacramento Executive Airport, which is where your private plane is hangered, right? I'm also going to have a team of tech people meet you at your house to install secure telephone and fax transmission equipment. All communications about Project One must be done by secured and encrypted means."

And the pace seemed to quicken.

"Yes, sir."

"Now remember Alex, we have billions to spend, it's off budget, if you need something just get me the wiring instructions. We know you had a sizable inheritance from your father in 2005, and you haven't blown it, so we're assuming your character is beyond reproach. There will be no audits. Credit cards are on the way for you and Curt, they have six figure credit lines, pay for nothing out of your pocket. Any questions?"

"Not at the moment."

"If any come up, you know where to find me." Carney stood and stuck out his hand. "I can't tell you how fortunate we are to have you heading this up, good luck and have a safe trip back home."

So there was a little bit of an "attaboy."

"Thanks Howard."

Curt and Alex next made their way to Admiral Torrance's office, threading their way through a building so large and overwhelming that Curt was beginning to wonder if they would ever get there. But it was only the latest surreal moment in a long, surreal day.

"Alex come in and this must be Curt."

Torrance shook Curt's hand. For someone who spent most of his days in an office, he looked like he could still convincingly order Curt to drop and give him fifty. So Curt made sure his grip was substantial.

"So are you two off to Sacramento, did you get enough stick time in that Lear to get comfortable with it?"

"It's a piece of cake, after an A-10, it's like driving a Cadillac."

"Alex this redeployment plan is invaluable. Now can you give us one for survival shelters? I don't have to tell you that once this gets out all hell will break loose. We have to be finished or nearly finished if we're going to have any chance at climbing back out of our holes and restarting our country."

"What's the current time frame?"

"The President has scheduled a news conference for two weeks from tomorrow to announce a major shift in foreign policy and the redeployment plan. That gives us time to contact all the division commanders as you suggested so they won't be blindsided. After redeployment starts, the probability of a leak increases, probably geometrically. There is literally nothing you can't ask for, just get it to Howard and it is done. You have my office number and my Land/Sat number, and I'm available to you twenty-four seven."

Curt was feeling light-headed, both at the amount of work to be done and what was riding on it. But his father just nodded.

"God speed, Alex," the Admiral said. "And Curt——take care of your old man."

"Always sir."

Chapter 5

TEAM BUILDING

The President sat down at his desk waiting for all the invited to take their places. Arlen Hendry was first to arrive and took a seat on the couch. Next, Arthur Cantwell, Secretary of State, was ushered into the room, greeted the President, and sat down across from Hendry in one of the wing backed chairs. Admiral Torrance came in with apologies five minutes late—traffic was stacked up around Washington that day.

"I brought all of you here today because we have finalized our redeployment and survival plans. In particular, what do we tell the rest of the world? And when? Now? When we've completed the redeployments and put into play our survival plans? I want to know your thoughts."

"Mr. President," Hendry said, "you know my position on this. If we were going to disclose, it should have been immediately. To disclose now, while our plans are in progress, could well sabotage those plans."

"Arthur? Your position?"

"I have to disagree with Arlen. Every day that goes by means another day the other countries aren't preparing. I don't think I want that on my conscience."

"Evan, I know your position, is there anything that you can add?"

"There is one other thing I think both Arlen and Arthur have missed. When this gets out there are going to be countries that take stock of their abilities to care for their populace. Many will come to the conclusion they simply don't have the wherewithal to meet the demands like we can. For example, China can't feed it's people now, the United States, being the breadbasket of the world…will look awfully tempting. We had better get our house in order before we announce anything to anybody. It may be nationalistic, but I'm really not willing to sacrifice my own nation on the risky possibility of saving someone else's."

"Admiral, you really think the Chinese would invade the United States?" Secretary Cantwell asked.

"If you recall in the middle of the first decade, Mr. Secretary, the Chinese began securing oil imports from all over the world to support their exploding economy. It was their aggressive activity in that area that started the dramatic rise in oil prices. They would stop at nothing to get that oil. And they will stop at nothing to secure food for over a billion and a half people. Don't forget not only China would be looking at us with envious eyes, but India has over a billion souls to feed as well. Both have huge, well trained armies, and both are nuclear powers. No, I adamantly oppose early disclosure. Get the redeployment done and let General Hanken implement his survival plan."

"All of you have valid arguments for and against," the President said. "At this point I think it best we maintain our stance on non-disclosure. When we feel we have repositioned ourselves from a military standpoint and can provide for the security of the nation, then I'll feel more comfortable revisiting this issue. And as for my conscience, Arthur, well…I was elected to make hard decisions. This one's just bigger than most." The President stood. "Thank you, all, for your input."

Alex eased the jet in for a smooth landing at the Executive Airport and taxied to hangar nine as instructed by the tower. Mitch Reilly, airport manager, was standing, waiting with his hands shading his eyes as the turbines whined to a stop just short of the hangar opening. Alex and Curt went through the shutdown checklist and met him at the exit doorway of the jet.

Alex shook hands with the man, trying not to rush him. He was feeling the clock ticking right down to his bones. "I understand you have something for me?"

Reilly nodded to the hangar behind him. "This is your private hangar, paid ahead for three months. General, I received this package last week from none other than Howard Carney, the Deputy Secretary of Defense. Am I right that he's just one step away from being the top dog right?"

"That's correct."

"Wow. Well, Howard put a note on here it says, this is an open contract for services, you bill it, General Hanken signs it, and we will wire the funds in ten days to an account you specify, no questions asked. In all my years as an airport manager I have never seen such a contract. You must be doing something real special for DOD."

Alex winced. He was going to have to let Howard know he needed to have a flunky make arrangements if he wanted to remain inconspicuous.

"Mitch," he said, "listen, there are some things I'll need. I'll try to give you a 48 hour notice when I plan to fly, but there will be times when an issue comes up suddenly. I can see needing a one hour turnaround. So I want a Level 2 ground maintenance preflight check performed each time I land, struts, rudders, brakes, fuel pump and oil pumps, hydraulic lines, avionics integrity and an environment system check."

"Wow again. I'd have to put two mechanics on the plane."

"Bill it, and I will sign it."

Mitch ran his eyes over the plane with a look that Alex usually reserved for women.

"This is a real beauty a new C-21 Lear, now I realize it's not the A-10 you're used to, General, but you didn't have leather seats, a refer, and a coffee maker in you're A-10."

"True. Besides, people had a tendency to shoot at me in the A-10. In my old age I've decided to take it a little easier."

"And you deserve it. By the way do you want to keep your King Air in its old hangar?"

"Yeah, that'll do for now. See you later Mitch."

Alex and Curt took separate taxis to their homes. Curt needed to get hold of Cynthia as soon as possible. Alex immediately called Dr. Chenowith to set up a meeting. She was on another call so he left a message for her to call him. Next he called Pete Cernak at the BLM in Coeur d' Alene and set up an appointment.

He was packing some fresh clothes when a small black telephone next to his bed—his new secure phone—rang. Alex Han—"

"Why the hell didn't you call sooner? Don't you know the world's coming to an end?"

"Dr. Chenowith, I presume?"

"That question wasn't a joke. I've been waiting for your call for three days now."

"I'm sorry, but I only heard about you yesterday, and I've been a little busy since then. You're not at the top of my punch list." He said it before he recognized the pun, then decided he didn't mind the pun a bit.

"So General Hanken— it is General isn't it?"

"Yes Dr. Chenowith— it is Dr. isn't it?"

"General, I fear we have gotten off to a bad start."

"You think? I would have hung up a long time ago, but we have a job to do, and I'm willing to put up with a lot to get it done."

"Ah, now that's the stuff of a military hero. That Silver Star and all those other medals they must be a heavy burden to bear."

"No more so than this conversation Dr. Chenowith."

There was a long pause. "I like you. You dance well."

"Terrific. When can we meet?"

"Pick me up at my office in Building Six room 122. I'll take us to a quaint place that is secluded and private, where we can talk without fear of being overheard."

"Perfect. See you tomorrow Dr. Chenowith."

Alex hung up the phone and sank into his easy chair. With the world ending he didn't need a caustic, intellectual prima donna. What next? Would they ask him to establish a run away teen safe house?

Well he had other things to worry about. Like how to keep the neighbors from suspecting something was up…he didn't want the Wilsons to spend the next few years in involuntary detention. Also his investment portfolio would need to be liquidated, leaving enough cash in the bank to pay bills and living expenses. The rest should go into gold, platinum, silver and diamonds. But, then again maybe that would all be for nothing. If people were struggling for food, they weren't going to care about Kruggerrands. He would call Howard for any suggestions, or if there were any prohibitions against accumulating precious metals since he had inside information about a future event.

After reading the detailed instructions left by the technicians, he picked up the secure phone—and how did they install it without the neighbors noticing? They put a high gain microburst dish on his roof for God's sake! He began to realize that standard operating procedures were no longer in effect. He speed dialed Howard.

"Howard."

"Hey Alex, I see you are on your secure line, those guys work fast."

"Yeah, listen, this may sound crass but I was wondering…. I have a substantial portfolio."

"We know."

"Of course. But given what is on the horizon I was considering moving into precious metals, I mean taking physical delivery. Would that present a problem?"

"Alex you have a fabulous mind, and the answer is no, there are no prohibitions for someone in your position. In fact I'm going to give you the number of a man at the US Mint to call. He'll give you some surprising information."

"Thanks Howard. Bye."

Alex dialed the number and spoke with the gentleman at the US Mint. What he found out left him gasping for air. It seems that just yesterday the man had received notification from the Justice Department that Alex was a Level One designee. Which apparently meant that the US Mint would be shipping gold and silver coins, along with platinum ingots to him as soon as he had secured suitable storage space.

"Um...how much are we talking about?" he asked.

"Somewhere in the range of six and ten billion in precious metals, and fifty billion in cash of various denominations."

Okay. Howard had said that price was no object. Alex was beginning to see what that meant.

The man gave him instructions on what type of secured storage he'd need, which the US Treasury would pay for. The man went on to say that their expectation was that all of the Level One designees would have their facilities in place within nine months. Alex thanked him for his time and clicked off the phone.

My God. Things were moving far too fast. He needed to get up to speed, and stop being so damned overwhelmed.

Then he began to think about what this new information actually meant. He was one of a number of Level One designees, all of whom were being given a chunk of the national mint. The United States was literally being broken up into pieces and spread all over the country. It was like an insurance company not concentrating its business in one area; the US government was spreading the risk. Alex got up out of his chair just about the time his residence phone rang.

"Hello."

"Is this General Alex Hanken?"

"Yes."

"General, this is Jeffrey Macklin from Cal Tech, I need to talk to you privately as soon as possible,"——Macklin gasped for air——"Both of our lives may be in danger."

"Professor Macklin calm yourself. Can I call you right back on a secure line?"

"No, it's got to be in person. I'm on my way there now."

"Hang on. I have appointments all day long and I fly out of town tomorrow for three days. I'll be back Monday and can see you then."

"Very well, I'll see you then." The line went dead.

Well, that was unexpected.

Alex immediately called Howard back.

"Howard I've got a small problem here, one of those professors, a Jeffrey Macklin, just called me saying that both our lives were in danger. He wanted to see me right away and I put him off until next Monday."

"Here's what you do. Call Ted Jeffers at this secure number. He'll handle this for you." "Thanks Howard." The name Ted Jeffers rang a bell but he couldn't remember exactly from where. He'd been through so much in the last few days. He dialed the number and the familiar screeching noise of a scrambled call could be heard.

"Jeffers."

"Mr. Jeffers, this is General Alex Hanken, Howard Carney said you would handle something that just popped up."

"General, what can I do for you?"

"About twenty minutes ago a Professor Jeffrey Macklin of Cal Tech called me to say our lives were in danger and he needed to see me right away."

"Oh Christ, Macklin's finally flipped, his boss Eldon Huart died of a heart attack and he's conspiracy happy. General forget about it. I will take care of this, and you do your job. And if anything like this happens again—call me immediately."

"Thanks. And forgive me but I know your name, I just can't place you?"

"I'm the Director of the FBI and from now on it's Ted."

"Okay Ted, good to talk to you."

Alex hung up, feeling even more disoriented. He was on a first name basis with the director of the FBI? This was just...the further into it he went, the more bizarre it got. And just where was he in the chain of command?

No that was ridiculous. He was a retired serviceman with a gift for logistics, that's all. He was being treated with deference because he was doing an important job. That didn't make him an important person. He shook his head. Having the US Mint hand you several billion dollars can go right to your head.

Alex got a call from Curt asking if he and Cynthia could come over that evening so he could explain to her what was going on. Cynthia didn't know anything beyond the redeployment plan story. It was up to Alex to break the more ominous news to her. Alex went to the grocery store and dropped some cleaning off and waited for Curt and Cynthia to arrive for the evening.

Alex went outside on the patio and looked up at the stars. Where were they? Where would they be coming from? And when they were gone, what would be left?

Curt found his father out on the patio, staring at the stars. "Dad Cynthia's in the kitchen waiting."

"What? Oh, sure."

His dad seemed perfectly calm, but Curt knew better. His dad had never been one to just stare at the night sky. The fear was there, underneath the surface calm, held in check by millions of details that needed to be taken care of.

Curt knew this because he felt the same way. Whenever he stopped planning and really thought about what was coming, he started to tremble. He was doing it now. He held his hand to his chin to quell the nervousness swelling up in his stomach.

Then his father put a hand on his shoulder. How's Cynthia sound?"

Curt was grateful for the change in focus. "She kind of balked because she said she had to work tomorrow, so she couldn't stay late. I told her she may never be late again in her life, after tonight." They both managed a forced grin.

Cynthia greeted his father with a big hug and the three of them got comfortable in the den. His father then told her the whole story once again, with Curt sitting next to her, holding her close.

Cynthia began to tear up. She tried to wipe them away during Alex's explanation, but they kept coming. Finally she just leaned on Curt and would occasionally squeeze him for reassurance.

His father then surprised him, telling Cynthia that her background included her parents, and that the powers to be were a little nervous about that.

"I know, Dad," she said. "I'm not going to let them get in the way of whatever it is they want me to do."

Alex nodded. "Good girl. I'll let them know."

"If this world was coming to an end. I want to spend the rest of my days with Curt. Can we afford for me to quit my job?"

His father looked a bit odd at this. "Ah, yes."

"So now we can plan our wedding Curt."

"The sooner the better," His father walked over to Cynthia and gave her a big hug. "And it will be a big, fancy, outrageously, expensive wedding."

She giggled and put her arms around Alex's neck and told him. "Oh Dad, I love you."

Cynthia wept the entire trip to their condo. Curt tried to console her but she couldn't stop. How could she stop? She was way too young to be facing her mortality?

"Cynthia, baby doll," Curt said softly, "it'll be okay, we'll get through this."

"Oh Curt, everything we've done, all that we were planning… it's for nothing. I've tried to be a good person, better than my parents. We'll be no better off than they are. It's just…so unfair." Her sobbing turned to small whimpers as Curt held her in his arms.

The next morning, Curt and Cynthia showed up at Alex's back door fifteen minutes early, looking both subdued and resolute.

"Is there something wrong?" Alex ushered them into the kitchen. "Have you been having second thoughts?"

"No, we had a tough night, thinking about what may have been. It's just a shock, not being in control of our own future anymore."

Alex had already spent a lot of time on this. He sat down across from them.

"Listen to me, both of you; no one has ever been in control of their own future.

"But we can always make decisions in the face of...circumstances—where we go, how we go, what we do and don't accomplish. Our ending story belongs to us, even if we can't always write the context."

Cynthia seemed calm. Remarkably so. "But the context here is the end of the world."

"All right," Alex said. "I'll grant you that extreme. But what we do about it is still in our hands. We can sit around and wait for what is handed to us or we can meet the challenge and do what we can. I for one refuse to go quietly. I have the two of you to think about and your futures. I will give my life doing everything I can to ensure that you have one."

"Dad, I love you so much," Cynthia said, "and you're right we're being childish."

"Did I say that? You're scared about what may come. You have regrets about things undone or maybe unsaid. There's nothing childish about any of that. I am on the same emotional roller coaster. But you can't let it seize your survival instinct. Don't let it take that spirit of accepting a challenge from you. If we're going to die, then let it happen while we're giving it our best shot."

"Dad we're with you," Curt said.

"Good. Now a couple of practical things. Howard's arranged to pay you two each $150,000 a year. You will start getting auto deposits next week in your checking accounts."

"That's about ten grand more than I'm making now," Curt said.

"That's a whole lot more than I make in a year," Cynthia mentioned.

"Especially if you forget about taxes and your 401Ks. I've got a luncheon with this Dr.Chenowith today, then tomorrow we all fly to Coeur d' Alene and start earning our pay."

The drive out to Davis from his home was a reminder of how much agriculture there was in California—field after field of crops. What would it look like in three years?

When he located Dr. Chenowith's office and knocked on the door, a young woman opened it. Must be a graduate student.

"I'm General Hanken; I'm here to see Dr. Chenowith."

"Sandra, there is an absolutely gorgeous man out here to see you," she said.

"Terri, behave yourself."

And then Dr. Chenowith walked out of her office. She was nothing like what he expected "Pleased to meet you, General," she said. "Ready for lunch?"

"Oh Sandra, are you taking him to Edna's, I want to go please?"

"Don't be ridiculous," Dr. Chenowith said. "You're a grad assistant. You're supposed to starve."

As Alex drove to the restaurant, she pointed out various sites around the Davis area. Edna's was a small place—a private home that had been converted, from the look of it. But a vine covered patio with tables gave it some charm. It was a little chilly outside so she asked for a table in the corner overlooking the patio. The waitress took their drink orders and left the menus for them to look over.

"General Hanken, this place serves classic American cuisine—, pot roast, meat loaf, fried chicken, and it is all excellent."

Ah, the stereotypes. "I'll take your word for it. I'm more a Cordon Bleu man."

"Really? Give me a good steak any day. I hope Terri didn't embarrass you."

"Not at all. Though, I can't recall ever being called gorgeous."

"Well to be honest, you are very handsome man, not at all what I expected."

"What did you expect?"

"Short—, most pilots are short. Balding,— most Generals I know are balding. Okay, now it's your turn."

"I must admit, you're not what I expected either."

"And?"

"Well I was expecting a doughty, flower-dressed, gray streaked hair, hunched back earth mother."

"Hunched back?"

"From carrying the weight of the world."

"Oh my gosh, you are a real prize."

"And what do you see?"

Despite himself, he was actually starting to enjoy this. There was more wit here than he expected, and plenty of spirit. "I see a very attractive woman in front of me."

"Well, Gen—

"Can we drop the General? Please call me Alex."

She nodded. "I'm Sandra."

"Perfect."

The waitress came with their drinks and took their order. He ordered pot roast, and she ordered the same. He couldn't stop looking at her eyes, they were light smoky blue and she had astonishing strawberry— blond hair. Her skin was lightly tanned but clear, he guessed her age to be in the mid-forties, but she was in what appeared to be terrific physical condition.

"So what should we talk about?" she said.

"Sandra just how much have you been told."

"Well I'm a designated person, so I know everything you know, I wish I didn't."

"Yeah, same here." At least he didn't have to reinvent the wheel.

"Sandra I'm flying up to Coeur d'Alene tomorrow to start looking for potential survival facilities. I know this may be short notice, but I'd like you to come along and assess the area as an agriculture center post event. I plan on being up there for two or three days."

"Well, I don't have anything more important on my schedule. I just put in my sabbatical notice, and today was my last day at UC Davis."

"Fantastic."

"When I get back to the office I'll pull the Ag stats on that county and the surrounding counties, I've never been there before, it should be interesting."

"Excuse me for being forward, but is there someone that you have to account for?"

"Husband or a boyfriend? Or girlfriend?"

"I'm sorry, I don't mean to intrude. It's just that I've had to deal with my son and his fiancée and trying to figure out how I was going to skirt around all these issues without alerting them. I didn't manage it."

"No offense taken. And to answer your question, no, I just jettisoned a suitor. A male suitor."

"To a pilot the word jettisoned, can be both good and bad."

"I am going to enjoy working with you. So are we driving up or what?"

"No we're taking the plane they gave me."

"What is it, I'm a pilot myself?"

"It's a C-21— military version of an eight seat Lear. Brand new." She was a pilot? No wonder it costs so much to attend a university, all the professors are out playing around in their private planes.

But her eyes.

"Hey first class I'm going to like this I can tell."

"The plane is for our exclusive use, and the government picks up all the tabs no questions asked. But we're not flying down to Rio in it."

She sobered. "Wouldn't dream of it. We're going to be busy."

They finished lunch and Alex took her back to her office. He told her he would confirm hotel reservations for the entire party and to plan on wheels up at nine in the morning. She gave him her home and cell phone numbers and asked if she could leave her car at his house while they were away.

The drive home was an exercise in self-discipline; he kept drifting back to her eyes. They were so mesmerizing…

He couldn't even think about going there. He had to stay focused…And besides, he hadn't been available for Ellen. He was going to be a lot less available now.

Tomorrow they started the arduous task of finding suitable locations for an as yet to be determined number of people who were going to be needed to save the world.

Chapter 6

LOCATION, LOCATION, LOCATION

Alex called Sandra that evening.

"Hi Alex, I'm putting together some clothes for the trip, and by the way, there is a USDA office in Coeur d'Alene that I can use for a work hub."

"That's terrific. Listen, I wanted to let you know that we're going to have some passengers coming with us."

"Let me guess, Curt and his fiancé."

"Oh did I mention that? Sorry. Last evening he and Cynthia agreed that they would work on the team. They're scared to death, but if the world is going to end they wanted to be together. Curt knows systems and communications hardware, plus he is a pilot. Cynthia has her Masters in math plus she is fluent in Spanish and two dialects of Chinese. I figure you and she can work together on your end of the project. She is really bright."

"That sounds perfect. Tell her to brush up on game theory and Nonlinear Dynamics theory, she'll need it."

"Nonlinear…"

"It's a branch of Chaos theory. Oh, and you didn't ask but I have a daughter. She will graduate from Cal Berkeley next year, and she, too, speaks several foreign languages. In fact her primary degree is in linguistics, and her secondary emphasis was international relations. She always wanted to work at the UN."

"Wow, you must be very proud of her."

"Of course, but I don't want to bring her in now. I want her to finish her degree. And enjoy a couple worry free years."

"Okay, then can you be here about eight in the morning?"

"Sure thing, I'll see you then."

Alex hung up the phone and thought how stupid it had been not to ask if she had any children. Her eyes must have distracted him. Alex thought about calling Jeffers again; he didn't like the part about never hearing from Macklin again. But Jeffers was right, his mission was too critical. He needed to stay on task, and not be distracted by events that didn't concern him.

Alex sat down at his computer, paid all his upcoming bills online for the next year, and went to the internet to check on any topics concerning asteroid impacts and/or impact outcomes. He came across an article written by a Professor Edward Killian of MIT; it was filled with technical data and formulas, but was well enough written that a layman could follow his arguments. The article pulled no punches, and graphically depicted some of the more disastrous scenarios. Alex felt this was a man that he should talk to and wondered if he was already on the team. When he got back from Idaho he would call Howard about it. Alex retired that night thinking about Ellen. He was kind of relieved that she would not be here to endure what was to come.

Six a.m. and Alex was up making coffee. At seven Sandra was at the front door. He told her he would open the garage door for her to pull her car in. As she got out, she noticed his auto. "Smart Car? Nice. Also not what I expected."

"Oh?" he said. "What did you expect?"

"Some huge vintage muscle car—a Charger, a Mustang. An attempt to recapture a lost youth on four wheels."

Ah, "Well come on in and have some—"

She nodded toward the garage's other bay. "What's under the tarp?"

"Well it's not…It's kind of an unfinished project…"

She dropped her bag and tugged the tarp off of his 1966 Carroll Shelby Cobra roadster in mint condition. And nearly collapsed, laughing.

"It's not about my youth," he said. "It's homage to an age long gone."

She was beginning to get control. "Of…course it is. I bet it's a hoot to drive as well."

"If you're good, maybe I'll let you find out some day."

They went into the house through the kitchen, where she inhaled the scent of coffee. "Can I get a cup of that?"

He poured. They sat down at the kitchen table and engaged in small talk until Curt and Cynthia arrived. Introductions were made, then they were off to the airport.

With all the luggage on board, Alex turned over the engines, went through preflight, and then taxied for takeoff. Curt was in the right seat, Sandra and Cynthia were in back, relaxing in the plush leather seats. "I'm told there are bagels and refreshments in the refrigerator." He said. "I understand there's' a coffee maker as well."

After about thirty minutes, Sandra poked her head into the cockpit.

"Captain, I'll be your stewardess for this flight. Can I get you anything like coffee, tea or a pillow?"

"For now, all I want is bottled water, the other things maybe later," He grinned, as much at Curt's unease as at Sandra.

Sandra settled into the seat opposite Cynthia. "Alex is really a dynamic man. I'm looking forward to working with him."

Cynthia nodded and smiled. It looked like she had more on her mind than working with him. Cynthia wasn't sure how she felt about that. Alex didn't need distractions right now.

Eventually, Sandra pleaded a sleepless night and tried to doze off. Cynthia wished she could do the same, but it was hard when, every time you closed your eyes you found yourself envisioning the unthinkable.

"Curt take over for a bit."

Alex came back into the passenger compartment and found Sandra hunched over the side of her seat. He went to an overhead compartment and got a blanket and pillow, then hit a handle and Sandra's chair flopped back, startling her. Alex put a blanket over her and the pillow under her head. She looked up at him with those smoky liquid eyes and thanked him.

Cynthia watched the heat between them, and knew it was just a matter of time. She had to warn Curt that his father was being stalked by a barracuda. After grabbing a bagel, Alex went back to the cockpit, and a moment later Curt came through the cabin and slid into the seat next to her.

"How you holding up?" he whispered.

"Well enough, I guess. Have you noticed the chemistry between those two?"

"Yeah isn't it great. She's a stone cold fox."

"Curt!"

"Ssshhhh. Keep it down."

Cynthia dialed her voice back a little. "She has designs on your Dad. He has a big bull's eye on his back, and she has him in her sights."

"You say that like it's a bad thing. Dad needs some company, you even admitted that, and besides she is supposedly one of the smartest people in the country."

"Well, maybe so, but it bears watching."

"Hey Dad is a big boy and knows what he's doing."

"You just remember what you said. I don't want to see your Dad hurt. He's had enough pain in the last few years."

"Cynthia honey, maybe this is exactly what he needs. And if it isn't, he'll do the right thing, like he always does."

"Now let's snuggle."

Sandra was holding in her laughter at what she heard. Cynthia was right to be so protective of Alex. But in all fairness, Alex had been on her mind ever since the luncheon in Davis. He was smart, witty, very handsome, a gentleman, and had a commanding presence. She would mark her time, and work this relationship slowly.

With that thought, she drifted off to sleep.

When the Coeur d'Alene municipal airport tower acknowledged Alex's message that he was thirty minutes out, Alex yelled for Curt to wake up, and get everybody ready for landing. As they taxied to the hangar Alex had leased for three months, he told them they were going to Hertz to rent two cars, then drive to the hotel and check in. Then he and Curt were going to grab some lunch and meet with Pete Cernak. Sandra was going to head to the USDA office to see what their setup was.

During lunch Alex announced that he had an appointment with Pete Cernak of the BLM at 3:00. He suggested Curt go with him, and Cynthia go with Sandra to the USDA office, and they would all meet back there at 6:00 for dinner.

An hour later, and Alex and Curt were scanning the lobby of the hotel for Pete Cernak, who said he would be wearing his green BLM shirt. And there he was, sitting in one of the lounge chairs. Pete saw them and stood up to shake their hands as they approached.

"Pete, Alex Hanken, and my son Curt, my project assistant."

"Let's see, where can we sit undisturbed?"

"Right over there at the corner of the bar is a table nobody ever sits at."

"Sounds like you know this place pretty well."

"Yeah, I come here for dinner and drinks a lot."

Once seated, Alex began to lay out what they were looking for—abandoned mines that might withstand earthquakes, floods, volcanic eruptions, even a nuclear strike. He told Pete that the military was embarking on a worldwide strategy to create survival bunkers for personnel and supplies in the event of a national catastrophe. He'd put a lot of thought into the cover story, but it still sounded weak, even to him.

But Pete seemed to accept it. He'd already done his homework and told Alex he had identified fifteen sites on BLM land that they should visit. He unfolded a map.

The nearest one was eight miles northwest of the city. Alex said he wanted to get started around eight in the morning and see as many sites as time allowed.

"We'll see you in the morning out front of the hotel." Alex stood and shook Pete's hand.

After Pete was gone, Curt leaned toward him. "You think he'll catch on?"

"Yeah probably sometime down the line. Hopefully we'll be so far along by then it won't matter. Listen, I'm going to go change into some street clothes and check some paperwork before we go to dinner. Put whatever you want on the hotel room Uncle Sam has got the tab."

"Great, see you at dinner Dad."

During dinner Sandra told of her and Cynthia's visit to the USDA office. She felt that it was a good start at putting together some ideas. She also went on to say Cynthia was a big help in deciphering some of the hydrologist's formulas. Alex asked what about historical data on the annual rainfall and snowmelt runoff into the lakes and rivers, and which lakes were spring fed and their historical levels. She told him she would get that tomorrow along with topography analysis and soil content for the 50 mile radius around Coeur d'Alene.

Alex was pleased. It sounded like everything was going smoothly, and that the team was able to work together well. He decided to go to his room and rest his eyes. The flight had taken a toll on them. Curt and Cynthia said they were going downstairs, there was a band playing in the lounge. Sandra announced she was heading to her room as well.

As Alex and Sandra walked down the hall to the elevator she said. "Given what we have to do, I actually enjoyed my first day on the job."

"I think we'll make a great team. Everybody seems to get along well."

"Even Cynthia loosened up, after I told her I wasn't planning on putting you in my trophy collection."

Hello? "Oh really? What did she say to you?"

"That she loved you, and couldn't bear the thought of you getting hurt after... your wife's passing. I'm so sorry to hear about that. It must have been awful."

"It was, but we've got past that. She's a sweet girl, especially given that her father is an alcoholic, and her mother a speed junkie. I think I'm her safe harbor, a surrogate parent you might say."

"And you're happy in that role?"

"Of course. Wouldn't you be?"

"Well, I think it's different between a father and daughter. Mothers tend to end up as backstops for daughters. They only seek you out when there's trouble."

"From what I've seen, I bet you're a good mom to Elizabeth."

"Thank you. But you seem to be just about the All-American dad to Curt. You can tell he worships the ground you walk on."

"Yeah he's a good man, and I think he'll make a good husband and father, if he gets the chance."

"Don't say that."

"I think we've got to get used to it if we're going to keep functioning."

"Anyway, I'm tired and we have a lot of reports to go over tomorrow. See you in the morning."

"Goodnight Sandra."

Morning arrived too soon for Curt and Cynthia. They were about fifteen minutes late getting downstairs, the two had danced well past midnight.

"Dad I'm sorry about that."

"Did you have fun?"

"Yeah."

"Good. Are you ready to go to work now?"

"Yes Dad."

"Then that's fine. Let's go."

The ride out to the first mine was dusty and bumpy and the BLM truck seemed like it had no shock absorbers. As they approached the entrance to the first mine Alex looked at the surrounding hills and valleys looking for danger signs, such as below elevation entrance or landslide evidence. Alex wasn't expecting to see that. The mine entrance was enclosed in steel shutter fences, with huge air duct piping coming out along the ceiling to the exit.

This was not your old time mine you saw with pictures of dirty clad men standing around with pick axes. These had railcar lines and evidence of high tech mining techniques that had been utilized. Huge rooms were excavated with massive grinding machines, which was perfect as far as Alex was concerned. Pete walked them in through the gate he unlocked, and guided them into the first open room area—about twelve by twelve, with a six foot ceiling. Alex was already feeling claustrophobic. There was a seventy-five feet long corridor about seven feet wide before the next room opened up. It was better about forty feet wide and maybe twenty feet long, but the ceiling was about ten feet up.

Alex stretched. "How much moisture do these rooms see?"

"None. None of the mines we're going to see have seepage problems. I assumed that any that did would be off the list automatically."

"And you were right." It was always a pleasure to deal with someone with a brain.

After they'd toured three more, similar rooms, Alex asked.

"Say Pete, how hard would it be to open the entrance and the corridor to about twenty feet?"

"No problem. A mining crew could do that in three maybe four days."

"Curt make a note of that and reference this mine number."

They left for the quick trip to the next mine. Thankfully, there was an actual paved road part of the way, until they turned off to the mine entrance road. Alex could see the entrance was well above what he wanted— about thirteen feet in height at the entrance. Inside there were several small office like rooms on both sides of the corridor, then a cavernous opening that Pete said extended for over one thousand yards. It was a good thirty feet wide and almost twelve feet to the ceiling.

"General, you could put an awful lot of men and material in here and it's bone dry."

"Curt note the mine number put it down as an A-1."

There were six other mines of similar size and dimensions that met with Alex's liking, except the last one. It had a steam vent that kept the back half of the mine fairly humid and warm. Alex had Curt make a note of it as well, and the comment about the steam vent.

"Pete, if we had to stay underground for an extended period of time where could we get fresh water from?"

"About a mile over that way is the Spokane River and back behind us there are two lakes just over that crest, which is about a mile and a half."

"Any idea what it would cost to run a six inch water line from any of those places to these mines?"

"We'd have to put it out to bid."

"All right, here's what I want you to do. I want you to contact a contractor, have them provide a bid on these first six mines. Skip this last one with the steam vent I'm not sure I can use it."

"It would make a nice sauna."

"In the bid, I want separate numbers for each mine, then combined for all six, and I want the bid to come from the river source, then the lake source and that would include stringing electric for the power source wouldn't it?"

"Well General, there are electric trunk lines all over this area. I don't think the contractor will have any problem finding a hook up close."

"And the lakes are they free of any mine runoffs or contaminants?"

"Oh yeah, they are all spring fed. You could almost drink it right out of the lake."

"Have any of them gone dry in recent times and what about the river?"

"Well, river water will never be as clean as lake water, but the lakes have never gone dry. They are fed by an aquifer that runs all the way up into Canada. The river, well I've been here for thirty-five years, and it has never dropped below twenty feet."

"Good. That's enough for today let's head back to the hotel. Curt I want you to prepare a summary of all our discussions."

While Curt was busy on his laptop preparing his report, Alex took Pete aside.

"Pete understand me, this is just the tip of the iceberg. We'll be putting in cement floors, finishing the walls in some mines, building sleeping dorms, kitchens, freezer units for cold food storage, bathrooms, installing water purification systems. Some mines will have to be vented, we will need electric power, lighting systems, cabling for data systems."

"Boy General, you're talking some serious money here."

"I have an extremely large wallet. Now here's my point. Setup whatever you want with these contractors, but the work must be done on time, and it must be of the highest quality possible. Money is not a problem, so do not cut corners. Do you understand me?"

Pete thought for a moment.

"Sure. There are a few contractors that we can use locally for some of the small jobs, but most of them will be from Spokane or Seattle."

"Now here is something critical. Each facility must have a secured double door system, with the inner door being a blast proof door at least twenty feet from the first door."

"That is definitely a Seattle firm."

"Are we on the same page now?"

"I'm with you General."

"Plan on meeting with me in the morning say around nine at the hotel."

"Will do."

As Alex and Curt entered the hotel Curt asked. "So Dad, did I just hear you tell Pete that it was okay for him to accept kickbacks and you'd look the other way?"

"That's right."

"And you're not bothered by this because…"

Alex still wasn't ready to mention the pallets of cash that the mint would be flying out in a few weeks.

"He could do it anyway, and we would never find out. This way I put him on notice that I know what he's doing. Now he has to take ownership if anything goes wrong."

"Ah I see. You just hired a project manager."

"And a good one, I hope."

They found Sandra and Cynthia having a drink at the bar.

"Hey what the hell is this drinking on the job?" Alex said. "Shocked. I'm shocked…"

Sandra grinned. "What are you having?"

"Barkeep," Alex said, "a Chivas Regal please, and put the ladies on my tab."

"You got it General."

"So what did you come up with today?" Sandra inquired.

"I think I've found all the locations I will need."

"Wow that was fast."

"The guy we were working with made it easy. I only had to pass on the last site because it had a natural steam vent in the back of the mine."

"Oh?" Sandra said. "Humid and warm was it?"

"Around room temperature wouldn't you say Curt?"

"Yeah, maybe a little warmer than that."

"Really?" So you passed on the mine that is ideal for seed germination and production?"

"Um…maybe."

"Can I go see it tomorrow?"

"Sure."

Alex proposed a toast to a successful day; they finished their drinks, and went to their rooms to clean up for dinner. Afterwards, Alex told everyone to be down at the hotel lobby at nine in the morning, and then he looked at Curt and Cynthia.

"That's 9 a.m. Pacific Time."

"Okay Dad, we hear you."

"Alex." Sandra said, "I want to go over some things with you."

"Your room or mine?"

"Mine, I've got my laptop there with my notes from yesterday and today."

"Your lead madam."

As soon as he entered her room, Alex could smell her distinctive perfume. She kicked off her shoes near the bed, then motioned Alex to come over to the table and called up a series of annotated maps.

"The hydrologist reports were very encouraging. The area is fed by multiple underground springs and aquifers originating out of Canada. The Spokane River's fed by snow runoff from the western Rockies that also extended into Canada. Within a fifty mile radius of the mine sites, we've got enough soil fertility to support potatoes a wide variety of legumes, carrots, beets, corn, and across the Spokane River into Washington State, rice and even wheat. Irrigation's not a problem. There is an abundance of lakes deep enough to sink submersible pumps, and the Spokane River was easily accessed to put in pumping stations as well. Unless the whole area takes multiple direct hits, we'll be in a good position to replant enough food to feed 40,000 people. All we'd need..."

Alex was always very good at multi-tasking. As he absorbed everything she said. All the while he sat there listening his mind took in this woman before him—her lips as she talked, the light dancing off her blond hair, making it almost shimmer. And those eyes, those smoky blue seductive eyes, that glinted every now and then like twinkling stars.

"Well," he said when it became necessary to say something, "that's just about the basic staples of the food chain with the exception of fruits."

"Silly, you ever heard of delicious red apples? They grow them right across the river in Washington and you can grow pears and peaches as well."

"Well there you go. We can look at your potential greenhouse tomorrow and we're done for this trip."

"I can't believe how much work we did, and my God Alex, your eyes are so emerald green."

Alex immediately recoiled. "Um...yes, I know. Listen, I'm tired, busy day, so I'll see you in the morning."

"Was there something I said?"

"It's nothing...... don't worry about it, I'll see you tomorrow... goodnight."

Alex left just slowly enough that it couldn't be said he fled. When he got to his own room, he leaned against the door, in the dark; trying to forget all the times Ellen had told him how his eyes reminded her of green emeralds.

He apologized for it the next morning, in their elevator on their way down for breakfast.

"Alex, you don't have to explain," she said. "I was being too forward."

"No, no, I really enjoy your company. It's just that sometimes I… let my wife's memory creep into my life at the most inopportune times. I'm sorry. I hope you weren't offended."

"Hey big boy you have to do a lot more than that to hurt my feelings. Alex we're in a desperate struggle to survive, I need someone like you in my life right now more than ever, if it's just to know that someone cares. Even if it's only as— a good close friend. It might help bring some sanity into a world that may soon go insane."

"Sandi, we'll all get through this together."

"Sandi, I like that, I'll call you snookums."

"Please…… I would never recover."

Everyone was downstairs waiting. They piled into the BLM suburban and drove out to the mine Sandi wanted to see.

"Pete," Sandi said on the hike into the mine, "how far back does this mine shaft go to the steam vent area?"

"Oh, I'd say it's about eight or nine hundred feet."

"Fantastic. I can feel the humidity now. We're about halfway now?"

"Yes."

When they got near to the end Sandi could feel the heat and she stopped.

"Alex I can't believe this, it's absolutely perfect for a green house."

"Any incidents of methane gas?"

"No never," Pete said, "it's a true hot spring somewhere back in the mountain. While the mine was operating it was tested 24/7 for eight years, and there was never a trace."

"Alex we can use this."

"Very well," he said. "Pete, those six mines we looked at yesterday and this one, we want them for our project."

"I'll let the higher ups know that you will be taking them into your custody."

There was a tour of the other six mines so all could see how large they were, and then everyone went back to the hotel. Alex and Sandi sat down with Pete in the hotel lobby.

"Now Pete, about you. How long have you been with the BLM?"

"My thirtieth year just this past January."

"Are you eligible for retirement pay?"

"If I choose."

"So if I offered you a job for say the next eight to ten months, would you consider it?"

"What would the job be?"

"Onsite project manager. You would report to me and Dr. Chenowith, and I will pay you $250,000 for ten months of your life. What do you say?"

"Did you just say a quarter of a million dollars?"

"That's right."

"General, you put that in writing and I'm yours."

"Okay then."

Alex stood up and shook his hand and told him to provide his bank account number and routing number and he would wire an advance of $25,000 on Monday.

"Will one of my checks do?"

"Yes perfect, it has the account number and routing number."

"Listen General, if that $25,000 shows up Monday you don't need to sign anything. I'll trust you from there. What do I do now?"

"I'll call you Monday at your office after the funds have been wired. We're flying back in the morning. You have a great weekend Pete."

"You just made it a whole lot better. Have a safe flight back."

As Pete walked away, looking slightly dazed, Sandi chuckled. "I thought he was going to choke when you said you would pay him a quarter million." She gave Alex a sly look.

"How much are they paying you, if you don't mind me asking?"

"Nothing. All my expenses are invoiced to Howard and all the vendors are paid directly by wire transfer. It's either on the card or invoiced, nothing comes out of my pocket."

"I do have to front Curt and Cynthia until their salaries kick in, but I have enough in the bank for all concerned."

"And how much is that might I be so bold?"

"Enough to keep me in cracker jacks for life. And I'll let you in on a little secret. I have to have a bank styled vault installed in one of the sites."

"With tumblers and all."

"Yes, you know why?"

"Tell me."

"In about six months the US Mint will be shipping somewhere between six and ten billion in gold and silver coins and platinum ingots, plus fifty billion in cash of various denominations."

"Oh my God, you're not serious?"

"Remember it's for safekeeping. But we can go in every now and then and wallow in it."

"You're such a teaser," Sandi said, laughing.

Elsewhere, things were about to take a disastrous turn for the worse.

Chapter 7

THE "J" STREET DANCER

After Jeffers got off the phone with Alex, he called agent Stephan Browers, the AIC in LA.

"Browers, Ted Jeffers in DC."

"Yes sir."

"We got another problem out at Cal Tech."

"Professor Macklin?"

"You win the prize, he is about ready to go whacko on us, I want you to black bag him to one of our safe-houses and get in touch with our good doctor. We want Macklin to completely lose it, so we can have him involuntarily committed. That way we can keep him doped until it's safe to let him go."

"Consider it done sir."

"Good man. Keep me updated."

"Yes sir."

When Browers, along with another fellow agent, arrived at Macklin's office, they found it stripped. Just a desk, and a chair, and a lamp. No books, no wall charts, no files, nothing.

So he was in the wind. He called Jeffers back and reported what he had found.

"Agent Browers this is a level three alert, you've been briefed on Project ONE. Mobilize a task force sufficient in size to find and seize this man, before he can divulge information that is damaging to the national security of this country. Use whatever means is necessary, do you understand?"

"Yes sir." Whatever means necessary? This is a professor, not a mass murderer. But Jeffers had always been straight with him, so he would go along.

The hunt was on for every person who ever knew Macklin. All phone records, bank statements, ATM records, and credit card transactions within the last two years were run down and checked then rechecked. Every flight, every bus, every taxicab, every train station was blanketed by agents with pictures and descriptions. In all, over 275 agents were on the trail of one middle-aged professor.

Six hours into the search, they got a tip from a waitress at the Coco's restaurant in Glendale. Macklin had come in yesterday for lunch and paid with a credit card. The waitress remembered the charge; it was $13.13, a double unlucky number. The card was traced to an Agnes Worthington, who turned up as a secretary at Cal Tech, specifically the secretary for one deceased Eldon Huart. Macklin had either stolen her card, or she had given it to him, no matter. There was an authorization for one hundred dollars pending at a Best Western in Bakersfield, California. Then an authorization for thirty dollars at a Coco's in Fresno.

He was headed north. Browers reported in to Jeffers.

"Okay, I've got a pretty good idea where he is headed. Set up surveillance at this address in suburban Sacramento. In the meantime, flood the highways between Fresno and Sacramento, use the highway patrol as a dragnet on I-5 and 99, get his picture out to all law enforcement agencies between those two cities and keep me posted. Get up there immediately and personally oversee this operation."

"Yes sir."

As soon as he hung up, Browers ran the address and found that a neighbor had reported s suspicious individual sitting in a car outside the address. The house belonged to an Alex Hanken.

Jeffrey Macklin was nervously fidgeting with the land sat phone he had taken from Eldon's office. Finally, he couldn't take it anymore. He dialed his home in Sherman Oaks.

"Honey it's me," he said as soon as he heard his wife's voice.

"Jeffrey where are you? The FBI have been here looking for you. What have you done?"

"Nothing honey, I've done nothing. It's what they've done. They killed Eldon, he didn't have a heart attack... they killed him!"

"Jeffrey, I don't understand, who killed him and why?"

"The FBI or the government killed him, because they're trying to cover up something that Eldon and I found out. It involves national security and is very dangerous to anybody that knows anything about it. That's why I never told you."

"Oh, Jeffrey! Please come home."

"I can't. I've got to go. I love you."

He cut the connection.

If they had been to his home, they knew he was on the run. They also knew his car, he had to ditch it. Macklin pulled away from Hanken's house and headed downtown. He found a promising looking street "J" street, but, there was little parking, not even enough for his tiny car. He drove further down the street and took a left, then spotted what looked like a medical office building. He pulled around to the back, and found a covered spot reserved for a doctor, parked the car, got his belongings out, and walked away.

He knew he had to get out of the city. They would be scouring the streets for him. As he turned the corner back onto "J" street he suddenly ducked behind a bus stop shelter. Two men drove by slowly in a nondescript car, scanning the street. They had already tracked him.

Macklin pulled out his cell phone punched in the internet, Google maps. There was a place to hide, the library, just two blocks down. Macklin went through the rotating doors, and walked up to the information desk.

"Hello, may I help you?"

"Yes. Are your archives in the basement?"

"Why yes, they are, but only staff are allowed down there. Is there something we can get for you?"

"I'm Professor Macklin from Cal Tech University in Pasadena. I am in desperate need of an article that was published by one of our deceased colleagues. He worked at a local company called Aerojet, are you familiar them?"

"Yes, my son used to work there. Well, Professor let me verify—"

"Here's my badge, if that helps."

"I'll pull up the Cal Tech site, just a minute..., Jeffrey Macklin, Professor Cal Tech. there you are. I just need to make a copy of your ID Professor, and I'll take you down to the archives."

"Thank you so much."

The woman took Macklin down on the elevator and explained how to use the computer to research articles. He thanked her, and watched as the elevator doors closed. Then he disappeared as deeply into the stacks as he could.

Finally seated on the floor somewhere in the anthropology stacks, Macklin tried to think. They'd been to his home, so they knew he was on the run, but how did they know he was in Sacramento?

He was probably spotted at Hanken's house way out in the county. And then he remembered some of the geological survey maps he'd seen that had been generated by the land sat system. And the tech who had told him the real resolution the satellites could achieve. So they'd spotted him with the satellite, maybe followed him down the street to there.

He had to get out of the library.

Macklin scurried around, the row after row of research material looking for a possible exit. No windows, no doors, a bathroom... there was a window. It had a steel grate on it, but if he could get the grate off; it was big enough for him to squeeze through. Macklin pulled out his Swiss Army knife his father had given him for his eighth birthday, and began to remove the screws holding the grate in place. It was difficult balancing himself on the toilet seat. The screws had been painted over many times and were hard to get started, but one by one, he removed most of them, until he could bend the grate away from the window.

The window was nailed shut. Damn, who did they think was going to break into a library?

He used the knife to pry each nail out of the wood, until one of his blades broke. With another he finally removed the last nail.

Macklin pushed up with all his might and the window squealed open. He crawled out the window into a very narrow alley, looked down the alley and saw a transit bus go by, slowing down as it went out of sight. He hurried down the alley to the street and saw the bus waiting at a bus stop. He hopped on, dug out three dollars and fifty cents, and bought a day pass. Since there was no other seat available, the bus was packed with commuters, he had to take a seat directly behind the driver.

He glanced down at the floor beside the drivers left side. There was a clipboard with Macklin's picture on it. They had a bulletin out on him.

His mind raced. They had to have every type of transportation around Sacramento covered. He had to get out of this city somehow.

Okay, what were his options? He knew he could no longer use his credit cards for food or hotels, they would track him with those. He needed cash, more than the three-hundred dollars he could get at an ATM on a daily basis. His Visa had a ten-thousand dollar credit line, but he didn't know how much he could get on a cash advance.

Once he got the cash, he would have to be long gone before they could get there. They were passing a shopping mall on the right, and there was one of his bank's branches. He got off the bus and walked into the branch, it was crowded, it was payday, and it was Friday, and the teller lines were long. Maybe that would work to his advantage. If he could just find a new teller, they might not verify his cash availability and give him several thousand dollars.

The guy in line behind him was grumbling about how long it was taking. Macklin turned around and caught his eye. "Yeah, I'd noticed. Do they have a lot of trainees today?"

"No they're just idiots. The young girl second from the right is the only one I don't recognize."

Macklin nodded.

When he finally reached the front of the line he was motioned by a stern looking woman with no smile on her face to step to her window. He told the guy behind him to go ahead, since he needed to check something first. He repeated the same with the next two customers in line, until the young girl motioned to him.

"Hi," he said, "I'm from Pasadena, I need to get a cash advance from my card so I can buy my daughter her car for school, she goes to Sac State."

"Hey, so do I," the teller replied.

"I don't know how much I can get, can you check?"

"Sure, but first slide your ATM card and enter your pin."

He did as he was told, trying to hold his breath.

"Let's see, Mr. Macklin. Your visa has a twenty-five hundred dollar cash advance limit on it. Is that enough? I notice you have an equity line of credit with $26,500 available."

His line of credit? He didn't know he could access it remotely. "Well, I need ten-thousand cash to buy the car. Can I get that much on the equity line?"

"Sure, let me get my supervisor's okay for the amount, and I'll be right back."

He watched as she spoke to another woman seated at a desk in a nearby office. She punched up something on the computer in front of her, then signed a piece of paper, and gave it back to the teller. The teller then disappeared behind a wall for a couple of minutes, and returned with a stack of hundreds. She asked Macklin to sign for the advance, and the currency transaction report since it was ten-thousand dollars or more, which he did—they would already know he'd taken the money.

She counted out ten-thousand dollars in hundreds, then asked if there was anything else she could help him with.

"No, that will be fine, thank you."

Macklin walked as quickly as he dared out of the branch, then flagged down a passing taxi.

"Where is the little airport… not the big airport?"

"Oh you mean Executive airport."

"Yeah."

It was only a two mile ride to the airport, Macklin gave the driver a twenty, and told him to keep the change, then went into what looked like a pilot's lounge and asked a gentleman who he would talk to about a charter flight.

"That would be me. I have a charter service."

"Look, I'm in a real bind here. The damn airlines have canceled my connecting flight to Portland, and my daughter's wedding is tomorrow morning. I'm supposed to host the rehearsal dinner, as well as pay for it. It's tonight at 8:00. Can you get me there, and how much would it cost?"

"Well sir, we've got some pretty rough weather up that way, it might get bumpy."

"Believe me, it'll be a lot bumpier if I miss this. I'll pay you twenty-five hundred dollars up front."

"Let me get my hat and coat, and file a flight plan. In about fifteen minutes, we'll be ready."

As the plane flew off into the setting sun toward Portland, Macklin looked down at the Sacramento skyline and wondered if Hanken would find…*it*? He wasn't going to think anymore, he was totally exhausted and fell asleep.

Macklin was roused when the plane banked sharply to the right.

He was instantly alert. "Is there a problem pilot?"

"Uh sir, we have been ordered back to Exec Airport"

So they'd finally tracked him down. But he was not going to let them kill him like they did Huart. He pulled out his Swiss Army knife and stuck the barrel end against the back of the pilot's neck.

"Pilot you know what this is?"

"No sir."

"It's a .32 caliber. Now, I will blow your brains all over the windshield, unless you fly me to Portland."

"Sir I'm not trying to distract you, but please look out the right side of the plane."

Macklin glanced right to an impossibly huge fighter jet just behind them.

"Sir," the pilot said, that is an Air Force F-16 with orders to escort us back to Sacramento. If I deviate from my present heading he has orders to shoot us down."

This was it. He would be dead in an hour unless he did something extraordinary. But what?

"Okay pilot, you see that highway down there? You put us down on it right now."

"Sir, maybe you didn't hear me, but that F-16 will turn us into kindling if I try that."

"Bullshit, they are bluffing, do you really think your government would kill an innocent citizen? Besides, if you don't put this plane down on that freeway, I'll kill you and myself. I've got nothing to lose."

"Sir, you need to know we may die anyway if we hit an oncoming vehicle, that's not a freeway, it's a two lane road."

"Then we're going to find out just how good a pilot you are."

The pilot put his plane into a steep dive and lost the F-16 in the clouds. At about twenty-five hundred feet he broke out of the clouds in a steep decline down to about five hundred feet. Then he leveled it out, and started the glide down to the two lane road.

Just then the F-16 buzzed by and flew off into the night.

Macklin began breathing again. They really had been bluffing.

It was raining; the wipers could barely keep up with it. They were less than one hundred feet off the ground when the plane hit the power lines that ran across the road; it sheared the left engine completely off the plane igniting the fuel lines. All the F-16 pilot could report was seeing a yellow ball of flame. The FBI helicopter that had been dispatched arrived at the scene and the lead agent reported in.

"Browers?"

"Yes."

"Sir the plane has crashed into power lines. Both pilot and Macklin positively identified. They're DOA sir."

"Thank you."

Browers put out the call for all agents to stand down. Then he called Jeffers.

"Mr. Jeffers?"

"Yes."

"Macklin issue resolved. His plane hit power lines trying to evade an F-16 we scrambled. Both pilot and Macklin are DOA."

"Thank you Browers, good job."

Ted Jeffers hung up and stared out of his office to the perfectly manicured grounds. Damn, damn, damn. He had given the orders that led to the death of two innocent people. He knew he had to, he knew all about the greater good, but it didn't help when he had to do something that went against everything he'd ever trained for, everything he ever believed in. America was a nation born of revolution, damn it, and governments were supposed to fear the people, not the other way around.

He didn't know how much longer he could keep this up.

Don Cray knocked on the half-open door.

"Hey buddy you look down."

"Jesus Don, the bodies are piling up on this Project O.N.E., I don't know where it's going to end."

"It will end in July 2017. We're not dealing with a drug cartel here, or some two bit dictator in another third world country, we are talking about the survival of the US, maybe humanity. There is no sacrifice too great to ensure that. Is that your granddaughter's picture on the credenza?"

"Yes."

"So, you're willing to trade your granddaughter for some left coast liberal professor? That's what this is all about, Ted, making choices. We do it every day."

"I have never had to make choices like this. Never."

"I think you need to get away and go fishing for a couple of days."

"I can't. There is some kind of bullshit going on every damn day. I'm putting out fires as fast as they're lighting them."

"Hey that's all you can do. Hang in there."

After Cray left, Jeffers sat quietly looking out his office window. Just how many more bodies? How many more will have to be sacrificed to keep this quiet?

And when the truth was finally announced? He'd seen the plans and projections, and could imagine the rest. The chosen few—government officials, agronomists, craftsmen, soldiers, technicians—would go into their bunkers and seal themselves off from the rest of the world. Then would come the chaos, the fear, the anger, of those left behind. It still wasn't clear just how many the asteroids would kill, but there were fair estimates on the effect of the mayhem before they hit, and it was in the hundreds of millions.

And right then, he made his decision. He would be one of them. He would get his family into a shelter. Then he would take command of whatever agents would follow him and try his best to keep the peace. To prevent what slaughter he could. Maybe it would make up for what he was doing now.

And, then, if he was in an impact zone…well, at least there was something to be said for dying with honor.

Chapter 8

GOING HOME

★ ★ ★ ★

Admiral Torrance sent one of his famous T-grams out to every overseas commander, in every theatre, where US forces were stationed. After that he had the Chiefs of Staff conference call of their direct subordinates to reemphasize the need for total adherence to the timelines set forth. The redeployment was in full swing.

But not without its detractors.

"What the hell are they talking about Reed?" The Army Chief of Staff told General Sam Holden, Commander United States Forces, Korea. We're going to abandoned Korea?"

"Look," General Reed said, "I know how you feel. But the following units are to begin redeployment back to the states through Osan Air base. Kunsan will keep the 8th Fighter Wing and the 8th Medical operational, until the others are redeployed—the 8th Garrisons at Daegu, Humphreys, Yongsan, and Red Cloud, and the Civil Engineering Squadron at Kunsan."

"I don't like this, something is up. I mean, we've been in Korea for over sixty years and in forty-five days we're just gone— poof?"

"I know. But you and I are soldiers, and these are orders. You do what you gotta do."

"I better not find out that the goddamn Congress is behind this. I just can't believe that Torrance didn't throw an absolute fit over this."

Ambassador Jamison Loudner, Ambassador in charge of the Seoul embassy, had been expecting this call. He was surprised it hadn't come sooner. "Yes, send him in." Now it would start, the lies, the subterfuge.

His counterpart in the South Korean government came in and bowed deeply. "Mr. Ambassador, thank you for your time."

"Mr. Secretary, how may I help you?"

The secretary took a seat. He looked absolutely unperturbed, even knowing that his country was being left essentially defenseless against the North Koreans. "The President of the United States has sent a communiqué to our President indicating a sudden and complete shift in foreign policy sir. He says he intends to withdraw all or substantially all American troops from South Korea within forty-five days. How can this be?"

"Mr. Secretary, the United States has called South Korea one of its most favored allies for nearly sixty years, but there comes a time when we must turn our attention to issues not just facing other countries, but within our own country. The US is still facing major challenges after suffering through one of the worst economic downturns in our country's history. We are heavily dependent on oil imports, prices have soared, the people of America are suffering, and they are calling for a change. The US spends nearly $296 billion dollars a year in support for American troops on foreign soil. That money is badly needed to support our own people. Quite simply, we have no choice. If it's any consolation to you and your President, US armed forces are also being withdrawn from Germany, Japan, Italy, Kuwait, Great Britain, Denmark, Taiwan, Greenland, Qatar, and Uzbekistan. We estimate there will only be twenty-five hundred to three thousand troops on foreign soil, and those will be stationed at our various embassies across the globe.I wish I had more encouraging news to give you."

"I see." The Secretary still seemed perfectly calm. Loudner would have killed for that kind of control. "We were so shocked at how fast this developed. A phased withdrawal would have been less disruptive, but of course it would have been more costly for your government. Thank you for your time Mr. Ambassador I will relay the information to our President. But I would alert you that our President Yoon may still want a direct dialogue with President Betts over his change in policy."

"I understand Mr. Secretary. I'm sorry. I wish it were some other way."

Similar conversations were taking place across the globe at embassies, in political offices, and with heads of states. Frantic foreign dignitaries were speeding their way to Washington D.C. for an audience with the President. Newspapers and television reports were emblazoned with headlines that the US was pulling out all foreign-based troops on a scale not seen since the end of World War II. Pundits from all over the world spent hours theorizing why the US was undertaking such a drastic move.

Finally, the President addressed the nation in a forty-five minute speech. He outlined the difficulties facing the country, and the challenging decisions that had to be made to restore America to its glory. The decision to bring the troops home was not made lightly. But given the options facing the nation, he had no choice but to go forward with the recommendations. The President concluded by saying that the day would come when this great nation would rise again, and take its place as one of the admired leaders of the world.

Military installations on foreign soil became the target of protests and there were isolated acts of violence. But the redeployments were well structured and came off smoothly. Military air cargo and naval vessels were dispatched worldwide, as a massive and unprecedented movement of men and equipment got underway. Stateside military installations were readied to accept the influx of some 255,000 troops. At the recommendation of Alex, an early-out program was offered to anyone not mission-critical with less than ten years of service, and a cash payment of ten-thousand dollars tax free. The Pentagon felt that nearly 200,000 troops would take advantage of the offer, and filter back into civilian life.

Of course, this was being done by a Democratic president, so opposition leaders voiced their expected concerns and conservative talk show hosts whipped up a frenzy of calls for a full investigation into these unprecedented actions and, once the investigation had uncovered the obvious perfidy, the impeachment of the President. On the other side, the liberal media praised a bold and courageous move for a nation under severe stress, and pointed out that it guaranteed the president's re-election. The great charade was working perfectly as planned.

Alex had invited Sandi over to watch the President's speech and to prepare for a debriefing call to Howard the following morning.

"Why the perplexed look?" she asked.

"We're facing a worldwide disaster, and the American people have no idea what's coming. And the first thing those in the know are doing is bringing all military personnel home. Granted, I wasn't privy to the insider decision making process, but I can't get my head around why Torrance didn't fight this. But, we've got our marching orders. And after all it is my plan."

She gave him a peck on the cheek. "And it is working splendidly."

Alex insisted that Sandi stay the night so she could be ready for the call first thing in the morning and have all their notes in one place. Besides, Sandi didn't have a secure line at her house in Davis. She was tired from all the day's hectic activity and turned in for the night.

Alex stepped outside on the patio for some fresh air, and walked over to pick up what looked like a piece of trash that had blown into his yard. It was an envelope with his name in big black letters. He took it inside and opened it. There was a hand written letter inside. He couldn't remember when he'd last seen one.

As he read the letter his anxiety level began to rise. The letter was signed by Jeffrey Macklin. Was Macklin a certified nut case or were there merits to his argument there was a cover-up taking place within a cover-up? He decided to sleep on it. He would call Howard tomorrow and report on the trip.

At six the following morning, he knocked, then backed his way into Sandi's room with a tray.

"Good morning. Who wants coffee?"

"You are a doll for having this ready," Sandi said.

"Get used to it, that's my regimen."

"I can learn to like this. But aren't you worried that some nosy neighbor might see me and start talking to all the other busybodies."

"Well, if they do, they do. Let them speculate all they want, makes me look good." He poured her a mug of black coffee. "Remember, the conference call with Howard at seven. I'll lead off with a report on the facility location issues, then you give them your findings from the USDA visit and the hot greenhouse mine site."

"Sounds like a plan. Now get out of here so I can shower and get dressed, and then go over my notes before the call."

Alex had decided he wouldn't mention the Macklin letter to either Howard or Sandi just yet. He wanted to do a little snooping around on his own. In the meantime, Alex called his bank and asked his private banker to wire the twenty-five thousand dollars into Pete Cernak's account. Sandi returned, ready for the call, and Alex put the land sat on speaker phone, and speed dialed Howard.

"Howard its Alex, and I have Dr. Chenowith here with me."

"Boy Alex you run a tough ship. Dr. Chenowith how early did you have to get up to make this call."

"Pretty early."

"Okay, what do you have for me?"

"Howard, Pete Cernak was invaluable. We've got six locations that are perfect, give or take some simple internal modifications. But the primary location can house anywhere from fifteen hundred to two thousand people."

"Holy mackerel Alex, that's fantastic."

"I'm calling Pete Cernak this a.m. to go over all the logistics concerning renovation of the survival facility and the remaining storage facilities."

"How much storage space do you think you have?"

"With the five other mines that can be converted, about three million square feet."

"And all these locations are water proof and solid?"

"Absolutely. We went over USGS strata analysis and USDA hydrology reports to confirm stability and fresh water access capability. The ballpark price on bringing fresh water to all facilities is three million."

"Hell that's nothing. But the three million square feet, now that may very well cause a shift in who and what we assign to that group of facilities. How soon do you plan on getting started?"

"That is what I'm going to discuss this a.m. with Cernak, since this is BLM land no permits are needed from local officials and we spoke to BLM legal staff, they waived any environmental issues. So we're ready to go. I want to start the water pipeline and the floor cementing in all locations within thirty days. Then we bring in the steel fabricators for the blast proof doors, and after that it's all interior work. I plan on cueing in for a six month build out date for all six finished facilities. Dr. Chenowith will discuss her facility with you shortly."

"And you have all these contractors in mind?"

"We'll use some local people for minor work. For the big jobs we'll bring in the vendors from Spokane and Seattle. Pete Cernak has tremendous contacts in both cities across a broad range of skills and expertise.

"While I'm at it, I want to hire Pete Cernak away from the BLM, and put him in charge as the site project manager. I offered him $250,000 for a ten month job, and I just wired him $25,000 as a good faith gesture."

"Very good, Alex I'm impressed with how you've taken charge. You bill all that salary stuff to me, including the $25,000 you sent out this morning. Now, Dr. Chenowith what do you have for me?"

She outlined her findings concerning crop production post event, water access issues, and the steam vent mine.

"Excellent." Howard said. "Dr. Chenowith I'm looking at your profile and it says you haven't committed to a site yet. Did this trip influence you in any way?"

"Oh yes. I definitely want to be assigned to the sites we just visited."

"Excellent, I'll change your designated contact to me, and load you in as one of the designated people for that site."

"Alex will you be around this afternoon?"

"Yes, sir."

"I may call you back, I've got some ideas rolling around in my head, and I've got to talk to Admiral Torrance first. Thanks, bye."

Alex hung up and turned to Sandi. And was surprised to find a smile on her lips that was almost coy. "Alex I think he thinks there's something between us."

"Yeah, probably. The question about where you wanted to be designated was a probing type question. Sandi, remember, all of our phones are monitored. They have satellites that can see a freckle on someone's nose. And probably know how many times we go to the bathroom every day. If the powers to be had a concern I'm sure Howard would say something."

"That's a little scary."

"They have to keep airtight security on this."

"I know. I just treasure my privacy."

"Well, you may have to give that up. Listen, I need to get on the phone to Pete and get him started on contacting contractors."

"Okay, I'll run out to Davis and gather some more material. Should I bring some clothes over here?

"The neighbors are going to talk anyway, so you might as well. And bring a nice dress. We may go out on the town."

"Sounds delightful, see you later big guy."

Alex watched Sandi pull out of the driveway, then went through the satellite phone's call sequence again. A minute of buzzing and beeping later, Pete Cernak picked up.

"Pete, Alex Hanken."

"Good morning, General."

"Okay new rule. When it's just me and you, it's Alex. I can still be a general when the public's around."

"Got it Alex."

"First, did you check your bank?"

"I didn't have to, they called me about fifteen minutes ago and said the twenty-five thousand came in on a wire."

"Great, then let's get started. You have pen and paper ready?"

"Shoot."

"I want you to contact cement contractors and get a bid on pouring floors in each of those six facilities. I want the floors to be six inch concrete, reinforced with 1/2 inch rebar, with the exception of the main personnel facility you know which one that is, we marked it. In that facility I want a design with sufficient space for eight individual private shower stalls, in two different locations within the facility, for a total of sixteen shower stalls. Got all that?"

"Got it."

"In the very back of the main facility I want you to pour a twenty-eight foot wide by thirty-five foot deep floor that is twelve inches thick, and/or capable of bearing at least one ton per square foot. On the twenty-eight foot wide side, I want a ramp six foot wide with a fifteen degree up slope."

"You're going to put a vault in there aren't you?"

"Yep."

"I'll take care of it Alex. The cement mix will change for load bearing floors of that kind, but I'll make it right."

"Good man. Now, get the water pipe people out there. I want a six inch line to all facilities as we discussed. Oh yeah, and put a restroom in Dr. Chenowith's facility."

"It's already in the works. I figured that place would need something like that."

"Next, contact Stifel steel in Seattle. I want engineers out there to measure each facility for those doors."

"Okay."

"Then get a hold of your mine drilling buddies to bid on drilling those 45 degree angle holes in the roof of the steam mine. I'm going to have Dr. Chenowith fax you the dimensions she wants."

"Finally, I want all these contractors to meet with me a week from this coming Wednesday, with bids and timelines in hand. I don't want to meet second line people. I want principles."

"Week from Wednesday, key people only."

"And in your spare time," Alex said with a smile, "start tinkering with the format inside the main facility–sleeping, eating, relaxing, exercising, allow for a separate room for communications and systems equipment, a separate room for the power generator. That room needs to be vented with a one way out vent system for exhaust fumes. We will need to install a sprinkler system as well. Finally, build a twenty by twenty foot bedroom with a ten by ten foot office attached. That will be my place— rank has its privileges."

"Absolutely."

"Okay let's talk about you. You have a degree in Architectural Engineering and Mining."

"Right."

"Can we rely on you for schematics or should we outsource them to another firm?"

"Alex I am so pumped to do this. I've waited almost twenty years to do an outside job. I've done plenty for the BLM, but nothing with a private firm."

"Great. Now on a more serious note, our background check indicated you've had some issues with alcohol in the past. Tell me about it?"

"Sure. A couple of years ago I got into a real depressed mood and started drinking more than I ever had before. I got hit with two DWI's in nine months. The last one sobered me up to reality. I still have a social drink every now and then, but I'm not an alcoholic by any stretch of the imagination."

"Enough said, I'm counting on you to carry out the most critical elements of this project. I need you sharp and clear headed at all times."

"As God is my witness Alex, you have nothing to worry about."

"Okay, any questions?"

"Just one. Alex there are going to be times that I'm running here and there. I'll need someone to be able to answer questions, or forward info, or fax things."

"Go hire yourself an assistant, max salary $35,000 per year, plus benefits. This is a contract job. And get yourself a nice office close to the lake. Also secure whatever design and blueprint software and equipment you need to do your job. I don't want these designs or blueprints floating around out in public."

"That's all I had."

"Well, let's roll up our sleeves and get to work."

Alex got off the phone and took his first deep breath in weeks. Pete sounded more than capable. If they could duplicate Coeur d' Alene, they could cookie cutter the entire national plan.

He could picture it. Tens, maybe hundreds, of installations around the country, each capable of holding a couple of thousand people, who could emerge after the worst case scenario and grow food for tens of thousands. And those tens of thousands for a million. And who would choose those tens of thousands? And what would happen when the word got out?

Sandi answered her phone.

"Hey you," she said, "how's it going?"

"Terrific, when do you think you'll be back here?"

"I should be there around three."

"All right I'll let you go. You like fish?"

"Love'em. They make wonderful pets."

"Ha ha. We'll go down on the river to a place I like, called Sal's, see ya in a bit."

Getting a date was easier than he thought. Alex was beginning to feel more comfortable around Sandi. But, he worried about compromising the mission. Once you threw romance into the mix... things changed. He simply could not afford to have emotional issues rearing their ugly head in the middle of a marathon race to survival.

His land/sat phone rang.

——"Hello."

"Alex, its Howard, have you got a minute?"

"Sure."

"Did you talk to your new project manager?"

Alex filled Howard in on what he had discussed with Pete that morning.

"You see, that's what we are talking about, project management is not a walk in the park, it takes a special mind to conceptualize and organize tasks. You'll have a couple of one star generals under you. Harlen Monroe, the base commander at Ft. Lewis, is one of them. Remember, that's where I said you can get your military supplies and equipment and the personnel from."

"Yes, I remember."

"The other thing is that you found such a large area of secured storage space we want to move in some heavy armor, tanks, helicopters and other equipment from Ft. Lewis to your site. Why don't you set up a meeting with General Monroe and go over what you have and see how much can be moved out there."

"I can get that arranged. Is this to become an Army Depot of sorts?"

"You might look at it that way. You'll have critical civilian personnel there as well."

"You know Howard, the civilian airport runway is fourteen thousand feet. That wouldaccommodate a lot of F-35's from McChord AFB."

Howard paused a moment. "Good, yes. But you need hardened hangars don't you?"

"The ones they put up in Saudi Arabia during Desert Storm were erected in thirty days. With a good crew we could put thirty of them up in four months."

"Hang on let me teleconference the Admiral."

After a few moments, Howard said, "Evan I've got Alex Hanken on the line with us. Alex tell him what you just told me."

Alex relayed to the Admiral his idea about moving some McChord AFB squadrons of F-35's to the civilian airport in Coeur d'Alene.

"Brilliant. If you need help with the civilian authorities let me know. Start construction as soon as you can."

"Yes sir."

"General Hanken, as we move forward toward an uncertain future, I want you to know your efforts are going to mean the difference between success and failure. Keep up the outstanding work you're doing."

Well. Alex hadn't expected that. "Yes sir, thank you sir."

"I'm done, Alex." Howard said. You have anything?"

"Actually, yes, I was wondering if I could contact a gentleman that seems to be an expert on asteroid impact analysis. It might give me what I need to better prepare for the event."

"What's his name?"

"He's an MIT Professor....let's see, where did I put his name? Edward Killian."

"I was afraid you might say that name," Howard said. He's has been placed on a 'do not contact' list. Quite honestly he has some dangerous ideas about public disclosure. We ran a few situational ideas by him to test his reaction and he went into a rant how the government is cloaked in secrecy. He is definitely not a good security risk. But there's a meeting—when is that meeting— ah yes here it is— three weeks from tomorrow at the White House. All the key players including the President and Vice-President will be debriefed by a group of scientists on potential damage scenarios and temporary versus permanent effects. Would you like to be in the room?"

"Definitely, and I should bring Dr. Chenowith. We both need to know as much as we can about what's coming."

"Absolutely. And how many rooms would you need?

Alex almost swallowed his tongue.

There was a pregnant moment, then Howard laughed.

"Alex, I'm pulling your chain. We know all about you and Dr. Chenowith spending the night together and that is perfectly fine with us. Listen if you can find love in all this mess, we're all for you."

"Howard it's nothing like that."

"Okay my friend. Then its adjoining rooms, talk to you soon."

Over dinner Alex discussed his day and asked Sandi when was the last time she was in Washington D.C.?

"Let's see, a couple of years ago, I think."

"Well, we're going there three weeks from tomorrow for a conference."

"Wow that was sudden."

Alex went on to explain what Howard had said, then he told her about the conference at the White House and who was going to be there

"Yeah, then Howard asked me if we would need only one room."

She dropped her fork. "Excuse me? He said what?"

"He let me twist in the wind for a few seconds and then said they knew all about us."

"Oh my gosh Alex, there's nothing…Well at least they don't actually know everything. But…this just keeps getting more unreal as it goes along. Alex we're going to be meeting with the most powerful people in our country."

"Sandi they're just people. Most of them were just lucky enough to be in the right place at the right time. You and I are just as intelligent as most, if not all, of the rest who will be in that room. Well, except maybe the scientists."

"Well maybe so. But still, this is going to be a bit overwhelming."

"Sandi, you don't have to go, I didn't mean to include you if you would feel uncomfortable around those people."

"Don't be silly, if I can deal with you, I can deal with anyone. Besides I've testified before congress many times."

"That's the spirit."

The next morning Alex busied himself with getting a conference call set up to speak to the thirteen site commanders that had been assigned to him. He also called Pete to have him get bids for the hardened hangars. Pete told him he had heard from all of the contractors they needed and many would be out this Thursday and Friday to survey the sites. Pete also said some of the contacts implied there would be something in it for him if he could push the contract their way, and he told them to shelve that talk. If they got the contract, he would be their worst nightmare for a foreman. Those projects would be completed with the highest quality of workmanship and on time, or else.

Alex felt more reassured after the call. The plan was almost beginning to look plausible. They could actually put away enough people and material to rebuild the country in the worst-case scenario. As long as nothing went wrong.

Chapter 9

SPIES

President Vladimir Kleskova sat at his desk as the Director of Internal Affairs Konstatin Bocovich approached and took a seat.

"Mr. President," Bocovich said, "no doubt you have been watching this spectacle with the US redeployment underway?"

"What do you make of it Konstatin?"

"As you might imagine, we have grave doubts about the true intentions of the United States. We all know they have had financial issues, but they are still one the most powerful economic forces in the world. Now that the Middle Eastern nations have injected so much money into their economy, it is only a matter of time before they right their ship. If this had been undertaken two or three years ago, I could see their point."

"So you feel there is a hidden agenda."

"Yes Mr. President, I do."

"What do you propose?"

"Let me relate something to you Mr. President. Two weeks ago, a scientist by the name of Ivan Borosky was found slain in his home in St. Petersburg. According to the Major Case Squad forensic team he was killed by a high velocity bullet fired from a silenced gun. Two days later his assistant was found dead, floating in the river outside of town. She had been bound and gagged. Her apartment home had been the scene of a struggle. Both of their computers at the Russian Academy of Sciences had been cleared of all data, and secured locked files had been compromised and removed. The day before Borosky's death, he made a call that was traced by the investigating team, but the call terminated at the London International exchange office. It would take extremely sophisticated technology to wash this phone call out, and leave no trace."

"Such as that owned by the CIA." Kleskova concluded.

"Let me go on. The assistant's personal computer was left untouched by the assassins— it was found under her bed. She kept a personal diary on a daily basis; in it there was an entry that said Ivan Borosky had contacted a Professor Eldon Huart of Cal Tech in Pasadena, California. When the lead investigator attempted to reach Professor Huart the day after Borosky's death, he was told that Professor Huart had suffered a massive heart attack and died. Mr. President the Americans are killing their own citizens to cover something up that Borosky had contacted Huart about. One more piece of information. According to the diary Borosky told his assistant that Huart had provided the access codes to the Cal Tech mainframe so he could send his data directly to Huart for his evaluation. Those were her exact words. Mr. President that would have left a trail from the Academy's computer system, but there has been an intrusion by a very sophisticated virus that destroyed that data transmission…and only that transmission. They have gone to extraordinary lengths to cover any tracks.

"So we began monitoring activities of the FBI around the Cal Tech campus and last Friday, a Level Three alert was issued for a Jeffrey Macklin, who was a colleague of Huart's at the University. He apparently fled to northern California, where our satellites picked up a transmission between air traffic control and an F-16, with orders to shoot down a civilian airplane. The plane crashed trying to evade capture, it was not shot down, and both occupants were killed. One of them was Jeffrey Macklin. Mr. President, the Americans are hiding something with major national security implications. We must do everything we can to discover what this matter concerns, because it could have major implications for our nation."

"I see. And I agree. Director Bocovich, you are authorized to use any means at your disposal to determine the nature of this concealment effort by the United States. I will call the Secretary for Security and tell him of our conversation. In the meantime, why don't you call our Chinese friends and see if they can be of assistance. After all, the more people on this the better."

"Thank you Mr. President."

As soon as he returned to the intelligence directorate, Bocovich ordered the computer center to run a correlation between the names Huart, Macklin, and Borosky. The report was back on his desk within an hour, with a single solid, 100% correlation. Asteroids.

He then ordered a second correlation between the United States, asteroids, missing person's reports, and recent deaths, within the last two weeks. The computer came up with Louis Felson, Eldon Huart, Jeffrey Macklin, Darlene Smith and PBS as 100% correlated. Bocovich knew he was getting close, but he asked for one more task, which was to expand the explanation of the correlation findings. It produced; Louis Felson, moderator of the PBS special 'Asteroids and the Universe,' missing persons report on file with the Washington D.C police. Darlene Smith, receptionist Washington D.C offices of PBS, missing persons report on file with the Washington D.C. police. Both missing persons reports were filed within twenty-four hours of each other.

Bocovich contacted the Academy again, and asked if there were there any threats at this time of an asteroid striking the earth. They said not to their knowledge. He recognized the qualification, pressed a bit, and found that no one country had the capability or technology to scan the entire universe at any one time. Instead, there is an informal system of shared knowledge between observatories worldwide. They pass along any pertinent findings from their area of concentration about any possible NEO activity. He thanked them for their time, and returned to his office in Moscow. He assigned several of his staff to poll observatories around the globe and ask if there were any imminent threats from an asteroid strike...there was none. Cal-Tech was contacted and Professor Conley responded in kind...as the US Secrets Act compelled him to do.

This was a drastic move by the United States. He still wasn't certain what they were up to, though he was able to guess. And now that he knew what to look for, there would be no way they could keep it secret.

The question was, if he were right, could it be kept a secret?

Don Cray called Ted Jeffers and said they needed to meet in the secured room off of his office with Arlen Hendry, the President's National Security Advisor. An anonymous source had let Cray know that a rogue CIA agent named Edward Ketchum had botched the assassination,overlooked Kinova's laptop under her bed and missed the link to Cal Tech. Ketchum's days were numbered as far as Cray was concerned, but Hendry didn't need to know that just yet.

"Arlen," Cray said, "my sources tell me that the Kremlin's FSB office is launching a full investigation into the Borosky, Huart and Macklin incidents. They believe the US is covering up something major and it's related to the redeployment announcement somehow."

"You think they're on to something?"

"I don't see how. We've cleaned both cases; you got the reports from Ted and myself."

"Then how did they connect those three?"

"They probably just did a correlation hunt. But even if they did, it would come up with dead ends."

"Can we see what they've seen?" Hendry asked. "Can we run our own correlation?"

"Yes, sir. In fact the Russians stole the program from us about fifteen years ago."

Cray excused himself and had a technician enter the data and the computer spit out exactly what the Russian security officer had received. Ten minutes later he returned with the reports.

"Son-of-a-bitch Ted," he said. Missing persons reports on those two you nabbed were on file at the DC police, and they both were filed within twenty-four hours of each other. Two dead Russians and two dead Americans."

"Christ, no wonder they're busy, I would be too if I found this out. We've got a problem Don."

The next morning, Alex put in a call to Harlan Monroe, the commanding general at Ft. Lewis, Washington.

"General Hanken, good to hear from you. I understand you're the man in charge—just got the designation from the Deputy Secretary of Defense. Apparently, I'm supposed to treat you as an extension of Torrance himself."

"General Monroe are you on a secured line?"

"Oh yeah, this is my land sat unit they installed day before yesterday, so you can always call me at this number."

"Good, did they fill you in on O.N.E.?"

"Unfortunately. My God Hanken, can you believe this? Now the redeployment makes more sense. I wouldn't want our troops on foreign soil helping other nations try to recover from a disaster, while we have a desperate need right here at home."

"Exactly."

"What I don't understand though is why the dispersal within the stateside commands?"

"Think about it for a moment. They don't know for sure where the impacts will take place. So, rather than have critical forces and equipment concentrated in certain areas, they are spreading them out. It's like an insurance company or bank spreading risk in its portfolio."

"Well, I guess that's why they're up there, and I'm out here. You notice where they're sending me."

"Yeah southeast Idaho, right near Mountain Home AFB."

"Makes me wonder why they didn't just tap the base commander there."

"I'm not in that loop. But I can assure you that one criteria is that they're damned sure you can do the job. Consider it a pat on the back."

"Yeah, and a kick in the ass."

"It is that," Alex said. "You have a construction unit at Ft. Lewis?"

"Yes. Why do you ask?"

"Well, we have a fourteen thousand foot runway at a civilian airport here in Coeur d'Alene, and Admiral Torrance wants me to build enough hardened hangars to house thirty F-35's from McChord AFB."

"Boy this gets more and more involved by the damn minute, yeah, I have a thirty man construction squadron. A couple of those guys have experience building hardened ammo dumps. That just might be the ticket."

"Okay then, Harlan, I'm going to ask you to put these men on a restricted list, no transfers, no temporary assignments. Just park them until I need them, which could be in about two to three weeks."

"Consider it done, General. Park, the equipment as well?"

"Yes. We may use local equipment, but have yours on standby. And, Harlan, when it's me and you, it's Alex."

"Sounds good Alex."

"I'm headed down to my site next Friday to determine what I need to get done."

"I'm putting together a conference call for Thursday at 0900 hours for all the units under my command. Be sure to attend."

"Absolutely."

"That's all I had for now. Good talking to you, call me if I can help in any way."

"Will do Alex."

Pete called back about an hour later and said the civilian airport was privately owned by a Herman Schmidt. Alex thanked him, and put in a call to Ted Jeffers at the FBI.

"Hey Alex, what can I do for you?"

"Ted, I'm under orders to use a civilian airport as a fallback base. I just found out it is privately owned by a Herman Schmidt. He lives in Seattle, maintains a drop box in Coeur d'Alene."

"Okay, I'll run a computer check right now if you can hang on for a minute. If that doesn't work we'll do a background check. I assume you're looking for leverage?"

"The more the merrier."

"Okay, got him. And, whoa, we got a hit and a flag. Let me look that code up…And…you've hit the jackpot. The DEA has an ongoing criminal investigation, starring your guy. He's running a known drug smuggling operation out of that airport. Alex, all you have to do is call the Attorney General's office and tell him you need that airport and the story behind Mr. Schmidt. He'll order a seizure under the RICO Act, and you will have your airport free and clear."

"Just like that."

"Well, it may not be strictly legal, but by the time they sort it out…"

"Ted, how can I thank you enough. This makes my life a lot easier."

"Glad to help. Hey, how's the fishing up there?"

"That area is God's gift to fishermen, you should come out."

"I just may do that."

Alex put a call into Robert Simons, the US Attorney General, who promptly conferenced the DEA director.

"Bob," the director said, "we're in the middle of an ongoing investigation. This could compromise two years' worth of work."

"This is not up for discussion," Simons said, "I am ordering you to execute this case immediately. Pick him up, put him on ice for now, and seize the airport."

"I'll need some time to get this done."

"No, you won't. This is a Level One Presidential Emergency. Today, you understand me?

"His attorney's will be all over us."

"I don't really care. Seize the airport and pass it to General Alex Hanken on orders from the Chairman of the Joint Chiefs.

You are also to give him all the cooperation he needs for a smooth transition, do you understand that as well?

"Notify all the civilian pilots having airplanes there to vacate their facilities within forty-eight hours. Failure to do so will result in their planes being seized and sold as abandoned property. Seventy-two hours from now I want you to tell General Hanken his airport is ready for inspection."

"Yes, sir."

"General is that okay with you?" Simons said. Alex was a little breathless. He had just been given an airport by some of the most powerful officials in the country on the strength of a phone call. And they were treating it like it was routine.

"Mr. Attorney General," he said. "I couldn't ask for more, thank you."

"Good." Without another word, the Attorney General hung up. Wow.

Sandi walked in.

"My daughter's coming in for the weekend, so I'll be tied up."

Alex wasn't quite listening. "That's fine."

"So, I heard you on the phone all morning. Talk to anyone interesting?"

"No not really. Just Ted Jeffers, Director of the FBI and Robert Simons, US Attorney General."

"Oh really? A couple of flunkies huh."

"Yeah. But Simons gave me an airfield."

"Well, that makes up for it, then."

There was no humor in the capitol. Don Cray was brainstorming with Ted Jeffers about how to derail the Soviet's attempt to uncover the real story behind Borosky, Huart, and Macklin. Someone had to also explain Felson and Smith. Ted jumped in and said.

"No, Don we need to separate the two cases somehow. One can be tied to the redeployment, the other can't. Otherwise, it would look like we're completely out of control and we don't want the Soviets thinking that."

"How about this? Felson is with PBS, but his background check shows him as working for the Washington Post as an investigative reporter for eleven years. What if an unnamed source told him of the redeployment before it was announced, and he was going public with it."

"Okay, I like that. We can build a case for bagging them because the White House exposed itself as trying to muzzle him. We had to cover that up, so we bagged them, I think that will work. Now for the Three Amigos, what about them?"

"I think we need to do a search of these people, the work sites, and their common projects. Find any news headlines or stories about anything connected with all three. See if there's a common thread."

"Yeah, good idea. Your computer or ours?"

"No, let's use ours here at the CIA. It does more international sweeps than your program does. This will take a couple of hours… I'll call you."

It took about six hours to run the search for common elements besides asteroids that linked Borosky, Huart and Macklin. Cray called Jeffers and said he was coming over to his office from Langley with the computer output. They convened their meeting in Jeffer's secure office annex.

From inside the building a Russian agent spoke to his counterpart two blocks away.

"Alexi, I can't pick it up. They're in the shielded office."

"Damn, we need to tap the electrical conduit into that office."

"Security has been tripled. Have you not noticed? We'll never get in that building beyond the front carousel. It will be impossible."

"Dimitri, you are forgetting we have someone inside."

"Yes, but how can she manage to get into the conduit trunk area? It requires an entry code to several doors—each door has a separate code—that changes daily."

"Leave that to me. Close down and come back to the office."

"Okay Ted here's what we have. It seems that four years ago the UN Committee on space exploration decided it was going to award a thirty million dollar grant to the team or university or institute that could provide the best bang for its dollar scouring the heavens for NEO's or Near Earth Objects. This was to be a ten year funding, with a twenty million dollar immediate grant for equipment upgrades. So we were looking at a fifty million dollar pot of gold. Guess who was in competition for it?"

"Oh, the Russian Academy of Sciences in St. Petersburg, Russia, and the Cal Tech extension at Mauna Kea, Hawaii."

"You win the cookie. Anyway, it seems Cal Tech got the grant, but the then Director of the Academy lodged a complaint with the committee alleging that Cal Tech had fudged its data and he had proof. His assistant was none other than one Ivan Borosky."

"Okay, this is getting good."

"It gets better. That Director, an Issac Petrovinka died suddenly three days after lodging his complaint. Ivan Borosky was named to replace him. Now here's an article written by a Swedish reporter who attended a conference in Geneva six months later. He wrote of witnessing from a distance, a heated conversation between Borosky, Huart, and a guy named Edward Killian. At that time Killian headed up the Cal-Tech program. Killian now heads up the astrophysics lab at MIT in Boston.Okay, that's the groundwork. Here's the punch line.

"Go on, you're on a roll."

"What if we dummy up some financial transactions—say wired funds from a bank in Hawaii or LA, to an account in Russia of a cousin of Borosky's who lives in St. Petersburg. We can allege Borosky was blackmailing Huart, and wanted more money. I have an agent, an Edward Ketchum who is about to be let go... so to speak. We can have Huart contact him for a job in Russia; he knows Ketchum works that corner of the earth. As a matter of fact Ketchum did work in Russia eight years for us. Say Huart offers a million dollars for the job, which is to snuff out Borosky and his assistant, destroy all his files and computer records, leaving no connection between Huart and Borosky. We can then take this to the Russians and fess up that one of our agents went off the reservation and became a freelancer and did the dirty deed. We'll give them Ketchum…he's living in southern Italy. We have an account in Paris under his name that we control. Ketchum doesn't even know about it, there's over 485,000 euros in it. We can show that to the Russians as well. That combined with the redeployment early disclosure story, should satisfy them enough that they'll back off and stop snooping around."

"Cray what kind of sick mind comes up with this stuff?"

"Yeah…yeah. We should take this to Arlen Hendry, and see what he thinks."

"Yeah let's do that."

Cray and Jeffers walked into Arlen Hendry's office and went over the whole scenario. Hendry wanted to know how quickly they could get all the phony account transactions set up. Cray said it would only take a couple of days, it was just programming input. Hendry gave them the go ahead for the account, but, wanted to speak to the President before they informed the Russians.

Hendry sat down with the President and went over all that had transpired in the last three weeks from Borosky's, Huart's and Macklin's death, to Felson and Smith's detention. The President asked how many spies were involved. Hendry told him Don Cray's office was tracking six new intelligence agents in the Washington D.C. area alone. Another four in the LA area around Cal Tech in Pasadena.

"My God, we are only three weeks into this thing and look at all that's happened. How are we going to keep a lid on this?"

"We'll keep the lid on for as long as we can, sir," Hendry said. "And if we lose it, well we have contingency plans."

"Arlen thank you. I am going to place a call to Kleskova so, get me the info as soon as it is ready. We've got to nip this in the bud before they find out too much."

The President placed his call to the Russian President early the next morning. The call went pleasantly enough, until he began to mention the redeployment.

"Vladimir," the President said, "what I'm about to tell you, no one knows except my intelligence people and Arlen Hendry."

"I see. May I call in my Secretary for Internal Security, Konstatin Bocovich, so he may witness this call?"

"Of course. I would prefer it."

A minute later, Kleskova gave him the go ahead. He started relating all the facts surrounding the conjured up tale by Cray. It took nearly forty-five minutes, because Bocovich kept interrupting with questions. The President would respond by telling him he was coming to that issue in a moment. He wanted to stay in chronological order so they could see how this unfolded.

"And now about the redeployment. I have been inundated with inquiries from nearly every nation on the planet, asking what motivated this extreme action. My response has been to tell them the absolute truth. That the United States of America has for too long been the policeman of the world, and is spending nearly three-hundred billion a year just to keep US air, naval, and ground forces in various locations around the globe. Our country suffered a severe blow with this last recession, one that's divided the country. Our people have suffered; they've lost jobs, lost their life savings...their homes.

Americans have always been a resilient people. We withstood the rigors of a Great Depression and WWII, just as your people did. But this recession as they called it, was more insidious. It affected more people, on so many levels. I cannot justify spending another dime outside this country, until I can restore integrity and confidence in our economy and the government...my people demand it. As God is my witness these incidents have absolutely nothing to do with any perceived or actual cover-up. Now my CIA director has informed me that he is offering the rogue agent to you, even though we had nothing to do with it. Our diplomatic pouch will be there tomorrow with all the exhibits for you to see. The whereabouts of former agent Edward Ketchum will be revealed.

"I see," Kleskova said. "I'm glad we could get this resolved."

"So am I," President Betts said. "Thank you for your time Vladimir."

President Betts hung up the phone and sunk back in his chair. He had just lied as convincingly as he ever had. He hoped. This had to work.

"Mr. President," Bocovich said, "while you were on the phone with the American President, I had my people pull files on known US agents. Edward Ketchum did operate here and he was spotted in St. Petersburg on several occasions in the last ten years."

About that time a young woman entered the office with some paperwork and handed it to Bocovich. He looked at it for a moment, looked up from the documents and nodded to Kleskova.

"It appears that two days before Borosky was killed two Americans arrived by plane in St. Petersburg. One of them was an Edward Ketchum.Here is an account statement for a Constantine Andropov at the Peoples Bank of St. Petersburg, showing a balance of 47,000 rubles, which would be over ten years of salary for this taxi driver. Constantine Andropov is a cousin of Ivan Borosky. It appears that the US President maybe telling the truth."

"Yes...I admire President Betts. It was a tragedy to see the United States going through much of what we did in the middle and late 90's. His country is under severe stress, and regardless of what our fellow comrades think, the world needs a strong America."

"What about the agent Ketchum?"

"Director Bocovich, I leave him in your capable hands."

"Thank you. Good day sir."

It took about two days before the foreign intelligence agents began to drift out of the country. Cray and Jeffers met for drinks after work that day, and congratulated each other on their successful ploy. Hendry was relieved; he was a little more confident that they could pull this off. Arlen Hendry was not so naïve as to believe that this little victory was going to last very long. Hanken and his team were now moving ahead with survival shelters on an unprecedented scale. Someone was bound to notice sooner or later.

They just had to make sure it was as late as possible.

Chapter 10

TERROR FROM THE SKIES

After his conference call with his site commanders, Alex promised to visit each one in the coming days, and go over their site plans with them. In the meantime, he had flown to the Idaho site, and been given the keys to all the offices at the Coeur d'Alene airport. All but one plane, an aging Cessna 172, had been removed. The FAA was notified that the airport was now a designated military installation, subject to expanded airspace restrictions. Alex then contacted a company that specialized in prefabricated modular bank vaults about having one shipped to the site for assembly. Delivery timeline was thirty-five to forty days, so he placed the order.

The next week and a half was spent visiting sites nationwide that had been designated by Homeland Security. All of them had issues. Most were easily addressed, there were few issues that an unlimited budget couldn't handle—but there were unique challenges that required Alex to rethink the best approach. Pete had contracted with a company to start pouring the cement flooring in the mines, with the main site being specially adapted for the incoming bank vault. General Monroe was contacted at Ft. Lewis to have his construction engineers pull hangar blueprints from the McChord Air Force base archives. The engineers were then to visit the Coeur d'Alene airport facility and mark off the construction site. In the meantime, Alex ordered fifteen mobile home trailers from the FEMA yards in Texas to house the construction crews. He was really getting the hang of this unlimited purchasing authority thing.

Alex informed General Monroe that the hangar construction start date would be in two weeks, after he returned from Washington. Alex signed contracts for all the assigned tasks he had given Pete, except the interior build-out for the main facility. Pete was still working on the blueprints for that. He had some ideas for Alex to consider when he returned from Washington D.C.

On the plane flight to D.C. Alex and Sandi discussed potential questions that might come their way and how should they respond. Sandi was most concerned about the environmental impact of the event—how possible landslides, tsunamis and floods might strip topsoil and how climate changes would affect the growing season.

Alex countered with his concerns about infrastructure damage—bridges and roadways, fuel distribution pipelines, waterways cluttered with debris. Even if they got agriculture back on its feet, they had to distribute the food somehow. Either way, this meeting would give them a clear idea of what was coming for the human race.

The meeting was convened in the cabinet briefing room at the White House. In attendance was the President and Vice President, the National Security Advisor, the Secretary of Defense, the Chairman of the Joint Chiefs of Staff, the Director of FEMA, Alex and Sandi, and two Professors from the Cal Tech Astrophysics Department. The President opened the meeting by introducing everyone at the table and laying out the agenda for the next three hours. He asked for everyone to hold their questions for later, since the material to be covered by the two professors was intense and complicated, and he didn't want to get off track. With that, he introduced the first speaker, a Professor Andrew Conley.

Conley, to his credit, opened by asking for everybody's prayers for the families of Professor's Huart and Macklin. He then began.

"I am going to go through the most probable scenarios of an asteroid impact on land and the resultant effects on the environment—using as little technical jargon as I can. At this point we cannot calculate the probable impact zones, though we should be able to identify them with 95% accuracy within three to four months. Currently we are tracking approximately forty asteroids that would strike the earth sometime between mid-July and early August 2017. Of those, there are three asteroids that are two to two and a half miles in diameter. There are 18 asteroids in the 1000 yard range, and the remaining appear to be small enough to be ignored for the purposes of planning. Let me begin with the following caveats. Impact analysis is dependent on projectile diameter, density— is it ice, porous rock, dense rock, or iron—and angle of entry— the higher the angle, the more damage. Most of the projectiles will come in at 45 degrees. We can with certainty, predict that the entry velocity will be somewhere between twenty-five to thirty kilometers per second—approximately 55,000 to 67,000 miles per hour. The density…we'll have a better idea in about six months when we can get deep space spectrometry readings. The most dangerous of course would be the dense iron asteroid, simply because it would survive more intact after breaching the atmosphere. I am not going into the largest. Instead, I'll give you the results of the more prevalent ones of around 1000 yards in diameter. You can imagine the effect of one of the larger ones yourself.

"So, with all that said here we go. A one km asteroid striking the earth at those speeds at a forty-five degree angle will release the equivalent of 300,000 megatons of energy. By comparison our largest nuclear weapon has been measured at just 60 megatons."

There was an audible gasp from everyone at the table.

"There would be a blinding flash," he said. Approximately one billion tons of earth—or projectile material as we call it—would be sent fifty miles into the atmosphere. The concussion would shatter eardrums for a thousand mile radius, radiation burns would extend to a radius of one thousand to fifteen hundred miles. The blast wave would destroy all standing buildings out as far as two-hundred fifty miles. The resultant firestorm would incinerate most of the biomass for a thousand mile radius. The heat generated will create a rain of death—fused earth debris that turns in to super-heated balls of glass. These would become lethal projectiles travel-ing at several hundred miles an hour. And this is just in the first seconds of impact.

"The fallout that begins after that will contain highly acidic rain, and pellets, or sproules because of the ionization of the atmosphere. The atmosphere will go into a "nuclear winter" con-dition, thereby arresting plant photosynthesis. Crops and most of the indigenous vegetation will perish. The sun will not reappear for between one and two years. Those humans not killed by the initial impact, will fall prey to famine and disease. We can expect somewhere around a twenty-five to thirty-five per cent worldwide fatality rate.

Alex couldn't help himself. "One strike," he said.

"That's right." Conley seemed unnaturally calm, but who knew how long he had been living with this already. Ladies and gentle-man we have eighteen of those coming at us. Now I would like to introduce my colleague, Professor Jared Kumar. He will provide insight into what we can expect from a water impact."

"Thank you Professor Conley." Kumar, who looked more like a greengrocer than a scientist, was also very calm and collected about himself. Or perhaps deadened would be the best word.

"Since the earth's oceans cover nearly two thirds of the earth's surface, statistically there will be a greater chance that most impacts will occur in the oceans. Does that mean there will be less damage? Not necessarily is the answer. At the speeds and angle Professor Conley spoke about an asteroid striking the ocean eight hundred miles from the eastern coast of the United States, would vapor-ize three hundred square miles of ocean. It would crash into the ocean floor creating a crater with a one hundred mile radius, and eject nearly five hundred million tons of sea floor material into the atmosphere. It would set off seismic events from Chicago to Rome, and would create massive lightning storms because of the ioniza-tion of the atmosphere. Storms that have never been witnessed by modern man—they would last for months. We know there would be worldwide acid rain that begins to fall, but quite honestly we do not know what the full effect would be with so much water vapor rising to such heights. There has never been a recorded event of such magnitude. The plankton life cycle would be severely if not completely diminished, which would cause all but the very tiniest of sea creatures to perish.

"The most immediate threat is from the resultant tsunami. I could give you the deep water pressure numbers, but that doesn't put it in perspective as to what the Atlantic coastlines of the world could expect. An asteroid of that size striking the ocean would create a wave height of approximately 980 to 2000 feet in height, traveling at nearly 500 miles per hour. Once it hits the continental shelves of the US and Europe, it would rise another two-hundred feet. Exhaustive wave analysis performed in the last twenty years, has shown that over that distance, the wave would dissipate to around 650 to1650 feet in height when it strikes the Eastern seaboard of the US. Going from south to north, Florida would disappear under three hundred feet of water for almost an hour. The wave would rush in destroying and killing everything in its path for nearly two hundred miles inland from Miami to the northern tip of Maine, eliminating all coastal cities. What most people don't know about tsunamis is that there are multiple waves that are created, and they would continue to hit the coastline every ten to fifteen minutes, for up to an hour. These follow-up waves would diminish in size as time goes on, but when you are talking about a nine hundred foot initial wave, you can imagine the following waves can be as devastating as well. If there is no evacuation, thirty-nine million people would die. That's within the first hour."

Heads shook in disbelief, hands were wringing, color began to drain from some of the faces at the table. It was too horrific to imagine.

Kumar was undaunted. "The gulf coast region along the Florida panhandle, the southern coasts of Georgia, Alabama, Mississippi, and Louisiana would suffer extensive damage as far as fifty miles inland. Another one point nine million people would be at risk. This event would also trigger a nuclear winter lasting one to two years, and most of our colleagues agree it could be the catalyst for another ice age.

"Turning our attention east, starting at the Gold Coast of Africa, Algiers, Gibraltar, Portugal, Spain, France, and Norway would incur significant damage to as far as one hundred fifty miles inland. The British Isles would be essentially scrubbed clean—"

"God!" someone yelled. "Stop it! Just stop it!"

There was a very heavy silence, then the President cleared his throat.

"I know this is hard to even imagine," he said. "But it's our job to imagine it. Ladies and gentleman we are going to take a thirty minute break. Then we need to get back and finish this."

During the break Alex introduced Sandi to Admiral Torrance. Admiral Torrance was, as Alex put it, an old guard military traditionalist, naval academy, family tree with a history of distinguished military service, and wartime experience in Desert Storm and Iraqi Freedom. After a two year stint as the Naval Chief of Staff, he was elevated to Chairman, Joint Chiefs of Staff. He was a very big man physically, standing nearly six foot five and weighing probably, Alex guessed, around 250 lbs. His voice tone was somewhere between a bass and a baritone and tended to boom.

"Dr. Chenowith it's a pleasure to finally meet you," Torrance said. Alex has had very high praise for you and from what I hear you two work together magnificently. These are...well you've heard what we're up against. Or country needs professionals like you and Alex to pick up the gauntlet. We are all counting on you."

"Thank you Admiral, working with Alex has been very rewarding. And knowing that our efforts may help save lives and restart civilization...it's almost more than I can imagine."

"I know what you mean. Now, if you'll excuse me."

As soon as he was gone, Sandi leaned toward Alex and whispered.

"You know, the two of you have similar tones to your voices?"

"Is that a good thing?"

"Sure. It's a commanding voice, intimidating to other males, yet to women, reassuring and sexually arousing."

"I take it, you're talking in general." He glanced back at the conference room.

Sandi looked back, and her face fell. "Oh, God, yes. If there was ever anything less arousing…I'd forgotten it for a moment. One strike in the Atlantic, and Florida and England are completely gone?"

"Do you want some more ice water? I'm dry mouthed after hearing how many different ways we are going to die."

"Yes, and it's not just the fear that is making us thirsty, I bet everybody's blood pressure is maxing out right now. Let's go sit down the conference looks like it is about to restart."

Once everybody was assembled—still a little pale faced but calm—Professor Kumar began again where he had left off.

"Now we turn our attention to the Pacific. An asteroid strike in the Pacific Ocean would essentially be the same as the Atlantic, with a few notable exceptions, and one dire difference. From Malaysia all the way up the Asian East coast to Beijing devastation would rain supreme. Most of the major population centers within two hundred miles of the coast would be obliterated by a seven hundred to eight hundred foot tsunami. The Marshall Islands, Guam, and Hawaii would be devastated beyond recognition. Japan would be for the most part destroyed. Eighty per cent of the island would be submerged under one hundred feet of water for several hours, since the nearness to the Asian continent would create a rocking type effect between the Japanese Islands and the mainland and the subsequent follow-up waves.

"We would anticipate Australia and New Zealand to be struck along the northern and western borders, but the ocean remains fairly deep around Australia, and there would not be the rising of additional feet that occurs when the tsunami hits shallow water. We don't believe that the devastation would be as great as along the Asian continental coast. Our estimates of the immediate death toll would be somewhere around one hundred million people. The west coasts of the Americas, from the very tip of South America up to the Alaskan peninsula would suffer similar devastation. San Diego, Los Angeles, San Francisco, Portland and Seattle/Vancouver would incur massive damage if not total destruction. As far inland up to one hundred fifty miles will see significant damage to structures, roadways, and dams. We estimate the death toll at around thirty-five million for the Americas in total."

The consternation and fear were back as badly as ever.

"Dear God have mercy on us," someone whispered.

"All the same after effects—— acid rain, nuclear winter, plankton interruption would occur. The dire consequence I spoke about would be earthquake swarms. As many of you know the Pacific continent boundaries are dotted with volcanoes—it is sometimes referred to as the "Ring of Fire". A strike near any of the many fault lines in the Pacific could trigger an earthquake with a magnitude of 9.5 on the Richter scale, which would be devastating enough in itself. But it could trigger volcanic eruptions all along this Ring of Fire.

"The Pacific regions from the southern tip of South America north to Seattle and from the Northern coast of China south to the Malaysian island chains could turn into a cauldron of spewing magma from the earth's mantle. If enough volcanoes erupt, it could take several hundred years to clear the atmosphere. If that were to occur ladies and gentleman, mankind would vanish.

"Finally, there is a lesser-known theory and not embraced by all scientists— including Professor Conley and myself—known as the "Final Straw." That theory says that if an asteroid of sufficient size were to strike the Pacific Ocean with enough force, say in the Eastern Pacific Rise fault, it could actually crack the mantle of the earth, causing an explosive discharge of the earth's core, sending the earth hurtling out of orbit at fantastic speeds. Of course immediately extinguishing all life.

"So there are scenarios where, no matter what we do, we're doomed," Alex said.

"Sadly, yes. But the chances of them happening are fairly slim, and we'll know more about their probabilities in a couple of months.

"Now the event I mentioned to you earlier an above ground explosion. We now know that the 1908 Tunguska event in the isolated part of Siberia was such an occurrence. As an asteroid enters the atmosphere it undergoes tremendous forces due to the extreme speed and the accompanying buildup of high temperatures. These forces come together so as to cause physical changes to take place in the very make-up of the material that constitute the asteroid itself. When that happens the asteroid simply explodes. The Tunguska event height at explosion has been narrowed down to about six kilometers from the ground. It flattened and scorched about eight hundred square miles of wooded area. We also know that this was a relatively small asteroid with only a three to six megatons release of energy.

"If an object this size—and we estimate that there could be as many as fifteen to twenty of them in this pack—were to explode over New York, it would destroy the city. The real danger does not lay with the size. It's the proximity to the ground and the resultant fireball that pushes down toward the earth. We don't feel the three largest and the eighteen smaller asteroids we used in our presentation represent a threat of this kind, since they are of such size and density that they will survive the turbulent entry into the atmosphere. However, as I mentioned there are smaller asteroids in this pack, and in such numbers that an atmospheric explosion or explosions will take place. That is our presentation for today thank you for your time and attention."

The President rose. "Fifteen minutes and then we'll have some questions and answers." When they reconvened the President thanked both professors and began with a question of his own.

"Professor Kumar can you be more specific as time passes, about just how far inland these tsunamis will travel if our east or west coasts are affected?"

"There are physical barriers running along the interior of those areas. For example the Appalachians in the east and the Sierra Nevadas in northern California and the San Gabriels in southern California. There are valleys and low lying areas throughout all the ranges. The resultant topography will act to condense these incoming water streams into enormous jets of concentrated water. Rivers will change course, new canyons will be gorged out, existing dams will collapse. When we say we expect the tsunamis to travel 150 miles inland, we are taking into account these barriers. But, you must realize that many underground aquifers will be invaded by these ocean waters spreading flooding far beyond the mountain ranges."

Sandi motioned for a question and was acknowledged by the President.

"Professor Conley some of the studies that I have read indicate that we'll be left with layers of sediment as much as six inches in deep containing acidic sproules. Can we expect these sproules to decay over time or do they stay acidic indefinitely?"

"Your expertise is in agriculture isn't it?And you're concerned about post event crop production. Well, we know the acidic levels in sproules from an ice or porous rock asteroid are not going to be as high, nor as concentrated as in an asteroid that was of dense iron. So, yes, they do decay in just a couple of years in a less dense asteroid aftermath. In the dense iron asteroid, the sproules may stay acidic for a hundred years and the soil they contaminate would be dead for that same amount of time."

"What do you mean by dead soil," Admiral Torrance asked.

Professor Conley gestured toward Sandi.

"Crops rely on bacteria in the soil to generate heat and release the needed nutrients," she said. "If the soil is too acidic, the bacteria can't thrive and, nothing will grow. The soil is essentially dead."

"General Hanken and I have discussed this, and it would seem appropriate that we have stores of bacteria laden soil in locations throughout the US. After removing the dead top soil, we could reintegrate the bacteria laden soil into the properly prepared soil, so that we can jump start the crop production process."

"How will you know how much top soil has to be removed?" The Admiral asked.

"A simple pH test should tell us."

"General Hanken has already ordered the equipment for his sites, and that includes air and water testing equipment. That was his suggestion."

The meeting was adjourned for a luncheon and Alex asked what steps were being taken to possibly intercept the threats and the President gave him the plans as outlined in his previous meetings with NASA, the JPL, and the Air Force Space Command. But, offered the more realistic outcome that some of the asteroids would surely get through and the need for he and Sandi to oversee and implement the far reaching survival strategy.

Sandi and Alex boarded their jet and headed back west with the knowledge that people were counting on them much more than they had realized. Sandi sat in the right seat and they began a long conversation about themselves. They were somewhere over the flyover states, with the autopilot on, when Sandi came into the cockpit and took the right seat.

"Alex," she said, "we need to talk."

"Yeah, after today...yeah."

"Three weeks ago—I am sitting in Davis—alone— wondering what my life would become. Then I find out that the world may be coming to an end. I think to myself, oh well, a fitting end to a boring life."—

"No, don't."

"I'm not finished. Then you come in with your charm and warmth and take charge attitude. It is so hard for me find words to describe how I feel right now. I am torn between the horror of what may happen, and yet the incredible sense that maybe, just maybe, I've found the man I always wanted to be with. There's fear, confusion, and an overwhelming sense of need for you in my life right now, even though I'm not a one-night stand kind of gal. Am I making any sense or just rambling out loud?"

"Of course you're not rambling. I'm feeling the same sort of things, except that I don't think I'd be as articulate as you are. I know it's just human nature to cling to the familiar during a crisis, but I think what's happening between us is real. I think being there for each other will make us better able to handle the task ahead of us. If we survive then we build on what we have. If we don't, we at least had each other for a time when we needed someone the most."

"Alex was this destiny or fate or something?"

"I don't believe in either. I believe God gave us the intellect to understand our situations and then make decisions based on what we learn. What happens then depends on our decisions. You and I will make decisions as we go forward and they will take us where they take us."

"Yeah…I suppose it's easier to believe in fate. Makes us less responsible."

"Gives us less control, too, so I guess there's a tradeoff."

They flew through the night a bit longer, the only light coming from the instruments.

"So," Alex said, "what decisions brought you to where you are?"

Sandi was quiet a moment. "Well, I suppose it started in college, my sophomore year when I married a graduate student at UC Davis. My God, I loved him. I became pregnant with Elizabeth in the summer before my senior year, then finished my veterinary degree shortly after her birth. It was then on to residency at the university animal husbandry facility and eventually a doctorate in agro-economics and a position at the university."

"And the graduate student?"

"Elizabeth was six years old when she walked into our bedroom to find her father in bed with one of his students. He didn't notice her there. I found out that evening when she asked me why her daddy was kissing that other lady."

"Oh. Wow."

"Yeah, wow. There was the typical outrage, the begging for forgiveness, the suggestion of counseling, which didn't work, and finally I made one of those decisions you were talking about and threw the bum out.

"After that, Elizabeth became a lot of my life. The bum kept up with his visitation rights for about a year then began to skip weekends and missing recitals. When he forgot Elizabeth's eighth birthday, I threw him out for good. Four months later while driving home in a dense fog, he was hit head-on by another car that had strayed from their lane. He was killed instantly."

"I'm sorry."

"I wasn't. He had made his own decisions. Fortunately, he was so disorganized that he never changed the beneficiary on his life insurance with the university. I used the proceeds to buy my house, and an out of court settlement on behalf of Elizabeth funded her schooling. And even after Elizabeth was out on her own, I never really considered another man. At least, until now."

"What with the world ending and all."

She laughed, but there wasn't a lot of humor in it. "How about you? What's been passing through your mind?"

Alex was tempted to tell her, but he wasn't sure whether or not the plane was bugged. It was safe to assume it was. Because he'd been obsessing on the handwritten letter from Macklin.

Was it the ravings of a paranoid conspiracy nut, or was there something to the scared little man's ranting. He had found out just today about Macklin's death in a fiery plane crash. And Macklin's letter had told about Eldon Huart's heart attack, even though Huart ran two miles a day, played racquetball twice a week, and ate a diet that would make Jillian Michaels proud.

But he couldn't say that. Even if it weren't true, for a man in his position to even express doubts could be dangerous.

"I don't know that I was thinking much of anything," he said after a moment. "Mostly just trying to wrap my head around what we learned today. That and hoping nothing will go wrong."

Chapter 11

THE DISBELIEVERS AND
THE BLACK WIDOW

Sergeant Andrade Kolna sat at his desk sipping coffee and smoking a cigarette. The Borosky case had been on his mind for weeks. A professional hit on his turf—it still rankled. He wondered how Moscow was handling the investigation…if they were handling it at all.

He finished his coffee and was putting out his cigarette, when a call came in from Vasily Kernoff, the major case squad lead investigator. It was the Borosky case… he knew it before he even picked it up.

"Sergeant Kolna would you like to hear what the US President had to say about the Borosky/Huart case?" Kernoff asked.

"I'll be right over."

Once he arrived at the major case squad office, he poured himself another cup of coffee and lit another cigarette.

Kernoff sat down at his desk and slid an ashtray across.

"Sergeant Kolna what I am about to tell you is considered a state secret and not to be divulged to anyone."

"Understood."

After Kernoff had finished relaying everything he had heard from President Betts, Kolna stamped out his cigarette in the ashtray and looked Kernoff straight in the eyes.

"That is complete bullshit, and you know it. There is no way a rogue agent employed all the sophisticated counter measures that were taken to hide the tracks and bury the evidence. The CIA itself had to be directly involved. I can never believe it otherwise."

"Yes. Neither will I. But the Secretary of Internal Security believes it."

"He's goddamn bureaucrat, who couldn't find a crime scene clue if it had a flashing red light on it."

"Sergeant Kolna I have a little room in my budget for special investigations. Call it mad money if you will. Should you want to take this any further, I'll fund the investigation. With this one condition…no one in Moscow can know what you're doing."

"Consider it done. I will start with the taxicab driver here in St. Petersburg."

"That was going to be my first recommendation. Keep me informed but keep it quiet."

"Thank you, I will, Vasily."

Finally, a chance to root out what was behind this brutal slaying and the resultant cover-up. He first found the address for Constantine Andropov, a taxi cab driver in St. Petersburg and Borosky's cousin and presumed partner in crime. Kolna walked up four flights of stairs to Andropov's small one bedroom apartment, feeling a little winded…too many damned cigarettes…and he knocked on the door.

"Who is it?"

"Constantine Andropov?"

"Yes. Who is it?"

"Sergeant Kolna, St. Petersburg police."

"What have I done— I've done nothing wrong?"

"I am not here to charge you with anything and to my knowledge you have done nothing wrong. I simply want to ask you some questions."

"About what?"

"Constantine open the door and let me in and I will tell you. Otherwise, I will find something to charge you with. Now open the door."

The door opened and Kolna stepped inside a litter strewn apartment that smelled of sweat and smoke so thick he could hardly breathe. Constantine was a slight man, with a caved in chest, already going bald, his stringy hair an unkempt mess. His nicotine stained fingers betrayed his habitual chain smoking. How did he get up those stairs every day?

"You were recently contacted by the security people from Moscow?" Andrade asked.

"Yes, it was about my older cousin Ivan Borosky. I told them everything. They asked me about an account at the People's Bank. I told them I am a taxi driver. I don't make enough money to have a bank account. I've never had a bank account in my forty-eight years of life." Look around me. Does this look like I have enough money?"

"What can you tell me about your cousin Ivan?"

"There's not much to tell. I saw him, I guess four or five years ago. He ordered a taxi to pick him up at the Academy. We talked on the way to his house and made promises to keep in touch and that was all. I haven't talked to him or seen him since that date."

"Okay. Then did you know his assistant, Anna Kinova?"

"No."

The answer was too quick—Andropov was anticipating the question. So Kolna waited a few seconds.

"Let me ask you again——— did you know Anna Kinova… his assistant? A beautiful, young, intelligent, talented woman who was brutally murdered by unknown assassins?"

The tears began to well up in Constantine's eyes…Kolna knew he had hit a hot button.

"Come on Constantine." Kolna kept his voice soft, confessional. "You'll be telling me what I already know."

"Yes." He buried his head in his hands, shoulders heaving.

After a minute, he gathered himself, looked up, his eyes red, a long strand of hair, now matted with tears, across his forehead.

"She was my daughter." He pushed his hands to his face. The tears came again.

This was not expected. Kolna walked over and put his hand on Andropov's shoulder to console him. He gave him a couple of minutes to get control of himself.

"Constantine, your daughter's last name was Kinova. Did she marry?"

"No!" This time it was anger that caught Kolna by surprise.

"She changed her name eight years ago."

"Why?"

"Because she was embarrassed by me, I was just a lowly taxi driver."

"And her mother?"

"Her mother abandoned us when Anna was six. We never heard from her again."

"And it wasn't a coincidence she was working for cousin Borosky?"

"After Anna left me, she sought him out, looking for a position. He agreed to help her, but she was succeeding on her own merits. It was one of the things he and I talked about when we met."

"You did a very noble and courageous thing to raise your daughter by yourself. You have nothing to be embarrassed about and I'm sure Anna would agree if she were alive today. Thank you for your time."

Kolna walked down the stairs into the cold morning air, his breath creating a small cloud before his face as he walked to his car. He thought that this family had all the tragedy it deserved. He decided he would make another trip to the Academy to talk to the Director.

While at the Academy, he browsed through Borosky's office looking for anything that might have been overlooked. The assassins had removed all the cabinet files and wiped the PC's clean. The desk was askew, slightly pulled from the wall. Kolna peered down behind the desk space against the wall, there appeared to be a small thumb drive with MP-3 capability lodged between the wall and the desk leg.

He retrieved it, and asked one of the staff if they had a playing device for the MP-3. A staff person brought a player, Kolna sat down and began listening. Expecting Borosky dictating notes he was surprised when a female voice began speaking. It was undoubtedly Anna's. She detailed a recent visit to an observatory in Chile. Then the subject changed to some conversation she had with Borosky about a mathematical formula for something Kolna could not make out— and for that matter, couldn't pronounce. Then came some comments about impressions she had of Eldon Huart and how much Borosky admired him. She went on to say that apparently Professor Huart had offered to help Borosky in a joint effort with some grant funds to buy an expensive piece of equipment, an adaptive optics filter, whatever that might be. Her impression was that Huart felt embarrassed by the riches his Cal Tech unit had received from a large grant and wanted to share with Borosky. A further entry, with an impression that Professor Macklin was a very timid man, almost scared of his own shadow.

The rest of the tape was devoted to technical things Kolna didn't understand. He went to the Director and asked if anyone here would have known about the adaptive optics filter, donated by Cal Tech. He told Kolna that he was very familiar with the piece of equipment, and it was tagged as having been donated to the Academy by Cal Tech and Professors Huart and Macklin. Kolna asked him if he had ever heard Professor Borosky speak of Professors Huart or Macklin. The Director told him Borosky spoke often of Huart, rarely about Macklin. He said Borosky often praised Huart as a genuine great scientist and an unselfish decent human being.

To Kolna, this didn't sound like parties on the opposite sides of an extortion scheme. He decided to go to the evidence vault and look over Borosky's and Anna's personal effects.

When he arrived at the major case squad building, he was intercepted by Kernoff, who asked what he had learned so far. Kolna told him everything he had uncovered, and that he was headed to the basement to look over the personal effects of Borosky and Anna Kinova for any clues that might have been overlooked.

"You know," Kernoff said, "this all looks like a classic cover-up. If we uncover it again, we may not like what we find."

"Perhaps," Kolna said, "but two innocent Russian citizens are dead, and two Americans are dead. That's four families that deserve the truth."

"Tell me, Kolna, would you be interested in a transfer to the major case squad? We could use good men like yourself."

"Well, I would—."

"Before you decide, the new person coming on board will be assigned to a two month training program run by the Los Angeles police department's major case squad. I have heard that's not far from Pasadena, where Cal Tech is located."

"You know I've been looking for a more challenging position," Kolna said. "I accept."

"You will not go alone. You'll travel with a former FSB agent. She will travel as your wife, you two will be combining a vacation with your training. I will also send you some special equipment to the Agriculture attaché's office in Los Angeles by diplomatic pouch. It may aid you in your investigation. Elena will know how to use everything."

"Sounds like you've done this before."

"Thirteen years with the KGB before the collapse. It's like riding a bicycle. Now, go wrap up any pending cases, and pass them along to your second in charge. You leave in two days."

Andrade wondered if he had ever had the right to say no. Not that he ever would. This was his chance to make a name for himself. "I'll check back with you before I leave."

Kernoff waited for Andrade to leave his office, then dialed the number in Moscow.

"Hello, is this Petrov?"

"Yes."

"Kolna accepted the new position, and Elena will accompany him."

"Excellent, keep me updated and keep this off the radar."

"Yes sir."

Kolna met with Elena the day before they flew to America to discuss the case and how they would approach it from an investigative standpoint. Kolna was impressed with Elena's quick grasp of facts and knowledge of utilizing unique techniques to speed along the overall investigation without compromising their cover. Kolna was also somewhat taken aback by Elena's attractiveness. She was 5'8", around 115 lbs, big beautiful round brown eyes—and in excellent condition it seemed. She said she ran five miles a day to stay in shape. Kolna, could barely walk five miles much less run it, but he was in pretty good shape otherwise, going to the gym and lifting weights three times a week and swimming the other four days. Those damn cigarettes.

Elena showed him her passport with the new last name of Kolna, she even had a marriage certificate dated four years earlier…and a birth certificate for a son born just two years before. Kolna asked her how she had obtained these fake documents so quickly. She told him that he would be surprised at how quickly things can move. Especially, if you have the backing of the right people. Kolna immediately grew suspicious of Kernoff. This was probably set up weeks ago without his knowledge.

Elena was thirty-two years old and was recruited by the KGB at age fourteen. Eventually she was assigned to foreign intelligence work in Europe. She was fluent in French, English, and German. She also volunteered at their first meeting that, for her, men were more of a nuisance than an object of desire. Still, she felt Andrade seemed very competent and they would make a good team and looked forward to her first mission in America.

During the long flight from St. Petersburg to the US they would alternately discuss the trip and doze. Kolna got a little more anxious as they got off the plane in New York. As they headed toward the US Customs station his anxiety grew. Elena and Andrade handed their passports to the agent.

"What is the purpose of your trip to the United States?"

Kolna standing there frozen for the moment, until Elena cleared her throat. The shame of seizing up in front of her drove him on.

"I am here to attend the two month Interpol sponsored Major Case Squad training program in Los Angeles. My wife is with me so we can combine it with a vacation."

"Yes, I see you have the extended visa for the training. Welcome to the United States."

Andrade and Elena walked to the next gate to catch their connecting flight to Los Angeles. As they did, she leaned over and whispered to him "You know you sounded like a robot?"

"It's my nature. And it wasn't nervousness, I was prepared for any contingency. I get a little hyper when people I have never dealt with are in a position to wreck your plans."

"I see," Elena smiled.

"What are you smiling at?"

"Oh nothing. Just remember, there are over 350 million people in the United States, any one of whom can ruin our plans if not careful. And one thing that the Americans say—in fact, it is part of their advertising. Never let them see you sweat."

When they landed in Los Angeles Andrade was puzzled as to why they didn't have to go through customs again. Elena explained that the flight from New York to Los Angeles was within the continental US. The US Customs people don't check those flight passengers. They collected their baggage and exited the airport to the car rental terminal.

"Mr. Cray, I thought you might want to know about this, we got a facial and first name hit on an Elena Grodny at US Customs at La Guardia."

"Elena Grodny? Huh."

"She was traveling under the married name of Kolna, with an extended visa for training with an Interpol-sponsored session in Los Angeles."

"Was she with anyone?"

"Yes, her husband, an Andrade Kolna."

"What was the origin of their flight?"

"St. Petersburg."

Home of Borosky. Cray was getting an uncomfortable feeling. "Do a background on this guy Kolna, and get back to me as soon as possible."

"Yes sir."

Cray then placed a call to Ted Jeffers and recommended he put a tail on the Kolna's. See where they are staying, get taps in place, and a 24/7 tag along for a few days to see if they are up to anything.

"Why the concern Don?"

"Elena Grodny was one of the KGB's and FSB's most infamous undercover agents. We know for a fact that she neutralized two German agents and we suspect she took care of three of our agents and a couple of French over a ten year period. She was nicknamed the Black Widow."

"Um…let me guess."

"You got it. She'd screw the agent's brains out, then kill them as part of the afterglow. This is not someone you would take to the high school prom."

"You said was. She was an infamous agent. How sure are you of the past tense?"

"I find it hard to believe that she has settled down to become a housewife. It just doesn't fit her profile. I mean this gal was a top drawer agent. I wish I had a couple just like her, cold blood and all."

"You got any flight info for me Don?"

"Yeah, they will be arriving at LAX around 3:40 pacific, American flight 103, out of La Guardia, I'll fax you her picture so you can ident them quickly."

"Okay Don, we'll pick it up from there."

Andrade and Elena picked up their car they had rented, got a map, and punched in the address of the apartment complex into the in dash Nav system. She let him drive. His ego was fragile enough already, and they hadn't really started working together. And besides, it left her free to keep her eyes open.

As they drove out of the lot, Elena picked up the white sedan with two men in it. Tails, no doubt. Then, after a few minutes, the white sedan made a left turn behind them and was gone, but Elena picked up a gray sedan with two male occupants. Jesus. You would think the FBI could be a little more creative. That tail followed them for another ten minutes, then traded off for another sedan with two men in it, that eventually traded back to the original white sedan.

When they arrived at the complex they had to check in at the complex office and get instructions.

"Oh, by the way," she asked the fresh-faced undergrad behind the desk, "did the people come by and install that equipment we needed in our apartment?"

"Yes ma'am they just left a few minutes ago."

When they got into their car to drive around the complex to their assigned apartment Andrade leaned over. "What equipment?"

"We've been followed all the way from the airport. Our apartment is probably bugged and the phones are tapped. When we get inside the apartment speak only Russian. Talk about the flight here, what a nice place this is, the training class, tell me you love me, just small talk of no consequence, do you understand?"

"The white and gray sedans?"

Elena was impressed. "Good, then you know we need to play a game with these people. When we unpack, I'll show you some countermeasures we can take."

While Andrade put the bags on the bed, he played his part well, chit-chatting about the amenities and what he expected to learn. She quietly unpacked her one heavy bag and pulled out a small compact disc player and a plastic holder with a selection of fifteen or twenty cd's each in its own sleeve. She went over to the dresser and plugged in the cd player. Then she retrieved an even smaller cd player and put it on the kitchen counter and plugged it in. She then pulled out a notebook and turned to a clean page.

"These cd's are fake background noises," she wrote, "bedroom sex, TV programs to let them think we are watching TV, general conversational stuff."

Andrade nodded, then motioned for the notebook.

"Please don't tell me I'm going to have to listen to sex tapes. I can only take so many cold showers without raising suspicions."

She took the notebook.

"In my job with the KGB, I was forced to sleep with six different men, they're all dead now."

She turned to him with her eyebrows upturned as he read it. He read it and a frown came over his face. He didn't want to use the notebook he just said out loud.

"The truth?"

"Yes."

She could tell by the look on his face, that this was more than disappointing. It was disturbing his morals. So she had hooked herself up with an honorable one. She went into the kitchen and put on a cd that started out playing a news caption then a rerun of "I Love Lucy". That should give them time to discuss the next day's agenda. He would go to the training facility and check in. Since he was only going to participate in the explosives part of the program, he could find out how much downtime they would have available to pursue the case. She would stay behind the first day and organize the efforts to thwart the wiretaps and bugs, so no one got tipped off on the other side.

She came back and whispered. "Remember we have a two-year old son, staying with my mother while we are here."

"Yes, Alexi."

"Tomorrow ask people about sightseeing in the state, not just Los Angeles."

She gave him a very long list of things to do and an equally long list of things not to do. The last item on the list of things not to do was, don't get involved with her, he deserved better.

They went out to a local Denny's for dinner, they dropped by a Ralph's grocery store and bought food and supplies for the apartment. After returning, they played their little game with the fake conversations, and then went to bed. She put on the cd of bedroom sex, and then small talk after, put in ear plugs and went to sleep immediately.

After a disturbing night—he couldn't relax both because he was lying next to a beautiful woman and because she had killed six lovers—Andrade got up and showered. As he was dressing, he noticed that she was watching.

"Good morning husband. How did you sleep?"

"Very well my lovely wife. And you?"

"Oh it was a deep sleep, filled with dreams."

"Good dreams I hope?" Andrade felt like a pimply youth stumbling through a high school play.

"Yes, they were dreams of you, my husband."

"Well good. I'm off to the training facility and will return as soon as I can."

"Aren't you going to kiss me before you go?"

Andrade was growing weary of this charade, he made a half-hearted effort at faking a smooch with Elena and walked out of the bedroom. She got out of bed and followed him into the living room.

"Andrade that was not a very good kiss for your wife, who loves you very much." She walked up to him and kissed him on the lips, long and hard. "Oh, that was much better."

Andrade waved his finger back and forth. What kind of game was she playing? She could've just faked the kiss, after all they weren't under video surveillance.

He drove to the training facility where the major case squad program was being held, found the administrative offices, and asked to see the instructor in charge of the program. A middle aged man came out and introduced himself. Andrade asked to see his schedule, since he knew he was not going to attend all the courses.

"Yes, I see you've already completed nearly all the units through the sessions held two years ago in Berlin. The only one you are to attend is the one-week explosives detection, disarming, and analysis class. It meets three weeks from now."

"So I have three weeks before the next session starts? Well, looks like my wife and I can do a little sightseeing."

"Oh, you brought your wife with you? Good. You've got Disneyland, Knotts Berry Farms, Universal Studios, and all the Hollywood stars' homes."

Andrade got back into the rented car and drove out of the facility parking lot. Another tail followed him and he picked up the handoff several blocks later. He decided he would just drive around for a few minutes to see how many teams they had following him. After about fifteen minutes it appeared to him that they only had two teams on him that morning, and he drove back to the apartment.

Elena gasped as Andrade came through the door.

"What's wrong?" he said.

"You scared me. I didn't think you would be back so soon. Why are you back so soon?"

Andrade put his fingers to his mouth to signal be quiet, she turned on the cd player in the kitchen, which began playing the sound track from the Price is Right. They sat down at the kitchen table and he whispered into her ear, "My training doesn't start for three weeks. Even then I am set up to attend only that one class for one week. Then we have another four weeks to work our case investigation."

She gave him thumbs up signal that he found strangely gratifying.

"I was tailed again, two teams."

She nodded. "Now that I know we've got three weeks, we need to set up a plan that will allow us to both get out of the apartment without raising suspicion. They've got to believe you are going to class and I'm just jogging around the complex for exercise. Let me think on it for a little while." Then out loud. "Would you like some eggs and bacon for breakfast?"

"Yes," he said with sincerity. "That would be nice."

She turned down the cd player.

"So when I went into the office they told me that the first day session doesn't start until one p.m. because so many attendees are late because of traffic, he said. "And some are having to deal with administrative issues relating to enrollment, and late airline arrivals."

"So you are going back at one today?"

"Yes."

"Are you ready for some coffee with your breakfast?"

"Yes that would be great my lovely wife."

She smiled and gave him the thumbs up again.

He was surprised to find that Elena was actually an accomplished cook when she placed a very nice omelet with bacon and English muffins in front of him.

"What a wonderful cook you are, and one of the many reasons I married you," he said.

She laughed silently with her hand over her mouth.

When he finished he motioned for her to turn up the volume on the cd player and come closer to him. He whispered while unfolding a map of the facility.

"As you can see there are multiple buildings at the campus. This is the administration building. See the parking on this side? There is also parking on the other side of the building that cannot be seen from the outer road. My thought would be to rent another car, and park it on this blind side of the admin building. When I arrive every day, I park our current car out front where it can be seen, and I can be observed going into the building. Then I walk out the other side unnoticed and get into the rental car and return to pick you up somewhere near the complex. It will be necessary for you find out if they are watching you. If so, evade them so I can pick you up and we can then go to work."

Elena sat back in her chair and thought for a moment.

"How will we shake the tails long enough to go to another rental car agency?"

"Simple." He went into the bedroom and came back with a page torn he'd torn out of a magazine on the flight from New York.

"You see, this company will deliver the car to whatever address you ask. They take you back to their office to do the paperwork, and then you are off. I will have them pick me up at the facility parking lot in the back and get the second car. Every day, I will park the car in back just about the time the sessions are over with, walk through the building out to the front, and get into our original car. They won't know the whole time I was gone."

"I can see you've done some thinking about this Andrade. You should have been a spy for the FSB."

"What I need you to do while I go back to the facility and arrange to get the second car is look around. See if you can discover any surveillance teams and find a secure location where I can pick you up unnoticed."

"Okay then that's what we'll do. Tonight when you return, I will go over this area with you and we can decide together where it would be best to pick me up every day. Maybe rotate the locations, so we don't get into a pattern that some civilian might notice."

"Good." Then out loud. "I've got an hour and a half before I should leave. Let's take a walk around the complex together and see what's out there."

On the fifty-first floor of a high rise in the Battery Park area, two men walked quietly down a corridor of private executive suites.

"Torrance seems to be placing an awful lot of trust in General Hanken," one said.

"Yes. I talked to Howard, and he says this guy is perfect—highly organized, great military discipline, and more importantly…a true patriot."

"Well, I hope so. When all this comes down, Hanken is going to have an awful lot of firepower at his disposal."

"I understand your concern, but Torrance knows his people and has absolute faith in Hanken."

"Torrance is old guard. Hanken was a combat hero. Evan could be placing too much reliance on that past experience as a predictor of his future loyalty. I think we need someone closer to Hanken in the event he doesn't see things the way everyone else does."

"Very well. I'll contact Howard and have him set it up. Should we let Torrance know?"

"It's better that he not."

"What about these two Russian agents?"

"Jeffers at the FBI and Don at the CIA are handling it."

"We don't need attention right now. There are already too many moving parts, and the stakes couldn't be higher."

"I agree. Everything should resolve itself this summer Carter."

"Brett, let's get some lunch. When's Boyd due in town?"

"He and Crane will be here tomorrow."

"Good. We can wrap up a lot of loose details. Like Hanken"

Chapter 12

THE DYNAMIC DUO

★ ★ ★ ★

Once back in Sacramento, Alex prepared for their trip to visit the Midwest and eastern facilities, then called Curt to fill him in on the upcoming itinerary.

"And one more thing, I want you to use your telecommunications background to set up a self-contained communications system between the thirteen facilities in the Western and Midwestern districts. Forget the Eastern districts. Post event communications with those facilities will probably be limited, or completely down, due to atmospheric conditions."

"Cost is not an issue right?"

"Right."

"Then I can give you voice, data, and video with telescoping relay towers to avoid any blast waves that might hit an area. Once cleared, I just hit a button on a master console and all the antennas with multi-directional disks unfold to a height of fifteen to twenty feet. Motorola has a great system that they put in place for the Army during the Iraqi Freedom campaign."

"Very good."

"We'll want plenty of redundancy to cover outages from blast damage."

"Well, as I said, you've got whatever budget you need."

Alex's next call was to Pete."

"Alex how are you?"

"Busy. I hope you are too."

"Well, those army engineers got here yesterday, and they're already lining out the hangars. And the battalion guy said they'll be ready to pour foundations day after tomorrow. We contracted with the biggest concrete fabricator and a steel beam company in Spokane. Those two put their heads together with the battalion commander and, in about two hours came up with a design that will allow them to literally put these things together like tinker toys. They'll be four times stronger than the ones called for on the plans that the commander got from McChord."

"Outstanding. How soon can they get the fabrication done?"

"Both of them were pretty comfortable with all thirty being trucked out here in thirty days for assembly. I gave them a little profit incentive for certain deadlines."

"That is what I need from you Pete, drive that process. Now, I have some more to put on your plate. Is the construction commander around?"

"Yeah, he's right here in the airport office with me, you want to talk to him?"

"Does that phone have a speaker?"

"Yes. Hang on."

"General Hanken," a voice said, with the hollow sound of a speaker phone. "This is Major Atkins."

"Major Atkins, you and Pete are being given another project associated with the hangars you're building. Are you aware of what's going into those hangars?"

"No sir."

"We will be bringing thirty F-35's, which get pretty thirsty when they fly. Two things needed, refueling tankers and fuel storage. I'll be bringing two C-17 refueling tankers to this facility. We need hangars for them, get the specs on the height and width and get them built. Second, we need eight underground fuel storage tanks for JP-8 fuel. Each tank needs a two hundred thousand gallon capacity. In addition, I will need two fifty-thousand gallon underground tanks to store #2 diesel. Did you get the trailers for your men?"

"They arrived in the middle of the night. The boys are busy setting them up as we speak. These trailers are much nicer inside than the dorms these guys are used to."

"Well don't let them get soft on you."

"Don't you worry about that sir. One question General, do these hangars have to be hardened?"

"Not the same way the fighters are. The C-17 has a tail height just under sixty feet. Probably reinforced concrete walls about ten feet around the perimeter, then steel canopy material like the ones at McChord where the other C-17's are based."

"Good, I'll get the boys on the horn tomorrow that are doing the hangars, and have them put the design together."

"Pete, at facility number one and three I want two helo pads each forty by forty with a paved runway eight feet wide from the entrance of the facility to each pad."

"I'll catch my concrete crew and give them the revised contract."

"Gentlemen, my son and his fiancé are coming up there tomorrow to check on progress. I will be out of hand for two weeks. Curt will be your liaison during my absence. Any questions?"

"No sir. We've got more than enough to keep us busy."

"Pete how are you coming with the interior design for living facilities?"

"I've got the toilet and shower facilities sketched in, tomorrow morning I meet with the modular people to combine the living quarters. We're going to have tons of room left in there for the kitchen, food storage, general supplies, communications center, and work spaces. It's just a matter of how much you want devoted to each."

"Bear in mind this will be a closed facility. I have a contract engineer from an air and oxygen purification company coming in. They're the same company the Navy contracts with for submarine environmental systems. There will be engineers from General Electric contacting you to provide a bid as well for a self-contained power system. They will need to know how many living quarters, ventilation needs for cooking and sewage run off, so try and get those plans ready as soon as possible."

"I'll have them completed by day after tomorrow, with electrical, lighting and conduits for computer and communications cabling. The steel company in Seattle has already come and gone for the facility doors. I should have a bid on those within a week."

"Good." Major, anything you need from me?"

"Well, maybe some water trucks to keep down the dust. Ours are pretty busted up and really of no use."

"Then go buy you two new ones."

"Really?"

"Yes really. What else do you need?"

"Well sir, those two tanker hangars are going to be tough to build without some mid-size cranes, and we simply don't have any."

"Then how many would you need?"

"One will work fine, two would be ideal. But those things are expensive to rent sir."

The Major clearly wasn't getting the scope of the project. "Is there a major equipment dealer in Spokane that has what you need?"

"Yes, sir."

"Then go buy two of them."

"Uh sir, those are like $250,000 a piece."

"Pete, fill in the Major on how we operate, and get the invoices submitted with wiring instructions pronto."

"Yes, sir."

"Major when I return in two weeks I want a complete breakdown of your personnel, their specialty, their rank, age, marital status, and children if any."

"Yes sir. Can I ask if a rumor is true?"

"You can ask, but I may not answer."

"We hear that 1st Special Forces is now under your commend."

"That is a true statement."

"Well then sir, I am proud to be under your command."

"Glad to have you on my team, Major. Pete anything else?"

"No, General. Have a good trip."

"Will do gentleman, let's go to work. See you soon."

After Alex got hung up, Major Atkins, still a little shell shocked from Alex's rapid fire orders.

"Pete, this guy is the Commanding General of 1st Special Forces. Do you have any idea how high up in the Pentagon that gets? I mean he is something special for sure."

"Major I can vouch for money being no object. I've submitted invoices to some fax machine number in D.C. and man, two days later the money hits the vendors account. These people aren't playing around. I've never seen such urgency."

"He was serious about the two cranes?"

"You start laying out the footprint for those two tanker hangars, then head over to the equipment dealer in Spokane, pick out what you want, get the wiring instructions for their bank, and get me the invoice. They'll have their money in three days. Have you got personnel trained to handle those types of cranes?"

"Four of them are certified for up to twenty-five thousand pounds"

"Good. As the General said, we've got work to do; I've got to get in touch with the contractors who built those maintenance hangars for Japan Airlines at the Seattle Airport. And locate that company that builds those underground tanks."

"Pete you know what the General is doing. He's building a stand-alone military command, and it has something to do with this worldwide redeployment. But why the hurry? What's the hair-on-fire emergency?"

"Major, you think too much for your own good."

When Alex asked Sandi about packing for the two weeks they would be gone to the eastern and Midwest sites she said she needed another laptop with some software she wanted to download from the University. She would go by the computer store, and then go to the university; she would be gone most of the day. How did he want her to pay for the laptop? Alex went back to his bedroom and came out with five thousand in one hundred dollar bills and asked if that was enough. She laughed and said she would try and make it last.

As she was leaving Curt called.

"Dad, I spoke to the people at Motorola, they have nine of those highly sophisticated telescoping towers and all the attendant communication hardware and software for as many sites as we wanted. So I said, how about thirteen sites, covering ten states? The guy got another engineer on the line and he said no problem, except that this is government contracted and restricted to military use only. I asked for his boss's name and number so I could have the appropriate people contact them about the equipment. So now what?"

"Leave it to me, I'll call Howard. You sound distant are you on the land sat?"

"Yes, I'm calling from the site."

"Curt, you called me on my personal phone."

"Oh Jesus. I'll call back."

Less than a minute later, the new phone warbled. By then, Alex had settled into his office with a fresh cup of coffee.

"That is better. Remember, never call into a personal line and discuss the project. Hang on I'll teleconference Howard."

"Howard?"

"Alex, how are you?"

"Good I've got my son Curt on the line and I'll let him tell you what I asked him to do and what he found out."

Curt relayed the story behind the desired communications equipment.

"Consider it on order. Curt, you fly out to Motorola and inspect the equipment, make sure it fits your requirements, and order any modifications you feel are necessary. Alex, nice job of thinking ahead. Anything else?"

"No as usual Howard you are the problem solver, you make my job that much easier."

"Have a great day guys."

Alex spoke briefly with a stunned Curt who couldn't believe how things get done so quickly on a guy's word. Alex reminded him that Howard Carney was the number two man at the Department of Defense and wielded incredible power throughout all levels of the government and defense industries.

"So, after you and Cynthia get back from Idaho, schedule a trip to the Motorola facility. I want you to be coy about exact locations of the facilities. Give them a general idea of the area and take into account line of sight obstructions. I would imagine the Colorado Springs facility will present some issues with the Rockies standing in the way. Look for them to provide a complete package price, hardware, software, installation, and testing. Oh yeah, and Howard sent you a government credit card. I got it yesterday. Use it for any and all things on your trips. And Curt, no gentleman's clubs please."

"Are you kidding me Dad? If Cynthia ever found out she would turn me into a gelding."

"And not a jury in the world…Now is there anything else?"

"No Dad, I'll call you before you leave."

"Okay son."

Alex sipped the cooling coffee and busied himself with personnel profiles of the Midwest and eastern facility managers. It didn't take long for him to spot potential problems—a couple of managers who just didn't fit the mission. But, he would not prejudice his decision, he would wait until the evaluation visits were complete.

And now, he'd put his next phone call off long enough.

"Harlan, Alex Hanken."

"Alex how are you? I'm currently at Mountain Home Air Base."

"So how are the facilities shaping up?"

"We'll have everything in place in four to five months. Your project model made it so much easier. I would have never thought of half the things you did."

"Thanks, and that's great news. Listen, Admiral Torrance wants me to transfer fifty of the 1st Special Forces under my command to the Coeur d' Alene. I've got FEMA trailers that will be there in two days for them. I haven't had a chance to review the troops, and I leave for two weeks day after tomorrow. I need some help in getting these orders cut and choosing the best of the best for the fifty."

"Alex, I'll be back at Ft. Lewis late tonight, if you can have me the orders for permanent assignment over your signature on my desk tomorrow morning, I'll call in the brigade commander, and we'll do as you suggested. Now do you want them to have their equipment and supplies, like ammunition and radio gear, humvees, parachutes? In other words, do you want them field ready?"

"Combat ready. Have them bring tents for ammunition and weapons storage. We'll park all the vehicles at the air facility in the vacant general aviation hangars. I want at least a Major, as officer in charge, with a sergeant major as company senior NCO. Have them diversified as to specialties—light weapons, heavy gunners, mechanics, explosives, vehicle drivers, radio techs. I want this to be a stand-alone outfit."

"I know just what to do. Get me those orders, and we'll have them there in about ten days, fully mobilized and equipped.Boy is this thing moving fast or what?"

"I still get a little dizzy from all that is going on Harlan."

After he'd hung up. Alex slumped back and stared at the phone, literally feeling a little dizzy. After all that he'd done in the last few weeks, all the personnel and money he'd moved around, this order for fifty specially trained troops was the hardest thing he'd had to do yet. He knew why Torrance wanted them there and under his command. If word of the survival shelters got out before they were complete and sealed, he might have to defend them. From mobs of American citizens whose only crime was they didn't want to die in the coming disaster. It was a side of this whole project that he was able to ignore most of the time.

But he couldn't ignore it. He had to get used to it.

With that out of the way he decided it was time to call General Corrigan and get the Coeur d' Alene issue resolved.

"General Corrigan's office."

"This is General Hanken, would you please reserve some time for me to speak with the general in the next few days."

"Are you coming to Washington?"

"No, I will call him from here on the west coast."

"Well, he's available right now. Would you like for me to check?"

"Yes. Go ahead."

"General Hanken, General Corrigan is on the line for you now."

"Alex what can I do for you?"

"Phil, most of my career was spent putting plans before people like you and then letting whomever run with it however they wanted. Unfortunately, this time around, the onus has been put on me to not only develop the plans, but I have to execute them as well. The President and Admiral Torrance felt that I should be out front, because we are operating on a tight timeline. Phil, we can't stand on formalities now, they both knew that when they put all of this on me. That's one of the reasons that Torrance asked you Chiefs of Staff to plow the road for me...we simply don't have the time to discuss things like moving a squadron of F-35's to Coeur d' Alene.

"I know under normal circumstances protocol would have been for me to run this by you first. But Phil, you're a designated person, you know what's coming, protocol is out the window...we are in a race with time. And every time we have to stop and question something, that time is gone forever. I know you are feeling that your power has been usurped by having Torrance place me above you...but Phil we don't have a choice...somebody has to do this and I need you and the other Chiefs on board."

"Yeah, but Alex, a new airbase, how much did that cost?"

"Nothing."

"Excuse me."

"I said it cost us nothing."

"How did you manage that?"

"I'm not at liberty to tell you how, but when the Attorney General says it's yours, you thank him for making your life a little easier and move on."

"Why move them Alex, you've got a perfectly good air base right there at McChord."

"Yes Phil, and it sits right on the Pacific coast and if there is a Pacific strike we'll lose the entire base. All my planning has tried to take into account what may happen and how can I minimize losses and maintain the security of the nation at the same time?"

"It just seems like we're moving too fast."

"Phil, I would trade places with you any day. This is like being in the middle of a tornado with thousands of things flying about you. And you are constantly trying to keep all of it in one place. We are moving forward, I need your leadership and experience to help me contend with the myriad of complexities in our military."

"Alex, I guess it's a daunting task you face, I'll do what I can to help."

"Phil, thank you for understanding, talk to you soon."

It would be several weeks later and General Corrigan would realize that…Hanken had done it again.

Fortunately, Sandi called then and mentioned that she got her new laptop and was currently at the UC Davis Ag research offices and downloading three programs she would need for soil analysis.

"What type of equipment will you need for soil analysis or equipment in general?"

She gave him a list of four analyzers and two field items she would need. She also mentioned the hot green house would need some specialized tables, deep enough for soil and seed germination, as well as an automated misting system, the type they use at UC Davis.

"Get the vendors for the lab and field equipment, the tables and misting systems, have it shipped to the airport in Coeur d' Alene. Call Pete, tell him of any special water connections involved with the misting system and also if there are any drainage issues."

"Oh, and I'm going to need a five thousand gallon plankton growing tank for the green house, and a storage tanks for fish eggs."

"Order it."

"And I need a big hug from you. Oops sorry."

"Don't be—I need one too." Especially at the moment. "When do you think you'll be done?"

"Give me a couple more hours."

Alex left Sandi to line up vendors for all the necessary equipment and supplies she would need to fully equip her greenhouse. She was doing what Alex had already done—creating the model for the national plan. In the meantime, Alex was doing some last minute organizing himself. Curt called. He and Cynthia were flying to Idaho around 1 that afternoon. Everybody was busy, they all had their agendas to attend to. Just how much busier could it get?

But he really could use that hug.

Alex and Sandi rarely talked about the future unless it was in the context of planning for survival. Both knew they hoped for the best, but deep down feared for the worst. So they busied themselves with the tasks at hand and used every opportunity available to them to reinforce the other. It was the best way they could cope …with everything.

Alex had always been confident in his own abilities, but doubt was beginning to creep into his subconscious. The sheer size and magnitude of his assigned missions, varied as they were, presented the most serious challenge he had ever faced. And it didn't help that, if he failed, if he forgot something critical, it could mean the end of the world. Even though he often worked himself to exhaustion, he still had trouble sleeping. But what could he do?

Chapter 13

FIND HANKEN

The next morning, Andrade left for the training facility, parked his rental car out front and walked through the building to the opposite side waiting for the rental agency to pick him up. When Andrade returned, Elena suggested they go to the attaché's office and pick up the diplomatic pouch and container with the equipment they would need for their investigation.

At the attaché's office in downtown Los Angeles, they were asked to have a seat. Andrade looked at his watch. It was getting late, he didn't want to be the lone car driving up or leaving the training facility. Finally, a gentleman came out introduced himself, and took them into his office. He hoisted a large and clearly heavy suitcase out from behind his desk. Andrade and Elena thanked him and left the office. Andrade dropped Elena off at the apartment, drove back to the training facility parked the new rental in back, waited about ten minutes until the class attendees began pouring out of the building, and walked through the building out front, got in the original rental and drove back to the apartment.

He carried the heavy suitcase into the apartment and set it down on the bed. Elena opened the suitcase. There were several packets containing fifty thousand US dollars each, two .40 caliber automatic pistols with one hundred rounds of ammunition for each, phone tapping equipment, debugging equipment, several microchip bugs, two headsets for communication within a twenty-five mile radius, two sets of eyeglasses, that would pick up conversations up to fifty feet away, and three lipstick case sized cameras with a six inch remote monitor. A pair of twenty four power binoculars with heat sensitive technology for night vision. Two satellite phones for secure communications between themselves and St. Petersburg.

Andrade whispered to Elena. "No wonder this thing was so heavy, the only thing missing is a handheld missile launcher."

She motioned to be quiet as she pulled out a piece of equipment and walked into the living room. She pointed to the air vent above the front door. The display on the piece of equipment was blinking green evidencing some kind of bugging device in the vent. She walked around the apartment, then back into the bedroom, and found the other device on the headboard of their bed. Cleverly buried in the wood carving, it was not only a voice but a video bug.

"Let's go out to dinner my love."

"My beautiful wife what would you like for dinner?" Andrade carried on the charade.

"Fish. I think a nice fish dinner."

"That sounds good to me. There's a place called Gladstones in Malibu that is supposed to be pretty good. It's right on the ocean. Give me a moment to clean up and then we can go."

While walking out of the apartment, she leaned toward Andrade and whispered.

"I'm worried."

He raised his eyebrows.

"While you were out, I walked entire neighborhood and saw nothing that might be a surveillance car or van. The homes and buildings surrounding the complex also appear to be normal."

"So? They are relying entirely on the bugs?"

"Perhaps. The bug in the bedroom was not only a voice, but video and a video feed requires video monitors at fairly close range. They are somewhere around here in a home, apartment, or van. We need to look for unusual antennas on buildings or inside cars or on van roofs. And be more careful in the bedroom."

They left for dinner and watched for anyone trailing them, and sure enough, a light colored vehicle followed them all the way to the restaurant. Over dinner she startled Andrade when she said, "I think I need to talk to our shadows."

"Elena is that such a good idea? We can give them the slip every day."

"Not if I don't know where they are, and right now I'm not sure where they have surveillance set up."

After finishing dinner they drove back to the complex, and decided to drive around the parking lot to see if there was anything unusual. At one point, she nudged him and pointed. And there it was, a telephone company van. Normally that would not be suspicious, but this van had a small three winged antenna attached to the rear tire guard. And it was a little late for house calls.

"Pull up next to it."

"Elena are you sure about this?"

"Just pull up beside the van."

Andrade did as she asked, and Elena got out of the car, walked over to the driver's side, and knocked on the window...no one appeared.

"Come on guys, I know you're in there."

A couple of minutes passed and the back door of the van swung open, and a man in a telephone company work shirt stepped out. "Can I help you ma'am?"

"Yes, you can start by removing the bugs you placed in our vent above the front door and the one you hid in the headboard of our bed." She stared directly into his eyes without flinching.

"I'm sorry, I'm not sure what you are talking about."

"Okay look, my name is Elena Kolna, formerly Elena Grodny. This is my husband of four years, Andrade Kolna. We're here for him to attend an Interpol sponsored Major Case Squad training program at the Los Angeles Police Academy. I am with him so we can vacation in the US before airline tickets get so expensive we can no longer afford it. I am a former KGB and FSB agent, and I'm sure I set off all kinds of bells and whistles at the New York airport. So tell your Director...I think his name is Jeffers, isn't it?—that I have my marriage certificate and my child's birth certificate. I am retired; I am no longer active as an agent for Russia or any other country. You may have the right to follow me anywhere I or my husband go, but you do not have the right to invade my bedroom, so that I can't even be intimate with my own husband. Either you remove the bugs, or I will."

The man in the telephone company suit stood stiff and silent... never uttered a word.

Elena got back in the car. "Okay, now we can go. We'll give them time to report to their direct supervisor and see what they want to do."

Andrade was still mystified at this tactic on her part, but he needed to trust her. She had far more training and experience in this field of work.

Half an hour later, there was a knock at the door. Elena answered. It was the telephone company man from the van.

"May I come in Mrs. Kolna?"

"Yes, please."

"Yes, well...my superior has asked me to remove the surveillance devices from your apartment, he also wanted me to remind you and your husband that we reserve the right to monitor your activities while in the US. Would you please provide a copy of your marriage and birth certificates?"

"Certainly I have brought extra copies just in case we needed them for any reason, I will get them for you, while you are removing the bugs."

After he had stripped the bugs out of the apartment, she gave him the copies he requested.

As he was leaving, he said, "And by the way, my boss said be sure and visit Disneyland."

"Thank you. And please tell Mr. Jeffers that Mickey Mouse was a KGB operative. Goodnight, agent."

She turned to Andrade who was standing in the kitchen marveling. "Tah-dah." She swept the apartment one more time, and it came up clean for hidden devices.

"We will need to keep up the double car routine just in case," she said. "So what do you think?"

"I must admit, your approach was probably the best move we could make, but I had my doubts. We'll still have to be careful, especially around the Cal Tech campus. Remember these guys murdered four people recently."

"I know, and we will get to the bottom of this, I promise."

The following morning, Elena made breakfast again, and Andrade did the double car switch and picked her up at the complex. They headed toward the Pasadena campus for interviews with Huart and Macklin's staff, masquerading as reporters for a St. Petersburg newspaper. Elena even had id's showing their position at the paper. He took a circuitous route to the campus, but was unable to spot anybody following them. Once there, they introduced themselves to Eldon Huart's secretary and said how tragic they thought his untimely death was. And that was partly the angle of their story because of Professor Borosky's untimely death so close to Huart's. If you added in the untimely death of Professor Macklin, it was an extreme blow to the scientific community.

"Professor Huart's death, it was ruled a heart attack correct?" Elena asked the secretary.

"Yes it was. But, you know, Eldon was in such good health. He walked two miles a day, played racquetball three times a week. It was such a shock."

"Did Professor Huart say anything to you about his conversations with Professor Borosky? Anything at all? Even the smallest item could be of great help in telling the story of these two great scientists."

"The only thing that I heard Eldon say about this call with Borosky was, "heaven help us." And he was going down to the computer center to get the data. That's I really all I know about this whole matter."

"When you say this whole matter, what do you mean?" Andrade asked.

"Well, the fact that Eldon was in near perfect health, and there was an FBI agent questioning him when he died. I do remember now how Eldon looked when I told him an FBI agent was here to see him."

"And how was that?"

"Scared. I've never seen him look that way, unless it was the time Professor Macklin had called him a couple of days before, with some kind data he had. I remember Eldon telling Jeffrey to calm down and get off the phone and to meet him at their favorite Coco's in Glendale."

"Ma'am do you have a recent picture of Professor Huart or Professor Macklin we could use?"

"I can pull their photos off the web site for you."

After getting the photos, they thanked her for her time and left.

"So, Elena are you hungry? I hear the Coco's in Glendale is a good place to eat."

"I'm eager to see their menu."

After they arrived at the restaurant, the waitress seated them asked for drink orders and left. When the waitress returned, Elena showed her pictures of Huart and Macklin. "Have you ever seen these two men before?"

"Oh yeah, those are the two professors from Cal Tech the FBI asked about."

"The FBI? What did they want, do you know?"

"Yeah, they wanted to look at the receipts for the day that the one guy came in and left in such a hurry. He used a credit card and they wanted to see the actual charge."

"Which one was this?"

She pointed to Macklin's picture. "Yeah they were both in here a couple of days before that, and wanted a secluded place to sit so they wouldn't be bothered. But some guy came up and sat down at their table and it looked like they were having a real intense discussion about something, I mean this guy—she pointed to Macklin's picture again. "He was really agitated about something."

"Can you describe the man who sat down with them?"

"No not really."

"Thank you so much for your help," Andrade said.

After finishing lunch, they both agreed they needed to make a call on Macklin's wife, and see if there is something at his residence of value. By now, it was obvious that something big had happened and both were killed for what they knew. Who was this mystery man that sat down at their supposedly private conversation? They knew that it was futile to look for any evidence at Cal Tech, with the FBI and CIA working in tandem any trace of information had been scrubbed by now. Jeffrey Macklin's wife lived a short distance from the Cal Tech campus. They drove to the address given by Huart's secretary.

"Mrs. Macklin," Elena said, "hi, I'm Elena Kolna with Neva News. St. Petersburg, Russia. May I come in?"

"Yes. Is this about Jeffrey and Ivan?"

"That's right. Please accept our condolences and sympathy for the passing of your husband."

"Thank you, but my husband didn't just pass away; he was killed just like Eldon Huart was murdered."

Andrade and Elena's instincts had been right... they had hit the jackpot.

"Mrs. Macklin," Elena said, "what makes you think they were killed and by whom?"

"First of all Eldon Huart was in perfect health, I talked to his wife three days before he died of a sudden heart attack. He'd just had a complete physical exam the month before, and was pronounced in remarkable health. That was no heart attack. As to whom I suspect...I believe our own government was involved."

Andrade looked at Elena and said. "We should be honest with her, and tell her the truth."

"What truth?" Macklin's wife asked.

Elena came over and sat down by her.

"Mrs. Macklin we're not from the newspaper in St. Petersburg. We're investigators from the Major Case Squad at police headquarters in St. Petersburg, Russia. We're trying to get to the bottom of Professor Borosky's death."

"So what does that have to do with Jeffrey and Eldon?"

"Mrs. Macklin," Andrade said. "Let me tell you a story." Andrade began with the phone call, the assassinations, the records that were erased, the Level three alert level, the F-16 ordered to shoot down a civilian plane, the whole story as they knew it. Not halfway through, Mrs. Macklin began to cry. By the end, she was cursing and mumbling over and over. "I knew it, I knew it, I knew it all along. Those bastards killed my Jeffrey and Borosky, that poor Anna. She sat in the very chair you are sitting in Mr. Kolna, not just six months ago, when they visited for a conference. We had them over for dinner one night, she was such a sweet girl and so bright and full of life, they killed her too, my God how can a government do such evil things?"

"Mrs. Macklin we need your help," Elena asked.

"I'll do anything in my power to help you get to the bottom of this."

"First, I need to run a check on your house for bugs or surveillance devices. Will you allow me to do that?"

"Of course. You don't think they would have tapped my lines or anything like that do you?"

"There's one way to find out. I'll get my equipment out of the car, and we'll see."

Elena first swept the house for bugs then turned her attention to her phone lines.

"Come here Mrs. Macklin, see the flashing green light? Your phone lines are tapped."

"Bastards. How can I help?"

"Mrs. Macklin your husband met with Eldon Huart at the Coco's on this date and a waitress mentioned that they wanted to have a quiet secluded table for privacy. But she remembered that a gentleman came into the restaurant and walked right up to their table and sat down. The waitress also remembered that your husband seemed really agitated. Would you have any idea who that man was?"

"No, no I'm sorry."

Andrade had been thinking about the stranger since the waitress mentioned him, trying to find a way to identify him, and he had a thought. After all, what did Americans do when they first met?

"Mrs. Macklin," he said, "is there any place in the house that your husband would have kept things hidden, a book or a journal, a card index?"

"You mean like a little black book of his girlfriends? Jeffery was scared of his own shadow, he never—wait a minute, his address book."

She disappeared into another room for a few minutes and returned with a battered black leather bound book. Andrade leafed through it and found a business card. For an Alex Hanken. His address was in Sacramento.

"Mrs. Macklin you have been a great help to us," he said. "Thank you so very much, and again we are sorry for your loss."

Andrade was feeling pretty confident on their trip back to the apartment. Tomorrow, they would make plans to go to Sacramento. But how this Hanken character was involved? Well, they would soon find out.

In a celebratory mood, they stopped by a liquor store on the way to the apartment and picked up a bottle of champagne. Alex poured Elena's glass full and they toasted each other on their day's success, and to their future exploits as a team. As the night wore on, and the champagne ran out, their inhibitions fell away.

"Andrade," Elena said, "our bed is no longer bugged. You must prove to me that you're worthy to take on the task."

"Task?"

"You must make me feel like a woman. Make love to me."

With that, Andrade picked her up and carried her to the bedroom. They both staggered a bit as they undressed, but the next several hours, he convinced her that she was a woman. He was equal to the task, which she never doubted.

"Don?"

"Ted."

"Hey Ted."

"Don we may have a problem. We just monitored a call from Macklin's widow to Huart's widow. She apparently met with two policemen from, are you ready for this, St. Petersburg, Russia and indicated that both their husbands were killed by the US government for a cover-up of something."

"Goddamn it!" Cray dug through his overflowing inbox and found the report on Andrade Kolna stuck under a personnel review," He gave it a quick scan, then stopped. "Oh Jesus Christ Ted, Sergeant Andrade Kolna was the crime scene team leader in the deaths of Ivan Borosky and Anna Kinova."

"We have a major problem, I'll send my boys out on this one unless you have a really crack group of people to handle this. It could get ugly, given what I've read of Elena Grodny."

"Don there's something else. They know Alex Hanken is involved somehow."

"Well that's it then, Hanken is Admiral Torrance's handpicked boy. There better not be a hair on his head out of place, or you and I will be sent to the gallows. Let me handle this, it goes across international lines anyway."

"Hang on Don, I just got a flash from DOD. Alex Hanken's military records were just hit by an online snoop."

"That's it, I'm sending my top team to Sacramento. You find Alex and put a twenty-four hour security lockdown on him."

"Will do, Don. We need to know what is happening at all times. Alex Hanken has become our top priority."

As soon as Jeffers hung up, Cray contacted the San Francisco office of the CIA and had a long discussion with his top west coast agent and his team. He left them with explicit instructions to end this matter expeditiously and quietly, with no loose ends. He never wanted to hear the names Andrade and Elena Kolna again.

It was midmorning when Kernoff got a call from Moscow.

"Hello this is Petrov. Alex Hanken is a highly decorated General who is now the Commander of the 1st Special Forces, the 101st Airborne, three entire army groups, plus all the nuclear and air forces, which means he was hand-picked by the Chairman of the Joint Chiefs and the President."

Kernoff called Andrade. Despite the late night last night, Andrade was fully alert.

"Handpicked for what?"

"We cannot guess, but they have given him enormous power. Another thing, the code name Project O.N.E. is associated with him. One of our operatives in Washington D.C. picked up a partial conversation between Ted Jeffers, FBI Director and Donald Cray, CIA Director two weeks ago, and again the code name Project O.N.E. came up. My friend we have stumbled onto something quite big. Be extremely careful."

"Yes sir."

Lilly Macklin lay prone on her bed, a sock stuffed in her mouth, as the drug to stop her heart was administered between the middle toes of her left foot. It was over in about fifteen seconds. She felt nothing. It would look like a heart attack to any ordinary coroner.

Melody Huart, distraught over the untimely death of her celebrated husband, allegedly committed suicide with a gun her husband never owned—— although ATF records showed he had purchased the gun five years ago. Cray's people were incredibly efficient.

Ted Jeffers put in a call to the Pentagon to speak to Admiral Torrance.

"Ted how are you?"

"Admiral I'm fine, but I felt you needed to know what was going on," Jeffers proceeded to tell him what had transpired the last two days.

"Okay, I don't care if you have to put a thousand agents on this, you find General Hanken and cover him up from head to toe. He is not to be harmed in any way. At the moment, that man is more important to this country than the President and I put together. Are you reading me? What is being done about those Russian agents, do we know where they are?"

"Don Cray is putting his crack team on it as we speak."

"Hang on. Let me call Don while you're on the line."

Moments later, Jeffers heard Don Cray's voice. "Admiral."

"Shut up Don, and listen to me."

"Yes, sir."

"How in the goddamn hell did these Russian agents get to my boy Hanken, and how in the hell weren't you aware of their activities? Listen son, Alex Hanken may be the most important person on the goddamn face of the planet right now, and you're letting Russian agents run around this country like they fucking owned it. You make them disappear do you understand me?"

"Yes sir, my team will be in Sacramento in ten minutes, they will handle this immediately."

"They had better. Do you know the whereabouts of General Hanken?"

"We just found out he is in route to Pennsylvania in his jet along with Dr. Chenowith."

"You just found that out, did you say?"

"Yes sir."

"Christ! Ted, I don't care if you have to use one of your agents as a suppository and shove them up Hanken's ass, I want you to know 24/7 where that man is. He is to have maximum coverage from your agency. Is everybody on the same page with me now?"

They both answered quickly.

After Admiral Torrance rang off, they kept the connection between them open.

"Well, Ted how does it feel to have your balls kicked up between your shoulder blades?"

"Jesus, I thought he was going to form a firing squad. This job is going to kill me yet."

"No, the Admiral will take care of that. Well, I'll be up for the next forty-eight until this thing is put to bed. Make sure that agent has plenty of Vaseline on him."

Chapter 14

MEAN TIMES

"Good afternoon. It's Howard."

"Carney. The only time I hear from you Carney is when you have a problem."

"Yes well we all have our little problems don't we? I imagine yours still has not gone away now has it?"

"Fuck you Carney. What the hell do you want?"

"There is change in the air. Things are going to happen soon and a certain person will be smack dab in the middle of every-thing. I need someone to keep an eye on that certain person."

"Keep an eye on them. What the hell does that mean?"

"Use your imagination. I'll expect updates on his movements and anything you might overhear about his strategic plans or his personal disposition toward what will be unfolding."

"Is this who I think it is?"

"If you think it's General Alex Hanken, yes."

"Carney, you are out of your fucking mind if you think I am going to spy on this guy or better yet snuff him out if he gets out of line."

"No, I'm not out of my mind. You'll do this or it's a one way ticket to Leavenworth and you'll never see your loved ones again."

"Damn it Carney, why me? Haven't I done enough for you over the years."

"Look, you're the one that screwed up and I'm the one that kept the feds from dropping a life sentence on you. That option still exists under federal statutes and I will not hesitate to send you away forever. This is mission critical and you have the experience and will be close to the man at all times."

"You know Carney I just may come to D.C. and put a bullet between your eyes."

"Save your bullets and do what I ask and all will be forgiven. How many years has it been now since that unfortunate incident?"

"I can't let you continue to blackmail me, you'll never stop. So I'm telling you now this is the last time I'll ever agree to any assignment you have."

"Call me with a weekly update."

"Whatever."

Elena and Andrade chartered a private plane to Sacramento. It just so happened that was the Executive Airport where Alex's hangar was. The pilot was in a good mood and talkative and asked why were they going to Sacramento. Elena told him they were going to see an old friend, a General Hanken.

"Oh, I know the General. Or at least know of him. He has a King Air and a Lear at Executive, and he flies up to Coeur d'Alene a lot."

"How do you know that?" Elena asked.

"I see the flight plans that are filed with the ops people."

"My dear," Andrade said to Elena. "I think we need to work Coeur d' Alene into our vacation plans."

It was near dark when Andrade and Elena arrived at Alex's house. Mitch Reilly had told them that Alex had flown out this morning to Scranton, Pennsylvania. Andrade pried the lock loose on the patio door. Elena found the land sat equipment right off. She searched Alex's desk for anything of interest. Nothing.

"He has highly sophisticated communications equipment, the CIA and Pentagon are the only ones that have this. This is getting us nowhere. Let's leave and head for Coeur d' Alene. Maybe something will turn up there."

They had placed their luggage including the specialized equipment suitcase in the trunk of the rented car. Elena could hear a constant buzzing coming from the suitcase. She opened the trunk of the car, and the buzzing got louder.

"What is that,' Andrade asked.

"The worst possible news we could get."

Andrade looked puzzled as she opened the suitcase. He saw a flashing red dot on the left frame of the suitcase itself. Elena slammed the trunk shut, and told Andrade to get in and drive away quickly, don't speed, but get out of this area immediately their lives were in danger.

Andrade swallowed hard. "CIA?"

"Yes, their best team out of San Francisco is probably headed here right now with orders to kill us both."

"Elena are you going to keep me guessing or will you fill me in on what is going on?"

"Andrade, please just drive, and I will tell you as soon as we have a moment that I feel safe…right now we are in extreme danger."

"All right. Tell me when to stop."

As they charged down US Highway 50. Elena picked out the business card of the pilot that had flown them to Sacramento and called him.

"How much to fly us to Coeur d'Alene without a flight plan, I can't tell you why just now, but trust me, the US Government will be very appreciative."

"Well, I'm always looking for a little extra to pay bills, but I can't get you to the airport there. That's now a military air base with restricted airspace. I can get you into Spokane and it's only twenty minutes from there."

"That'll work."

"How's five thousand?" the pilot asked.

NEW EARTH: PROJECT O.N.E.

"Fine. Be at the airport where you dropped us off in fifteen minutes."

"Lady I'm already here. Get your bags in the luggage bin, and I'll be ready to taxi."

"See you in fifteen, then."

Twelve minutes later, Andrade and Elena were stowing their luggage and the equipment suitcase and stored it in the baggage compartment of the twin engine airplane. The pilot rushed to the departure runway and took off immediately. The tower noticed the plane taking off but couldn't make out the tail number, or the make of the plane. They figured some amateur pilot on his/her first night flight forgot regulations. They would issue a citation when the pilot returned. Elena counted out five thousand in hundreds, and shoved it over the shoulder of the pilot.

"Much obliged ma'am, and you don't need to provide me with any explanation. Just sit back and relax, and I'll let you know when we are about an hour out of Spokane."

"Thank you, we are very tired and need some rest."

"No problem."

Elena leaned her head on Andrade's shoulder and whispered.

"You said you trusted me."

"Yes."

"Well, the flashing red light is a signal to any field agent that they have been discovered by hostile elements and are in extreme danger."

"Elena we are with the Major Case Squad. We're not field agents."

"You mean you're not a field agent."

"What?"

"I'm an active agent with the FSB. I report to Petrov Ingosich. His office ordered this whole operation. Andrade, whatever is going on here is big, and this General Hanken is an important part of, if not the key player. We may have to sacrifice our lives in trying to find out what the truth is behind this cover-up. Mother Russia could be affected."

"And last night that was just part of the job?"

"No, no, no. That was genuine on my part please believe me. You are a wonderful man, intelligent, honest and honorable. It's a combination I have rarely seen, and I find I am very taken by you. Now, rest my love. We have some very trying times before us, we both have to be clear headed."

Alex had just gotten clearance from Wilkes-Barre Scranton International Airport for landing when an F-22 pulled up beside his Lear and indicated by fingers number, the number seven. Alex switched his radio to channel seven, the secure military band.

"General Hanken, you read me sir?"

"Five by five. Go ahead."

"Sir, I'm not sure what's going on, but I have orders to shoot down any plane within five miles of you, and there are four other birds out there sweeping the area with the same orders. I'm to escort you safely into Scranton. There will be a contingent of FBI personnel waiting for you on the ground and they will take you and Dr. Chenowith into protective custody. So don't be alarmed. Just do what the agents tell you to do."

"I assume you were told nothing else."

"Sir, I just read you the exact words passed on to me from FBI Director Jeffers."

"Very well pilot, your name?"

"Captain Philip Ford sir."

"Your call sign Captain?"

"Uh…that would be Southern Comfort sir."

"Well Captain. I hope you haven't taken your call sign to heart tonight. I'm beginning my descent now, and thanks for the escort."

"Yes sir, I mean no sir, well sir, I…think you know what I mean."

"Yes I do, over and out."

Sandi looked at Alex with a wrinkled frown on her forehead.

"What's going on?"

"We'll find out soon enough, I think."

"Okay. Little scared right now."

"Who was that on the satellite phone? You looked upset."

"Oh it was Liz….boyfriend problems. I told her not to call me on that phone unless it was an emergency. 'But Mom it is an emergency,' she says, 'he hasn't called me in three days.' Alex be glad you had a son."

Alex studied her. She wasn't telling him something. He hoped Liz wasn't pregnant—neither of them needed a complication right now.

As he taxied up to the designated terminal a stream of black SUV's and limousines surrounded the plane and agents began pouring out of them. There were four FBI helicopters circling overhead and each agent on the ground had an automatic weapon drawn. When the jet finally came to a stop, four agents came to the cabin door and threw it open.

"General you and Dr. Chenowith come with us immediately, leave everything where it is."

As they got up out of their seats, each agent took one arm and hustled them out of the plane. Alex guessed nearly twenty agents were surrounding them. They were rushed to one of the waiting limousines and literally thrown into the back seats and covered by an agent. The doors slammed shut, and they sped off into the night.

"Sorry General and Dr. Chenowith," one of their handlers said. Are you okay? Are you hurt in any way?"

"Other than my dignity, I think we're fine."

"Again, I apologize. We were under cover orders from FBI Director Jeffers."

"So I assume Jeffers will be along soon to explain why?"

"He's on the way here right now. We've got to get you both to a secured facility, so bear with us."

The highway into Scranton had been completely cleared of traffic. Alex could make out a highway patrolman every half mile or so. Jesus, the President didn't even get this kind of treatment. What the hell is going on? They made an abrupt exit from the highway, traveled several blocks, metal overhead doors, a down slope, several right turns, then to a complete stop.

The door opened, and the agents walked both of them into a nicely appointed room with leather chairs and couches and piped in music. A young female FBI agent came into the room.

"Good afternoon. My job is to make both of you as comfortable as possible. If you need a bath, or a massage, coffee, or food, or just some sleep, I'll see to it immediately."

"Ladies room?" Sandi asked.

"Come this way Dr. Chenowith."

Alex kicked off his shoes. His feet were aching after the long flight. The FBI attendant came back and noticed his shoes off.

"General, let me call in our massage therapist. She's fantastic."

"Sure."

By the time Sandi returned from mother nature's call, Alex had his feet up, and a young lady was working genuine magic on them.

"So," Sandi said, "I turn my back on this guy for ten minutes and he turns the place into a massage parlor."

Everyone including the armed agents guarding the doors laughed. It broke the tension that had been building ever since the airport.

"Sandi, this young lady is magic."

"I could use a back rub myself."

The agent in charge, without any hesitation, said. "Get the other massage therapist in here immediately, with a full table."

And in came another young lady with helpers this time carrying a table, supplies and towels, and multiple privacy screens.

"Dr. Chenowith undress, and cover yourself with this towel. The privacy screens will allow no one but me to see you, but the agents have to stay in the room, okay?"

Five minutes later, Sandi was groaning softly from behind the screens. "You know Alex, if this is protective detention, I feel a lot less sorry for criminals."

"Enjoy it while you can. We may be a lot less relaxed when we find out why we're here."

Chapter 15

THE BLACK WIDOW'S BITE

Elena nudged Andrade to wake up. She hated to wake him since one of them needed their sleep. She had not closed her eyes since they got on the plane. Her mind was too busy trying to figure out how she and Andrade could survive this mission. Funny. She had never thought of including someone else in her survival plans. But it felt right now. For the first time in nearly ten years, Elena felt very close to a fellow human being. Andrade wasn't using her for his own ends, wasn't competing with her to show off his ego. He was simply working with her to do an important job as best they could, with respect and affection. She had forgotten such a thing was possible.

So now she would fight to keep them both alive.

"Mr. Duvall," she said, "I need to tell you something. Can you put the plane on auto-pilot or something?"

"Not a problem. Go ahead."

"Mr. Duvall."

"Hey, call me Mack."

"Okay Mack, here's the truth. We are both agents for a foreign government, sent here to investigate the murders of two of our citizens and two American citizens. We believe these murders were committed by the CIA to cover something up. That something is so important the US does not want our government to know about it but...the American people are being kept in the dark as well."

"Yeah. Go on." Duvall was clearly a little squeamish.

"Right now CIA agents are probably on the ground at the airport in Sacramento. And they will—if they haven't already— narrow down the field such that your plane will be the target of an intense search. So, because of us you are in extreme danger. Please accept my apologies."

"Jeez." He moved from squeamish to outright scared.

And now to make him more scared. "Make no mistake about it Mack; these CIA agents will have orders to kill both of us, and unfortunately, anyone that might have knowledge of our mission. That means you are a target."

"Well that's just perfect. You're telling me that I just gave up my life for five grand."

"Possibly."

"Well, ladies and gentlemen. I've got to radio ahead to Spokane and have the authorities waiting. At least you won't be killed by the CIA, and I can probably wiggle out of this with a fine from the FAA."

"I can't let you do that. It would mean certain death for all of us."

"If I may?" Andrade interrupted and told Mack the story of Jeffrey Macklin and how he died.

"Are you telling me that the US government would go that far just to cover-up something?"

"They assassinated one of our top scientists, then brutally murdered his assistant. So, yes they are doing just that."

"What do you want from me?"

"We need to find a place where we can set down unnoticed. Somewhere near Spokane or Coeur d'Alene, but where we wouldn't be picked up by radar before we land."

"I know a place. It will be tricky landing there at night, but I guess we don't have a choice."

The CIA agent shoved Mitch Reilly backwards into his office and shut the door.

"You're the airport manager?"

"Yes."

"A plane landed here approximately four hours ago with a man and woman in it. I want you to find that plane immediately, and give me the status."

"I...can't do that immediately, the tower guys have their records. I'll have to cross check with them. It'll take an hour or so."

"Not good enough."

"Look I don't have the manpower to do a physical count and get tail numbers and cross check the tower with arrivals and departures."

The agent pulled out what looked like an oversized cell phone and speed dialed. "This is Crossbow, contact the FAA, and close down Executive Airport in Sacramento stat." He slipped the phone in his pocket. "Now you're not so busy. Go upstairs get inbound and outbound traffic signatures, and bring all tower personnel down here right now."

"Yes, sir."

When Mitch had everyone gathered in his office, agent Crossbow spoke.

"Sometime between fifteen minutes and four hours ago, a twin engine plane from Burbank landed at this airport with a pilot and two passengers. The pilot was Mack Duvall and—"

"Mitch," one of the controllers said, "what is all this crap about and who the hell are these guys?"

Before Mitch could say anything Crossbow had flown across the room and pinned the controller against the wall with his feet dangling off the ground.

"I'll tell you who I am...I'm your worst nightmare...I'm the guy that'll make you wish your mother aborted you."

Crossbow then threw the controller like he was a tennis ball across the room into another wall. "Has anybody else got any more stupid comments? Good. Gentlemen, find me this airplane and the pilot, you have fifteen minutes."

One of the controllers raised a hand. "Uh, Agent Crossbow, we had a twin engine plane takeoff without a filed flight plan about three hours ago. It was dark and we couldn't get the tail number. We assumed it was some amateur on his/her first night flight, because they didn't even contact the tower for takeoff clearance."

"That was him," Crossbow said. "What was the heading?"

"Well, we think it was north by northwest, but he was staying under radar and we lost them about twenty minutes out."

"Good work guys." Crossbow suddenly appeared human.

"I want a blanket on every airport north of here all the way up the coast to Vancouver and as far east as Cheyenne. Provide the tail number of that plane, alert the FBI to engage their search teams immediately."

Mack Duvall was frantic, trying to get his head around the mess he had gotten himself into. He might as well face it; she was probably going to kill him before the CIA did. Or maybe these two were bank robbers. Yeah, she had all those hundreds she gave him; they were on the run to get lost in the northwest maybe into Canada. She wouldn't kill him for that or would she? His mind played tricks on him, until he noticed they were getting close to the place he had planned to land.

"Ma'am, I'm going to try and put us down at an old friend of mine's crop dusting strip. It's grass and there are no lights, so it's going to be bumpy and scary as hell."

"Leave your landing lights off...I don't want anybody seeing the plane come in."

"Lady you must have a real death wish, but here goes."

Duvall put the plane into a steep dive and pulled out of the low altitude cloud cover just about two hundred feet above ground. That would drop them off the radar scopes in the FAA traffic area. Then it was just a matter of spotting landmarks in the dark.

It wasn't easy. His friend Jim lived several miles from his nearest neighbor and about fifty miles south of Spokane.

Then he spotted the river, glistening slightly in the moonlight leaking through the clouds. After following the river for about five minutes he saw the T in the road that marked the way to Jim's place. He banked hard south along the small two-lane dirt road. Next came the hangar, silhouetted against Jim's house lights.

"Ma'am I hope you're ready," he said. The moon is peeping in and out of those clouds. We may catch a break and have a little moonlight to help us out… hold on we're going in."

Duvall made one pass over the field then banked hard left to come around for the final approach.

"Duvall cut your engines as you land," Elena said. "We don't need the noise to alert any people near."

"Jeez, what else, you want me to land on just one wheel?"

But the moon cleared the clouds and he could see the grass field clearly. Maybe their luck was holding on. The fence popped into view, he cleared it by about fifty feet. Then he cut his engines and floated down to the ground. A slight slip to the right caused the plane to skid a little. Duvall used the brakes to correct the slide, since he had no engines to compensate.

He rolled the plane to a stop ten yards from the hangar and let out a big sigh of relief.

"We're here folks."

"Great flying Mack. We've got to get the plane in the hangar."

As they unloaded the plane and stretched their legs, they could see a flashlight beam flickering toward them from the house about fifty yards away.

"Duvall," Andrade said, "who is that, your friend?"

"Oh yeah, I'm sure it's Jim. He lives alone."

As the figure moved closer Duvall yelled out.

"Jim, its Duvall"

"Mack?"

"I just dropped by for some coffee and donuts."

"The hell you say. Engines give out on you?"

"No, Jim, something else. This lady here will explain."

Elena stepped forward and shook Jim's hand and then told him the whole story. He kept scratching his head as she spoke, but he let her finish before he said anything.

"Mack my boy, you realize we're all dead, if she's telling the truth."

Elena walked over to Duvall.

"This is an over the counter cell phone. It can't be traced by satellite for about forty-five seconds. That's all I'll give you. You have the number for the airport manager's office in Sacramento?"

"Yeah, in my book."

"You call him and I'll think you'll find out that what I've said is true. But plan what you are going to say before you make the call. I'm going to take the phone away from you after forty seconds. Andrade would you be a sweetheart and put the equipment suitcase on the wing of the plane."

As he opened it she said, "Now Mack you and Jim look at this equipment and tell me. If it's, let's say we were bank robbers on the run from the law, would this be the kind of stuff a bank robber would use?"

Mack got an uneasy feeling that this gal was in his mind, she knew what he was thinking—before he was thinking it.

Jim peered in.

"Yeah, that there is a bug sweeping device, and I don't mean the roach kind of bug. What's that flashing red light?"

"We received that signal by satellite as we were breaking into Alex Hanken's house. Our superiors received credible information that we had been discovered. It essentially tells us we need to run for our lives."

"The CIA was on to you?" Jim asked.

"Either them or the FBI, with orders to terminate us."

"Okay, let me call Mitch Reilly."

She gave Duvall the phone and he dialed the number. His mouth was so dry he could hardly muster a spoken word.

"Is Mitch Reilly there?"

"This is Reilly."

"Mitch, Mack Duvall."

"What in the hell are you up to Mack?"

"Don't talk, I don't have much time, just listen and answer. Are there any agents there?"

"They're thicker than Baptists at a tent revival, and they know who you are, and your occupants. And these guys mean business partner. Hell they shut down the whole goddamn airport on this guy's word alone, some kind of half breed Asian, he's meaner than——

"Mitch, if I don't make it out of this, tell my wife and kids I love them."

She snatched the phone out of his hands and terminated the call.

"Well?"

"You're right; they're all over the airport. They know who I am, and you two as well. Reilly said some half breed agent was running the show and he was a real mean dude."

"Did he say half breed?"

"His words. An Asian mix."

Elena said nothing for a minute. She looked absolutely calm, but Duvall got the impression she'd just gotten a serious shock.

"All right," she said, "is everybody satisfied?"

Duvall and Jim both nodded.

"What's next?" Jim asked.

"We need to get this plane out of sight and into the hangar."

It only took a couple of minutes for Andrade, Jim, and Duvall to wheel the plane around, and moved it into the hangar next to Jim's plane, an old Stearman tail dragger he used as a crop duster.

"Ma'am," Duvall said, "I need a smoke, I'm so damn nervous right now."

"I imagine Andrade would like one as well. Why don't you both go outside and indulge. I'm going to ask Jim some questions about the area and how we might get out of this with all of our lives intact."

Duvall and Andrade went outside for a smoke and began talking about his family and how long he had been flying. Elena waved

Jim toward the table and chairs he kept in the far corner of the hangar. She asked him a lot of questions about the roads leading out of there and what kind of farming was most prevalent. It all seemed like casual conversation, but he knew she was working out her escape route. But what should he do? These guys were KGB, or whatever they called them now. They were certainly wanted, but he didn't buy that cock and bull story about the government killing off scientists. Fortunately, he was ready.

Jim turned his head to see if Duvall and Andrade were still outside, and as he did he nonchalantly reached to pull out the .38 special he'd tucked into his back overalls pocket.

Just then—he felt a stinging sensation and the taste of salty blood came up in his mouth. He pitched forward and part of him realized his throat had been cut deep enough that he couldn't make a sound. The .38 police special that he planned to shoot Elena with fell harmlessly to the ground.

Elena went to the equipment suitcase, pulled out the silencer, and attached it to her gun. Duvall and Andrade were coming back into the hangar.

The bullet struck Duvall at an up angle just below his left cheek, it crashed through his upper jaw bone into his brain, and out the back of his head. He was dead before he crumpled to the ground.

Andrade leapt back, then began frantically wiping at the skull and hair bits on his jacket. "Goddamn it Elena, what did you do that for?"

"Jim was going to kill me if I gave him the chance," Elena said gritting her teeth while picking up Jim's pistol. "I didn't think Mack here, would be as cooperative with his friend dead."

"We could have tied them up or something, not slaughtered them like cattle. Elena we're no better than the people chasing us, if we resort to these kinds of tactics."

"I don't want to die, do you?"

"Of course not."

"Then bear with me. Someone could come by and free them. Duval knew we were interested in Coeur d'Alene and Alex Hanken. We would've had no chance of ever finding out anything

182

more than we already knew. The CIA would be on us before we knew what happened.

"I...it's still...I don't like it."

"You think I do? You think I enjoy this? She was practically shouting. She had no idea why his opinion of her was so important. "Andrade, what we have here is something bigger than I have ever worked on before. This is so dangerous and so important to the US. They have put their most experienced— most skilled and most ruthless agent on it. His name is Crossbow. He will be relentless in tracking us."

Andrade just stood there, still cleaning bits of human debris off of himself, looking at her like she was a stranger.

"Andrade," she said, "Crossbow is the son of an ambassador and a refugee from Mao's China. He is physically powerful and psychologically troubled. He has been disciplined four times for excessive violence and has not been promoted as a result. The fact that they have put him in charge shows their desperation."

"You...you sound like you know him."

"All field agents know him. He's called 'The Yellow Death.' His superiors do not know about it, but he has been responsible for the deaths of five KGB and FSB agents over the years. And they were not killed cleanly. He beat them to death with his bare hands."

At least Andrade was looking at her as if she were human again. She was getting through to him.

Then he said, "And what is he to you?"

Damn. She'd forgotten how smart he was. "When he entered the CIA, he had a mentor, one Robert Knowles. I had an...encounter with many years ago."

"An encounter that left Knowles dead?"

"That's how it was portrayed, but that happened while I was in a hospital bed in Moscow recovering from a bout with malaria. Somehow my name got attached to him and his demise, but Crossbow thinks I did it."

"So, if he finds you..."

"My death will not be quick."

"All right then," he said, "We must cover every possible clue, and leave nothing behind—clean the area of blood and any traces of struggle, bury the bodies far enough away from here that no one will find them once they discover the plane."

She took a deep breath of relief. Andrade was back with her again. "I have Jim's keys to his Ford, so we have transportation to get to Spokane. We'll dump his vehicle in the river so it can't be found easily, and get another vehicle. We will probably have thirty-six to forty-eight hours to get as much information as we can, then get across the Canadian border to a safe house in Vancouver."

"Elena, as I said before, I trust you. But you need to know, I can't bring myself to the violent level at which you are operating."

"My love you don't have to. Let me carry the burden. Just be my support and help me as I ask for it, okay?"

"Very well then, let's get started on this cleanup of the crime scene, which is something I know a great deal about."

Together they literally scrubbed the scene clean, even taking off Duvall and Jim's shoes and creating footprints to the house for all four people. Once in the house, Andrade forged notes on a piece of paper in Jim's handwriting, pressing hard enough to imprint the address of a person in Seattle on the page underneath and tearing off the top page. Elena placed a phone call to the person at that address. It was late and the recorder came on, just as she had hoped. The trace would lead them to that address as well—unless Crossbow got wind of it, he would never buy that old trick. They put the bodies in the bed of Jim's Ford F-150, and left looking for a place to bury them without drawing undue attention.

The massages were almost over when an orderly approached Alex carrying a phone.

"General, Director Jeffers for you sir."

Alex grabbed it. "Ted, what the Sam Hell is going on?"

"Alex I can't talk with you in front of the agents. The main thing is that you're safe and we want to keep it that way. You could be there another couple of days until this thing blows over. I was going to fly there tonight and debrief you, but we're socked in with fog, and it won't lift until tomorrow around noon they think. Is there anything I can do for you in the meantime?"

"I was scheduled to meet with site commanders tomorrow and the next day. Can you touch base with them and let them know I've been delayed?"

"Absolutely, which sites were they?"

"Uh…" He put one hand over the phone. "Agent can you get my briefcase? It's the black one over there against the wall?"

"I'll get it for you."

"Thanks." Alex opened the case and pulled out his punch list. Here it is Ted. Tomorrow was site E-5, and the next day it was site E-3."

——"Ok, got it, I'll pull the commanders private lines and call them right now.

Anything else?"

"Yeah. Are my kids in any danger?"

"Not as far as we know. I'll try and get there tomorrow afternoon and debrief you both, but while you're there just ask for anything and it's yours, with the exception of going outside."

"Okay, I'm tired and it's been a long confusing day. I'm hitting the sack."

"Goodnight, Alex."

Alex hung up, and the orderly whisked the phone away. "Sandi are you relaxed enough to go to bed now? I'm turning in?"

"Sounds wonderful. How about these poor people? Will they get to rest?"

"Dr. Chenowith you don't worry yourself about that," the AIC said. We have over a hundred agents here with nothing to do but ensure your well-being. You run along to bed and get a good night's sleep, and we'll keep a steady watch over you all night."

Sandi was so tired she didn't even bother to ask Alex what was going on. Or maybe she realized it wouldn't have mattered. Alex was fast asleep as soon as his head hit the pillow.

Chapter 16

COEUR D' ALENE REVISITED

Elena and Andrade drove for several miles until she motioned for him to take the dirt road off to the right. They drove until they came to a wooded area and she directed him into an opening between the trees. Andrade thought that was not smart—the truck tires would leave imprints in the soft grass for anybody to see in daylight. As he drove over the ridge in the field toward the tree line he could see another ridge about three feet tall he would have to cross over. When they arrived at the tree barren area she got out and looked around.

"Found it."

He leaned out the truck's window. "Found what?"

"A well head cover for the rice fields."

He got out and joined her in levering the concrete cover off the manhole-sized tube that disappeared into the ground. It was just big enough to fit a human body into and let it plunge two hundred feet into the cistern below. It would take days for the stench to be noticed by anyone.

When they had finished disposing of the bodies Andrade asked.

"How are you going to erase the tracks the truck made in the soft dirt and grass getting over here?"

"You see this box over here by the well head? This is an automatic timer, and during the rice growing season they keep the fields flooded. You simply set the timer and the pump kicks in and the water flows to the designated field by way of underground pipes. She pulled out a lock pick and had the control door open in less than a minute. Look, see the diagram on the door of the box? If you want to do it manually it gives you the layout of the fields and which control head to turn on for that field. Let's see this field is number three, and we turn the switch to number three and set it for minimum fill, we don't want it to take all night to at least cover the field. Now flip the on switch and we leave."

As they crossed back over the field dykes, she would have him stop and she would use a large shop broom that was in the bed of Jim's truck to brush away the truck tracks left on the tops of the dykes. Once on the main road Andrade could no longer hold back his question.

"Okay, just how is it that you knew about this particular field? And how those pumps worked? And that these were rice fields?"

"Simple, I asked Jim. As far as this field, I just noticed the dykes as we were driving and saw the dirt road, so I knew we could probably find a well head somewhere around those fields. I was just lucky that the opening to the well pumping station was wide enough for their bodies to drop down into the water shed below."

"Remind me to kiss you later."

"Oh you, you kiss me now, I haven't had a kiss all day."

They kissed, and he almost ran off the road. She was such a child sometimes, yet he had just seen her kill two men without a qualm. How could such a warm and loving person do such things?

They came upon a four lane highway and took a right headed east. A few miles down the road they began seeing road signs that advertised a twenty-four hour truck stop.

"Andrade, we need to stop and get a map and find the shortest route to Coeur d'Alene, then ditch his truck because they'll be looking for it. I want to look at a yellow pages also and see how many rental car agencies there are. We need to separate when we hit Coeur d'Alene. They will be looking for a man and woman traveling together. There it is, park around the side. I'll go in first and look at the yellow pages, you follow a minute or two later, and buy a map."

He gave her a full five minutes, sitting in the darkened pickup, smelling the unmistakable diesel fumes from the big rig trucks all around him. When he went in, she passed without a glance. He purchased a map and came back out to the truck.

He unfolded it, then looked for some kind of light in the truck but couldn't find one. "Could you please check the glove box for a flashlight?"

She found one and handed it to him, and he found what he was looking for.

"You see a way to Coeur d'Alene?" she asked.

"Yes, but more importantly I found the outer road that runs along the Spokane River. We will go there first and look for a spot to leave the truck."

"You mean dump it into the river?"

"No, look at the sky it's getting near daylight. We would be spotted by someone. River fisherman are the same the world over They get up early in the morning, drive to their favorite spot, park their vehicle on the side of the road, and walk down to the water. They have their fishing gear in one hand, and a chair in the other, some with a radio to listen to music, or their favorite sporting event. The vehicles line up for miles. We will find what looks like a favorite of the locals and make a note of the area. Then I will drop you off at a rental agency.

"You will drop me off at this one. It's open twenty-four hours a day seven days a week."

"Excellent, change of plans. We will find a place that looks good to drop the truck off. Then we will drop you off and get a car, you follow me back to the spot we found, and pick me up. Then we can head into town, find a hotel, and get a little sleep before anything opens."

"Andrade you're a genius."

They found the perfect spot along the river. There was even a paved parking lot with several hundred parking spots. As they pulled up near the all-night rental agency, Elena got out and went in.

"Hi, I'm so glad you are open," she said, putting a touch of Boston accent in her English. "My car broke down. This very nice man said he would drop me by here, so I could rent a car."

"Yeah well, you're lucky lady. This office will no longer be open twenty-fours a day starting next Monday."

"Really? Why is that?"

"The airport's closed."

"Yeah, I think I heard something about that on the radio. Didn't they just convert it to some kind of military base or something?"

"Not just some military base. The rumor has it that they are sending F-35's from McChord. Looks like they're building hardened hangars for at least thirty of them, plus just yesterday a group of humvees went by and their insignia was 1st Special Forces."

"Is that good?"

"They're the elite fighting force for the Army. The commanding General is a four-star guy named Hanken."

"How do you know that?"

"His son Curt comes in regularly and rents cars. He was just here the other day and picked one up."

"Does his son come here often?"

"I asked him about that the other day, and he said with all the projects they have going, he'd be coming up here a lot. Hey I can't quite place your accent, are you from New York?"

She made a couple of quick adjustments. "Wow, you're really good. Yes Manhattan."

"I thought so. So I need a driver's license and some kind of credit card."

"I don't use credit cards since my id got ripped off. Does cash still work?"

"Sure, but I'll need a good size deposit of at least a week's rental."

"Here's a thousand. Is that enough?"

"Plenty. Just sign here and initial those three marked spots, and here are your keys. It's just outside the door, in slot four."

"Thank you. Could you recommend a good hotel?"

"Yeah, well that guy's son always stays at the resort on the lake. Just up the road, you can't miss it."

"Thanks again."

She got into the rental car and followed Andrade back to the parking lot by the river. There were already several cars parked there. Andrade parked the truck, locked the doors, and threw the keys into the river, then they swapped the plates with another truck about the same year.

She told him about the resort hotel by the lake. She would dye her hair there but they needed to get some sleep first. Elena checked into the hotel room under her fictitious name, and returned to get Andrade. He brought all the luggage including the equipment suitcase into the room by himself. He then announced he was tired and going to sleep, which he did almost immediately.

They slept until around 9:30 that morning. Andrade was showering when Elena stepped in on him. She told him there was a water shortage, and they needed to do their part to conserve. They showered together with Elena enticing Andrade playfully the whole time, until finally he picked her up and had her straddle him. She was in ecstasy, the hot water streaming down her back, Andrade deep inside her and holding her in his arms. She made love many times in the course of her profession, but now for the first time in her life, she was consumed with a passion she didn't recognize. She didn't want it to end, but it did, with a thunderous electric pulse than ran through her entire body, and left her nearly breathless.

Finally, she had found a man that could take her to a place she had never been before as a woman.

While they were dressing Elena filled Andrade in on what she had learned from the night clerk at the car rental agency. She asked him to order room service for breakfast, she was going to run down the street to a drug store she saw driving in, and get some hair coloring and some scissors.

When she returned she had two full bags of items.

"Hair coloring and scissors?" Andrade said.

"Well I found some other things I wanted. You know women things."

"Oh yeah, never mind, I don't want to know."

"Andrade you're terrible, but I love you anyway. I spent my life just accepting men as they were, and being constantly disappointed. This time I got everything I wanted. Do you understand how I feel about us?"

He took her in his arms. "If we get out of this, I will spend the rest of my life making you happy. Seeing you smile and watching you enjoy our lovemaking is all the reward I would ever want."

"Oh how I love the way you talk to me." She came over and kissed him, then took a bite of his English muffin. She went into the bathroom and began cutting her hair into a shorter style, then applied the hair coloring.

Two hours later she was a streaked blond with highlights, instead of a black haired beauty.

"Are you ready?" Andrade asked.

"Yes, let's get this over with."

Their plan was to find Curt and then track him to see if they could overhear something of importance. That all changed when she asked the front desk clerk about Curt and he responded.

"You just missed him, he was here for lunch. He's probably over at Pete Cernak's office."

"Where is that, and who is Pete Cernak?"

"Pete Cernak's the project manager for all this stuff going on around the mines and down at the new airbase."

The mines? Really? What sort of stuff?"

"Man they are bringing in cement trucks by the hundreds, running fresh water and electricity to those old abandoned mines. Something the military is doing. They have armed guards out there now from none other than the 1st Special Forces, guarding the mine entrances and all the construction around the airport that is underway. You can't get within a hundred yards of the place and they will challenge you with guns drawn. We've never seen anything like it."

"I see. And where did you say Pete's office was? Maybe I can catch Curt there."

"Just right down the road a piece, the first left in that business park, I think in the three story building."

"Thanks."

Andrade pulled the car into the business park, and parked in front of the three story building. Elena checked the tenant list next to the elevator, and found Pete Cernak's name and suite number.

When they walked into the office the receptionist asked.

"How can I help you?"

Elena noticed the name plate, Olivia Cernak.

"You must be Pete's daughter?"

"That's right."

"We're good friends of Curt Hanken, and we just missed him at the hotel. The front desk clerk said he might come by here to see your Dad."

"No, Curt hasn't come by yet, but my Dad may know where he is. Let me ask him."

A minute later, she waved them into an inner office. Elena said—quietly in Russian—"Stay behind and make sure the daughter doesn't leave." Then she followed the daughter into the office.

"Hi Mr. Cernak," she said with a trace of California's 'I'm from nowhere' accent, "my husband and I are good friends of Curt's, and we just missed him at the hotel. Your daughter said you may know where he is, so we can let him know we finally got to town."

"Really? How do you know Curt and his fiancée Trish?"

"We've known Curt for years from our time in Sacramento."

Pete Cernak was not much of an actor. She could see immediately from his reaction that Curt's fiancé was not named Trish. She pushed the door shut, pulled out her pistol, and motioned him to sit down at his desk and say nothing.

"Mr. Cernak, I'm with the Russian secret police. I have already killed two people in the last twenty-four hours, don't make it three."

"What do you want?"

"I want to know what relationship General Hanken has with these abandoned mines and what they are being prepared for."

"Sorry lady but you might as well shoot now."

Elena went to the door while holding the gun on Pete.

"Bring her in here."

Andrade shoved Cernak's daughter into the room, his gun on her spine, and forced her down into a chair next to Elena.

"Now Pete let's try again. If your answer is the same as before, I will blow your daughter's hand off. I did notice her trophies out front, she appears to be quite a tennis player. That would be a shame." She said this as she was screwing on the silencer for the gun.

"No wait, please...Olivia, I'm sorry...you can't"...Cernak broke down and cried.

"Pete, ...Pete, look at me," Elena said in a stern voice. "It doesn't have to be this way. Just tell me what I want to know and then we'll leave. It's as simple as that." Andrade thought to himself— things are never that simple.

"Look lady, I am just the project manager, honest. What they, or the military is up to is all classified, and I'm not cleared to even ask what it's about. I just have the plans and the construction schedule and the list of vendors, that's it."

He really was not much of an actor. This was the truth. She was relieved because she wasn't sure Andrade would let her shoot an innocent girl. Assuming she could let herself do it.

"Okay Pete, I believe you. Let's see the plans and the vendor list."

Pete began pulling out the schematics and the current list of vendors. She ran through the plans, picking out what were clearly living unit modules, shower and toilet units, and a room with a communications center. But what struck her was a room labeled 'General Hanken's quarters.' So he would be on the inside.

"This is a survival bunker isn't it, it's set up to support a large group of people?"

Pete did not respond.

She found another schematic with a large area labeled 'Sandi's green house.' It had a natural steam vent and sunlight openings cut in the roof of the mine. Pete had put a note at the bottom indicating how many growing tables could be installed and the vendor that could supply them. Another mine plan had penciled in the margins. 'Arms and weapons storage must be vented.'

She saw the plans for the airport, and again Pete had penciled in the storage tank locations, indicating a 200,000 gallon capacity for each tank with JP-8 jet fuel. My God. One point eight million gallons of jet fuel, and fifty thousand gallons of #2 diesel, thirty hardened hangars for F-35's, plus two giant hangars for C-17 tankers.

"This vendor Stifel Steel out of Seattle, you have B-doors, what does B-doors mean?"

"It stands for blast doors," Pete responded.

"Good, you're doing well. Empty out your top drawer."

She noticed a hard bound binder and asked him to give it to her. In it were daily notes Pete had been keeping, so he could debrief Alex when he called. One note caught Elena's eye, just entered yesterday. 'Curt to fly to Motorola and order micro telecom equip for main and other twelve facilities in Midwest and western region.'

"There are twelve more facilities like this one being set up in the United States?"

"I have no knowledge of the other facilities, other than that they exist."

Twelve survival facilities, with extensive food growing preparations and room for a sizable military force, with equipment. That added up to one thing. Despite the lack of evidence elsewhere, the asteroids were coming, and the United States was preparing for the worst.

Elena pulled a small camera from her pocket and took quick photos of all the plans. The analysts could mine them for information later. She rose from the chair.

"Pete, you and your daughter are going to take a little trip out to where Curt is, so I can get some more answers."

The three of them with Pete's daughter in tow all got into Pete's truck and drove out to the main facility. Driving up to the mine she noticed two armed soldiers standing outside.

"Pete, if you want to live, get us through those guards and into the mine," she said quietly.

"Hello Mr. Cernak," the guard said. "Who are these people?"

"Well I've got my daughter here to take some steno notes for me, and these two are vendors, who are preparing a bid on some work to be done inside."

"Very well sir. Proceed."

They drove up to a huge tunnel in the side of the mountain, with men and equipment flowing in and out.

"You did well, Pete. Will there be any guards inside?"

"Usually there's one that accompanies anyone while inside the facility."

They began walking in and the sheer size of the facility inside astonished Elena. The floors had been completed, and there were chalk markings in various colors outlining piping, conduits, doors, and walls. Elena noticed on the floor a marking that said b-door, then another similar marking about twenty feet further in that said inner door. Just one blast door would suffice for even a nuclear threat. So what kind of power were they expecting the impact to be?

They heard voices close. Elena pulled her pistol and held it behind her back. As they neared Curt and his fiancé, Curt turned and saw the group..

"Pete, what're you doing bringing your daughter in here? You know better than that, and you didn't call me and tell me any vendors were coming"

Just at that moment a soldier stepped out from behind a crate to the right of Elena.

"Stop where you are, or I'll fire."

Elena wheeled to her right and squeezed off three quick shots from the silenced pistol. One of the bullets struck the soldier in the thigh, the other two hit him in the left arm and right shoulder. He fell to the floor incapable of holding a firearm anymore.

The fiancé let out a shriek. Elena pointed her gun at her, and she quieted down.

She then went over to the soldier she had shot, pulled his med kit out of his pocket and stuffed gauze in the thigh wound.

——"You'll be okay; none of these are life threatening. Try and keep pressure on this one."

"Oh my God Curt," the fiancé said, "we're all going to die."

"Curt, if you want your fiancé to live, shut her up right now."

Curt stepped forward to shield Cynthia.

"Now that I've introduced myself, let's all have a nice long talk about your daddy and what he's planning to use this and the other facilities for."

"They're Russian agents," Pete said.

"I gathered. Look you communist bitch, you'll get nothing from any of us."

Elena's eyes lit up and she walked swiftly over to Curt and power punched him in the sternum, then kicked him in the groin. Curt fell like a rag doll onto the floor.

"Two things you need to understand," she said. "I am not now, nor have I ever been, a member of the communist party. Second, I may be a bitch, but I don't like being called one." She punctuated this with a kick in the kidney.

Cynthia fell to his side screaming.

"What do you want from us?"

"Just what I said. I know Curt's dad is the driving force behind all of this, and I want to know the details."

Curt rose to his feet gasping.

"We will never betray our country. Fuck you, bitch."

So, the boy had stones. Admirable.

Then Andrade stepped in front of Elena with his gun drawn and motioned all of them to stand against the wall. She hesitated, then realized that this was Good Cop stepping in. She glared at him, slipped in a quick wink, and stepped back. It was nice to work with a partner.

"Curt," Andrade said, "this entire mission of ours started with an investigation by me of a homicide in St. Petersburg, Russia. It turned out that it was no homicide—it was an assassination. Your government came into our sovereign territory and killed two innocent Russian citizens, one a noted astronomer Ivan Borosky, and the other a young woman assistant named Anna Kinova.

He looked straight at Cynthia.

"Young lady would you like to know how they killed her? They gagged her and bound her hands behind her. They didn't even have the common decency to put a bullet in her brain. They threw her off the top of a dam, still alive, and let her body be crushed as she slid down the dam spillway, then drowned in the river below. Now here is where the really good part comes in. Your government is so concerned with covering up whatever this is all about, that they arranged the assassination of Professors Huart and Macklin of Cal Tech University in Pasadena. They feared our Professor Borosky had discovered what they knew and were collaborating on public disclosure. Your own government is killing its own citizens to cover this up. General Hanken is a part of this cover up—to what extent we don't know, and may never know. But I tell you this; our government will not stop until the truth is known, and neither will I."

"My dad would never be a part of something like that," Curt said. "He's an honorable man, with very high moral standards. But, I can't, and will not divulge anything to you."

Elena stepped forward with her gun raised, but Andrade lowered her gun with his hand.

"Enough. We have a lot of information, it's time we go."

Elena looked into his eyes and realized he was right. They knew enough.

"Curt get some rope."

Curt couldn't find enough rope for all, but did find a roll of duct tape. Elena and Andrade bound their hands behind their back, and feet together, and taped their mouths. Andrade wondered about the two guards outside, but when Elena said she would handle that, he acquiesced.

But before she left, there was one quick thing she had to do. She leaned down close to Curt. "We know the asteroids are coming. We can see how destructive they will be from the shelters you are building to protect against them. Yet your government is keeping this knowledge to itself. Have you thought about what that means to the billions of people who could be preparing right now? Think about that when you are feeling so proud of your government."

She and Andrade made their way back to the entrance, walking as if they owned the place.

The sentry on duty stopped them.

"Where is the rest of your party?"

"They're in there arguing about some change to the plans," she said. "We have to go back to our room at the hotel and get a piece of measuring equipment to complete our bid. We'll be back in about thirty minutes."

"Very well ma'am."

And they were out. Easy as that.

Andrade could not keep from speeding down the road. Elena sensed his tension she put her hand on his thigh and asked him to calm down.

"We will go to the hotel, get our bags and head for Seattle. Then we'll rent a private charter boat and get to Vancouver and the safe house. Don't worry it will work out."

They gathered their things at the hotel, got in the rented car and turned onto US 90 West toward Seattle. Elena knew Crossbow would not be far behind, and if he found her she would be in for the fight of her life.

Chapter 17

THE CHASE

Agent Crossbow called into his office and asked to have a DMV report run on any and all cars owned by Jim Sanders. The FAA had supplied his name as the owner of the crop dusting business.

"No, run it right now while I'm on the phone," he said. "Okay, got it."

The pilot stuck his head out of the cabin.

"Agent we'll be landing in about fifteen minutes."

Crossbow nodded, then called ahead to have the choppers fired up and ready for immediate take off.

When they landed, his team sprinted to the choppers, and they were off to the crop duster's airfield south of Spokane. Approaching the area they noticed a flooded field down below and what looked like ambulance and police cars with their lights flashing. Crossbow contacted one of the other helicopters and told them to investigate that scene, even though he was pretty sure what they might find. The FBI team that was already in place at the hangar had said there was no sign of people. Flooding a field would be a good way to hide tracks.

Five minutes later, he landed at the little airfield near where neighbors had reported hearing a low-flying plane the night before. He confirmed that the extra plane in the hangar was Duvall's, then his team spread out. He headed for the house.

One of them turned up with the note pad and the imprint. Crossbow studied it a moment. "They're trying to lead us away. No Russian agent is going to slip up like that. They're headed to Coeur d'Alene. Let's go."

The team he'd left near the flooded field reported in.

"Yes sir, apparently the field manager for the local rice farmer was notified by someone that his irrigation pumps were on, so he came down here and found out that someone had turned the pumps on manually."

"Where did they find Duvall and the crop duster's bodies?"

"In the well head , sir. Professional hit all the way."

"Okay, we're headed to Coeur d'Alene."

Ted Jeffers entered the secure facility where Alex and Sandi were being kept in protective custody. Then ordered the agents in the room to leave so they could have some privacy.

"Alex, Sandi how are you being treated?"

"Fantastic," Alex said. Good night's sleep and a great breakfast."

"Okay, I assume you want an explanation, so here it is in a nutshell. Two Russian agents started snooping around Cal Tech, investigating the deaths of Huart and Macklin. Somehow, someway, they got to your name as being involved, and we tracked them to Sacramento. One of the agents is a known former KGB operative, and she is one nasty character. We couldn't take the chance that she might get to you, so we initiated a security lockdown, at least until we can track these two agents down."

"Ted, Curt and Cynthia were in Coeur d'Alene. If these agents know I'm involved, they'll probably find out about that site. Can you assure me—"

"There are nearly twenty FBI agents headed there with another twenty-five CIA on their way, and I'm told the CIA agent in charge is the best they could ask for in this situation. There should be no problem."

"I'm counting on that, Curt is my only son, and I consider Cynthia like my own daughter."

"Bear with us for a few days more, until we're sure this fire is out."

As soon as Ted left Alex and Sandi, he called Don Cray.

"Have you got them yet?"

"No, but we believe they're in Coeur d'Alene right now, and three teams of my people are ten minutes out, with another thirty flying in from the east coast. We'll get them."

"Alex's kids are up there at the site right now."

"Holy shit. Call you back."

So the General's son and his son's fiancé were at the site, probably at the main facility? And now Crossbow was to make sure nothing happened to those people or Torrance would have his head.

Crossbow immediately called Cernak's number. No answer, not even a voice mail. As their team flew over Coeur d'Alene Lake, he saw the construction taking place at the airport and ordered his pilot to land. When they got to the ground Crossbow jumped out and found the officer in charge, Major Atkins.

"Major Atkins, Agent Crossbow with the CIA. We have reason to believe that Curt Hanken's life may be in danger, and that he is possibly at the main facility site."

"I'm sure that's where he is," Atkins yelled over the helicopter noise.

"Do you know where that is?"

"Yes."

"Then get in."

Two minutes later there were two very startled soldiers with guns drawn, as the helicopters landed in front of the mine. Major Atkins got out and told them stand down, then asked…

"Is Curt Hanken inside?"

"Yes sir, he and his fiancé, and Pete Cernak and his daughter."

"Have there been any other people?"

"Yes sir, but they left. Jesus, they said they would be back in thirty minutes, that was three hours ago."

"Stay put soldier," Crossbow ordered.

The agents rushed into the cave and—thank God— found all four bound with their mouths taped. As the agents freed them from their bonds; Crossbow asked if any of them were hurt.

"Only my pride," Curt said. "That female Russian just kicked my ass all over the place."

Crossbow actually smiled. It was Elena Grodny.

"So what did you do to piss her off?"

"I called her a communist bitch and she went postal on me,"

"Curt, remind me to buy you a drink sometime," Crossbow said. Now, for the time being, these four agents are going to take you to that big hotel and get a room and you are to do exactly as they say, they are there to protect you."

"We already have a room at the hotel."

"Which you will not go near, until one of the agents tells you it is okay to do so. Now, we have to get back on the trail of those two Russians. You go with those agents in the other helicopter and wait for word from us."

"Uh, Agent Crossbow," Pete said, "she got a look at several of the facility plans, the vendor lists, and my notebook.,"

"How did she get that information?"

"She had a gun pointed at my daughter."

Crossbow turned. "You shouldn't have given in. She might have been bluffing. You there, get this soldier to the hospital right away."

As the helicopter pulled away from the mine Crossbow called Cray, and told him everyone was safe and they were in pursuit. It looked like they were about three hours behind. He suspected they were headed for Seattle, then on to Vancouver for refuge in the known safe house the Russians kept there. He was turning around the FBI force coming in from Seattle and having them cover all transportation into and out of Seattle and the Columbia River. He knew they had a rental car because they found the abandoned F-150 that belonged to the crop duster near the Spokane

River just a few minutes before. Agents were checking all the car agencies there right now to get a description of the car.

Then, before Cray could hang up Crossbow said there was one more thing.

"She got her hands on some pretty detailed information about the facilities and vendor lists."

"Oh Christ. Find them quickly, and kill them. This is a Level One threat."

"Yes sir."

They would shut down Seattle. There would be no easy way to get in, and no way at all to get out. She and Andrade would need another plan. They would have Spokane covered as well, and the Columbia River would be closed as a viable escape route. She pulled out her cell phone to call the satellite for relay to Ingosich. She dared not use her satellite phone, the CIA could triangulate their position much easier than with an over the counter cell phone.

"This is Petrov."

"It's Elena, listen, we are in grid sector 136-18. Have friends in Canada call back with extraction plan, out."

"Got it, you'll hear shortly, have you any concrete information?"

"Plenty. The strikes are coming, and they will be big. The Americans are making elaborate preparations. Twelve survival facilities around the country well-armed. We've got the details."

"Good. Get back as soon as you can, and stay safe."

As soon as she hung up, Andrade said, "Extraction plan?"

"The FBI and CIA will have Seattle and possibly Spokane covered like a blanket. They will also have the Columbia River basin under surveillance. At this moment they are getting a description of this car from the rental agency. We have to dump this car and get another, and I'm waiting on the safe house to call with a plan to extract us before we get to Seattle. Take the next exit, we have to get off the road to avoid being spotted."

There was an exit coming up soon according to the road signs and Andrade took the exit. At Elena's suggestion, they pulled into the tavern lot with the neon sign flashing.

"Okay, what next?"

"You trust me Andrade?"

"I have said so and I meant it."

"My love, we are fighting for our lives. I'll do anything to preserve what we have between us and protect our country. Do you understand that?"

"Yes, what do you plan to do?"

"I'm going to get us another vehicle, and you cannot get in the way. Promise me you will follow my instructions, and not interfere, no matter what you see or hear."

"If I see you in danger—"

She put her hands to his lips.

"No, no, no my love, I can handle myself, you must trust me."

She stared directly into his eyes and kissed him long on the lips, then got out of the car and went into the tavern. She left her cell phone with Andrade just in case the safe house called with further instructions.

Inside what turned out to be a typical working-class tavern, Elena sat down at the bar, pulled out Andrade's pack of cigarettes and lit one up.

The bartender came over to her.

"Hey little lady what can I get you?"

"Double Crown, straight up."

"You got it."

The bartender prepared her drink and walked back over to her and sat the drink down.

"That'll be $6.00."

Elena pulled out a $100 bill and slapped it down on the bar.

"Let it ride."

"I'll break it down for you sweetheart, is that ok?"

"Sure. Keep five for yourself."

"Much obliged ma'am."

He brought the change back and set it down in front of her.

"So what brings you to these parts, I know you're from back east somewhere."

"New York. I'm celebrating my divorce becoming final."

"Well I'm sorry to hear."

"Don't be. He was a class A prick."

"Now you're not going to let this prick ruin your life are you? You're still young and attractive, and there are a few of us men who aren't pricks."

"Tell me what it is about men that come home to their wives, who have washed their clothes, cooked their meals, borne their children, kept the house clean and organized, then serviced them in bed, only to have them go out and bed down with some slut?"

"If I knew the answer to that I could make millions on the talk show circuit. I'm guessing it must be something to do with their ego."

"I'm not turned off men just because my ex was a certified asshole. In fact I'm looking forward to a fresh new way of looking at life. I'm going to explore the world and enjoy my freedom as a liberated woman. Give me another one...what's your name anyway?"

"Al."

"Well Al, keep em coming. This is my party."

"All right then, but watch it if you're driving, okay?"

She noticed four men sitting down at the end of the bar talking between themselves, one of them kept staring at her. She needed to set her trap. Al brought her another drink and she asked where the ladies room was. He pointed it out around the end of the bar in the corner. She took her drink with her, when she got inside, she poured the drink down the drain. When she returned with her empty glass, she noticed the bartender talking to the four men at the other end of the bar. They were laughing and chuckling about something. Perfect. The only question now was which one will take the bait.

"Hey Al, another one."

"Coming right up."

When he got to her spot she said, "Hey all, why don't you go tell that guy in the blue shirt that if he wants to stare at me, he should come down here and keep me company so he won't strain his eyes."

"I'll do that."

Al walked down to where the four men were sitting, and whispered something in the ear of the man in the blue shirt. He got up from the bar and walked toward Elena. He was okay looking and that would make it a little easier.

"The barkeep said you wanted some company, my name is Lonny."

"Well, Lonny, sit down and tell me your life story. What'll you have, I'm buying."

"Al an Oly please."

"Ah a beer drinking man. You must be a lumberjack."

"Jeez lady how'd you know that? What's your name?"

"Lucky guess, and my name is Cat, you know like pussycat."

"So are you the kind of cat with claws, or do you just purr a lot?"

"My claws come out only when I'm fucking a man's brains out," she whispered to his ear.

"Now that sounds like something I'd like to see."

"Which? My claws, or my pussy?"

"Both."

"Al keep the change, it was great talking to you, and Lonny let's blow this joint."

They walked out of the tavern and he pointed to where his car was parked. Ford Fusion, maybe six years old. Conveniently nondescript. It would do.

She put her arms around his neck and said.

"Take me out in the woods and fuck me, I've never fucked outdoors."

"I know just the spot Cat. Get in, and I'll show you."

He took off out of the parking lot, gravel and dust flying, and headed down the tree lined road. Andrade was following well behind. Lonny pulled off onto an old logging road that came to a dead end about a half a mile into the thick forest.

"Well, here we are Cat, let's get busy."

"Not here, not in the car. Outside remember?"

"Oh yeah, okay, outside."

He got out and she was right behind him, he turned just in time for Elena's first punch to strike him dead on his lower jaw.

He staggered. Then Elena crashed her gun butt into the side of his head. He fell backwards unconscious.

She pulled the car out of the road and turned it around just as Andrade drove up.

Rolling down her window. "Andrade get the luggage out and put it in this trunk."

He loaded all their belongings into the trunk, gave her the cell phone, and drove the rental car deep into the woods, until finally coming to rest in a shallow stream. He walked back to where Elena was waiting, and glanced once at the unconscious young man.

"I'll take him back into the woods and tie him up real good and tight to a tree," Andrade said. Elena nodded and she pulled the car onto the logging road, waiting for Andrade.

When they were back on the road, Andrade was silent for several minutes.

"That was one we did not need to kill."

She realized he had expected her to kill the young man.

"Andrade, I do what I need to do. Please don't think about it, I beg you."

"Very well. The safe house called. We are to take the Quincy exit off I-90, on the other side of Spokane, then north to a town called Chelan. It's a small river town. They are flying in a pontoon plane to land on the river and pick us up. The plane is green with a blue tail. We are to be waiting at the dock by the big wooden bear statue, appropriately enough. They will be there at 4:30 p.m. sharp."

"Great." He still didn't look entirely comfortable. "We're going to make it Andrade, aren't you happy?"

"I'm happy that you weren't injured my angel."

Crossbow knew Elena would never try getting through Seattle. She would try an unorthodox route to Vancouver.

"Sir, we've got the rental car description."

"Good, pass it along to the FBI and Washington State Highway Patrol, put out an all points on the car, and the two agents."

"Yes, sir."

But she had probably already dumped the rental car. If she was as good as the reports on her indicated, this would be one of the most challenging missions he had ever undertaken. She was a seasoned agent and one of the best. His own excitement grew at the thought of meeting her one on one for the first time and…what would he do afterward.

"Give me that map of northern Washington State and the Canadian border."

How would he enter Canada undetected? It was a wide open territory. There were small rivers and rugged backwoods dotting the landscape all the way from Spokane to Seattle and all along the Canadian border. He decided he would play his hunches and place agents at four possible locations. He dispatched two FBI helicopter teams to separate small towns on the Columbia River, one CIA team by river boat up the river, and he led his team to a small river town just north of Quincy.

The pilot told Crossbow he couldn't get down to the river's edge; it was too close to the trees. The closet place he could land would be about a mile and half back up the road, in a small field adjacent to the forest.

"I don't give a damn about the trees. You get me and my men into that town, now!" Crossbow barked.

"Okay, but I'm not guaranteeing your safety agent Crossbow."

"I'm good with that. Go."

The pontoon plane emerged from the outlet of the river at Chelan, skimming just over the water, then banked hard to come in as close to the dock as possible. It was 4:29. Elena spotted the distinctive green and blue colors of the plane.

Then, off in the distance, the unmistakable noise of a helicopter's beating blades could be heard.

She and Andrade glanced at each other, then back to the plane taxiing toward the dock. Elena knew. It was Crossbow. The bastard wouldn't give up. The plane looked like it was in slow motion.

Not having come this far, not after all they had been through.

Crossbow was urging the pilot to follow his gestures.

"Get us closer, right there, put us down, right there."

"Crossbow, I'll hit those damn tree branches, and we'll all fry."

"Then get us close enough to jump, right there, in that opening."

"Ten feet off the ground? Those trees are forty feet tall!"

"Do it!"

The pilot reluctantly lowered the helicopter. There was a breeze coming from the north, he could compensate for that, but then a gust hit the area and the helicopter swung sharply to its left striking two trees with the blades. His engine compression red light came on, he couldn't auto rotate, he was too close to the ground.

"Hold on, we're going down."

The right landing leg hit the ground first. The ship pitched to the right, and the already damaged rotor blades dug into the earth, slamming the chassis into the ground. Crossbow and two of his agents were thrown from the passenger cabin, just out of reach of the still spinning blades.

Crossbow got up and shook himself off. The chopper lay on its side, the engine finally silent. He couldn't see the rest of the team, but the pilot seemed to be moving.

Then, in the silence, he heard the approaching seaplane.

He kicked the nearest agent, not hard. "Get up!" We've got to get down to the dock.

Elena and Andrade were loading their suitcases onto the plane, when the pilot yelled.

"Forget the suitcases, get in, there was a helicopter hovering over there just a few minutes ago."

"Okay, all in, let's go." She pulled out her gun and the pilot full-throttled the plane away from the docks—he apparently wasn't going to bother with a taxi run.

"Unload on that plane!" Crossbow yelled.

A hail of bullets flew toward the plane. The aluminum hull amplified the sound of the impacts. Crossbow emptied three full clips from his MP-5 before the plane lifted off the water.

The engine noise and the bullets striking the plane were deafening to both Elena and Andrade, but the plane kept rising steadily toward the east. They'd made it.

Chapter 18

BUSINESS AS USUAL

"Yes Admiral," Ted Jeffers said, "everybody is safe and unharmed. The agents are somewhere in Canada trying to make their way back to Vancouver and a safe house they maintain there. They won't be coming back."

"All right, here's what I want you to do I want two of your best agents with Alex and Sandi 24/7 until I tell you differently, is that clear?"

"Yes, sir."

"In addition, I want the same level of protection on Alex's kids."

"Yes sir."

"Now what are they doing about those agents?"

"Don Cray is speaking with the State Department right now, to get clearance from Canada to extend our reach into their country."

"Oh shit, all the State Department will do is take it under advisement and appoint a team of MBA's to study the situation. Tell Don to go directly to the President, and he will go directly to the Prime Minister."

"I'll call Don right now."

"Very well, and stay on top of this."

"Yes, sir."

Jeffers called Cray and told him what the admiral said.

"Yeah Ted, I got the impression that those people were going to take too long to make any difference, so I contacted Arlen Hendry. He said just what the Admiral said, the President is calling the Prime Minister as we speak."

"Okay, well at least we didn't lose anybody on this one."

"We lost two civilians and a soldier was shot up. And that bitch Grodny got her hands on a shit-load of information about the facilities—locations, armaments, the works. It's the bottom of the ninth and we trail 4-0 Ted."

"Yeah. Keep me in the loop."

"Will do."

Jeffers hung up and made another call, one he would enjoy making. "Hey, Alex, it's Ted Jeffers. Looks like things have calmed down to the point where you can get back on schedule. However there is one condition. The Admiral has ordered a 24/7 detail of two of my best agents to travel with you. I'm assigning the agent in charge at the facility as one of them and the young lady that is on guard right now I believe."

"Isn't she a bit young?"

"Twenty-six. Three years ago she graduated first in her class, set a record for pistol and automatic rifle range accuracy, in both casual and rapid fire. She got a gold medal in the hand to hand combat tournament at the end of the class course. She holds a black belt in Tae Kwon Do, she speaks Spanish, German, and Russian. And if that wasn't enough, she graduated magna cum laude from Virginia Tech. Her name is Tina Somers."

"Okay I'm convinced. But if these two are going to be with us 24/7, there is no way I can keep the details of this project secret from them without having to go to extraordinary lengths that will waste time I don't have."

"Yeah, you're right. Designate them. They're already covered under the Secrets Act."

"I don't have the authority to do that."

"Uh, didn't Howard tell you?"

"Tell me what?"

"Admiral Torrance said he wanted you to have designation authority, so you wouldn't have to waste time asking for permission. Just as you said, your time is too important."

"What's the other agent's name?"

"Bill Evans, I just got off the phone with both of them, they know their duties. Your and Sandi's well-being is their primary focus."

"Okay, then I'm going to reschedule my visits and get moving again, thanks."

"Talk to you soon."

Alex busily rescheduled his itinerary, then told his new keepers that they would be departing tomorrow morning for the first of fifteen stops, in fourteen days. Agents Evans and Somers left by helicopter to go retrieve clothes and sundries from their homes in Washington DC. Shortly after dinner, they returned to the secured facility where Alex and Sandi had spent the last day and a half.

Alex sat down with both of the agents, and told them he was designating them to the Project O.N.E. team. He proceeded to tell them the entire story behind the project, and what his duties were. He also told them they would be accompanying him and Sandi to the facility in Coeur d'Alene, as their assigned survival shelter. Alex was impressed to note that there were no emotions displayed by either agent. Not a grimace—not a gasp— not even a comment. They both sat there and intently listened to every word Alex said.

"Any questions?" he asked when he was done.

"No sir," they replied in unison.

"Wait a minute you two," Sandi said. "The whole goddamn world may be destroyed in less than two years, and you both sat there like frogs on a log. No tears, no questions, no nothing. Are you even human?"

Alex was watching Sandi closely. He could see she was upset and venting at the agents, but he let her go on.

"Don't either of you have boyfriends, or girlfriends," she said, practically shouting, brothers or sisters, mothers or fathers, pet dogs or cats or even a pet turtle? Don't you have anything you care enough about that you're upset at losing it?"

"Sandi that's enough," Alex said. "Don't take your frustration out on them, it's not their fault."

Sandi stormed into her sleeping quarters and slammed the door shut.

"Guys," Alex said, "let me apologize she's is a little out of sorts because—"

"There's no need, General," Agent Evans said. "We're trained in handling just these kinds of situations with high ranking officials."

"Well, better you than me."

"General," Somers said, "we know how critical you and Dr. Chenowith are to the success of our surviving this coming event. We are absolutely dedicated to ensuring that you complete your mission, if not for the sake of the country, then for our own survival."

Jeffers was right, she was impressive. "Good to hear."

"General may I say something to Dr. Chenowith?" Somers asked. "I know she's upset, but I think it's important."

"Young lady enter at your own peril."

There was a knock on the door.

"Yes?"

"Dr. Chenowith, its agent Somers. May I come in please?"

"Yes of course Tina." Sandi's first bout of crying was nearly over. She tossed aside the soaking tissue and tried to sit up. Alex was right, she had been unfair to those two young professionals, she supposed.

Somers came in, still looking unusually composed. "His name was Sam," she said.

"What?"

"My turtle's name was Sam. I had to let him go in the park by my apartment, because no one will be able to take care of him now." A single tear rolled down Somer's cheek.

"Oh Tina, I'm so sorry for what I said to you."

Sandi put her arms around her and hugged her, and they both began to cry in earnest. Sandi held her like she had held her own daughter so many times.

"Cry as much as you need," she said. "It's what makes us human."

"Thank you Dr. Chenowith," Somers said presently. "I'm sorry for interrupting you; I just felt you should know."

"You sweet child, you did a wonderful thing. Now, let's dry our eyes, so Bill doesn't see you all teary eyed."

"Don't worry about Evans, I beat him in the hand to hand combat tournament, and he placed second to me at the Quantico firing range competition. I've got his ego under control."

Sandi laughed, in spite of herself. "You know, I'm looking forward to having you with us. I feel much more secure knowing I have you two watching over Alex and me."

"General Hanken seems like a great guy. He's so down to earth for someone in command of the future of the country. When you two first arrived I assumed you were a couple the way you both interacted. But then I saw the sleeping arrangements."

"Funny how that's worked out, Alex and I haven't even kissed, but that doesn't mean that either of us wouldn't jump at the chance. I adore him, and a woman my age rarely gets a shot at a man like Alex. But, he's not ready and we are so damn busy…but I can be patient."

"I hope so. You would make such a great couple. I just hope I get the chance someday to meet that special guy. Though, I suppose, given what we just learned…"

"Oh don't write the future off yet. That's what Alex and I are working on, so you'll have that opportunity someday."

"The future, it seems tenuous now at the moment."

"You know what Alex said to me the first time we expressed our concern for the future."

"I bet it was something really special"

"He said we don't know what will happen in the future, but we do know this, that we can strive to make every moment we have together better than the previous one, and that's the promise we made to each other."

"Wow. I'd be patient for that, too."

Sandi smiled. "Yeah. Now, let's go back outside with the boys, and let me apologize to Bill for my outburst."

Sandi and agent Somers emerged from the bedroom and announced they had solved the world's problems and there was nothing to worry about. Alex sat back sipping his scotch and smiled.

"I couldn't think of two more talented people than you two, to tackle such a monumental task and succeed."

Alex took the opportunity to chat with agent Evans and find out about his background. Evans attended Notre Dame, graduated from their law school, and passed the bar three years ago. His father was a Captain in the Boston City Police department, his mother was a school administrator in the Boston Public School System. He was an only child, lost a brother at birth, then two years later lost a sister also at birth. After that his parents gave up on having any more children. They were a good Catholic family, attended mass regularly, and supported the Archdiocese with a substantial amount every year. Until his father dropped dead of a heart attack when Evans was fourteen. His mother was diagnosed with uterine cancer his sophomore year in college, and he lost her the summer before his junior year.

"Okay, everyone," Alex said, "we have an early start tomorrow, so I suggest we all turn in."

Sandi told Alex what she had learned about Tina's background. Her father was a Petroleum Engineer with Exxon/Mobil who was onboard the platform that capsized during the year hurricane Thomas hit. Her mother committed suicide three months later, when Tina was only a senior in high school. She graduated from Virginia Tech with a Masters in Engineering. She was an only child.

Alex thought for a moment.

"You see what we're dealing with? Both these kids lost their families. They joined the FBI, because that is a place where the best of the best compete against each other, and it is their surrogate family. We need to be sensitive to that."

"Well," Sandi said, "they didn't exactly lose all of their family." She told how Tina opened the conversation about her turtle Sam.

Alex spent the next couple of hours working out the logistics for tomorrow, but his conversation with Sandi stayed at the back of his mind. Finally he got up, corralled one of the many agents that were watching the facility, and sent him on a special mission.

The next morning after they all had packed and were ready to head to the airport, Alex approached the agent he had spoken to late the previous night.

"How did it go?"

"Mission accomplished. Everything is on board the plane."

"Outstanding."

Everyone boarded the plane and stowed all their personal effects and the agents seated themselves. Alex walked back from the cockpit and stopped in front of agent Somers.

"Agent Somers I have decided to give you an additional duty beyond keeping Dr. Chenowith and myself safe from harm."

Alex then pulled out from behind his back a bowl containing some water, and Sam the turtle, perched on his rock.

"You'll find lettuce and carrots and a box of turtle food in the refrigerator. And don't ever give up on the things that are important to you. You fight for those things to your last breath. It's what makes us winners, and more importantly...survivors."

"Sir, I...yes sir, thank you so much."

"All right everybody, we're out of here in five minutes," Alex announced.

Once they were in the air and at cruising altitude, Sandi joined Alex in the cockpit.

"You did a good thing back there, you know."

"I try."

"Yeah, maybe a little harder than most. But tell me the truth, was that actually the real Sam?"

"It's amazing what you can do with the power of the U.S. Government behind you. Bill had seen about where she let the turtle go, and turtles aren't prone to go very far. It wasn't hard to find the real Sam."

"Well, do you have any idea what that meant to her? You are the most wonderful man I know on this plane, that's currently flying it."

They both laughed, and Alex thanked God for Sandi's wit. He needed the light moments. They were in such a desperate race with time, and the odds sometimes seemed so insurmountable. And then, even if everything went perfectly, there was the horror of the aftermath to deal with before the rebuilding could begin. If he let himself dwell on it, he would wind up curled in a fetal position somewhere, whimpering quietly. He simply had so much to do, and little time to do it.

He put the plane on a heading for Little Creek Virginia to the 1st Division Naval Construction Headquarters. He was behind schedule, but he would make up for it somehow. As he set the glide path into the computer, the plane made a sweeping turn to the right and began its final approach to the field at the naval station.

Upon arrival, there was naval brass all over the place standing in formation, in their naval whites, with ribbons gleaming across their chests. The jet pulled to a stop on the tarmac and the Naval band began playing Anchors Aweigh. Alex was sure this was Admiral Torrance's doing. His first thought was that he didn't have time for pomp and circumstance, but then realized that he didn't know how many people here were aware of what was coming. He needed the pomp and circumstance as cover.

Alex stopped and snapped to attention and saluted the Naval Division's flag. He then spoke to the Rear Admiral Joseph Byers in charge standing in front of him.

"Permission to come aboard sir?"

"Permission granted General, and welcome to the home of the Seabees."

As they came down the stairs, Sandi said to Evans and Somers, loud enough for Alex to hear.

"You're going to see just how important your job is, by the way these people fall all over themselves to give Alex what he wants. He is the man who sits at the right hand of their god, Admiral Torrance."

"Are the stories about his exploits during Desert Storm true," Evans asked.

"You don't get the Air Force Cross and the Silver Star for playing in the band."

Chapter 19

THE SMELL OF BLOOD

Andrade turned to Elena. "You all right?"

She nodded yes.

The plane was on a level flight now, about two thousand feet up, headed east. She wondered when the pilot would bank back toward Vancouver, but it was so noisy in the cabin she knew the pilot couldn't hear her. Then the plane began to yaw side to side, up and down. Elena leaned forward to find out why the bumpy ride, and grabbed the pilot's shoulder.

And found her hand covered in blood.

"Oh my God Andrade, the pilot's been hit."

She scanned the instruments quickly. According to the artificial horizon, they were in a slight dive, and as she watched, the rate of descent increased.

"We're going down," she said tightly. "Help me."

Elena popped the pilot's seat harness and dragged him back. Andrade grabbed him under the shoulders and heaved him far enough out of the seat that she was able to reach the controls and pull the plane back level. She kept her grip on the wheel while

Andrade pulled the pilot clear, then hopped forward into the pilot's seat. In a moment, Andrade was in the seat next to her.

"You can fly this?" he asked.

"My experience is with small single-engines, and I've never flown a pontoon plane. I'd probably kill us on a water landing. But...do we have a choice?"

"I've never flown anything more complicated than a kite, so no."

She figured they had been flying due east for about fifteen minutes. The country passing by below was rugged, with dense forested hillsides dotted with huge rock formations. She couldn't see any place to put the plane down on water. Going back was not an option either. She banked hard left to come back on a westerly course.

"We have smoke," Andrade said with an admirable calm.

She looked past him and saw a small trail of white smoke coming from the engine. Not a fire. That was oil burning off. She scanned the instruments again.

"The oil pressure is dropping," she said. They must have hit in one of the lines—damn there it goes."

The engine began to knock, then white smoke billowed out from under the engine cowling and Elena killed the engine.

"Elena, what the hell are you doing?"

"I don't want to catch on fire. Start looking for any open place to put this down."

"It's getting dark, I can barely see."

"Hurry, we are now gliding, and losing about fifteen meters per second."

"Over there," he pointed. "An open meadow, along that hillside."

"I see it."

Elena pushed the rudder as hard as she could to turn the plane. With no power it was like driving a tractor trailer truck without power steering. She kept pushing and was beginning to line up fairly well with the meadow, when the rudder cable gave way under the pressure, they were about two hundred feet in the air.

"Andrade I love you, we are going in, get ready for bad things."

Andrade didn't get the chance to respond before the first tree tore into the right wing; it pitched the plane hard to the left. Then the left wing caught another, throwing the plane back to the right. Elena and Andrade were tossed back and forth like marbles in a can. The plane spun completely around and hit the forest floor tail first, shearing off the wings and pontoons, sliding some one hundred yards on its side, until it abruptly hit an out cropping of rocks and came to rest miraculously upright.

Andrade fought to get the pilot's body off of him. He had to get them out of the plane before it caught fire. Finally, mustering all his strength, he managed to slide out his door, sprung open in the impact, and run over to the other side to get Elena. Her door was badly crushed and wouldn't open. He struggled for a couple of minutes, then forced himself to turn away and hunt for something he could use for leverage. He found a broken spar, jammed it into a gap in the warped door, and managed to pop it open.

He dragged Elena from the pilot's seat and carried her for nearly fifty yards then collapsed. He began talking to her, noticing the bump on her head. Wounded, but she was alive.

Miraculously, the plane had not caught fire, so he ran back and found a first aid kit under the pilot's seat. He glanced in the back seats and saw her gun lying on the side of the bulkhead. He retrieved that as well as their two suitcases with clothes and equipment. It started to rain and he needed to get them to shelter.

A nearby rock formation made a natural overhang for them to crawl under and get out of the rain. There, Andrade laid Elena down on some of her sweaters from out of her suitcase. He studied her. How could such an angelic looking face belong to the person he had seen kill two people simply to buy them a few hours head start? How did she become this person? She could be so tender and loving then almost instantly become a ruthless killer. He realized he had never felt this way about another woman.

She was beginning to move around and moan with her injuries. Finally she opened her eyes.

"Elena don't move," he said. "Take it easy, you have a nice bump on your head."

"We're alive?" she whispered.

"So far, thanks to your perfect landing."

She managed a smile. "I'm so cold."

"Here, I've got some of our clothes out of the plane, I'll cover you up, and see if I can build a fire."

Andrade crawled further back under the rock overhang. Apparently, they were not the first to use it for a shelter. There was lots of brush and leaves and a couple of good size pieces of dead tree limbs. He pulled several rocks in from the rain to make a fire pit. Placing a bed of leaves and small twigs inside the ring of rocks he used his lighter to start it burning. Once the twigs caught, he put two big tree limbs on, and within fifteen minutes had a nice warming fire. He pulled Elena closer to the fire, and she began to respond to the warmth and wanted to sit up. Andrade told her to be slow. She propped herself up on her elbows.

"Every muscle and bone in my body hurts right now, and I have a headache."

"So sex is out for tonight then?"

She chuckled, then grimaced. "Don't make me laugh, it hurts too much."

"Here, I got the first aid kit from the plane. Take these two aspirin, and here are two bottles of water I salvaged, you're not bleeding from your bump on the head, and there are no broken bones…I think the pilot helped cushion our fall. But, you have a nice knot up there."

"I bet I look real good right now don't I?"

"You look beautiful to me, and always will."

"Andrade you're so sweet. How long has it been raining?"

"Oh, I'd say about half an hour, it's just barely misting now."

Elena sat up finally, and took her two aspirin with a couple of gulps of water. The warm fire was bringing her around to full consciousness, and soothing the bruised muscles all over her body.

"Andrade we need to inventory what we have, and make sure we get everything possible out of the plane that we may need."

"When the rain stops I'll go see what we can salvage."

"Crossbow? Director Cray."

"Yes, sir."

"We have clearance to set up surveillance at the safe house in Vancouver with the RCMP unit as backup."

"Sir, please don't tell me the Royal Canadian Mounted Police are calling the shots on this."

"No, they are there to assist you with civilian issues only. Any actual intrusion or apprehension on your part is to be done by you and your team. We're jamming the hell out of their communications, so nothing is going out."

"Sir, you realize Grodny will avoid that place if she hasn't gotten there by now. She'll know we'll have the place covered."

"We're in a wait and see game Crossbow. Get your team in place."

"Yes, sir."

Crossbow began to think. If she's not there yet, where would she go? His instincts had been right before, where would he go? He pulled out the map to look at the whole picture of the Northwest.

That's where he would go, along the coast and on up to Alaska. Then contact Russia to come in and pick them up by plane or boat at some little port town. The extra agents from the east coast had arrived. Although he had permission to set up the surveillance at the safe house, that permission did not extend to any other action within Canada.

To hell with protocol. He would send twenty agents, ten teams of two, by car to cover all the coast and islands of British Columbia. He decided against Alaska since the US Coast Guard was active along that coastline, and Elena would know that.

Andrade sat next to Elena holding her, while they warmed themselves by the fire. Elena imagined this was a camping trip with just her and Andrade, she loved the smell of the rain in the forest and the smoke coming off the burning wood. The clouds were clearing, and the moon was bright and peeking through the tree tops.

She moved so that she was sitting in between his legs and, could lean back on his chest. With his arms around her, she felt safe, her pain diminished by the warmth of the moment. They sat there for a good hour just taking in the night air, the crackling of the fire, the occasional water droplet from a tree branch hitting the ground. It was a peaceful refuge from the previous frenzied and tension filled days.

The fire began to die down, and Andrade got up to get some more wood. Elena checked her cell phone. Just as she suspected, no service available. She figured they were about a hundred twenty miles from Vancouver on a straight line. How they were going to get there she didn't know. She knew one thing for sure. They'd survived some pretty testy situations these last few days, and now wasn't the time to give in.

She checked her gun, a full clip and two clips in the suitcase Andrade had salvaged from the plane. When she asked Andrade if he managed to find his gun, he told her the dead pilot had pinned him down during the crash and his gun couldn't have fallen out if it wanted to. He had a full clip and one in his jacket. Elena stood up for the first time since the crash. She was already starting to stiffen up from all the thrashing around in the plane she endured. She was thankful that neither she nor Andrade broke any bones. They were incredibly lucky to be alive and in such good condition.

"What time is it Andrade?"

"Is this still Pacific time?"

"Yes, I think it is."

"Then it's 9:35."

"Come help me walk to the plane so we can see if there is anything useful."

"Elena let me do that, you need to rest."

"No, I need to move around. Otherwise I will stiffen up even more."

"All right, let me put this wood on the fire, and I will make a torch to give us some light."

Elena held onto Andrade's arm and they walked the distance to the crash site without incident. She actually felt better after the walk. Andrade crawled into the cabin over the dead pilot's body, and began looking around. He found a compartment door behind the back seats and opened it.

"We hit the jackpot Elena." He handed out two flashlights. "Here see if they work." He dove back into the compartment. "Oh, yes! A blanket, looks like two gallon containers of water, and, are you ready for this? American K-rations, four of them. A backpack with a compass in it. And what's this? A twelve gauge shotgun and a box of shells. I can't believe all the stuff that was in here."

They carried all the loot back to the campfire organized it and packed the backpack with nearly all the essential food and water, the pistol and shotgun ammunition. Andrade had the map still in his jacket. They decided they would start out first thing in the morning and head west by northwest.

"Well Andrade we got lucky, except for two critical items."

"And what would those be my love?"

"The satellite phones were shot to pieces."

"And what else?"

She laughed. "Toilet paper."

"I'll get you something."

Andrade walked back to the plane and a few minutes later came back with a box of tissues, a partial roll of toilet paper, and a handful of maps.

"My dear, your wish is my command."

"Goodness, you are quite the scavenger. I'll just be a minute."

She went into the brush to take care of her business.

After a couple of minutes Andrade yelled out.

"Be careful Elena, don't let a forest mouse jump in your birds nest."

"Stop that, you're scaring me."

After her commune with mother nature, they settled down to get some sleep. They had a long and arduous day ahead of them.

The morning came with the sounds of the forest all around them. Elk could be heard in the distance with their distinctive call of the wild. Birds bantered back and forth. The rustle of a slight wind moved through the trees. The unmistakable smell of morning in the wilderness.

Elena was stiff, but spent about twenty minutes stretching, and felt much better. Then they were off. Andrade carried the backpack and shotgun, and Elena had fashioned a rope tie down that held the blanket and some dry clothes for both, slung across her shoulder. Elena's mind refocused on their predicament and she told Andrade there is no way they could get to the safe house now. Crossbow would have it completely covered up with agents.

"They don't know we have crashed yet, we need to find a house or a cabin, and get to a phone so I can call the satellite. If I can get to Ingosich, he can arrange another pick up somewhere near. After about two hours of walking they came upon a well-worn dirt road that looked like it might be a logging road. They could hear heavy machinery just over the next hillside. Hopefully their luck would hold out, and they could hitch a ride to a small settlement nearby. As they reached the top of the next hill they looked down upon a major logging operation underway. Whole sections of the forest were gone, but it was like a patchwork pattern.

"If we come upon someone let me speak," she said. "Your English still has a noticeable Russian accent to it."

"It's not that bad."

They sat down and took a break and had some of the rations Andrade had found. Andrade smoked a cigarette after, finished his water, and belched.

"That was probably the worst meal I've had in my life. I'm not sure exactly what it was that I ate, except for the peanut butter and stale crackers."

Elena laughed, then picked up her pack. "We need to get moving." Her plan was to isolate the driver of one of the pickup trucks and force them to take them to a phone somewhere. As they got closer to the worksites, she could see what appeared to be a foreman talking to some of the workers. His truck door was open and he was draped over the door while he was speaking. The Americans were so informal at times. No discipline—the pigs. They crossed over another road just about the time the meeting with the foreman ended and the workers left. Perfect.

"Let's hurry, Andrade."

She crept up behind the foreman as he was speaking into a walkie talkie. As he finished Elena stepped out from behind a tree.

"Hey mister, can we get a ride?" She put some Southern California in her voice.

"Holy—Where in the hell did you two come from?"

"Oh, we camped about three miles over that way."

"Well I hate to tell you this, but you're on private property and you need to leave."

Elena pulled her gun and shoved it into his cheek.

"Now that was just plain rude. Don't you feel embarrassed how you've behaved?"

"What…what the hell do you people want?"

"You know I really don't like repeating myself." Her voice was mutating into Southern, a'la Bonnie and Clyde. "I asked you, could we get a ride and then you copped an attitude—"wait a minute, is that a satellite phone in the seat of your truck?"

"Yes ma'am, we can't get cell phone service way out here."

"Well, mister you let me worry about that. Roscoe, cover him while I call my babysitter."

Andrade shoved the shotgun under the man's chin and motioned for him to sit down in the truck. She picked up the satellite phone walked a good distance away. She dialed a sequence of numbers, waited for the beeps, entered more numbers. She could hear the dial tone and the automatic dialing.

"Petrov."

"It's Elena."

"My god where are you, are you okay?"

"The pilot is dead. The plane was shot to pieces by the CIA and we crashed last night. We're going to need another way out, we're about a hundred twenty km southeast of Vancouver."

"Yes, the safe house is covered up with CIA. And the Americans are jamming all communications in and out, let me think for a minute."

Elena waited for what seemed like forever. Then Petrov came back on the line.

"Elena do you have a map of the west coast that shows north of Vancouver?"

"Hang on." She walked over to Andrade, took the backpack off his back and found the map she needed.

"Yes, I have it right here."

"Look up the coast. You see the Queen Charlotte Islands, and the town of Masset?"

"Yes, I see it."

"You must find a way to get there by midnight two days from now. I will have a trawler disguised as an American crab boat come into the harbor and pick you up. They will flash three times on their spotlight. That will be your signal it is okay to board."

"Petrov, remind me to kiss you when I see you again."

"Just get back to us in one piece."

"I promise, I will."

Promises made, actions assured, Alex was plowing new territory at an alarming rate, he was becoming indispensable and people in certain circles were becoming nervous. Another call was made to Howard Carney to ensure eyes were on the boy wonder.

"You have confidence in this person of yours Carney?"

"Of course, and why are you calling me about this? You asked me to do something for you and I did, and now you're calling to check up on me like I'm some kind of child. I resent that."

"Howard calm down, no offense intended, it was just a follow-up."

"Okay, now you've had your follow-up. Let me get back to doing my job."

"Good talking to you Howard, as always."

Up and down the government echelon those individuals that knew of the coming event were beginning to exhibit signs of the stress and that stress seemed to mount daily. It would only get worse.

Chapter 20

BUILDING HOPE

A lex eased into the leather chair in the Admiral's office and was transfixed by all the memorabilia covering every wall in the expansive office. My God, was that a Civil War battle flag?

"General Hanken," the Admiral said, "when the Naval Chief of Staff calls you and tells you that Admiral Torrance has given you command of a project that has national security implications, and that the entire armed services are at your disposal…well, you tend to sit up and take notice. Never in my thirty three years in the Navy have I received such an order, nor have any of my cohorts at the other branches of the service. So General how may I help you?"

Alex proceeded to lay out his mission without divulging the underlying purpose. He went on to say what type of construction would be involved, what type of skills and equipment would be needed, and the facilities needing attention in the eastern district. He also explained that it was important for him to meet with each facility construction manager or commander so that he could evaluate their readiness to assume the duties.

The Admiral leaned forward.

"General Hanken I am an old guard Navy man, when I get an order from the top, I don't ask why, I just do what I'm told. But I would observe that you seem to be building a separate military unit as a reserve in case of a national disaster."

Alex sat quietly and stared directly at the Admiral. He was fishing, and Alex made it clear he wasn't biting.

The Admiral laughed.

"They told me you were a no nonsense commander, and nothing rattles you. I can see that now. I can have your six divisions ready in about two weeks for deployment to the sites you mentioned, fully staffed and equipped. As far as the unit commanders, I'll have all of them here tomorrow if that meets with your schedule."

"That's excellent Admiral. Now that we've discussed your part in this endeavor, can you tell me where I can get a good steak dinner for my party?"

"I'm glad you asked. I've got a great place just about five miles from town."

"You and your executive staff are invited as my guest Admiral."

"Thank you General, now let's take you on a tour of our base."

After lunch, Alex along with Sandi and the two agents were given the VIP tour of the Seabees home base. The Seabees had a wide range of duties around the world. But that was changing with the redeployment underway, and it worked in Alex's favor— it had freed up several divisions for his facility work.

During dinner the admiral was curious about the two agents, who were they, and what they did. Alex told him they were hand-picked by the FBI Director to be his and Dr. Chenowith's body-guards. Alex filled him in on their background and skill levels, and the Admiral asked had there been trouble, Alex would only say that there were foreign agents that were snooping around trying to find out what he was doing.

"I'm surprised Admiral Torrance didn't assign a Seal team as your escort."

"Funny you should bring up the Seals. I'm going to ask for at least four to five Seal teams be assigned to various facilities throughout the country."

"You can't get any better General. Even your 1st Special Forces group can't match the Seals."

"Disloyal as it sounds, I agree. The 1st is excellent at combat tactics and field of play execution, but they don't have the diversity of mission capability that the Seal teams do."

"Big of you to admit it. I can almost see why Admiral Torrance didn't choose a Navy man for this project."

The Admiral had four of his senior staff with him at dinner, so the restaurant had set up a private dining room for such a large party. Everyone was enjoying their meal suddenly, a man burst through the door unannounced. Before he could say anything, and before Alex was even aware she'd moved, Somers had her gun to his temple.

"Put your hands up and turn around or I'll drop you where you stand. Now!"

"Evans clean him." Alex only noticed that Evans had his gun trained on the man as well. He approached the man and patted him down.

"He's clean."

"Hey lady, I just wanted to say hello to the Navy guys." He slurred his words.

"It's all right," the Admiral said. "He's…kind of a local character. We've been tripping over him for years."

"Okay," Somers said, "you've said your hello, now leave this room immediately."

"All right, I'm sorry to barge in on your little party."

The man staggered back into the main restaurant.

The Admiral leaned over to Alex.

"Jesus General, maybe Torrance has a point. The Seals might be as good, but I don't think they're better."

"She was top of her class at Quantico, and you know, they turn out a pretty good product there, too."

"I'd love to see her in action against a Seal."

What the heck. He really did need a break, and it wouldn't hurt for everyone to see just how well protected he was. "Agent Somers, the Admiral says he would like to see what you could do against a Navy Seal."

"I would enjoy that General," she said.

"Firing range, or hand to hand combat?

"Ladies choice," the admiral said.

"Hand to hand sounds good to me."

"This ought to be interesting," Evans whispered to Alex.

"Understand Somers," Alex said, "if you get hurt, I'll have you shot."

The next morning Alex interviewed three potential candidates for site commanders. He was comfortable with all of them and told them their responsibilities under the Secrets Act, and let them know what they were in for. All of them were shocked, but none of them were debilitated. Good, it was a good group. He went further to tell them that they would be permanently assigned to his command, and they reported to him and only him. Additionally, there was no expense that couldn't be justified, the timeline was tight, and nothing else mattered. That was all the personnel he needed, as two of the new facility commanders said they could handle multiple locations that were close enough to maintain post event. The eastern region was now set, all he had to do was have the new commanders step right in, and take over the process that Alex had laid out for them.

Later that day everyone retired to the gymnasium, where the gladiatorial battle was to take place. Word had spread like wildfire around the base, and nearly three thousand officers and sailors packed the gym. Protective headgear, foot pads and light weight half gloves were the attire for the match.

Sandi, in the ringside seat next to Alex, leaned in to him. "You'll stop this if it starts to get out of hand, right? I don't want Tina to get hurt."

"I don't think anyone's going to get hurt," he whispered back. "I suspect Tina will be the one to stop the fight."

The Navy Seal was a tall and muscular young man. His arms looked like steel ribbons twisted into shape. A captain in dress whites who was acting as referee sent them to their corners, then signaled for them to come together.

The two circled one another for a moment, studying their opponents. Suddenly, a set of lightning fast punches. They broke apart, neither hurt, neither breathing hard. Alex realized this was just a feint, a way of testing each other's defenses. You could tell the Seal was impressed and a bit surprised.

The Seal tried a leg sweep, but Somers anticipated the move and jumped clear, landed on one foot and threw her momentum into a kick to his stomach. Then she launched herself straight up four feet in the air, spun around and brought her left foot against the Seal's temple, right on the sweet spot.

He was staggered. The crowd was stunned.

But Somers wasn't done. Before he could fall, Somers unleashed a devastating series of punches directly into the Seal's face. Most of the gathered could not even see the punches, they just heard them hit. The young man collapsed in the corner...out cold. Alex glanced at the timer. It had taken her fifty-four seconds.

The crowd was silent for a long moment. Then a thunderous chant arose from somewhere in the back and spread through the auditorium until it thundered through the rafters.

"Somers, Somers, Somers."

Alex and Sandi were on their feet and clapping as if she were their own daughter. Evans went into the ring and picked her up, put her on his shoulder, and paraded her around the ring to the cheers of the crowd.

"My God General," The Admiral shouted over the din. "I've never seen anything like it."

Somers, wearing a slightly sheepish smile, walked over to Alex and Sandi.

Sandi took her hands. "You were magnificent."

"I couldn't be more proud of you," Alex said.

Somers looked like she was on the verge of tears. Sandi put her arm around her, and walked her back to the locker room.

Alex sagged. He knew he needed the relief, but even though this whole distraction only took an hour or so, he felt he had to scramble to catch up.

Back to the grind.

"Wheels up in five," Alex announced.

With everybody on board and settled in, he taxied the jet down the runway, pulled the engine controls back, and roared off into the western skies.

"Where are we headed again," Sandi asked.

"We're going to take a little detour to Fort Campbell, Kentucky, the home of the 101st Airborne. I'm going to spend about two hours with the division commander, then it's off to Ft. Leonard Wood Army base, the 554th Engineer Battalion. That's in Missouri."

Upon arriving at Ft. Leonard Wood they were once again treated with pomp and ceremony, and Alex got the opportunity to meet with four of the lead engineers. He was impressed with their backgrounds, and decided to pull them in with the standard caveats he had given the Seabees. The number of people who knew about the coming event was growing. He hoped the FBI and CIA would be able to keep a lid on it.

From there he wanted to see the Meramec caverns facility, so they drove there in a military convoy. After inspecting the caves he asked Sandi for her impressions.

"I think it's too wet and seeping in there."

"My thoughts exactly, this was a bad choice, I think we should take a trip up to Whiteman AFB. It's just about sixty-five miles southeast of KC. We'll fly up there tomorrow morning. I'll clear it with the Air Force."

After visiting the facilities at Whiteman AFB Alex got on the phone to Admiral Torrance

"Admiral, Alex Hanken."

"Alex how are you, and I heard about the little competition that went on. Those Seabees are still talking about it."

"Yeah it was fun. Uh, Admiral, who chose the Meramec caverns site?"

"I'm pretty sure it was the FEMA Director."

"I'm afraid it's an untenable site. It's damp and moldy, the walls leak, the floors are uneven and soft core rock. It would take a year or more to get that place in living condition."

"What's your recommendation?"

"I just got back from Whiteman AFB. They have fifteen hardened control centers, the remnants of the old ICBM missile wing. They're sitting there, all on huge shock absorbers, with self-contained electric power systems, air ventilation and purification, and ample water table supplies. We could convert those things very quickly to take on thirty people and build storage units within to sustain people for two years. Plus all the control centers are interconnected by cable for communication. Whiteman is the home of the B-2 Bomber Wing, they all have hardened hangars and support facilities. There's one other thing. Whiteman was the only base in America to have a master control center actually on a base. That facility could be remodeled to hold up to a hundred people."

"Wouldn't that be concentrating too much at one location?"

"No. These fifteen sites are spread out over a 10,000 square mile area, about the size of the state of Massachusetts."

"What about the construction team?"

"It's already set up. The 544th Engineers out of Ft. Leonard Wood are awaiting my orders."

"Hell Alex, we were only going to put about two hundred ten people in all the facilities in the Midwest. Are you telling me that you can put a little over five hundred people in those facilities alone?"

"Yes, but much more. We have the facilities at Whiteman for not only the B-2's, but hundreds of other military vehicles and support items."

"You know what? Just do whatever you think and keep me posted. Stay focused as you are."

"Thank you sir, we are on track so far, and I'll keep it that way."

Alex called his three new Army construction people, and alerted them to be prepared to mobilize in five days, and to inspect the sites for recommendations.

Don Cray sat down with the President and Admiral Torrance.

"Mr. President, those two Russian agents made it into Canada, and we assume they are making their way to the safe house, which we have staked out.

"How did they get that far?" the President asked.

"I take full responsibility," Cray said quickly.

"Any sign of what they know and what they've been able to pass along?"

"They did penetrate deeply into the Coeur d' Alene facility. I'm sure they have enough to generate details on the size and defensive strength of the survival facilities. As to how much they passed on…they were still on the run when they entered into Canada. If they had given everything they had, they would have chosen a land route. I'm confident the Russians only have the outlines."

"That's still more than I'd prefer."

"Yes, sir. But, remember, the Russians are still unable to detect the approaching asteroids. That should confuse their thinking long enough for us to get the survival shelters habitable. After that, it's simply a matter of getting our people inside and pulling the door shut behind us."

"And letting the world outside go to hell."

"It's the only way to rebuild it afterwards, sir."

The President waved this off. It was a discussion they'd had many times before.

"Incidentally," Cray said, "our sources tell us that the Russian secret police have dubbed General Hanken as the most dangerous military leader since Patton. They have agents coming here to try and find out what he's up to and to make sure they know where he is at all times."

"And are they right? We are concentrating a lot of power in his hands."

"Mr. President," Torrance said, "I have known General Hanken for many years. He is the most thoroughly loyal, patriotic man I have ever known. I trust him implicitly to do what is necessary when the time comes. Which is why I think it's time we move forward with what we've discussed."

The President nodded. "Very well. Don, we are taking away his Lear and giving him Air Force 2. Wherever he flies he will be accompanied by an escort of Air Force or Naval attack planes.

Traveling with him will be ten Navy Seals to augment the FBI personnel."

"You'll let Ted over at the FBI know?"

"Of course, sir."

As the meeting broke up, Cray felt even better about his backup plan. Torrance might trust Hanken to do the right thing, but he was less sure.

It was a rule he'd picked up from weapons design training. No matter how reliable your missile, always build in a destruct switch.

Alex got a call from Admiral Torrance while packing for the trip back home.

"Yes, Admiral."

"Alex have you got a few minutes?"

"A few, yes, sir."

"We have credible reports that there are Russian agents coming to this country to find out at all costs, what your mission is. In other words you have a big red target painted on your back. The President and I just spoke and he agreed that we have to take extraordinary steps to ensure your safety."

"Well, you've already given me pretty good armor in those two FBI agents. They seem extremely qualified, Admiral."

"They won't stop an Igla."

It took a second to recall the Russian, shoulder-fired, anti-aircraft missile. "You think things are that bad?"

"Okay, you're not going to like what I'm about to say. Alex your home in Sacramento is no longer a safe place for you to live. We can't adequately secure the location without drawing undue attention to you and your immediate family. Secondly, the Lear jet we provided you does not have anti-missile capability and can't be rigged with it either, that goes for the King Air as well. So here's what we're going to do. We are going to move you to Petersen AFB—, you, your kids, Sandi, her daughter and the two FBI agents. We are also attaching a ten man Seal team to personally accompany you everywhere you go. I'm sure that young FBI agent will get a kick out of that."

"The Seals may, too."

"Your living accommodations will be more than comfortable—, the unit was originally built for LBJ as a secure hideaway. It has three master suites and six guest bedrooms and is literally built into the side of a mountain. You'll have two housekeepers and a fulltime chef with two kitchen helpers to care for all your needs. You will want for nothing. The President is already jealous and so am I.

"When you take a trip to here or a facility, you will be flying Air Force 2, the backup air command ship. It will have a full complement of crew. That way you don't have to wear yourself out flying coast to coast, you'll have time to relax or work if you prefer."

"Yes Admiral. But if securing my house will draw undue attention, what happens when I start showing up in the President's other plane?"

"We thought of that. Nearly all of the facilities are near some military base, where we can lock down security as tight as we want. From there you can helicopter to the sites with a Marine helicopter detachment for air cover. You will always have two fighter aircraft as cover and they will tag team you as you move across the country. Your flight ops person in charge of all the arrangements is Col. Bradley Cole out of Nellis AFB, he said he knows you."

"Brad and I go back to Desert Storm. He's a good man, sharp as a tack. Admiral what about my household and Curt and Cynthia's things?"

"As we speak Curt and Cynthia are on their way to Colorado Springs. Your household and their two condos are being packed and containerized for shipment to Petersen AFB. All your personal items will be marked so that you can retrieve favorite pictures and things. And, yes, your Cobra is coming as well"

"Whew, there for a moment I thought I was going to have to resign my commission."

Torrance had a big laugh then said, "So what I need you to do is turn yourself around and fly back here to Andrews. There you will board your new plane, and welcome aboard the new Seal team members. Now Alex these Seals have very specific orders from me about how to secure your activities, so let them do their job."

"Yes sir. We'll take off in about thirty minutes."

"You call Brad at Nellis, here's his number, and tell him your flight plan, and he will set up the return flight logistics to Petersen AFB."

"Yes, sir. I wish we didn't have to go to all of this trouble, just for me."

"It's not just for you, it's for the country, Alex. You're the guy who's putting all of this together."

"Thank you sir. Goodbye."

Admiral Torrance headed off for his testimony before the House Armed Services Committee. During his testimony, he outlined the status of the redeployment from overseas, he also gave a summary of his contentious meeting with the NATO members, who were highly critical of the redeployment. It seemed that now the US was no longer footing the majority of the costs for defending Europe, the financial burden would fall on the nations of that region. The ranking member of the committee asked Admiral Torrance if he could comment on the rumors that military units within the US were being realigned and commanders were on notice to downsize their units as quickly as possible.

"No Congressman, that is not true. We are realigning our entire military focus, with the intent to maximize the use of modern warfare technology. The future of our military is going to be technology based. It will not be personnel intensive. Military personnel will be highly specialized and thoroughly trained. We will have quick reaction teams at the level of Navy Seals and Special Forces to address unique threats. Our air and naval forces will continue to be the dominant fighting force in the world, but the day of the foot soldier is coming to an end Congressman."

"Then can you tell me how it is that you are spending so much money on rehabbing facilities throughout the nation, under the direction of this General Hanken, and not come before this committee and ask for more money?"

"It's quite simple Congressman. We have moved appropriations from new construction to rehab activities. Last year's budget allocated six billion for new construction. We have reallocated those funds to save time and expense, by updating existing facilities, rather than the expense of brand new facilities. These new facilities would not meet our future needs. In essence, it would be excess capacity, and not in line with our desire to streamline the military."

"So you are telling this committee that you are actually economizing the use of the American taxpayer's dollars. I can't recall in the last fifty years that has ever happened."

"Congressman, there's always a first time for everything," Admiral Torrance remarked.

"Yes, I suppose there is Admiral. Thank you for your time, and I look forward to other firsts."

"You can count on it Congressman," the admiral said.

Chapter 21

RENDEZVOUS AT MIDNIGHT

After Elena finished her call to Ingosich she walked back to where Andrade was guarding the foreman at the truck.

"Well how about that ride to, let's say, where all these workers out here park their cars?"

"Ma'am I told you I can't give you a ride in this company truck, I'll lose my job."

"You know something, Sparky? You must be the dumbest asshole on the face of the earth. You have a 12 gauge shotgun pointed at your head and you're worried about losing your job?"

The foreman got behind the wheel and Elena got in the passenger side front seat. Andrade slid in behind the foreman in the crew cab, his gun never leaving the foreman. It was astonishing how Elena was able to transform herself into someone else at the drop of a hat. And a little disturbing. It made him wonder if the Elena he thought he knew was even real.

"To the parking lot, James," she said. "And don't make any sudden turns because Roscoe here might just slip and the shotgun pointed at the back of your head might go off, and that would be a shame."

"Lady, I don't think you have any shame."

"Oh, are we waxing judgmental here? Because, I was referring to the mess it would make on the windshield and how it would be a shame for me to have to scrape your brains off the steering wheel. Now just drive and shut the fuck up."

Andrade was not sure whether Elena was playing the role or if she was really getting upset with the guy. The road was rough and dusty and they ended up behind a huge logging truck carrying cut trees to the saw mill. The cab was filling with dust to the point Elena was beginning to choke.

"Hey back off this guy in front," she said. "We're choking to death on this dust."

"Wouldn't that be a shame," he said with a grin.

Andrade braced himself for…whatever was coming.

"What are you some kind of clown, you think you're a comedian?"

Andrade had to admit, this guy was either brave or extremely foolish. "Look lady you've got the guns, you're in control, you can do whatever you want."

"So, if we didn't have our guns what would you do?"

Andrade just put his hands up to his face. Or maybe the guy just had a death wish.

"I'd kick your ass all over this forest." Andrade knew that did it.

"Stop the fucking truck."

"Elena don't," Andrade said.

"No Roscoe, this smart ass needs a lesson in courtesy."

The foreman pulled the truck as far to the side as he could on the logging road and turned off the engine.

"Now what?"

"Here take my gun," as she handed it to Andrade. "Get out, I'm not armed."

They both climbed out of the truck, and Elena squared off in front of him. "So bigmouth what are you going to do now?"

"Hell, if I hurt you he'll just shoot me."

She was standing about three feet from him. But with cobra-like quickness, she rocked forward and slapped him square in the cheek.

"Wow, what was that a bird flew over and shit on your cheek?" she said. "Let me wipe it off for you?"

He didn't see the second slap coming either, and she tele-graphed it. He was clearly scared now, and with good reason. She launched a fast punch to his abdomen that bent him over double and dropped him to the ground. She kneeled down beside him and grabbed his throat with enough force to convince him she could choke him to death if she wanted.

"I just survived a plane crash nine hours ago. Every bone in my body hurts. Every muscle is bruised and aching, and you want to give me a hard time? The next time you smart off to me I'm going to gut you from your nut sack up to your chin, do you read me mister?"

He nodded and tried to catch his breath after she let go of his throat. Then he got in the truck and drove.

"Now that we've settled that, would you please drive us to the employee parking lot?"

"Yes ma'am."

"Good boy."

Dear God. How was he going to keep Elena from killing this poor sap? Up until now, their killings had been, arguably, nec-essary for the good of the mission, which was absolutely vital. But this...They drove for another ten minutes and came upon an area that had been carved out of the forest by bulldozers. About ten cars and pickups parked there in more or less orderly rows.

"Give me your keys," she said.

He gave her his keys to his Toyota Tundra. She pressed the alarm button on the key module and the lights on the Tundra flashed on and off.

"Nice truck." "Now Mr. Crites is it?" She pushed her finger into his name tag on his company shirt.

"Do you have any maps in your personal truck?"

"Yes ma'am in the glove compartment." He was trembling. "Are you going to kill me now?"

"No."

The man seemed comforted. So did Andrade. It was only temporary though.

"Okay, now you go on over there and stick out your thumb, and pay no attention to us. Eventually somebody will come along and give you a ride."

The man turned and almost ran across the logging road to the other side, where an embankment dropped off steeply.

When he was standing at the edge of the embankment, Elena raised her gun.

"Elena don't—,"

"Before Andrade could finish his plea the bullet was on its way.

And it missed. The man jerked around at the sound, stared in relieved disbelief for a moment. Then lost his balance and tumbled backwards over the edge of the embankment, down the steep incline into the brushy area.

Andrade and Elena ran over to the edge and peered down. The man lay half hidden in the underbrush maybe fifty meters below. Andrade watched carefully and could see that the man was still breathing.

Elena was busy brushing the area where he had stood to cover any footprints. After a second he helped her. Then they locked the man's work truck, took the satellite phone, and headed toward the coast of British Columbia with Andrade at the wheel.

"Nice shot," Andrade said after a couple of miles.

"I did that for you, Andrade. It will take his workers a while to find him, though it would have taken longer if I had actually killed him. Now we'll have to dump his truck much quicker than necessary because we were so humane to him."

"And the beating you gave him?"

"Insurance. I humiliated him. Now there's a good chance he will simply forget the whole thing, hoping his truck will show up abandoned somewhere, and not tell the authorities we were there."

Andrade didn't know what to say. After a moment, he said, "I'm sorry. I thought you had snapped."

"Well, I was upset, and I did enjoy myself. And don't fool yourself, I could have killed him. I still feel I should have. This business you're now in doesn't award points for being a nice person. In fact, the nice ones get killed early on in their careers. Longevity in this field of endeavor is based on cunning, intelligence, skill, and ruthlessness."

Elena opened the glove compartment and began pouring over the maps.

"We need to take 97 north to Prince George, then 16/37 west to Prince Rupert and it looks like a ferry runs to Skidgate. And from there you take the main road north to Masset."

"Yeah but Elena, where the hell are we right now?"

"Don't worry we're bound to run into a main road, and we can always ask for directions."

She pulled more paperwork from the glove compartment and started flipping through it. She came across the registration for the vehicle; it stated that Ned and Gloria Crites were joint owners. A wife means a missing person's report if Ned doesn't show up. Elena figured they had about eight to ten hours of use with this vehicle before a missing persons report was filed, then they would have to find another vehicle.

The road was rough and they passed several logging trucks some empty, some full. Andrade didn't understand that. Had they missed a turnoff somewhere? Empty trucks and full trucks should be going in the opposite directions unless there were two timber companies operating around there.

Andrade alerted Elena that there was something up ahead of them. It looked like road crews clearing overhanging tree limbs from the road below. Elena told Andrade to pull over by the guy standing by himself. He slowed the truck down, and came to a stop next to the man Elena wanted to speak to.

She rolled down her window.

"Hey, how do you get to 97 south, eh?"

"You headed down to Spokane?"

"Yes, we are, we just bought this Tundra from a guy."

"Is this Ned Crites truck?"

"Why, I think that was his name."

"Hell, he just bought the thing six months ago."

"Well, Gloria pitched a fit and I guess Ned got tired of it, so he sold it."

"You know, that sounds just like Gloria."

"Always has been, always will be, eh."

"Okay folks, keep on this road for about six miles, until you hit a T in the road. Take a left and about fifteen miles you'll come across a railroad crossing. The road bends around and follows the railroad tracks, just stay on that road and you'll start to see the signs for 97."

"Thanks a lot, have a great day."

Andrade checked the fuel gauge. It was at about half a tank. He wanted to stop and look at the map to make sure they didn't get into an isolated section of road with no fuel stops for hundreds of miles. He mentioned that to Elena, and she agreed they would check at the T in the road for any signs of nearby communities and possible sources of fuel and food.

When they reached the T in the road there was a sign that said Grimmers Petrol Pit Stop two km, with an arrow pointed to the right.

Andrade pulled into the little one story establishment next to a single fuel pump. The sign on the pump said cash customers pay in advance. Elena went into the little store and found it was stocked with lots of food and different sundries. Standing behind the counter was a woman in her nineties. The woman asked Elena how much gas they were going to get. Elena wasn't sure, but the truck looked big, so she figured 120 liters. The woman requested she put down one hundred twenty Canadian. Elena only had US dollars, so she gave her three one hundred dollar bills.

By the time Andrade finished filling the tank and spare tank, the total came to one hundred eighty Canadian—about $220 US. The old woman told Elena she didn't have enough change to break the remaining hundred, so Elena picked up some cigarettes, and bottled water, crackers and cheese and other things to use up the change. The woman totaled the gas and goods and gave her thirty-four fifty Canadian in change. Elena asked her was there any place along 97 south to spend the night. The old woman told her not for a piece maybe ninety km from the cutoff, but if you went north there was a really nice hunters lodge that had cabins about ten km from the cutoff.

Andrade came in and grabbed the bag of groceries and put them in the jump seat behind his driver's side. They drove for nearly an hour before they hit the railroad tracks, then the road swung back to the east paralleling the tracks. Elena busied herself with the maps plotting their path to escape until she was satisfied they would get to Masset for pickup, without exposing themselves to any of Crossbow's agents.

She knew Crossbow would not sit in Vancouver and wait. He would figure out they weren't there, and send his agents up the coast of British Columbia. British Columbia had a lot of coast, but she didn't know how many agents Crossbow had available.

"Here we are," Andrade said.

She looked up, and there was the sign for Hwy 97, five km. "Our next stop is Penticton, which was about a two hour drive north. It looked like they had a couple of nice hotels there."

"What about the hunters lodge?"

"Too rustic. I need a nice place with a pool and spa, so I can relax my aching body."

They pulled into a Ramada Inn at Penticton, and Elena got them a room. She immediately got her shorts headed to the pool area and found the heated spa. In just a tee shirt and her shorts she relaxed in the spa for about an hour then returned to the room.

"Andrade are you hungry? I'm ready for dinner."

"Yes, I could eat a polar bear right now, fur and all."

As they ate dinner Elena went over the trip ahead of them.

"We will drive to Prince George tomorrow it's about a nine hour drive from here...and spend the night there. We need to switch cars in Prince George. The next day is actually get away day, it's a nine hour drive to Prince Rupert, then the ferry ride to

Queen Charlotte looks like a two hour trip. We'll get a room for a few hours, then get transportation to Masset, which is about an hour and a half. We need to be there by 11:15 p.m. that night. The trawler is coming into the harbor at midnight."

"Why don't we just drive straight through to Prince Rupert, take the ferry, and stay in Queen Charlotte?" Andrade asked.

"We can't afford to be in one place for too long. Remember Crossbow will have agents up and down the coast. We want to get into Queen Charlotte, then leave almost as quickly as we came in. Always keep moving, that way you lessen the chance of being spotted. If you're just hanging around killing time, someone will remember you."

"Yeah, I guess you're right."

They finished their meal and returned to the room where they both fell asleep.

Gloria Crites was pacing. Ned had never been this late before without calling her. She forced herself to wait until midnight, then she called the local police office to file the report.

"Hello Gloria, how can I help you?" Officer Tom Juno asked.

"Tom, Ned hasn't come home and that's not like him. I'm afraid something's happened."

"Okay, now, Gloria. We have to wait twenty-four hours before we can file a missing person's report, but there's nothing says I can't poke around on my own. When did you last see him?"

"This morning at breakfast."

"Well then, I can call out the troops around 7:00 a.m. tomorrow morning, but right now I'll send a unit up to the camp to look around. But, Gloria, don't get too upset okay? He's probably sleeping off a night at some bar down the road. He'll probably come stumbling in the house in a few hours. If he does you be sure to call us okay?"

Deputy Ken Wells took his time driving along the logging road with the cruiser's spotlight pointed in the brush, looking for signs of a car going off the steep side. He still hadn't seen a thing by the time he came to the employee parking site where

Ned's company truck was parked. It was locked up as usual, there didn't appear to be any signs of trouble, and his Tundra was gone.

He was about to turn back around and start visiting bar parking lots when he thought he heard a growling noise coming from across the road. He went over to the edge of the steep embankment, and shined his flashlight down into the brushy undergrowth. It was a wolf, and it looked like it had killed a small deer.

But it wasn't a deer. It was a man. He grabbed his radio.

"Tom this is Ken, Jesus, I just found Ned Crites body. I can't tell what happened here, if he slipped off the embankment or was pushed, but there's a wolf picking at his body. It's… it's as ugly as anything I've ever seen."

"Is his truck there?"

"What? No, the Toyota is gone."

"Okay, stay there. I'll call the detective's office, and put out an all points on the Toyota Tundra. It'll take them a couple of hours to get up there. Don't mess the crime scene up or we'll catch hell about it."

"You going to call Gloria?"

"Not until we have positive ID."

It was 4:30 a.m. before the homicide detectives arrived and began going over the crime scene. The lead detective told Tom he could call Ned's wife, and tell her the bad news. One of the detectives found a spent casing lying next to a rock.

"Will you look at this?" He held up the casing. "That's not a .44, and I'm pretty sure it's not a .38. Have you ever seen a casing like this?"

"Can't say that I have. Some kind of a specialized gun?"

"I know a guy at RCMP I can ask."

The detective studied the scene. It looks like Ned was standing over there at the edge of the road. If somebody shot at him, they missed, but he stumbled and fell over the edge. Looks like he suffered a severe blow to the head while falling down the embankment. The fall could have killed him. Yeah, this is a murder scene. Call it in."

"Whoever did this has his truck," another detective said. "Might be one of those reservation Indians."

"No, I don't think so," Ken said. "This scene was cleaned with the exception of the casing. We're dealing with someone that knows what they're doing."

"Let's see." The lead detective glanced at his watch. "It's 7:30, the road crews will be up and at it, so will the loggers."

"You stay here and interview the loggers as they come in. I'll go with Ken down the road and see if anybody saw anything."

The lead detective left with the local officer and drove down the road to see if any of the road crew might have seen something, but the man that spoke with Elena about directions was late to work that morning. The officer and the detective drove further down the road looking for any possible leads. The worker that was late walked up to his workmates and they informed him that the police had just left, and that they had found Ned Crites body. The man felt sick to his stomach, and said he needed to talk with them right away, got in his truck, and sped off in search of the officers.

Elena turned on the police band radio just to see if she could hear anything of value. There was huge amount of chatter, the sign that some major crime had been committed. She didn't have to listen long before she realized which crime it was.

"Did you get the all points out on Ned's truck?"

"Roger that. I can't believe he's dead."

"The detective here says they found some kind of weird gun casing at the scene."

Elena reacted immediately.

"Andrade pull off onto that road there."

"What the hell for?"

"They found that guy's body. They know we have the truck, they'll have an all-points bulletin broadcast out on it, we've got to get rid of this thing immediately."

Andrade did as she asked, driving down a narrow one and a half lane road until they saw a cluster of what looked like resort cabins with a main office set apart from the rest. Andrade pulled into the driveway and stopped just past the office. A lone vehicle was parked in the rear.

"You stay here," she said, "and pull the truck behind the building."

Elena walked into the office, but no one came to the front desk. The office was unfinished; the walls had sheetrock up, but no paint. She heard what she thought were boxes being opened in a backroom. She walked back there and came upon a native dressed woman opening boxes of linens.

"Hi."

The woman was startled. "Oh, you scared me."

"I'm sorry. I was wondering if this place was open for business?"

"No, we won't be ready until the end of May."

She quickly searched through the accumulation of random facts she'd built up over the years, looking for a point of contact. "Cree?"

The woman smiled. "Chinook."

"Ah, the river people."

"You sound like you know the first nations."

"I read a lot, it interests me. Are you here by yourself, do you live around here?"

"No I don't live here, this land was donated to our tribe, and we're turning it into a hunting lodge. The area's full of game—elk, moose, beaver, black and brown bear. I actually live about three hours north of Kamloops, but I'm staying here in one of the finished cabins."

Elena dialed up a nervous look. "You're not frightened being out here alone?"

The woman laughed. "These woods are like my living room, comfortable and homey. Besides, my husband comes down every Friday and checks on what's been done and what I may need."

"Oh I see, so in a couple of days your husband will be here?"

"Yes."

Elena made it painless. A quick chop to the back of the neck and she fell unconscious on top of the boxes she had been opening.

Elena picked up the woman's purse and fished out her keys. She walked out the front door of the cabin, then stopped, and turned around. They were not far from civilization. The woman could wake up. Someone else could come. The risk was small, but real.

Elena went back into the storeroom and put one round through the unconscious woman's skull. Then she left, locking the door behind her and throwing the keys into the woods.

"Andrade park the truck on the other side of that last cabin, so it can't be seen from the main road, and get all of our stuff ready to put in this nice Suburban."

She started the car up and drove over to where Andrade had parked the Toyota. They stowed all their gear in the new vehicle, and returned to the main road. Elena didn't talk about what had happened, and Andrade didn't ask. But for the first time in many years, she felt wrong …about a necessary kill.

She had no time for this now. She noticed there was a full tank of gas, so they wouldn't have to stop before Prince George. Good. There was no chance of somebody recognizing the woman's car.

"Hey I think somebody is trying to flag us down, he's flashing his lights on and off."

The officer pulled his patrol car to the side of the road and rolled down his window.

"I hear that Ned Crites was murdered last night."

"Yeah that's right. You have some information?"

"Yeah unfortunately I think I do. Two people a man, and a sharp looking lady, came by the worksite yesterday asking for directions on how to get to Highway 97. I noticed that their truck looked like Ned's and she said they'd bought it off him, that Gloria had thrown a fit and made him sell it."

"Did they say where they were going?"

"Yeah. She said they were headed to Spokane."

"I need you to sit here in the patrol car and give a complete description of those two people to this officer."

"Yes, sir."

After he got the description, the lead detective got out of the patrol car and called his partner.

"Okay we've identified the people, they are on the run, possibly headed south on 97 for Spokane. Call that in and alert highway officers to be on the lookout for a male and a female, both Caucasians. She's about 5'7", streaked blond hair, and the male is 6'1" or 6'2" about 195 lbs, muscular, black hair."

"Got it, I'll call it in right now."

"We're going on down the road and check to see if anybody saw anything else."

After the worker got out of the patrol car they proceeded further down the road until they came to a T intersection and saw the sign for Grimmers Petrol Pit Stop. It was the wrong way if you wanted to get to 97, but the detective wanted to check it out anyway.

Paydirt. The old lady told them about the hundred dollar bills and all the supplies she bought, nothing out of the ordinary she thought. The detective called his partner and said have the main office pick him up at the 97 junction.

Elena and Andrade passed through Kamloops around 10:30 in the morning. She was making good time, keeping the Suburban at 85 mph, but they were running into a construction zone and would have to slow down. Elena asked Andrade to take out a shirt or something and roll it up in the window so it would block his passenger window. They were about three hours from Prince George.

Andrade was busy working on the police band radio he took out of Crites truck, trying to hook it up through the radio antenna of the suburban.

"Hey, there you go it's working."

"Great, start scanning, see if our friends are around."

An RCMP helicopter swooped in near the 97 junction and picked up the lead inspector. There was another man in the helicopter he introduced himself.

"Hi I'm David Royals, RCMP Special Investigations Unit."

"So to what do we owe the honor of your visit, inspector?"

"Well it seems the boys down in the US have got a problem. There are two Russian agents on the run with extremely important information that the US doesn't want them to have. They caught up with them day before yesterday near Chelan Lake, and shot the hell out of their plane, but didn't bring it down, at least not right away. Our forest service spotted a downed plane about twenty miles due east of Chelan this morning. Looks like the pilot was hit during the firefight and died at the scene, but there were definitely two survivors. They set out on a trek that would have taken them directly to your boy Crites worksite."

"Here inspector take a look at this casing, tell me what you think?"

Royals looked at it closely turned it around several times, then looked closely at the rim damage from the firing pin.

"My friend what you have there is a .40 caliber bullet casing. It came from a Russian handgun that former KGB field agents carried."

"Are you telling me Crites was killed by Russian agents?"

"That's about the whole truth and nothing but the truth my friend. And they're not headed for Spokane. They're headed up the coast to either a plane drop or a boat pick up. The top dog for the US, an agent Crossbow— funny name for an agent—anyway, he believes they will try for the coast with a private plane and get picked up by a Russian trawler disguised as an American fishing vessel. We are going to blanket all the small airports between here and Prince George. Crossbow says they're probably not driving Crites' vehicle by now."

"Christ. They killed Crites just for his truck?"

"Crossbow says the female is a notorious agent with a long history with the KGB. She has been dubbed the Black Widow, because of her penchant for killing male agents after she beds them down.

Crossbow said shoot her at a distance, don't even think about taking her on at close range. Nasty sort it seems."

Royals broadcast the alert to all field officers.

"Did you hear that, Elena," Andrade said. "They are after us."

"What is David Royals doing here? He was SIS in London six years ago?"

Elena decided she was going to stop immediately and get gas. She had to think. After filling the tank, she drove around thirty miles north of Prince George and pulled into a rest stop.

"Elena what are we doing here?"

"Andrade, I'm trying to figure out a way to get us out of this."

"Simple really," he said. "Get on your cell phone call this hotel right now." He handed her a brochure from the stack she had picked up at the first gas stop. "See if they have a room in Queen Charlotte for tonight and tomorrow night. If they do make a reservation, since they are looking for a man and a woman, when we arrive at the ferry in Prince Rupert, we split up. You take the car on the ferry to the hotel and check in. I'll stay behind and take the next ferry alone, and I'll sneak into the room. You'll need to signal what room you are in by placing a note on the window that has the initials AK. That way I don't have to ask at the front desk and be seen.

"We have plenty of food in the grocery bags. If we want room service one of us stays hidden while it is delivered. We do not leave the room and we do not want cleaning service the next morning. Tomorrow night around 10:15 we get into the car and drive to Masset, and wait in the car at the dock until the boat arrives. That way no one will spot us."

"What a team we make," she said. "I love you, that's brilliant."

She called a hotel in Queen Charlotte and booked a first floor room for two nights. Once that was done she pulled back onto the highway and sped off toward Prince Rupert. Andrade was listening to the police scanner for any signs of progress.

When they reached Prince Rupert, Andrade picked up a call from a patrolman indicating they had found Ned Crites truck and a native woman who had been fatally shot. He reported they had taken her car and he passed along the description of the vehicle.

"Okay change of plans," he said. "We have to ditch this car, and take the ferry on foot. So, here's what we'll do. We'll unload everything from the car over there, you stay with it, call a taxi and have him load your things into his cab and take the ferry to the hotel. I'll take the car and hide it somewhere, then get back here and take the ferry at a later time. Be sure and put the signal in the window."

"Thank you for being there when I needed you Andrade, it means so much to me."

Andrade dropped Elena off by a waiting area with their bags, and drove off into the night to find a place to hide the automobile. He found a place that in his experience with the St. Petersburg car thieves, had worked so often when trying to hide a stolen vehicle— he put it in a corner of the Prince Rupert Police station parking lot, facing the building so no one could see the tags. He figured they would overlook it for days. He walked back to the ferry station and took the next one to Queen Charlotte. As he walked up to the hotel there was a sign in a room window with a big AK and a heart scribbled on it. Now it was just a matter of waiting until midnight tomorrow night and they would be on their way home.

Andrade gave Elena a long backrub to soothe her aching muscles.

"Andrade this is heaven, it feels so good."

"Elena tell me about yourself. Where were you born, your parents, your schooling? I want to know more about you."

"I was born in Pripyat. My mother was a street conductor on an inner city trolley, and my father was a slaughter house employee. I went to visit my grandmother in Moscow during the week that the nuclear plant had the accident and never saw my parents alive after that date. I was four."

"I'm so sorry. They died in the accident?"

"Not easily. They received, what turned out to be lethal doses of radiation poisoning. They literally rotted away from the inside. I was never allowed to visit them in their hospital."

"Oh, Elena…"

"I was placed with my grandmother in Moscow. I excelled at studies and gymnastics, until I was fourteen. That's when my grandmother died. I was sent to a special school for gifted students and kept up my school work and gymnastics. I remember I always competed hard against the boys at school and most of the time I beat them. Until Boris Krenko came to the school. He was a bully and he was faster than me. One day he came up behind me and put his hand under my dress and tried to pull my panties off. I was so mad, I turned around and hit him square in the face and knocked him out. It felt good, I was so proud of myself. The teacher on the playground only saw me hit him; she didn't see him trying to grope me. I was sent to the discipline office of the school and given a spanking with a leather belt. I refused to cry, because I knew I was right in defending myself and said so.

"That got me sent to the school psychologist. He looked at my academic record and athletic achievements and said he might have a special program that I may be interested in. It would more fully utilize my skills. I was given the address of this huge building in Moscow and a person to see. He put me through all kinds of tests. The staff asked me questions and wanted to see how I would react. They ran me through an obstacle course for three days in a row and each day the course got a little more difficult. I was put on a treadmill and they let it run for almost an hour some fast, some slow speeds.

"Every day there were the interviews over and over, sometimes three or four a day. Some were just asking how I felt about that day's activities. Then other days it got personal, like they would ask me if I had ever seen a penis, and what did I think of a penis, have you ever looked at your own vagina, have you ever thought about kissing another girl or wondered about what her vagina looked like. I was definitely not a candidate to become a lesbian. After nearly a week a man came to see me, a huge man with a big handle bar mustache. He told me I was an extraordinary young lady and they had a very special program that served Mother Russia in the highest possible way. They would escalate my schooling and physical development, and I would have the finest instructors and trainers in the world.

"Then he took me outside in the yard and pointed to a rabbit in a hutch. It was fat and grey, with ears that flopped over and a pink nose that never stopped moving. 'I want you to do something for me. You see that rabbit over there? It has a disease that could kill all of us at this facility. I want you to kill it before it can harm anyone.'

"He gave me an automatic 9mm Walther PPK and showed me how to hold it and fire it. My first two shots missed, but I realized how to correct and then pumped the rest into the rabbit at a very a fast rate of fire. He came over and took the gun from me and asked how I felt. I told him the truth, that I felt nothing. He had this big smile on his face and put his arm around my shoulder and walked me back into the building and told me that my training started the next day."

"That Andrade was the beginning of my KGB career. I became a specialist in foreign intelligence, a master marksman, a 3rd degree black belt in Tae Kwon Do, I speak German, French, and English."

Andrade said nothing of what he felt. He could now see that, despite her apparent lack of emotion, telling these personal details had cost Elena. And he was grateful for her trust in him. He would not push it not now. "Speaking of English, how did you acquire that New York accent? It is nearly perfect?"

"I watched American movies like the 'Godfather' and reruns of 'The Untouchables.'"

"Did you actually want to be a secret agent?"

"No, not at first, not until I saw my first James Bond movie with Sean Connery. I thought he was so dashing and so talented. I think I had my first orgasm thinking about him making love to me."

"What did you think of your first orgasm?"

She laughed. "Honestly? It scared the hell out of me. I thought I had worked myself up so much thinking about him I was having a heart attack, and would die a young teen."

Andrade laughed.

"Did you ever see the man that brought you into the program again?"

"Sure. He's still my handler. His name is Petrov Ingosich."

"The senior guy at the FSB?"

"That's him."

"What a story your life has been Elena."

She rolled over and put her arms around his neck. "My love, now that I have met you, my story is just beginning."

They kissed each other with passion and made love until both were exhausted, then both enjoyed a long restful sleep.

Elena and Andrade did as he had suggested, they stayed in the room all day. Elena decided they would leave their clothes and bags behind. They would pack the backpack with their guns and ammunition, the remaining $35,000 in US dollars and a few odds and ends of clothing. Andrade suggested they not call a cab company. It was too easy to trace their movements. Instead he said they should watch for someone coming in around 10:00 p.m. and parking their car. He would go out and break in and hotwire the ignition. That way they could drive to Masset on their own. Staying in the car would let them wait for the trawler without drawing attention to themselves.

It was important that they not get there too early, maybe fifteen minutes or so. She agreed but under no circumstances could they be late. Elena had called a local restaurant in Masset to ask about the layout of the dock and harbor, and was told that the there was a parking lot that let you walk straight to the dock. She asked if big ships and boats come in there very often, and the person indicated there was a commercial fishing fleet that docks there all the time.

And even better, it had started to rain. Good cover for their movements.

It was 9:00 p.m. when one of the agents Crossbow had dispatched to Prince Rupert rolled into the local police department to ask if anything unusual had happened in the last few days. On his way out he noticed a car parked in the shadows of the parking lot. It was the Suburban. He immediately called Crossbow to tell him he had located the car.

"Are you near?"

"No I'm standing under a door stop at the police department."

"Go out and feel the hood."

The agent stepped out into the rain and checked the hood.

"It's cold sir."

"Did you find any leads out on the islands?"

"No sir, we haven't gotten out there yet. We've been concentrating our efforts on the city and surrounding neighborhoods."

"Get your goddamn ass over to Queen Charlotte Island, right now."

"Sir, there is no one to take us there, and the last ferry to the island leaves in five minutes."

"Well, I suggest you get on that ferry right now, call me back when you arrive."

"Yes, sir."

Agent Carl Beeks sprinted through the rain to the ferry dock and hopped on board at the last moment. He didn't even have time to notify his partner, who was interviewing people at a restaurant two blocks away. Once he was settled on board for the two hour trip to Queen Charlotte Island he called his partner and filled him in on what Crossbow had ordered him to do.

"Hey, remember, cowboy, don't try and take these people by yourself."

"Yeah, I know. Shoot her from a distance." Beeks closed his phone, then used it to tap into the internet and did a little research. Then he walked toward the wheelhouse of the ferry.

"Where do the big commercial fishing boats dock? He asked. At Skidgate?"

"No, they dock at Masset. Is that where you wanted to go?"

"Yeah, I'm a paramedic. The crab boat *Finnigan's Hope* has an injured deck hand. I'm supposed to meet them in an hour."

"No problem, where is your medical bag?"

"I left it in the customer lounge, although most of the boats have just as much stuff as I do in their on board kits."

"I know the skipper of the Finnigan's, his deckhand must be really hurt. The whole crew is tough as nails and one of the best crabbers in the Northwest. Look, you and two other people are the only ones aboard. It only takes about fifteen minutes out of our way."

"I really appreciate that, the injured sailor will too."

At 11:15 the ferry dropped the agent off at the docks in Masset. It was pouring, and visibility was down to next to nothing. Not a good time to start looking. On the other hand, it was a small island.

Andrade had commandeered a guest's auto, as he'd planned. They left early because of the rain. They arrived at the docks at around 11:15, and Elena immediately noticed the ferry. She had asked the day before if it stopped at Masset and was told it only went to Skidgate.

"Andrade, something is wrong. That ferry doesn't make stops here."

"A lone man just got off and is walking down the dock toward us. Look he is on a cell phone in the rain. That's an agent."

"You're right. Pull the car out from under this light, over there in the shadows."

Elena jumped out immediately and crouched down behind the fender of the car.

Beeks had stopped at a tavern on the dock that was just about to close for the night, and struck up a conversation with the employee who was stacking the chairs for the night. It was 11:35 when he and the employee emerged from the place. He stood near the front looking for protection against the rain. The employee walked up to the parking lot, got in his car, and drove off. No one else was in sight.

He was about to call in to Crossbow when something hit him on the back of the head. The agent collapsed on the dock at Elena's feet. She put away her gun, checked to make sure he was breathing, then signaled Andrade, who brought the backpack to where the agent was lying.

She scrounged some rope—always lying around a dock. "Here tie him up, feet and hands. We're going to put him in the bed of that boat with a canvas covering. Help me pick him up."

They carried him over to the boat, lifted up the canvas cover and threw him in. He was starting to come to and made a muffled sound.

"Andrade, get the backpack. Hurry."

She pulled out a pair of her panties and shoved them into his mouth as a gag.

"Now don't you get too excited smelling my underwear," she said with a slightly exaggerated Russian accent. "And be sure and tell Crossbow he can kiss my Russian ass."

She covered the agent with the canvas and they walked to the end of the dock.

It was 11:59 when they spotted the boat in the distance. It flashed three times from its forward deck light. On time as always.

Once aboard, the captain told them it would take nearly eight hours to reach international waters, where they would rendezvous with a Russian sub. The commander of the sub would take them to Murmansk. From there they would fly to Moscow, everything was arranged. They could relax for the next few days.

"I would have never made it without you," she told Andrade when they were together in the tiny mate's cabin. "We are a great team and we accomplished our mission, now it's on to Moscow my love."

Crossbow was on his way by helicopter to Masset. He hadn't heard from the agent in over two hours. He landed in the middle of the Masset town square at 4:20 a.m. and, with several agents in tow, went immediately to the docks. He could hear muffled and faint yelling coming from a boat resting on the beach next to the dock. He ripped back the canvas to reveal one of their own bound and gagged, with women's underwear stuffed in his mouth. There were scattered snickers from the other agents.

"Drop the humor," Crossbow said. "He's lucky to be alive, and we just lost two Russian agents in possession of vital US secrets. There's nothing funny about any of this."

After they untied the agent, Crossbow asked him if she'd said anything.

"Yes sir, but I would rather not repeat it in front of all these guys, it's kind of personal."

"Beeks don't be ashamed. You were by yourself, and as I said, you are one lucky man that she didn't put a bullet in your head, what did she say?"

"Well sir, she said for me not to get excited at smelling her underwear."

"And she had a message for you sir. She said for you to kiss her Russian ass, uh sir."

Now there was silence. Crossbow could only grit his teeth.

Before he lost it in front of his men, he stormed off, his fists clenched, to the waiting helicopter.

Alex and Sandi would soon find out that there was no relaxation in their future. The entire military echelon of the US was buzzing with the news that General Alex Hanken was now heading up the most powerful arsenal known to man. He knew the logic of how it was happening. He needed to prepare for the event and do it damn quickly, and that meant that he had to have a lot of power that he could wield quickly and without fuss. And far too soon, any day now, in fact the news of the coming asteroids might leak and he might actually have to turn some of that power toward defending everything he'd built. The future of humanity.

But it still seemed like a bad dream. Less than six months ago he was a retired two-star hero of Desert Storm——How did this happen? And why him? Had the President, and more importantly, Torrance lost their collective minds?

The suspicions in the ranks of the military grew, but Alex was able to win over the key leaders, not only of the country, but the mission critical military personnel as well. So far, he'd been able to do the job, as much as he wished he didn't have to.

But he had the feeling it was only going to get worse.

Chapter 22

THE POWER

A lex eased the Lear into the parking spot at Andrews AFB as a team of Navy Seals came sprinting out to the plane.

"General sir, we have a convoy waiting for you," their commander said. "Please come this way."

Alex and Sandi were whisked away to the White House. After arriving they were taken to the Oval office where the President and Admiral Torrance were waiting. Sandi needed to excuse herself and a Secret Service agent along with agent Somers escorted her to the ladies room. Alex asked agent Evans to stay outside the door of the Oval office.

Admiral Torrance shook Alex's hand. "Alex how was the flight?"

"Good admiral, smooth all the way. Fighter hand offs went like clockwork. Colonel Cole did his usual outstanding job."

The President stood at his desk and extended his hand and they all sat down.

"Is Sandi with you?"

"Yes, she's in the ladies room."

"Good, I wanted to say this in private." The President paused. "General Hanken, it was once said by a Roman general that great events bring out great men. Admiral Torrance and I have watched you perform at a level far exceeding our expectations. Your ability to anticipate difficulties, to conceptualize a mission, and then put the appropriate resources in place to accomplish the mission has been remarkable. Your communication skills with Group, Division, and battalion commanders are reportedly excellent. We have heard nothing but the highest praise for you from your counterparts in the military services, and that is what we are here to talk about."

Torrance got up from his chair and strolled around the Oval office, stopping right next to the seated President. Standing tall and looking down at Alex.

"The President and I feel that you should take the reins in tandem with us," the Admiral said. "You know firsthand how we're reorganized and the field people are comfortable with you. The President has the power under the War Powers Act to appoint a civilian and/or military person to head up all military operations in a particular theater.

"Your command headquarters will be at Peterson AFB in Colorado Springs. You will assume joint command of NORAD and all the Sac Bases. Yes that means you will have your finger on the trigger. You and the President alone will have that power. The West Coast Seal teams should be housed at your facility at Peterson.

"The sea borne naval units will remain under my control here at the Pentagon, and naval aviation stations will stay under Admiral Halsey, yes that would be Bull Halsey's great grandson, if you were wondering."

It took a moment for Alex to speak. "I appreciate your confidence in me and I will start on reorganizing the units into complimentary divisions and spread our risk so to speak."

"Alex you have any questions?"

"Well, not so much a question, as an observation. I'm wondering how this will play out politically here at home. And how will our allies and enemies react to this concentration of military power? If I'm a congressman, I immediately call the President and ask who is this General Hanken, and why have you given him so much power? The Senate Armed Services Committee will undoubtedly scream bloody murder over this and grill both of you. Is there something I'm missing?

The President and Admiral Torrance looked at each other and smiled. The President spoke.

"Valid point, Alex," the President said. "We've met with congressional leaders in secret and assured them of your capabilities, and our complete and unwavering confidence in your ability to react to a situation or threat in accordance with prescribed directives. Our key congressional leaders have come on board with our position. Alex, I know all of this seems sudden, but you know what we'll be facing. We don't know how communications will survive, and we need someone knowledgeable and trustworthy to make decisions if thing go south. Sometimes you find a diamond in the unlikeliest places, and I rely on Admiral Torrance's vast military experience."

"Mr. President, Admiral, please don't confuse my concerns, with doubts about my mission. I'm an American, and a patriot, putting all else aside, I will do the right thing for this country."

"We have absolute confidence that you will Alex," the Admiral added.

"Your designation will be Grand Palace when you're flying. That's the current designation of the backup plane. The plane is waiting at Andrews for you and your party to board, and by the way, tell Sandi that her daughter Elizabeth is on the way to Peterson right now in the company of two FBI agents."

"Thank you Admiral. Good day Mr. President."

Sandi had been dutifully sitting outside the Oval Office with Somers and Evans waiting and wondering what was under discussion for so long.

"Alex can you tell me what is going on?"

"Not now Sandi. On the plane when we are underway."

Alex directed the Seal team to sit by the doors, and the FBI agents to sit in the section behind the Seals, and he told agent Somers not to pick on the Seals, just for a laugh. Sandi and Alex took their seats next to the Presidential suite. After they were air-borne, Alex and Sandi retreated to the private suite.

"Okay," she said, "you look worried. What's wrong?"

Alex held up a huge stack of papers that Admiral Torrance had given him.

"These are force strength reports for NORAD and the Strate-gic Air Command. I've been put in charge of the nuclear arsenal.

"Dear God, what does all of this mean Alex?"

"It means I have enough power at my fingertips to destroy any country at will. I've got to take a couple of days and sit down and figure how I'm going to deploy all these men and their equipment and at the same time provide shelter and food for the aftermath. This is like being in a whirlwind with a thousand documents flying around and you've got to get them in order… and quickly. Going from a retired officer to one of the most pow-erful military leaders in this country,—it just doesn't seem real to me nor plausible. Am I missing something here? Why would Torrance agree to allow the President to appoint me as the next in command, to be shared with him? They say they want triple redundancy. I just can't fathom why they're doing this so late in the game."

"I think," she said, "that you close your eyes now, and I'll give you a neck rub. You need to relax."

He sank into a leather swivel chair, and she began to work on the knots in his neck. She was right, this was the answer.

"You sell yourself short too often," she said. "You are a remark-able man, with superior skills in organization. People respect you, you have a command presence about yourself, and you always seize the initiative. The President and Admiral Torrance know this, they've seen it, they have hundreds of other officers to choose from with more time in the active service than you, but you alone bring all the right qualities to the table for this critical time in our nation's history. They wouldn't give you this much power if they didn't have complete confidence that you could not only handle the pressure, but would execute with certainty and professional-ism."

"Admiral Torrance said to tell you hi, and Liz is on her way to Peterson field right now in the company of two FBI agents."

"They took her out of school?"

"I guess."

"Uh, we may have a small problem when we get there. I'm not sure how she'll react."

"Well mom, she's your daughter."

"Oh no you don't. She's our problem now."

"Well as Scarlett said in Gone With The Wind, 'Tomorrow's another day.'"

There was a brass band and greeting entourage at the airstrip with the congratulatory handshakes and salutes. Then there was Elizabeth, Sandi's daughter. She came running, crying hysterically and claiming that she had been kidnapped and held captive by government agents. She looked at Alex.

"He ordered it didn't he, and you've been brainwashed, that's why you're still with him?"

"Liz calm down," Sandi said. "I'll explain everything to you, let's just get to the house, and unwind from a very long trip."

Curt and Cynthia rushed to Alex on the tarmac.

"Dad are you okay, we were worried about you did you hear about the Russian agents, and I'm sorry is that Air Force One?"

"Okay by the numbers. Yes, we're fine. And yes we heard about the Russian agents, and no, that is Air Force Two. It's how we travel now."

"What Russian agents?" Liz asked.

"Elizabeth, I'm sorry that you were pulled out of school against your will. I had nothing to do with it, the order came directly from the President before I was informed of the Russian agent situation. Now let's all get to the house and get settled in, and I'll tell everyone what's up." A major stepped forward.

"Sir, where did you want the Seals to be housed for the night?"

"What is the closest barracks to our living quarters?"

"That would be the temporary officers billeting."

"And what is it used for?"

"Parents, friends, girlfriends, and boyfriends of cadets attending the Academy."

"Major, the practice of subsidizing the social life of cadets while they're schooling is paid for by the US Taxpayer is hereby rescinded. You see to it that these men are properly billeted and cared for. These men are operating under direct orders from the Chairman of the Joint Chiefs, Admiral Torrance, do you understand?"

"Yes, sir."

Alex asked the team leader of the Seals contingent, a lieutenant commander Morris, to post two men at the entrance of the dwelling 24/7, eight hour shifts, no double shifts, he wanted people frosty while on duty. Alex informed him that he knew some of the men would feel bored with this job, that babysitting him and his family would seem like a letdown. But their mission was a critical one.

"General," Morris said, "when Admiral Torrance comes to your base and personally picks me and nine others out of two hundred to carry out a mission that he sees vital to the national interests of this nation, then we don't care if it's policing a playground."

"Thank you and welcome aboard our team. I'll fill all of you in tomorrow. Right now, let's all get some rest."

"Yes sir."

Alex drove to the residence with the Major who handled base housing.

"Major, I've got four Seal teams coming here, that's close to sixty men. We need to put them someplace. I want you to contact the head of FEMA and get two hundred of those disaster trailers sitting in Texas doing nothing, and I want them up here pronto."

"Yes, sir. How should I say this is authorized?"

"You tell them that General Hanken ordered it. We're on a timeline that doesn't allow me or anyone working with me the luxury of dealing with a bureaucratic system. My needs are immediate and are always related to the national security of this country. Remember that and you'll do fine. While you're asking about those

two hundred trailers ask them how many are in current inventory there and the rest of the country?"

Once they had arrived at the residence the Major began showing all of them around the castle, as Curt would come to refer to it. Three master suites, six guest bedrooms, a giant den with a massive fireplace, comfortable seating for up to twenty people, three private offices, a huge kitchen and dining room to feed twenty people, and an underground bunker accessed by elevator.

The 18,000 square foot house was built in 1964-65 at a cost then of twenty seven million dollars. The costs soared as then President Johnson wanted it on the base, yet he wanted it built into the side of a mountain and secured from the outside in the event of war. The outside frame of the house incorporated a steel shutter system that essentially sealed the house from the outside world.

Alex wanted full communication capability from the house as well as the command center at the base. That meant Curt needed to upgrade the computer and communications systems, not done since the Clinton administration. Alex also wanted a fully redundant computer system that could communicate with SAC and NORAD commands, as well as all Air Force installations with nuclear weapons delivery capability.

"Jeez Dad, are you setting up a dual command system. Why?"

"Curt, what did they teach you in Boy Scouts?"

"Okay, okay, I know, always be prepared."

Once the base logistics were underway. Alex flew every commander of each unit to Colorado Springs for a two-day meeting to debrief them on Project O.N.E.—let them know of the threat and the need for troops on the ground in the US, both before and afterward. Once the shock had passed, Alex could see the commitment in their faces and knew he had them on his team. Having all the branches there at once also helped the team concept begin to gel. By the second day he had a focused and dedicated group of leaders who would carry out this monumental task before them.

By the end of May he had submitted his reorganization plan to Admiral Torrance.

"Alex"

"Admiral sir, how are you?"

"After reviewing your report I'm doing fine. Alex, as usual an outstanding plan, especially integrating the 101st Airborne and the 1st Special forces together into eight different fighting battalions spread out from the west to the Midwest. Tank and helicopter support, air support, artillery batteries, it's just amazing. What was your thought behind this?"

"At first I broached the idea with your Chief of Staff, General Leemon. He was— how can I say— reluctant to go along with that reorganization and I had to do some real hard convincing to win him over."

"So how did you win him over?"

"I appealed to his strategic side. I put him in several scenarios post event and asked him how he would respond. I think it finally sunk in that a smaller, highly trained, and integrated force could respond quicker and with a broad range of specialties to meet nearly every contingency."

"Brad Leemon is a good soldier, I'm sure he wasn't trying to bully you. These guys have been hit with a lot in the last few months. But, Alex you handled it well. Now, you were explaining your rationale."

"The way I looked at it we couldn't defend both coasts at the same time either pre or post event. I would rely on your naval forces to slow down, if not destroy, any enemy coming from the east or southeast. If they did come ashore we would stop them at the Mississippi then drive them back to the Atlantic. If they came to the west coast, well heaven help them."

"Excellent, Alex. This allows me to concentrate my naval power to the east coast and southeast Gulf. Now the big question…when do you think this will be accomplished?"

"I have a timeline for you coming by courier, but my projections have a drop dead date of June 30 for all my divisions to be in place and operational."

"Forty-five days? Is that enough time?"

"I believe it is. Work's already underway, and not one base or unit is behind schedule. The rail yards are humming and the skies are filled with C-130's and C-17's."

"I know. Yesterday at the President's press briefing several questions came up about the unprecedented troop and material movements underway within the US. The President seemed to handle it quite well. Here's the reason I asked about the timeline, we've decided that we need to stress test the whole survival network before we really need it. All facilities will assume post event posture, close their doors and facilities to civilians, only assigned personnel will be allowed in. For the next forty-eight hours we will stress computer and communications systems, food distribution and preparation, water source checks, power systems, air purification systems, the whole thing. The President and his cabinet will go to their bunker, and the congress will go to their bunkers and spend the next two days experiencing what it will be like to live there."

As far as Torrance was concerned, the congress was a waste of time, there were a lot more important people than them, but he knew the President had insisted they be brought in otherwise there would be hell to pay. Besides, when Mount Weather was funded, congress, at that time saw to it that sufficient bunkers were built to house them and their staffs.

"How are you going to get all of those people to take two days off?"

"We aren't. The test is scheduled for the first week in August, that's the President's and Congress' holiday month. And the President has got the House Speaker and the Senate Majority leader already on board for the test. Most if not all of Congress will be at their assigned locations. That's why I asked if you are certain of the completion dates."

"Yes sir. I have a very high level of confidence that we will be ready several weeks before the scheduled test."

"Good. The overseas redeployment is almost complete, Korea, Japan and the Asian sites are done, most of Europe and all the

Middle East are completed. It's just a matter of weeks. We are getting record numbers that are coming back and opting out under the $10,000 bonus plan, so we're trimming our force levels to an appropriate size to accomplish our self-defense mission. That suggestion you had about the $25,000 plan for married personnel did the trick. We're now at a level of strength that I can feel confident about saying these are the best of the best. Alex, I'll let you know as soon as we've finalized our test date."

"Thank you Admiral."

Alex hung up. It looked like he might actually be doing it, creating a survival system that might keep humanity alive. But at what cost?

The worst times in all this nightmarish craziness were the ones that came right now. When he could immerse himself in the frantic details of the projects, he was all right—or at least manageable. But it was in the quiet times, when he pulled back and looked at the big picture, that he ran the risk of losing it.

If the US was attacked before the event, he could manage that—soldiers fighting soldiers. Except that the foreign troops, if they came, would be joined by armies of panicked civilians, as word got out. Would the police, National Guard, the Army continue to keep the peace in cities around the country if they knew their time was numbered? No. His fighting force, which looked so powerful on paper, might essentially have to fight off the rest of the world as it clamored to get one of the safe seats when the disaster hit. And he had to fight that fight with all his heart. If the bunkers were destroyed—which could well happen—then humanity was over.

And post-event? There would be survivors by the millions. Food stores would last a while, but with agriculture shut down, it would only be a matter of time, and they would know it. What would they do? Camp outside the bunkers and beg? Battle among themselves for the surviving resources? Blow it all in one huge, self-destructive orgy? All of the above?

No, there was no getting around it. The world was heading for hell, and he had to make sure there was something left afterwards.

He got back to work.

Chapter 23

THE PRELUDE

 ★ ★ ★ ★

Don Cray was not a happy camper when told that both Russian agents had escaped, because he would have to report that to Arlen Hendry, and he in turn would tell Admiral Torrance.

But when he told Torrance about the agents' escape, Torrance only said, "Well no matter. Things are in place or will be in place that would negate any discovery of the cover-up."

Russian President Vladimir Kleskova convened a meeting with the military heads of the Army, Air Force, and Navy along with Konstatin Bocovich and Petrov Ingosich of External Affairs.

"Gentlemen, we have a grave situation before us. Intelligence reports recently received have provided a picture of total reorganization within the United States military, leaving one man in command of a force that rivals our own. Each of you has before you a binder with all the pertinent facts regarding the restructure that has taken place and the appointment of General Alexander Hanken as the commander of these various military units. Your opinions please?"

"Mr. President," the Naval Fleet Admiral said, "this new General, has NORAD, the Space Systems Command, and SAC Headquarters. He has control of all the remaining nuclear warheads in the United States arsenal. He literally doesn't need the President to make war."

"That was my thought as well Admiral. The question is why?"

"I am looking at his tactical forces, all of these air bases, his helicopter inventory, his tank and mobile artillery corps—it rivals Patton's 3rd Army during WWII," the Marshall of the Armed Forces observed.

"And yet," the admiral said, "I don't see this as a threat to our country."

"How so Admiral?"

"We have been watching the movements of submarines out of the Pacific, and they are showing up along the east coast of the US, I think they have an east coast/west coast defense strategy. Their submarine group will act as the deterrent for the east and southeast borders and General Hanken's divisions will bring to bear his formidable resources on any aggressor that is foolish enough to try a western or northwestern attack. It would be suicide. No, I think the United States has moved into an isolationist mode, and they are reorganizing into a defensive posture."

"But have they given so much power to one man? And why have we never heard of this man before? This has never been done before in the history of the United States. Is this about the asteroid threat?"

"Mr. President," Ingosich said, "we have examined the possibility of the asteroid threat from all angles, literally. Our telescopes can find no signs of incoming asteroids. I cannot explain why the Americans are doing this, but I'm confident we can rule that threat out."

"Gentleman," the Admiral said, "the real power behind all this is the Chairman of the Joint Chiefs, Admiral Evan Torrance. He handpicked Hanken, and as all of you know, President Betts does whatever Torrance says."

"This is why I brought all of you together, to look at a dilemma before us. Is this even a threat, and if it is, how do we to combat it?"

"Director Bocovich, I want you to send those two agents that uncovered so much about General Hanken back in, and have them find out more about Hanken and his plans. We need to know what's going on there."

"We have already arranged for a reinsertion around the first of August," Bocovich said.

"Very well gentlemen, we are done for now. But we are just getting started on determining just who this General Hanken is and why he's receiving such unprecedented power."

Bocovich and Ingosich returned to their offices and discussed the reentry of Elena and Andrade into the United States.

"I am concerned Director, that we are pushing our luck with these two. They were extremely lucky to get out with their lives last time, and they are now known as working in tandem."

"And yet the President specifically mentioned sending those two. If we were to send another pair, and the mission failed, we would be shot as traitors."

"I see, then let me work on a plan. We have a few weeks before August is here."

Alex had completed his morning calls when Sandi came in.

"Liz is furious."

"Okay. What now?"

"Someone from the university told her that her degree had been conferred, even though she hadn't completed her final two classes and thesis. So she knew something was wrong and came to me and said she wanted you to stop interfering in her life."

"Sandi, I swear, I had nothing to do with this."

At about that time, Alex's door to his office swung open and it was Liz.

"Did you tell him Mom?"

Alex had enough of Liz's complaining. He had heard from Cynthia that she was nearly impossible to work with, and that all she ever did was find fault with everyone else's work. Alex stood up abruptly and startled both Sandi and Liz.

"How dare you barge into my office uninvited. And my name is not "him." My name is Alex. You need to sit down, shut your mouth, and open your ears for what I have to say to you.

Liz dropped into a chair like a poleaxed steer. So did Sandi.

Alex dialed it back, but just a bit. "First, I knew nothing of your being removed from school and brought here in protective custody. That was a direct order from the President of the United States. If you want to complain, take it up with him. Second, there were two Russian agents that had tracked me down to find out the nature of my mission. These agents ended up killing two innocent Americans, and almost killing Curt and Cynthia. They went on to Canada to make their escape and left two more bodies in their wake."

"Oh," Liz said. "You know, I had no idea—"

"Of course you didn't, because you spend most of your time whining about your perceived predicament, oh poor me. Let me tell you something young lady, we are facing the possible extinction of the human race, and you're walking around worried about your goddamn degree. You need to get perspective, get over your pity party, and get focused on what really counts. Quite frankly you've become a subtraction, not an addition to our team, and I will kick your butt back to your beloved university in a heartbeat. And when the Russian agents come calling this time—and they will be back—you can deal with them yourself. You try and explain to them how your life is so screwed up, and see if they give a damn. Now you get out of here and don't ever come in my office and show me such disrespect again. I have much more important things to do than baby-sit a twenty-two year old going on eleven, now go!"

She left quickly and closed the door quietly.

Sandi was staring at him. He wasn't sure if that was a good thing or not.

"Look," he said, "I'm sorry if I came off a little—"

"Why didn't I have you around ten years ago? Her teen years would have been much easier for me."

He slumped back into this chair.

"I'll try and make some time for her. Now that I've jumped at her, maybe a little tenderness might help her make the transition easier."

"Alex Hanken, you may be tough, but you are also a teddy bear when it counts."

She kissed him on the forehead. He looked up at those smoky blue eyes of hers and the sudden rush of emotion overtook him. He stood up and pulled her to him and kissed her deeply with passion, she melted into his arms, her head on his chest. The sense of well-being and security wrapped around him like a warm blanket.

"Sandi I'm so sorry I haven't done this before. Forgive me for neglecting our relationship. I promise you I'm going to try and devote more time to us. This whole thing is getting so intense and I have a nagging feeling in the back of my mind that something is amiss, but I can't get my head around it."

"Alex I have been waiting for months to have you kiss me that way. I must say it was worth the wait. Now I know what you are feeling. We both have our plates full with deadlines looming and pressures are building. This is the time we should cling to each other, be there for the other one. We don't have to be married; we just need to be there for each other. An emotional kiss, a nice big hug, a neck or back rub, a well-timed joke—all of those things we can give to each other to help us cope."

"You know something Sandi. You are very special to me and I need you."

"Then we both know how we feel about the other, we don't need to pass love notes in class. We're adults, let's take care of each other."

"It's a deal." Alex kissed her once again and Sandi walked out of his office.

Liz was upset, and it showed, as she walked past Curt in a huff.

"Hey Liz, is everything okay?"

"No. I just got called a subtraction instead of an addition."

"Ah, that would be my Dad having an honest talk with you. Listen Liz, my Dad is not critical of people to be critical. If he's called you on something, he's probably right and just wants you to learn from it. That's why so many people gravitate toward him, because they know he expects certain things from them, and if they perform, he will praise them and reward them. If they don't, he'll point out their mistakes and expect them not to repeat the same mistakes again. I mean let's get real, the President and the Chairman of the Joint Chiefs of Staff anointed Dad as the head honcho of this whole shooting match, you think he just might know a few things more than you and I?"

"I guess. I just can't get my arms around how big this is. And as your Dad said—and he is right I've been spending way too much time moping around instead of focusing on being a positive addition to the team."

"You just try and focus on what Dad assigned you, try and let all the other things slide by, we don't have much time Liz. We have a lot to do, and it has to be done right. You know what the stakes are."

"You're right Curt, but I keep having this nightmare. What if all we're doing is for nothing and we all perish in a ball of fire?"

"It's...yeah, it's possible. But what if we do survive Liz, and we've done nothing to emerge after the event? What then?"

"Better to be safe than sorry, you're right again. I'm sorry, but it's hard to hold all this in, and I don't have anyone to talk to."

"You have your mom, and my dad, Cynthia and I. You're not alone, we are all family, we need to look out for each other," Curt picked her chin up and gave her a hug.

That night at dinner there was the usual talk of the day's activities, and Liz was very engaged, Sandi and Alex noticed it right away, so Alex decided he should say something.

"There have been times where I was caught off guard by the higher ups doing things I would not normally do myself, like moving Sandi and I lock stock and barrel to this facility and doing the same with Curt and Cynthia. Of course poor Liz gets yanked out of her class by two FBI agents and whisked away to this mountain retreat with no explanation. Unbeknownst to me, someone has once again intervened, and we need to toast Liz on the conferment of her degree in Linguistics, regardless that she was given a break on her final thesis. The intent, I suspect, was to make her feel better about herself given the circumstances. Sometimes we have to accept the fact that there were good intentions behind what was done, regardless of how it was done. So Liz here's to your degree. Congratulations."

Everyone raised their glasses in a toast and Sandi was so proud of both Alex and Liz. Curt winked at Liz. Agent Evans though shook her hand while gazing into her eyes. Alex noticed that, when he did, a warm blush came over Liz's face.

Alex strolled down the walkway from the house with Sandi by his side. It was a beautiful late spring night.

"What are you thinking?" he said.

"Oh about this night...how nice it is, walking with you...and how good it feels."

"Do you know how much I care for you Sandi?" He put his arm around her shoulders and continued their walk.

"I've noticed that you're a bit more intense, more passionate lately, yes."

"Yeah, I've felt this way for a while, too, but I no longer have that tugging feeling that wants to hold me back. Does that sound right?"

"Yes it does. You're learning to let go of the past so you can live in the present, and it's a process. And it's not like you haven't had other things to do. It will take time, but you're coming through it, and I'm here waiting for you."

May was spent finalizing shelter requirements, troop deployments and several trips to brief Torrance and the President as to the status of Project O.N.E. The coming weeks were going to test Alex and Sandi's new love. But more importantly, they would test everyone's resolve.

Chapter 24

MESSAGES MISSED,
SIGNS IGNORED

In mid-June Petrov Ingosich called Elena and Andrade into his office for a meeting. The two had just returned from a three week vacation at a resort in the Black Sea area. Rested and very much in love with each other, they looked rejuvenated and fresh to Ingosich's eye.

"My friends, the President has ordered you two back into the US to track the activities of this General Hanken and discover the true mission of this man."

"Why Petrov?" Elena said. "We got you as much information as was possible. The inescapable conclusion is there are asteroids heading to earth and the Americans are preparing for it. Which is what our government should be doing instead of sending Andrade and I back to the United States."

"First, let me tell you that there is no threat of any kind from an asteroid strike. We have spoken to nearly every major observatory and space research institute around the globe. There is nothing out there."

"What... that can't be," she said, "Then what are the Americans up to?"

"Exactly. Since you returned things have gotten a little more complicated."

Petrov began outlining the military units that were now under the control of Alex. He watched the surprise spread across both Elena and Andrade's faces, as he listed the manpower numbers and weapons systems at his disposal. Then he said the one thing that intrigued Elena the most.

"My friends, our military leaders including the President, have marked General Hanken as the most dangerous military leader since Patton in WWII. Do I need to say more?"

"When do we leave?" Andrade asked.

"We're looking at the first or second week in August. That will give you time to develop an entry and exit strategy. When you have developed your plan, call me so we can go over it in depth. Then I can take it to Bocovich and the President."

"Very well Petrov."

Elena was immensely curious as she and Andrade walked out of the Moscow office of the FSB.

"Andrade what did you think of Petrov's request?"

"First of all I don't think it was a request. Second, I think it bears further investigation. This General Hanken has his finger on too many weapons. For us not to know the true intentions of the United States would be reckless at the very least and possibly fatal at the worst."

"My thoughts exactly. But the Americans are spending enormous sums of money on those survival shelters all for nothing...I can't believe something's not there."

"It would not be the first time the Americans have wasted huge sums of money."

"We will devise a plan to go in like we came out."

Andrade pondered this for a moment.

"You know you're absolutely right, no airports, no technology to notice us entering the country. No CIA or FBI tails. Good thinking my love. So now we have the entry plan, we have to devise a cover for us to operate under, and get close enough to Hanken to monitor his activities."

"I'm going to call Ingosich and see if we have any agents working the area. Why don't you contact our technology division and see what we can use to make our trip more productive."

Twenty minutes later, a couple who lived in Colorado Springs near the Air Force Academy for years and visited Peterson AFB every two weeks for some kind of equipment adjustment, were about to receive a visit from their cousins.

For the next three weeks she and Andrade filled out all the necessary tactical points and provided Ingosich a formalized action plan. The President was satisfied with the plan and instructed Bocovich to implement it as soon as possible. Petrov called Elena and informed her that the plan was approved, and they would be travel by boat into Masset on Queen Charlotte Island, British Columbia on August 1st.

Alex busied himself with follow-up visits in the east and Midwest before the test date. Finally he was satisfied—the facilities were ready. Army, Navy, and Marine personnel were now at their assigned locations. The Air Force bases had temporary facilities installed to accommodate the new flight and maintenance crews. The only thing that bothered Alex was they had no protection against airborne diseases like they would at his facility—the sealed mines in Idaho, or the underground bunkers.

The biggest expense and headache was shipping survival food and storing it. Sandi, Cynthia, and Liz handled that part of Alex's survival strategy and it ended up costing nearly $850 million dollars in food and storage facilities. By July 8th Alex reported to Admiral Torrance that everything was completed, personnel and equipment were in place at all assigned facilities. On July 26th, Alex got a phone call.

"Alex? Brad Cole."

"Colonel. How's everything?"

"Pretty smooth so far, I just wanted to run something by you that seems a little odd to me."

"Sure Brad, what is it?"

"You know Torrance wanted me to coordinate all of your personal flight logistics and command logistics."

"Yes, and you've done an outstanding job. I couldn't have pulled all of this off without your help."

"Thank you, but here's the reason for my call. Wouldn't it seem odd to you that someone is moving around twenty six C-17's and placed them all in 24 hour reserve stand-by status, fully fueled, specifically for August 5th and August 6th ?"

That was right around the time of the lockdown. That was odd. "Who gave the orders for that movement?"

"That's just it Alex, I can't trace it down to anyone. Either the people at MAC command don't know themselves or somebody is lying."

"Okay Brad, I'll make inquiries. It is probably something Torrance is doing and he didn't want to burden us since our plate is full already. But I'll check it out and get back to you."

"Thanks. I'm not a conspiracy nut, it just seemed odd that's all."

"On the surface it is odd, you're right. Get back to you soon."

"Thanks Alex."

Later that day Admiral Torrance announced to Alex that the two day stress test would be on August 5th and 6th during the congressional recess. Admiral Torrance checked to make sure the communication systems were working properly. Alex informed him that Curt had already run three test runs with all the connectivity between the regions performing as expected.

It was the perfect opportunity. "Admiral, do you know anything about some C-17 transport planes being moved around?"

"Oh, right. I didn't want to bother you with that. I am running a test along with our own stress tests to see how easy it will be to move key command staff to different locations when we're under duress or attack. I didn't want to burden you any further you've had enough going on."

"No problem, and thanks. Brad Cole at Nellis called me wondering what was going on, and I told him it was probably just what you told me."

They finalized the details. Everyone was to be at their assigned location by 0800 the morning of August 5th. Facilities with blast doors like Mount Weather would be sealed for the duration of the test. Admiral Torrance thanked Alex for all he had done for the country, and no matter how things turned out, he would always know that they gave it their best shot. He also thanked Alex for his loyalty, which for a commander, is critical in times of change and chaos. It was Alex's loyalty that the Admiral admired the most, and would very shortly depend on.

Andrade gave Elena his hand as they stepped off the disguised Russian trawler on to the dock in Masset at 11:00 p.m. on July 31st 2015. They were three days early. Both the submarine and the trawler made unexpectedly good time. Elena called ahead to have a taxi waiting at the dock parking lot to take them to a hotel for the night on the island.

The next morning they got up and called another taxi to load their baggage and take the ferry to Prince Rupert. Once there, Elena and Andrade visited a local Land Rover dealership and drove off with a slightly used Land Rover. Several weeks earlier Elena had opened an account by mail at the branch of Bank of Montreal in Prince Rupert and wired $100,000 into the account. After they picked out the vehicle they wanted, she went to the bank branch and got a certified check for the total costs and they were off to Colorado Springs. Elena figured it would take at least two possibly three days to get there by car.

They took the same route that got them to Prince Rupert—south on 97 this time, all the way to the American border. They even stayed at their favorite hotel in Penticton, before heading further south. They pulled into Colorado Springs at the home of one of the embedded Russian agents at 9:00 a.m. on the morning of August 3rd. They spent the rest of the morning unpacking and devising their plan to infiltrate Peterson AFB, and get as close to General Hanken as possible.

Curt and Cynthia were taking a scenic drive through Colorado Springs on the morning of the 3rd to take a break from the frenzied pace at the bunker. Suddenly Cynthia grabbed Curt's arm.

"My God Curt, it's them!"

"Who them, which them? And what's the matter, you looked scared to death?"

"Curt it's those two agents. They were standing in the living room of that house we just passed by."

"What?"

Curt stopped the car and turned around. As he slowly rolled by the house he could see the woman…Elena. She was unmistakable. He grabbed the phone and called Alex.

"Hey Curt how's the dri—."

"Dad those agents are here. We just spotted them in a house here in Colorado Springs."

"Give me the address, and drive away from there at a normal speed."

Two minutes later, Alex had Tina and the Seal Team leader in his office.

"I have a mission for you. Those two Russian agents have reappeared. They're in Colorado Springs at this address. I want you to apprehend them—alive if possible. You are authorized to use lethal force to protect yourself and innocent civilians if necessary. After you've got them bring them to the brig at the air base and lock them up. I must warn you the female is extremely dangerous. I would suggest at last ten of your best people be on this mission."

"General, I think you should let me lead this, I have specific training in these kinds of situations."

Alex hesitated only a second—he knew what it could mean to send Tina up against the Black Widow. But he had to trust her abilities. "You're right," he said. "Agent Somers is mission commander. Follow her orders, and God be with you."

Somers directed the Seals to reconnoiter the entire area and report back to her two blocks away. After she was debriefed by the scouts, she set the lookouts in strategic locations with sniper rifles. She sent two teams, each with three Seals, into the side yards of the neighboring houses. Entry would be through the garage on one side, and through the back door at the rear of the house. Somers and two Seals would go through the front door, and all of them would go on her command through the entry points at the same time.

She walked briskly to the front door, saw no one in the living room, tried the front door. It was unlocked. Colorado Springs was evidently small enough for people to trust their neighbors.

"Go, Go, Go!"

Elena and Andrade were lying down for a short nap when a team of soldiers broke through the bedroom door.

"Down on the floor, or I'll kill you where you sit! Now!"

Elena sprang with incredible quickness, noting while she was in midair that the leader of the team was a woman. A young woman, tougher, with sharper reflexes, and ready for her. Elena never saw the right hook coming.

Elena was stunned for the moment, but recovered and leapt once again. This time the woman hit Elena in the jaw. And that was the last she remembered.

Somers looked around the room, resisting the urge to massage her knuckles. Andrade had been thrown to the floor and had four good-sized Navy Seals sitting on him. And another operative was already slapping cuffs on Elena and frisking her for weapons.

She called for all team members to come forward and collect the other residents of the house. A convoy of humvees appeared at the front of the house and all the captives were loaded and sped away to the airbase.

Neighbors looked on in astonishment. The whole raid had taken all of six minutes.

Elena and Andrade and the two other Russian agents were put in separate cells at the airbase stockade. When that was taken care of the Seal Team leader came up to Somers.

"Lady, you are some kind of bad ass," he said. "I'll go on any mission with you, any day, anytime."

"You know what, that may be the nicest thing anyone has ever said to me." She laughed along with all the Seals, as they walked into Alex's office to report that the mission was successful.

An hour later Alex walked into a room with a Navy Seal in each corner of the room, a table with two chairs on one side, and a single chair on the other. Somers asked Alex to step to one corner while she brought in Elena and Andrade and sat them down at the table, with their hands secured behind their backs.

"Now here are the rules," she said, as soon as they were situated. "General Hanken wanted to speak to you, I didn't like the idea, but he insisted. If you make any threatening moves toward him a Navy Seal standing behind you will put a bullet in your brain. If you curse him or insult him in any way, I will break one of your arms in half. Are we clear on the rules?

"My dear you have a special way about you," Elena said without rancor, "but you were lucky today."

"No Miss Grodny," Alex said, stepping out of the shadows, "you and Mr. Kolna were the lucky ones. If I had sent the Seals in without Agent Somers, you would be lying on a metal table in a morgue right now."

"Now you can either be civil and live to see another day, or I can turn you over to the CIA agent in charge of your case. I believe he's known as Agent Crossbow. I'm sure you're familiar with him aren't you Miss Grodny?"

"So you are the infamous General Hanken?" Elena said. "Pleased to meet you General. And, yes, I am quite familiar with Crossbow."

"Well good, we have an understanding then."

Andrade motioned with his head that he wanted to say something.

"Yes, Mr. Kolna."

"General, why has your government been killing innocent Russian citizens as well as innocent American citizens? What have you been covering up?"

It was actually a fair question. "Inspector Kolna, I cannot tell you why my government did what it has done, and I regret the loss of any life, regardless of political persuasion or ideological position. And I can assure you of this, I had nothing to do with any of your citizens being harmed, and I would most certainly not have anything to do with harming a fellow American."

"You called me Inspector. How did you know that?"

"I know a lot about both of you. For example, Andrade, I know that before you met Elena you were a hardworking, honest policeman from St. Petersburg."

"And now?"

"And now you are an accomplice to a serial killer. A ruthless, heartless, cold blooded murderer."

Elena glared at Alex, and Somers made a move to take Alex away. But Alex waved her off.

"You're mistaken," Kolna said. "Elena may be many things, but she is not heartless. She kills when necessary and no more than necessary. How is she worse than your own government?"

"Andrade, save your breath," Elena said. "They are going to kill us...you must know that." And to everyone's surprise, as she looked at Andrade the tears began to stream down her cheeks.

Agent Somers stepped forward.

"General, this is a bunch of crap. Just call the CIA and have them pick this trash up, and haul it away to the dump."

But there was something here. Kolna was a good man, and he seemed even proud now.

"Agent Somers I'm going to ask you to leave the room with the Seals."

"Sir! No!"

"Shackle both of them to their chairs for security, I want to speak to them in private."

"Okay sir, but you whisper what you don't want me to hear, because I am going to stand in the doorway with a gun trained on them."

"Agreed"

Alex sat down at the table and looked at both of them and said in a whispered voice.

"Do you want to live?"

Andrade and Elena looked at each other in surprise.

"Of course." Elena leaned forward, her tears dropping on the table.

"Then listen to me very carefully. You are foreign agents captured on American soil. You have killed several innocent citizens. I could have you shot or bury you in solitary confinement forever if I chose to do so. I can't set you free. You may have to be here for another two years. There are things that are going to happen that I can't tell you about at this time, horrible things, never seen by mankind."

"The asteroids," Elena said. "Yes, we know."

Alex lost his momentum. "You know about the asteroids?" He lowered his voice again. "But why are you here? What—"

"Because," Kolna said, "there are no asteroids. Our people have searched the heavens and cannot find them anywhere."

"That's...that's ridiculous." Alex's mind spun over everything he'd heard in the last few months. "Our people must have taken steps to hide them, probably some technology magic."

Kolna shrugged as best he could with his hands shackled. "Our people tell us no. And they are not rushing to build their own bunkers, so I think they believe it themselves."

Alex realized that, fascinating as it was, this information didn't change what he meant to say. "Okay, let's set that aside for a moment. You're well aware of the destructive power of the arsenal that I possess. It rivals your own country's military power. It is imperative that other nations, who are scrutinizing our actions here in the US, understand that we are not in an offensive posture from a military standpoint. I need someone who has foreign intelligence experience who can get me solid information as to what other nations might be planning to do in response to our initiatives."

"General are you asking us to defect to the United States?"

"No. I am asking you to consider your options for now, take a few days to think your position over. When you're ready to talk, let me know." He raised his voice again.

"Okay Somers, you can take them back to their cells now. They are to be treated humanely is that understood. No rough stuff?"

"Yes, sir"

"And let Elena and Andrade have a couple of hours together tonight."

"You mean…a conjugal moment?"

"Yes, I guess that would be the term for it."

"Okay sir, as you wish."

Alex pulled all the Seals and Somers into the next room and debriefed them about his conversation. And on consideration, he added that it was important that the CIA and the FBI not know that they had the two Russians in their custody.

Something very strange was happening, and he felt more comfortable with more resources at his disposal.

August 4th—lockdown, minus one—was a day of intense preparation. Alex conducted one last conference call with all the facilities nationwide to ensure everyone was ready.

Somers knocked once and stuck her head in the door. "Sir, the lovebirds would like to talk to you."

"Be nice, Tina. Someday your Prince Charming will appear and you'll appreciate what two people in love can mean to each other."

"If I may be frank, sir, after seeing you with Dr. Chenowith, it does give me some hope."

"Good for you young lady, I'll be over there in about fifteen minutes."

Alex walked into the room where Andrade and Elena sat, the same table as they had a day earlier. Somers stood at the door as before and watched for any sudden threatening movement.

"General, let me first thank you for giving Elena and myself our private time together last night. I know that is not commonplace and it was appreciated."

"Yes, General, I sincerely thank you as well."

"Well now that you know a little about me, know this, I demand absolute loyalty from my people. In return, I give everything of myself to them. There is nothing I won't do to ensure my people are given the best shot at succeeding. Now with that said, tell me what you're thinking?"

"Both of us agreed that we are in a compromised position with few alternatives," Elena said. What is it that you want us to do?"

"I can't tell you just now. But it may be tomorrow, or the next day, or two years from now, but when I come to you and give you a mission, I want complete and total commitment. I will make this promise to you, I will protect you from harm by agents of this government and any other foreign government, and I will never, ever ask you to commit an act against Russia."

"Will Andrade and I be allowed to see each other like last night?"

"Yes."

"We have a deal General."

"Good." Alex nodded, then got up and walked out of the room accompanied by Agent Somers.

Somers was curious. "Did you just pick up two hardcore Russian agents and bring them over to our side?"

"Yeah, that about sums it up." Except that he was growing less sure of what "our side" meant.

"I'm going to watch your back though."

"I'm counting on it, Tina."

Alex needed to make several last minute calls before retiring for the evening.

"Colonel is your battalion in place?" Alex asked each one of the eight battalion commanders. All answered in the affirmative and were awaiting his orders.

Alex enjoyed dinner with Sandi alone that night, he wanted to have a romantic evening with her, since the next two days would be bedlam for both of them.

The next morning Alex was busy communicating with facilities across the nation to get updates on how the testing was going. He had provided a punch list for each facility, based on its own peculiarity of things to test for reliability. The President and his entire cabinet with the exception of the Secretary of Agriculture, were at Mount Weather locked in their bunkers. Congress was dispersed to their several facilities and sealed in as well. But during his checking, he found that Don Cray and Admiral Torrance weren't in Mount Weather with the rest of the cabinet.

That night, on a news broadcast carried by every television outlet in the country, he found out why.

Andrade and Elena had been right. There were no asteroids. Instead, as Admiral Torrance explained in patient tones, there had been an overthrow of the United States government.

In the luxurious offices of a prestigious Washington D.C. law firm sat eight men around a highly polished table made of sapele. The Circle, as they called themselves. They were the CEO"s and Chairmen of the three largest domestic oil companies, the CEO of the largest diversified corporation in the US, the CEO of the largest Pharmaceutical company in the world, and two principals of a well-known venture capital firm, with ties to two former Presidents and the Saudi Kings. Their number also included one lone high ranking government official…the Deputy Secretary of Defense, Howard Carney.

In late 1960, the departing President Eisenhower, addressed the nation in a broadcast carried by the three major networks. In that address he warned the American public to *beware the military industrial complex*. The American people did not heed that prophetic warning. In early 2014 after the airlines had been nationalized and there were rampant rumors of nationalizing the major oil companies and placing price controls on pharmaceuticals and other basic chemical stocks, a meeting was held, with all the players of the Circle present. At that meeting it was decided that the federal government could no longer be counted on to do the right thing for America. It must be replaced. Subsequently, the Circle met and devised their plan.

Early on the morning of August 5, 2015, twenty-six C-17 aircraft carrying crack ground troops from the 1st and 2nd Marine Divisions were dispatched to all the survival facilities to secure them with orders that no one got in, and no one got out, unless on a direct order from Admiral Torrance. The entire government of the United States of America was removed from power without a shot being fired.

How did the Circle pull off one of the biggest political cover-ups in the history of modern man? It began five years ago at the Mauna Kea Keck observatory where a young grad student working a late night shift recorded an incident in which comet Sedna/Kern p236 disturbed the asteroid belt sufficiently to create a short-lived astronomical spectacle. It was recorded by the young man for several hours and into the next day shift when he returned. Mauna Kea was the only observatory in the world that picked up this event, since that was their assigned area of space to cover. One of the grad student's drinking buddies was an employee of an influential venture capital firm and was always on the lookout for anything out of the ordinary. The grad student made a copy of the recording and showed it to the man and explained what had happened. He liked it and gave him $50. The man in turn shipped the recording with an explanation off to the New York office.

It was no easy task getting programmers and digital imaging technicians to reformat the event to include an asteroid strike. It had to match up on a second by second real time view of a scene that was unfolding before the astronomer's eyes—all the background stars and asteroids had to be in the right place. When the astronomer turned his/her attention to the coordinates of the event, a subroutine would kick in and reveal a digitally engineered depiction of the status of the threat and no one would be the wiser.

The days of the lone astronomer had passed with the advent of newer technology. They no longer sat perched on a little stool behind a massive telescope peering into outer space. Everything was digitized now, and the images captured went to a computer screen which the astronomer viewed. Computers meant software, and software meant hacking vulnerability.

The Circle knew the charade would eventually be discovered, but it only had to last around six months. The subroutine would run until the overthrow of the government, then a signal would be sent to the computer controlling the software, and the subroutine would erase itself.

The young grad student, who was an excellent surfer, mysteriously drowned one Sunday afternoon. The man who bought the recording from the grad student fell to his death from the twelfth floor balcony of his hotel. Since Borosky and Kinova shared some of the common area of space with their observatories and the Cal Tech Mauna Kea location, it was necessary to introduce the subroutine to their computers as well. As soon as Borosky and Kinova were eliminated their computers were wiped clean and no record of the findings existed anywhere but at Cal Tech. This was accomplished by a rogue CIA agent named Edward Ketchum hired by the venture capital firm in New York, whose two principals were members of the Circle.

Both Professors Huart and Macklin were duped by the program. Eldon Huart really did die of a heart attack and Jeffrey Macklin caused his own death by panicking. Their wives having discovered something mysterious about their husband's deaths were ordered eliminated.

As Admiral Torrance stepped to the microphone, Howard Carney lifted his glass in a toast to the Circle. After Admiral Torrance had finished declaring martial law and explaining why this drastic step was being taken, the subroutine was signaled to erase itself and it did so. No traces existed now, the people involved were dead, and there were no subroutines to track down.

"Gentlemen, we have done it."

"What about Hanken?" one of the men asked.

"Torrance should be able to bring him on board. And if not..." Carney shrugged. "We have a backup plan in place."

With that, the United States of America had fallen victim to its first coup d'etat. Alex Hanken stood transfixed staring at the television monitor. He had always thought highly of Torrance, and over the last few months, he'd grown to admire the man immensely. And now?

To his tremendous shock, the first thing that bubbled up was relief. There were no asteroids. The earth wasn't going to be destroyed, and millions of people were not going to die, and he didn't have to worry about protecting the bunkers from foreign armies or fighting off starving mobs. They weren't going to die; the people they knew weren't going to die. They were safe.

But then the enormity of what had happened began to sink in. There had been a coup d'etat. In the United States. Apparently led by a man he admired. The threat of an asteroid calamity was gone, but the news was still incredibly shocking.

And what was he going to do about it?

Sandi stepped forward.

"Alex, its Admiral Torrance."

"Tell him I'm not available right now, better yet, give me the phone."

He hurled the phone against the wall, shattering it in pieces. He had already heard more than he ever wanted to hear. He looked around him, at the room full of people watching him carefully— Sandi, Curt and Cynthia with love in their eyes but also fear, Tina and the Seals with calm readiness, the others with a mix of shock and confusion. All of them waiting to hear what he would say.

And what would he say?

Torrance was right, the country was in bad shape. But no worse than it had been in during the depression, or even the various crashes that had hit over the centuries. It's institutions had been stressed many times over the years—the constitutional crises of McCarthy or Nixon, or the chaos and bloodshed of the Civil Rights movement. They'd come through.

They could come through again.

But if a small group of powerful people could upend the nation's laws simply because they didn't like how they were playing out, then there would never be stability again. Torrance was counting on his loyalty, but Alex wasn't loyal to particular men or even particular institutions. He was loyal to a set of ideas. And it wasn't blind loyalty. They were good ideas, strong and powerful, capable of changing the world.

So there really was only one decision to make.

He stared at the people he'd assembled around him until he had their attention. Then he drew himself up to his full height.

"This Will Not Stand"

The End

www.ingramcontent.com/pod-product-compliance
Lightning Source LLC
Chambersburg PA
CBHW060533180626
46817CB00002B/558